Inca

GW00721714

To Chris.

Inca Prince

by

Colin Davey

HATT PUBLICATIONS
2003

HATT PUBLICATIONS

A HATT BOOK
Published in paperback in 2003

© 2003 by Colin Davey
ISBN 0954 4645/0/8

All rights reserved

This book is sold subject to the conditions that it shall not, by way of trade or otherwise, be lent, resold, hired out, or otherwise circulated without the publisher's prior consent in any form of binding or cover than that in which it is published without a similar condition including this condition being imposed on the subsequent purchaser.

Printed and Bound by
The Latimer Trend Group Ltd
Plymouth

Cover Illustration: Gillian Anderson

Ackowledgements

I would like to thank my daughters Claire and Nicola for encouraging me to write this novel and to my wife Anne who put up with hours of my irritating one finger typing. Also I am indebted to Jane Penfound and Susan Briggs who changed many of my grammar and spelling mistakes.

Prologue

Much has been written about the Inca Empire and yet so little is known of it. The Incas were an extremely advanced civilisation for their time and yet they left little writings or codices for future scholars to study. Most of the contemporary information comes from the Spanish who invaded them in 1532. The history of the Inca people was passed down through the generations by word of mouth in stories, songs and poetry.

The first Spanish invaders to arrive on the shores of South America were a motley collection of conquistadors under the leadership of Francisco Pizzaro who was an illiterate pig farmer. This contingent consisted of sixty-two horsemen and one hundred and sixty foot soldiers. It was the impact of the horses that made it possible for the Spaniards to conquer the Inca people who were completely overawed by their size and strength in warfare. Also the warriors had never come across muskets. Even now it is almost incomprehensible how some two hundred soldiers managed to overcome an army consisting of over two hundred thousand highly trained warriors.

Within a short space of time the Empire of the Incas was in ruins due to diseases that were brought in from Europe to which the Inca people had no natural immunity and by the killings and plundering of the Spanish soldiers whose main interests lay only in the finding of gold. The whole infrastructure of the Inca civilisation was gradually broken up by the marauding Spaniards, which in turn allowed the once conquered tribes in the surrounding areas to rebel and begin to take their revenge on their former captors. During this period of time there were reports of a group of Inca people who led by a Prince escaped from their Spanish captors and disappeared into the Amazonian jungles where they eventually established a new civilisation. This Prince was supposedly the direct descendant of the great Sun God Atahualpa who had been the divine leader of the whole of the Inca Empire.

There has been a great deal of speculation over the years as to where this group of Incas eventually came to resettle. Rumours of a Golden Garden of Eden where people were dressed in gold and beautiful womenfolk walked around half naked with exquisite works of jewellery hanging around their necks kept filtering out of the jungles. There were so many stories of a lost city, which was paved in gold that it eventually became known as El Dorado. The jungle tribes called it 'Piatta' which in their language means, "sadness, affliction, anguish".

The first party to venture into the jungles in search of the lost Inca settlement were the conquistadors themselves after they had destroyed the entire Inca Empire. They had been told by the Muisca Indians, whose present day descendants live in Columbia, of a tribal chief who, in an annual ritual, anointed himself in gold dust and then plunged himself into a lake. Gonzalo Pizarro who was the half brother of the Francisco Pizarro led this Spanish group of treasure seekers. He left Quito with over two hundred horses and five thousand pigs for food. A year and a half later he returned having not found the lost city and with only half of his original army of men most of who were suffering from disease. The legend of the Golden Man spread like wildfire throughout Spanish America and since those days many ill-fated expeditions have failed to find El Dorado.

Two latter day explorers became world famous for their quests of The Golden City. Percy Fawcett was a British army officer who came to South America to help the Bolivian Army to define their jungle borders. His real interest, however, was tracking down the Golden City that according to a Portuguese document, which he had acquired from a group of adventurers, was in Brazil. He also had possession of a stone idol supposedly of Brazilian origin and which according to psychics had actually come from the lost continent of Atlantis. The idol contained mysterious inscriptions, which he claimed were identical to some strange scribblings at the end of his Portuguese document. Armed with this conclusive proof of the existence of the Atlantian city Fawcett plunged into the green hell of the Amazon Basin in search of it. His family never saw him again. The whole party disappeared. Over the years various explorers reported that they had met Fawcett or had heard rumours of his whereabouts. Some reports stated that he had married a tribal woman of one of the tribes living in the jungle and that she had given birth to a white, blue-eyed son.

It was Hiram Holiday who made the first incredible discovery of the lost Incas. He set off from Lima with a large mule train carrying months of supplies and went in search of some lost ruins which the natives called Choqqueqiram, which roughly translated meant the 'cradle of gold' After many months exploring in extreme conditions he had his first stroke of luck. Sitting around his camp one evening, listening to the local Indians who were relating to one another about their superstitions with regards to old ruins and bones, Hiram heard one of them state that he knew of such relics quite near to where they were at that present moment. The Indian eventually led Hiram to a sheer cliff, which disappeared high up into the mists. At the base of the cliff he was shown a huge pile of human bones. After an exhausting trek and climb taking three days they eventually came out of the mists and jungle to be greeted by the magnificent site of Machu Picchu. This grand city was built at the edge of a sheer precipice almost like the nest of one of the majestic eagles, which soar high up in the mountain crags. The buildings were made of huge blocks of smooth stone, which had been so cleverly carved and assembled like a jigsaw that it was impossible to fit a thin knife blade between any of the joints. How the Incas managed to transport and raise the huge blocks into place remains an enigma.

The ruins still resembled streets, staircases, monuments, temples and houses, which were set into a breathtaking landscape. This truly was the last resting place of the Incas, thought Hiram Holiday but this was to be disproved many years later by Professor Jason Downing.

PART I

Chapter One

He stood there motionless in the tangled, steaming under-growth of the tropical forest. The morning chorus of chatter-ing birds accompanied by the high pitch screams of monkeys filled the still air like a reveille. The canopy some hundred feet above his head was so dense that only an occasional shaft of sunlight managed to pierce into the gloom of some of the most unimaginable conditions known to man. He had endured this for the past two years whilst he had been playing hide and seek with his enemies.

An ordinary being would never have been able to endure the torture that his body had been subjected to during so many months of absolute solitude in such an abysmal environment. The only resemblance to a human being was his eyes, which conveyed a keen sense of alertness. Although cramp had set in due to the huge amounts of lactic acid which had pooled within his muscles after the long, arduous chase through the spiky thorns of the undergrowth, he still possessed good body tone which in an emergency would mobilise him from a grotesque looking statue into a highly tuned fighting machine. The Chief Commander of prob-ably the greatest army in the world had produced no finer a soldier.

A sudden flurry above his head startled him but he did not move at all. After a few seconds had passed he gradually lifted his head and focused his eyes to where the sound came from, already anticipating that a bird had caused it. He was right. It was a Blue Jay that was perched on a slender branch pecking at some brightly coloured berries. He could see that the bird often chose this spot as the lichen on the branch was worn away with the constant gripping of it's sharp claws.

In the process of landing, after a precarious dive through a small hole in the thick canopy above, it dislodged one of the

1

most beautiful creations in the forest, a red and green orchid that floated to the ground at the feet of the soldier. As it fell it caressed his face and left a sweet smelling fragrance in the air about him. It was like a sign, which brought back painful memories of his Nakita, the most beautiful woman he had ever encountered. Momentarily his eyes began to moisten and his mind raced back over the last six years of his life. He could vividly remember the day when his life changed so drastically.

He had awoken earlier than usual and was immediately filled with excitement and the feeling of great anticipation. It was the fifth day into the last quarter of the moon. On this particular day of the month he had given specific orders to the Palace Ceremonial Guards that he was not to be disturbed under any circumstances as it was a time when he would be meditating. He knew that no one would dare to try to contact him during such a time, as he was the second most powerful person in the Empire after his father. His father was the "Sun God", leader of the greatest army the world has ever known, the army of the Incas!

The Royal Prince was in a transitional period of his life when he was being groomed for the time when he would take over from his father. Much of his previous years had been spent being taught by the elder statesman of the Inner Circle on the finer points of running a huge Empire, most of which he would never see. Now he was embarking on a much more exciting period in his life when he was being prepared for the times when he would have to lead his army into battle. During a short space of time he had already proved that he had talents superior to those of the selected soldiers of the Imperial Guard.

A faint creaking of the floorboards outside his room reminded him that he should check to see who had been assigned to guard him that day. He went to the door and gently turned the door handle. It made no noise but the actual movement of the knob was enough to notify the guard outside to be ready for the Royal Prince. As the door opened the guard stood to attention and faced directly across the hallway because to look the Prince in the eyes was forbidden.

"Good morning. May I thank you in advance for keeping guard over me this day." He looked at the guard and was extremely impressed by what he saw. In actual fact he was always impressed, such was the splendour of the Royal Guard. These men were the elite of the Inca Army. They had proved themselves many times in battle and as a reward they had been attached to the Royal Guard, which gave them many privileges and the respect of the citizens of the city. They were distinguished from the rest of the army by their amazing uniform. The main part consisted of a brightly coloured turquoise leather material, which gave the body a certain amount of protection. Over this was a magnificent golden chest plate, which glistened in the sun's rays.

When the full guard was on display one had to shield ones eyes, as it was if one was actually looking into the sun itself. The main armament was either a short sword or an evil looking lance. All wore a dagger tucked into a black leather waistband, which was decorated in golden suns. When they went into battle they also wore a leather sling over their shoulder for their arrows. The front echelon of the battle group would also be equipped with a short two-sided axe. It must have been a most frightening experience for any opposition to see a sea of gold approaching them, led by a wave of swinging axes. The reputation of this fine body of men had been spread to the far expanses of the kingdom and even beyond, so few people ever dared to cross them.

"No doubt you have been informed by your superior officer that at no time am I to be disturbed," said the Prince. " If anyone wishes to see me I will contact them tomorrow morning."

The guard gave a slight nod, which was accentuated by the tall plume of white eagle feathers, which were attached to his helmet. With that last command the Prince shut his door and began to plan his next twelve hours.

The guard outside the door was one of almost a thousand who were strategically placed in and around the Palace grounds in order to stop anyone from getting within eyesight of the Royal Family. It was an impossible task to even think of doing

3

so, and yet the Prince was about to do the reverse. He was going to get out of the Palace without being seen and return by the same method. He paced across to the far side of his room making a small cloud of dust rise from the floor.

The rooms of the Palace were decorated in brightly coloured silks and on the walls were beautiful murals depicting various parts of the empire. The furniture was ornately decorated in gold and fine gemstones, and the floors were covered in cool white marble. Many of the spoils of battle were used as decorations in the halls and corridors. Anyone coming into the Palace as a visitor was always astounded at the beauty, which surrounded them.

The Prince's room was the exception. Over a hundred years ago it had been the servants quarters until there had been a spate of thefts in the palace. The servants were given the blame and all were put to death. After that a fresh contingent was found which was housed outside of the official Royal Quarters. The old rooms were boarded up and remained that way until the present Prince decided that he would use them for his own quarters. Until then he had lived in the main block of the palace with the leading scholars of the Inner Circle who were responsible for the general daily running of the Inca Empire.

When he reached the age of twenty he was permitted to live anywhere of his choosing provided it was within the sanctuary of the Palace walls. It was usual for a new Prince who had come of age to have a new building erected to his own specifications and to be lavishly decorated. This was totally against the Prince's principles as he was never one for wasting finances, so he had opted for the disused servants quarters.

He could always remember the day when the workmen began to remove the old wooden boarding across the entrance to the rooms. The rough planks had been nailed into the wall with hefty metal pins in order to prevent any form of entry. Anyone making such an attempt would have had to make a lot of noise and would have been discovered immediately, so the entrance had remained undisturbed for well over a hundred years. What should have been major work in removing the planking proved

4

quite the opposite. The overseer of the work was a small man who on his initial inspection of the boarding was able to remove most of it on his own. The wood was so rotten with the constant attack from termites that it crumbled into dust when hit with anything hard.

As soon as an opening was made, clouds of dust mixed with dank smells drifted out of the darkened rooms and covered the workers. On initial inspection the room appeared to be completely empty but once an oil lamp had been brought in by one of the slaves a few pieces of furniture could be distinguished in the gloom. All of it was in the same condition as the wood across the door opening and had to be thrown away. The only other thing in the room was a faded old tapestry on the corner wall, which the Prince decided to keep, as it still possessed a certain amount of aesthetic beauty. It was in no state to be cleaned as the material was only just managing to remain together and so it was decided to leave it in its place on the wall.

The only furniture that the Prince had asked to be brought into the room was a low table on which he kept his few personal things, a chair where he did actually sit and try to focus on the daily problems that might arise, and an old wooden box in which he kept his clothes. All of his ceremonial dress was left in the actual Palace. He decided to have no lavish wall hangings. The only things he had hanging on the walls were his army clothing and odd things that he had picked up on his visits into the jungle. There wasn't even a bed, as he preferred to sleep on the hard floor, which was a mixture of dried earth and sand and was very easy to keep tidy. He had inherited these basic habits from his days when training to be a soldier. By denying himself the pleasures of self-indulgence he had remained extremely fit. When he ate he tended to keep to the foods that the ordinary soldiers were given and not eat the rich foods that were given to the senior members of the palace.

There was one other piece of furniture, which was placed in a corner of the room and hidden in shadow. It was a form of a trunk that had a hinged top, which the Prince opened and let fall back against the earthen wall. He bent down and proceeded to remove what appeared to be old clothing. It was in fact a set of hunting clothes made of thick brown leather. The main tunic had short arms, which were very baggy to allow full range of movement and to allow the air to circulate. The jungle was extremely humid and one tended to sweat a lot so by allowing a circulation of air, evaporation took place which helped cool the body. It had numerous pockets where various hunting gadgets could be stored. The belt had many openings in which to hang hunting knives, small bags and coils of rope. Also he had a quiver and a set of deadly sharp arrows, which he had obtained by trading with an Indian who he had come across during one of his expeditions with an army assault team. At the time he thought the Indian was out to kill him but all he wanted to do was to trade. It was during that incident that the Prince decided that he should commence learning the local languages of the jungle people.

During the first night he occupied his new quarters he had had great difficulty in getting off to sleep. Although the sleeping area had no form of ventilation it still felt very draughty. In fact when he lit one of the small torches it kept flickering and as he walked around the room with it in his hand it's flame became more distorted in certain areas, especially in the far corner. As he neared the old wall hanging the Prince noticed that the flame burnt more brightly and when he looked behind it, he came across some form of an aperture.

On first inspection the opening appeared to be a storage space, but when he placed his burning torch into the darkness he could see that there was a narrow passage leading away from its entrance. He crouched down and forced his upper torso through the space and peered into the darkness. From the glow of the torch he could see that the sides of the tunnel were quite rough which indicated that it had not been weathered by the action of water. On closer inspection he thought he could make out marks that seemed to have been made by some form of sharp implement, like a chisel. The aperture appeared to be man made and he was intrigued to see how far it actually went into the cliff face. He found out later, when talking to the elders, that many years ago one of the Inca Kings had had a tunnel built by a group of slaves, as a means of escape. On completion of the tunnel he had the whole group of slave workers put to death and the engineers he sent away on an extended holiday where they in turn were also executed. That left only the King who knew of the whereabouts of the tunnel. When that King died he took the secret of the tunnel with him. It was hundreds of years later that the servants came across it.

The Prince kept the opening a secret and many weeks after its rediscovery he eventually ventured into it: it was not a very inviting place as it stank of mouldy, rotting vegetation. He had to crawl for well over two hundred metres until the tunnel began to widen and the roof eventually disappeared out of the reaches of the flickering torch. On one occasion the fumes and smoke given off from the burning, oily rags of the torch almost choked him as he passed through a very narrow area of the tunnel.

A further crawl of forty metres found the Prince standing in a huge hall of stalagmites and stalactites formed over the centuries by the action of small droplets of water. Any noise that he made seemed to boom across the expansiveness of the cave and seconds later come booming back again after bouncing off the high walls and ceilings. On examination of the floor the Prince noticed that he was walking on a well-defined path and assumed that this was the way that the stolen goods from the palace used to be taken so many years ago by the servants.

During his first exploration of the cavern he nearly got lost when his flaming torch began to burn out and on that occasion he was very lucky to have found his way back. The next time he ventured into the labyrinth he made sure that he had at least another two spare torches so that he could be more adventuresome and go deeper into the numerous tunnels. He also made sure that he took a long length of twine to lie along the floor and a large block of charcoal to mark the walls if the twine ran out.

It took three more trips into the darkness before the Prince found another entrance to the tunnel. On that occasion he was on the verge of returning to his room as he was down to his last torch, when he noticed a glimmer of light ahead of him. He tried to work out how far he may have travelled from his room and assumed that he would find himself still emerging into the palace grounds. He did not want to show his presence to any of the guards so he cautiously moved forward with the minimum of noise, which proved quite difficult as he had put out the flame of his torch and was feeling his way along the walls in almost total darkness.

Eventually he came to a mass of undergrowth, which he gently parted and was astounded to find himself outside of the walls of the palace. No wonder the tunnel entrance had never been discovered as its entrance was inside the sacred grounds of the Royal Cemetery where commoners were forbidden to enter. The servants must have been either extremely desperate or daring, for to be found in these grounds would have meant sudden death.

The tunnel proved to be invaluable to the Prince for he had found a means of exploring his principality incognito. This would give him the opportunity of meeting his subjects and being able to discuss with them numerous topics on a man-to-man basis. He would be able to find out how his subjects felt about the Sun God, which might help him to eventually become a ruler for his people and not a ruler of his people.

As the months went by he gradually increased the distance that he would travel away from the protection of the palace. He managed to barter a hunting outfit on one occasion which allowed him to travel around the city unrecognised, as hunters from outside the city walls were continually visiting with their catches to sell in the market squares. It proved the perfect disguise, especially the cap that had a large peak and flap-down ear covers that covered most of his face.

He was now preparing to venture out for his sixth time. Once donned in his hunting clothes he cautiously began to part the old tapestry. The last two times he had gone through that process he had pulled on the fabric of the tapestry far too energetically as he was eager to get out of the palace and in doing so had pulled off a handful of the material as it was so rotten with age. He was also extremely fortunate not to have got bitten by a nasty looking scorpion, which had found its way up through the tunnel. This time all stayed intact and no horrible crawling insects dropped down upon him. He could now do the journey in half the time as he had learnt to memorise each twist and turn in the tunnel.

When he emerged from the dank subterranean tunnel system he could hardly see as the sun was low in the sky and shone directly towards him. He made no attempt to move until he was fully accustomed to the climatic conditions. His first concern was the sentry who was due to go past within the next five minutes so he hung back in the entrance of the cave well hidden by the undergrowth. Sure enough the guard appeared as usual, paused for a few moments and then walked on the next stage of his designated route. The guard had been a different one each time as it was a custom to have a relay of guards moving around at given intervals which helped to overcome the boredom. Each guard had his own favourite place to stop so the Prince had to be very vigilant. Once the guard had disappeared from sight he made his way around the perimeter of the graveyard where there was more cover and less chance of meeting anyone. There was in fact little chance of anyone being in the sacred grounds as it was out of bounds from sunrise to sunset. Any maintenance of the grounds had to be done in the dark by torchlight, usually only once a week at the most.

The tunnel always made him feel claustrophobic and often gave him a slight headache so he always looked forward to the first breath of fresh air from outside. At that time in the morning the air was always cool and carried the sweet fragrances from the jungle below. Once out of range of the palace grounds he would sit for a few moments and gaze out over the huge panoramic view below him. He never failed to marvel at the many different shades of green of the trees below, which were always changing under the influences of mist, cloud and bright sunlight. If the sky was overcast, he would be looking at a carpet of dark green and if it was bright sunlight the jungle would be a patchwork of all colours. If the winds were strong this would give the effect of a raging storm. He preferred a clear sky with a gentle breeze, which encouraged the eagles to soar high

9

up on the rising warm air from the jungle where they then gracefully circled above his head. Their wings were enormous and tipped white at their ends. The Prince thought it was such a travesty of beauty when their feathers were used by the Royal Guards as part of their head-dress. These birds were indeed the true gods of the Andes.

After a few moments rest he lowered himself down a very steep gradient, gripping small bushes and bunches of grass for support. At the bottom of the incline was a narrow path, which led down to the valley. This part of the journey could not be rushed as in places there were sheer drops to the valley floor thousands of feet below. Also at intervals of about six hundred metres there were guards whose duties were to challenge any travellers who were coming up from the valley. The Incas had chosen this place well, as a handful of soldiers could protect it from a whole army, there being no other way into the city.

Anyone who was a permanent resident of the city had a pass to show the guards. The Prince had had great difficulty in obtaining such a pass, as there was no need for him to possess one because he was Royalty and was always accompanied by the Royal Guard and therefore could travel anywhere he wished. He had got his closest aide and childhood friend to obtain one for him. His friend had assumed he needed it for getting young maidens into his quarters and so did not pursue the matter.

The guards he passed hardly paid any attention to him and the ones who did challenge him just glanced at his pass and did not bother to look into his face. Once he arrived at the base of the cliff he paused in order to decide in which direction to travel. He glanced at the tops of the trees to see which way the wind was prevailing and then decided to go against it hoping that it would help disguise his presence from any animal that he might begin to track.

After travelling for about an hour he paused for a few seconds in order to orientate himself and to listen for any unusual noises. Above the noise of the wind blowing in the trees and long grasses he thought that he could hear the sound of running water and decided to move towards it as he was beginning to become slightly dehydrated. He also thought it might be a place where animals might congregate. If there were animals there he had to make sure that he approached them from downwind. He looked at the top of the foliage of the trees and noticed that he was in luck as the branches were bending towards the direction in which he was travelling. The nearer he got to the sound of the water the slower he moved. He also began to take smaller steps and was particularly careful where he placed his feet in case he stood on a dried piece of wood, which might crack under his pressure.

He stopped again and listened for any sound of an animal. What he did not expect to hear was the sound of a human being. As he listened he noticed that the person appeared to be singing. Whoever it was, was obviously not afraid of attracting attention. The person knew that they were in a very safe environment and should anyone intrude upon them they could prove that they were very capable of looking after themselves.

He was now within about forty metres from where the melancholy voice seemed to be located. He knew that the stream or small river was very nearby as the foliage had changed from high trees with very little ground cover to thick bush and clear sky. As he moved even nearer the brush changed to high grasses, which made him change his tactics of approach. He knew that any movement that he made would give away his whereabouts as there was no wind now to disguise any swaying of the tops of the grasses. The best way to overcome this, he decided, was to backtrack until he reached the protection of the forest and to approach from the other direction which would put him in a more advantageous position. He could see at the far end of the jungle opening that the ground rose up into a small hillock which had excellent cover and which would enable him to look down on his quarry with little chance of himself being seen.

He quickly retraced his steps and then began to skirt around the clearing. As he neared the small hill he dropped onto all fours and slid through the stunted undergrowth until he had reached the top. Thankfully it was covered in grass through which he would be able to peer and not be seen. He was now in a prone position and remained that way until he was sure that whoever he was tracking had not seen him.

The voice continued to sing in a language that he did not recognise. During his forays into the jungle he had encountered many different tribes all of whom seemed to have their own languages. He had made it one of his priorities to try to learn at least a few useful words of their languages, as he knew that when he eventually took up his main roll in life it could prove very useful. What he could distinguish was the fact that the voice was that of a girl or woman and he was looking forward to getting his first glimpse of her. She was probably a girl from one of the Indian tribes that inhabited this area. They used to be extremely hostile but had changed their life style from hunters to traders. They were a very squat people and quite ugly, as they tended to go in for a lot of body and facial piercing. It seemed that the more they distorted their faces the more their self esteem improved. Little did he expect the extremely pleasant surprise that was about to unfold before his very eyes.

He eventually reached the top of the hill and lay there for a few moments in order to allow his weary muscles to recuperate with a fresh supply of oxygenated blood. Although he was exceptionally fit, the rarefied air during the first part of his journey followed by the huge change in temperature and humidity had taken its toll on the chemical system within his body. Once his heartbeat had returned to normal he reached forward and took hold of a handful of grass in front of his eyes and gradually parted it. Immediately he was astounded at the sheer natural beauty of the clearing below him.

Tall trees surrounded the clearing and at its centre was an area covered in exotic flowers of various shades of colour, which was accentuated by large patches of dark green mosses and short springy grasses. Through the centre of this meandered a small, extremely clear stream in which he could see long strands of grasses, which moved from side to side with the flow of the water. Occasionally a brightly coloured bird would dive down from the high branches above to quench its thirst or to take a quick splash in the stream in order to cool down and to wash out any uninvited insects.

Again he heard the sound of singing and his attention was drawn to the centre of the clearing where a large flat rock split the stream into two. The rock was quite smooth and just a few centimetres above the level of the slowly moving stream giving the impression that it was floating. The small bow wave caused by the movement of the water against it gave an optical allusion of it drifting upstream.

What he saw at the centre of the stone momentarily took his breath away. He would have been prepared for a dangerous animal or a ferocious looking headhunter but not a beautiful woman. She was sat cross-legged with her back towards him. He noticed that down the entire centre of her back she had some form of tribal markings as if made by an animal's claw.

She had obviously been bathing as her long slender back had rivulets of water running down its centre following the outline of her vertebral column. Her hair was jet black and glistened in the rays of the sun, which was now almost directly above the clearing. He could see small wet footprints on the stone indicating that she had only just climbed onto the rock, as the strong sun would have dried them up in a matter of minutes. She seemed oblivious to all around her and sat motionless allowing the sun's warm rays to caress her soft skin and gradually dry her off. The Prince could see that she was totally naked and as he surveyed the scene more scrupulously he saw at the far edge of the clearing a neat pile of clothing. He also noticed that beside of the clothing was what appeared to be a lethal looking spear and some form of knife that had a stocky handle and a long slender blade that glinted in the sun. This was not the usual type of woman that he had had acquaintances with in the past. He was truly intrigued and wanted to see her face. This was no ordinary native girl, he thought.

Five minutes had passed and still she had made no attempt to move. Under normal circumstances had he been in the palace grounds he would have thought nothing of walking straight up to the girl even though it would have startled her. He was after all the ruler of all his people and they were all subservient to him. Rulers of the Inca Empire had in the past taken numerous native girls for their own pleasures. The Prince was the exception however, for he believed that all women had their right to protect their dignity and he had never taken advantage of any of them. He actually felt extremely guilty lying there spying on the unsuspecting girl but he was unable to draw himself away. He felt compelled to wait to see if she would eventually stand, which he knew was inevitable, as she had to collect her clothes on the far side of the clearing. This would mean that she would have to turn at least sideways to him thus possibly allowing him to get a glimpse of her face.

Her skin was a dark brown and as she moved he could see the definition of a lean body, not too muscular, but one that purveyed pure physical fitness. The sun was nearing the time when it would move behind the tree line and the clearing would become quite dark.

The Prince took a deep breath in anticipation of her first movement when she would collect her clothing. Sure enough, just before the sun was about to disappear she moved her legs and commenced to stand up. She became even more beautiful as her legs were long and slender which matched her slim upper body. She stood for a moment and pulled her elongated strands of shiny black hair from around her back and twirled it up into a bun. She was about to step from the rock into the stream when she seemed to freeze as if she sensed that something or someone had dared venture into her personal clearing. The Prince knew that she was aware of his presence even though he had not portrayed any giveaway signals. He sank even lower into the grass but still kept her in his vision. From the position where he was lying there was no chance of being spotted as the grass gave the perfect camouflage and the sun would have been in her eyes if she had looked up towards him. He never expected her next move and it remained vividly with him for the rest of his life.

She slowly turned to face his direction and he could now see her in her true beauty. He had seen many native girls in his travels over the past years but none such as this. Her face was

14

absolutely perfect, high cheekbones, light sallow skin, quite a large mouth and dark slanting eyes. Across the left side of her cheek was some form of tribal markings, similar to the ones on her back, which had the effects of enhancing her beauty even more. It was the eyes that he noticed most of all. They would haunt him in future times. She seemed to be looking straight at him and he began to feel quite exposed. She knew he was there but made no attempt to run for shelter. She kept staring in the Prince's direction until the he became so uncomfortable that he decided that it was time for him to move.

It took the Prince about ten minutes to get well away from the clearing to a position where he could stand up without being seen. His initial feelings were ones of shame for having spied on the girl, but as he stood there this changed to slight anger and then bemusement. Here was the next ruler of the Inca Empire hiding from a native girl. What a ridiculous position he had allowed himself to get into. How pathetic he felt. In hindsight he should have stood up when the girl looked towards him and walked down towards her. She would then have taken fright and run off into the jungle. He had no intentions of going back to the palace feeling as he was at that present moment. At that point he made a decision to return the way he had come and confront the girl.

The journey back to the clearing took less than no time as he was travelling at a jog and paying little heed to disguising his movements through the undergrowth. He had decided his best tactics would be for him to burst into the clearing, thus taking the girl by surprise and giving her no time to run off into the forest.

On reaching the edge of the forest he increased his speed to a fast stride and without making hardly any noise at all jumped into the clearing. His plan had worked up to this point except for one major problem. The girl was no longer standing in the middle of the stream. She was nowhere to be seen. The neat pile of clothes had gone plus the spear and knife. There was no sign of anyone.

The Prince looked upon himself as an expert tracker but no matter how hard he looked he could find no traces of the girl.

He looked for any signs where the grasses may have been bent underfoot and for any telltale marks on the mosses around the rock. There was nothing. Only an expert in jungle craft could have disappeared leaving no clues at all that they had been there.

He began to search around the borders of the clearing looking at the bushes in the hope of at least one broken branch. There was nothing out of the ordinary. He must have searched for over thirty minutes and the longer he looked the more annoyed he became. How could a woman have tricked him? What a fool he had been. In his mad dash through the forest he had forgotten all the rules he had been taught when tracking a quarry. She must have heard him long before he reached the clearing.

The light was beginning to fade and he knew that he would have to begin to make tracks back to the palace grounds before sunset. He took one last look at the beautiful clearing and then set off at a brisk pace back the way he had come.

During the return journey he was unable to remove the picture of the girl from his memory. The more he tried to concentrate on other things the more vividly she appeared. He arrived back at the palace just in time for his absence not to have been discovered. By the time the sun had set he was expected to make an appearance at the dinner table along with the elders and he only arrived with minutes to spare.

All during the meal he found it hard to concentrate on the various topics that were being discussed and at one time there was an embarrassing silence when he had been asked a question which he had not heard as his mind was back in the clearing. This momentarily brought him to his senses and for the next hour he was able to function as normal. That night he was unable to sleep. He kept cursing the girl for upsetting his normal routine

When he awoke the next morning he felt absolutely shattered. There was no possibility of him taking any extra respite from the previous day's excursion, as he had to attend early morning roll call in the main square as part of his training to become a warrior. There were no excuses for arriving late even though he was the Prince. For this part of his education he was treated as an ordinary soldier.

The parade ground was cool for the moment as it was only seven in the morning. The sun had just crept over the craggy tops of the mountain range and cast long shadows over the thousand young men who were assembled in lines of twenty. They were dressed in a simple uniform of loosely hung cotton which would help them to keep cool during their exercises and allow full range of movement when taking part in hand-to-hand combat. The Commanders of the Elite Guard were true professionals when it came to training their soldiers in improving their fitness and strength. They even appreciated the importance of having a good warm-up which prepared the cardiovascular system and the muscles for strenuous exercise.

The warm-up took about half an hour. Initially they ran laps around the parade ground followed by a series of stretching exercises. This was followed by either aerobic or anaerobic training. There was then a short rest period in order to allow the body to replenish itself for the loss of liquids and to allow the men to eat small amounts of food containing high quantities of carbohydrates. Time was given for these foods to be digested in order for it to turn into glycogen, which was used for energy in order to replenish the muscle fibres.

During this day the Prince was due to spend an hour on the art of throwing the lance, an hour using a short sword and then a strenuous run to the valley below and back up again without stopping. On returning to the parade ground the soldiers then had to stand at attention in the heat until the last runner had returned. This was a good ploy by the training instructors as it encouraged the soldiers to look after one another thus developing camaraderie within the ranks, which in turn would produce a close-knit unit during battle.

The Prince was always in the top twenty runners to return to the parade ground and in order to take his mind off the heat of the sun he used to make a conscious effort to study the conditions of the soldiers as they returned. One of the things he detested most of all were the flies that were attracted by the hundreds of sweating bodies. Often he would come off the parade ground covered in numerous bites, which would itch for days on end. He had endured this onslaught of insects every time he paraded in the square until one day he was fortunate to end up after a run behind one of the oldest members of the battalion. This man was renown for his prowess in battle and for his ability to endure extreme hardships and this was the first opportunity that the Prince had been close enough to him to make any form of assessment of the man.

He had been standing, watching the soldier for almost a half an hour and in that time the Prince had been bitten more than a dozen times. He noticed that the old soldier in front seemed to be getting no bites at all. The flies were landing on him but soon left leaving no telltale marks on his skin. Why, he thought should this man be the only one on the parade ground, from what he could see, who was not troubled by stings from the numerous insects that frequented this place? When the parade was over he decided to tackle him on this. He had to wait until the time when they all took a welcoming dip in the cool spring water that was brought to the city by a clever network of stone leats. He sat down next to the older soldier.

"Please forgive my intrusion but I am puzzled by the fact that you never seem to get stung by insects on the parade ground. What mystical powers do you possess?"

The older man smiled.

"You're the first one to have noticed that in all the time I have stood in that confounded dust bowl. The secret is complete control of ones muscular reflexes and a substance called pig dung!" He laughed when he mentioned the latter. "You would assume that the flies would be attracted by the odours from the unpleasant smelling manure. Quite the contrary. If you were a fly would you prefer a sweating soldier with succulent blood or an old sow? I learnt that from my grandfather who served with the Inca Army in numerous areas of the Empire. He discovered it from one of the tribes who inhabited a part of the forest, which was infested with large mosquitoes. Many of his friends died during that insurgence into the jungle from the bites of those fever-carrying insects. He was one of the lucky ones who was given a liquid to rub on his skin by one of the friendlier natives. He survived and passed the remedy on to me. And now I am passing it on to you. I have been watching your progress with much interest. You have the gift of becoming a great warrior. You still have much to learn, however. Your perception today will be invaluable to you in future years when you will no doubt have to endure the hardships of the jungle below. What is your name incidentally? Have we come across one another before other than on the parade ground? I have got a good memory for faces and I am sure I have seen you somewhere."

The Prince was momentarily caught off his guard. Should he pretend to be someone else or own up to the fact that he was the Royal Prince heir to the Sun God? He was extremely impressed by this soldier, especially by the fact that he had been noticed by him during training. For once in his life his performance had been appreciated as a soldier and not as the Prince. He decided on the latter as the soldier gave the impression that he was a very honest type of person and may not have been very impressed with his new leader if he lied to him.

"I am the Royal Prince."

The soldier's face went pale for he immediately now recognised the person in front of him. He had only seen him at a close range on one occasion and that was when he was assisting the Royal Guard in the main palace square where hundreds of common folk had gathered to receive one of the rulers of the principalities. His first reaction was to drop to his knees and bow his head towards the Prince.

"Please don't do that. We are equals under these circumstances and it should be me kneeling before you, as you are by far the most senior soldier here and have achieved many heroic exploits serving for the Empire. Please stand up."

The soldier arose and was once more shocked when the Prince held out his hand for him to shake. This was not at all protocol. No one ever greeted the Prince with a handshake unless they were of royal blood. He was reluctant to take the hand but the Prince insisted.

"You have taught me much in a very short space of time",

the Prince continued. "How long have you been serving in the army?"

"All my life, sir. I was given to the army when I was of age, and have served her ever since."

"Why have you not become an officer in all of that time then? A man with all of your qualities should by now have been well up in the ranks."

"There have been times when I have not seen eye to eye with certain commanding officers and for my sins have made it known. I appreciate that this cannot be tolerated in an army and I have accepted the consequences. I have now taken a more resilient attitude to poor commanding and gone with the flow so to speak. The commanders have improved immensely over recent years but there are occasions when they could learn from the experiences of us older ones."

The more the Prince heard from this soldier the more he liked him. Few would dare express any form of comments in his presence, which might prove contradictory to the running of the country, which was laid down by the elders who represented the Sun God. He could see that he could gain much from this man who was in contact with the ordinary commoner. It could prove beneficial to him in making him a better leader in years to come.

"I appreciate your frank answers to my questions. I would like to talk to you again in the near future. In the mean time I would prefer it if you would not mention our conversation to the other soldiers as I would like to continue my training being treated as one of them."

The soldier nodded in agreement not appreciating how this encounter would change his life so dramatically. A month later he was promoted to the post of personal guard to the Prince and from that point forward a life-long bond grew between them.

The next two months were extremely busy ones for the Prince. His training doubled in intensity and he seemed to be spending far more time attending meetings with the Elders, as it was the silly season for visiting dignitaries. In actual fact being kept occupied for most of the day was a blessing in disguise for it gave him little time to think of the beautiful Indian girl. It was at night she was most in his thoughts. He had to see her again and so he decided that at his first earliest opportunity he would go once again down into the jungle.

The opportunity arose some four weeks later when he had two days free in his calendar due to a distinguished guest from an outlying settlement cancelling his appointment to meet the Prince. The meeting had to be postponed as trouble had flared up between two warlike tribes in that vicinity and it was felt unwise for the entourage to travel through that district.

As in his previous trip he got up early, packed some dried fruit from the previous night's dinner, changed into his hunting outfit and then went down into the damp tunnel. It was during this trip that he made his first mistake. He had become over-confident and was travelling quite quickly down the steep narrow path to the valley below and failed to slow at a very sharp bend in the path. He came around it just as two sentries were changing posts. He ran straight into one of them and knocked him to the ground. The soldiers initial reaction was not one of antagonism as they appreciated that the instigator was travelling away from the city and could not have been an intruder. They were however extremely annoyed.

The one who had been knocked to the floor got up and began to dust his uniform down.

"Not very clever coming around the bend at that speed. What's the hurry? You could have gone over the side. There is a sheer drop here." He pointed to the side of the path, which disappeared into the abyss below.

"I really am sorry for that. I'm late for meeting up with a hunting party. I will make amends by dropping off an animal on the way back up." This seemed to appease the guard who managed to smile.

"Make sure it's a big one even if it means a struggle up the path. I'm not going to forget your face for a long time especially if I get no fresh meat. Now be off with you before the animals disappear for the night. I doubt if you will catch any today, as they will hear you coming along the paths and crashing into trees." His companion laughed out loud.

21

"If you had bumped into me you would have been unable to continue on your journey. You got off lightly this time. I would have thrown you over the side," said the other soldier.

The Prince bowed his head in an apologetic fashion and moved off down the path at a much slower pace. He was really annoyed with himself for attracting so much attention. It would not happen again. Damn girl. It was her fault. No it wasn't. It was his. He remembered the words of one of his army instructors,

"If you make any mistakes in the battlefield it will cost you your life or the life of one of your fellow soldiers. There is only one person to blame for such a death and that is not your foe. A mistake is a luxury that none of us can afford!"

That episode had brought him to his senses. He was now once again an alert athlete in search of a prey. The remaining part of the descent took longer than normal. The other guards he came upon took very little notice of his presence even though he was the only other person on the path at that time of the morning. They were too preoccupied in cleaning their uniforms and swords for a possible early morning inspection.

He reached the floor of the valley at about noon and decided that as he had lost so much time in the descent that he should press straight on to his destination, the little clearing in the depth of the forest.

This trip was in vain as there was no one in the clearing. He had remained hidden on the small hillock for over three hours before giving up. He could not afford to stay any longer, as he had to hunt some form of wild life for the soldier he had previously bumped into. That man was justly pleased when he received a young fresh buck just before going off duty.

It took three more visits to the watering hole before he encountered the Indian girl once again. He had taken the normal precautions of approaching slowly so as not to disturb any grasses whose swaying actions might be picked up by a wary prey. He positioned himself in the same place as on previous occasions, lying on his stomach with his head just high enough to peer through the grasses without the top of it appearing over the skyline. There was little breeze so he would easily be able to pick out any form of noise made by anything or anyone approaching the clearing.

He had been in that position for only about ten minutes when his senses indicated to him that something was happening. He kept perfectly still and listened intently. Nothing stirred and yet he knew there was something out there. His hair on the back of his neck began to stand on end. Not a sensation that he was used to. He felt that he was being watched. Carefully he looked around his hide but could see nothing out of the ordinary. He tried to assure himself that nothing could get within range of him without him knowing. How wrong he was.

A sharp pricking sensation at his throat made him freeze like a statue. To move would have meant certain death. A bead of perspiration formed high up on his forehead and then trickled down the side of his cheek. Nothing else moved. It seemed like an eternity he had lain there waiting for the blade to dig deeply into his neck. There was no point in making any heroic moves. The only chance that he had was to remain perfectly still and hope that the first thrust would not be fatal. It was at this point that he would defend himself.

Suddenly the blade was gone. He had been at the mercy of whoever had been so brilliant at tracking him and now they were allowing him to possibly take the initiative. Were they waiting for him to make the first move before killing him?

Someone laughed behind him and he could hear from their movement that they had retired slightly away from him. At that precise moment the direction of the wind changed and the Prince caught the fragrance of an exotic flower. He slowly rolled over with one arm and leg underneath him in order to push himself up from the ground into a fighting stance. His other hand was at his waist where he could quickly reach his hunting knife. The person laughed again, obviously amused by his tactics. He turned and looked his attacker in the eyes. They were the eyes that had haunted him for the past three months. It was the Indian girl.

Chapter Two

Nakita was the only daughter of an Indian Chief of a tribe that lived in a village on the periphery of the jungle. At one time the Indians lived deep in the forest and were known for their warlike nature. However, since the Incas had established themselves by their sheer numbers and their ability to organise themselves so effectively in battle, the tribe had decided that they were no match for those armies and had given up their arms and in time became a trading village, and a most successful one at that.

The family of Nakita consisted of four brothers, her mother and father and two very old grandparents. The children were separated by a year, Zuma the eldest, followed by Nakita, then Zalai, Rastu and finally the youngest, Barulu. It was these brothers who were mainly responsible for her upbringing.

Her mother had little time for her, as she was so busy running the house. Cooking for five was a mammoth task in itself. She was also responsible for looking after the animals to produce milk, food and occasionally clothing. These also had to be fed and once a week moved on to better pastures that were few and hard to come by in the proximity of the forest. One had to be careful not to overgraze especially during the rainy season when there was a possibility of soil erosion that could mean no more grasses for quite a few years.

Theoretically it was Nakita's job to help her mother with the family chores whilst the boys were allowed to play hunting games. This she did, but as soon as her father left on hunting trips she used to disappear from the house and join in with her brothers. Her mother never made any fuss, as she was afraid that her husband would take it out on the girl when he returned.

The only time that Nakita had to herself was when the rest

of the family had retired to bed. She would then sneak out of the house and go to the side of the jungle where she would lie down and gaze into the crystal clear heavens. Over a long period she learnt all the constellations in the sky and knew in which position they would be even before looking up. She could do this no matter what time of the year. She found it very relaxing and it helped her to get rid of all of her anxieties. She continued to do this even during her adulthood.

When she was born her father was in two minds as to whether she should be allowed to live. A girl was of little use to the family as she could not hunt and bring home food. If it hadn't been for his wife's begging for the baby girl's life, he would have done just that, like his father and their fathers before them.

During her early years Nakita copied her brothers when they played their hunting games, but as she became more agile and stronger she began to assert herself and often was the instigator of a game. She made her own hunting equipment and by the time she was in her teens she could match all of her brothers' skills in hunting and tracking. She made twine from the jungle creepers for her bow, made a lethal hunting knife from the bones of a water buffalo whose skeleton she had stumbled across during one of her hunting games with her brothers, and designed a sling from which she could hit a target at a distance of fifty metres.

As they gradually grew older so the games became more adventurous. Instead of keeping to the tall grasses that covered the ground for miles around the camp they began to venture into the traditional tribal hunting grounds in the jungle. Here the animals were much bigger and much more ferocious than the small game that inhabited the grasslands. They had no intention at all of tackling such game if they came across it but they loved the excitement of being in a danger zone and an environment where one could see no further than a few metres ahead. It was during one such venture that they lost Zalai.

Their father was going away on a long hunt and would not be back for three days so the children decided to get up very early the day after he had left so that they could venture deeper

25

into the jungle where the largest animals were known to roam. Nakita was the first one up that morning which was no different to usual as her brothers were always the last out of bed and would stay there for most of the day if it hadn't been for their mother who used to hit them with a slender stick if she found them lying on after sunrise.

"Come on you boys otherwise I will go off on my own," called Nakita to her sleeping brothers.

They were up like a shot, as they knew that Nakita would have done just that, as she was not afraid to go into the jungle on her own.

"And do not forget to bring along your water bags. Not mentioning any names but one of you forgot the last time and spent the whole of the day moaning and begging for water!"

"No need to be so bossy. We know the rules of the jungle and don't need you to look after us," said Barulu the youngest and cutest of the boys. He was trying to assert himself but knew deep down that he would not go into the jungle without his sister.

"Well, I'm ready and have been for the past hour so let's get going," said Zuma who was asserting his authority over the rest. He always led the way on their forays into the jungle even though his sister was a better tracker. She never contradicted her brother's actions but was called upon from time to time to find their way back when they got lost.

Nakita looked at her brothers to make sure that they were suitably attired for the rigorous trek through the demanding undergrowth within the depths of the forest. They seemed to be kitted out in the right clothing and all seemed fully armed, not that they were going to take part in any serious hunting.

"Right, we're off. Nakita you take up the rear and the rest follow me."

Initially Zuma followed the track that they had carved through the dense jungle many months before. Each time they had to use their machetes to cut back new climbers and bush that sprung up almost as they passed by, so excellent were the growing conditions. Nakita was amused by the antics of her younger brothers who took every conceivable moment to hunt for small prey. During the initial part of the walk they would venture slightly off the beaten track looking for small animals but always staying within earshot of the main party. As they got deeper into the jungle however, these small sorties began to cover less distance until they stopped completely. The light had faded drastically due to the dense branches of the canopy high above which only allowed the odd beam of sunlight to filter through. In these areas her brothers closed in on one another until the whole group formed a tightly knit line within touching distance of one another. She appreciated how they felt for she too had experienced the ghostly feelings the jungle could inflict upon people. On her solo forays she had learnt to control her fears. Now it did not bother her.

All around them was still. The tall trees cut out any sounds made by the winds high above the dense canopy and no birds had need to venture down to their level. The only sounds made were the rubbings of the trees and lianas against one another as they swayed in the strong breezes. No one dared to talk.

Nakita suddenly whispered that they should all remain very still and quiet for a few moments. She had picked up a sound which was unfamiliar to her and which her brothers had not picked up. They stood like frozen statues not daring to move until their sister gave the command. Not even her eldest brother made any attempt to do anything as he appreciated the acute skills that his sister had acquired during her many forays into the jungle alone.

There it was again. They all heard something this time. It was the crackling of undergrowth as something stepped upon it. No one was quite sure from which direction the sounds were coming as they kept changing. Each sound was followed by a long silence as if the animal, if it was an animal, appreciated that it had made a noise and was waiting patiently before making the next move. The children had the feeling that some unknown predator was stalking them.

"I don't like this", whispered Rastu. The other boys turned and glared at him for breaking the silence. Rastu looked sheepishly at them and then at his sister who tried to give him a reassuring smile. She held up her finger to her mouth indicating that he should remain silent. After some three or four minutes no more sounds were heard other than the swish of the branches high up above their heads. It was Rasta who finally broke the silence.

"I think it must have moved on, whatever it was. It's getting late and we must be out of here before it gets too dark." The rest looked at him and nodded in turn. No one else wanted to speak until they were out in the open and well away from the jungle.

Nakita could see her brothers relax a little. As Zuma turned to retrace his steps there was a powerful rushing noise that seemed to emanate from above their heads. Suddenly the undergrowth parted to reveal a huge black, snarling face travelling at a tremendous velocity. Nakita was the first to react. She held up her machete just as the animal flew past her and felt the steel cut into the black, gleaming flanks. Warm blood sprayed across her arm. The injury had no effect on the animal at all. It had previously selected its prey and had decided to ignore all of the others.

Zalai took the whole brunt of the attack. He stood no chance at all. He probably felt nothing after the initial powerful crunch of the black jaws. In a matter of seconds he and the animal had disappeared back into the forest. There were no sounds after that. No screams came from Zalai, no sound of an animal crashing through the undergrowth, nothing at all. The rest of the party just stood in a bewilderment not quite grasping what had just happened, as it had been so swift.

Barulu began to whimper which broke the spell.

"Quick. We must get out of this place in case the animal should return. We must look after our younger brothers," said Zuma to his sister not wanting to remain any longer.

"You get out of the jungle, Zuma. I will search around to see if I can find Zalai."

They both knew that nothing would be found but both thought it was the right thing to do at that moment. Nakita knew that the animal would have travelled well away from its killing place by now.

"You are going to have to explain what happened here today to father and tell him that I will be back before sunset." She did not relish the thought of telling her mother and father and preferred to stay and look for the animal.

Zuma nodded, told Rastu and Barula to keep close to him and then made off at a quick jog back down the narrow jungle path. They kept up this speed until they were well away from the jungle and then sat down for a rest and a long drink from their leather water sacks.

"We should not have left Nakita on her own," said Rastu in a soft voice.

"We had no choice. We could not return to father without making an attempt to find our brother. That would have been a sign of cowardice, and in any case Nakita is the best tracker of us all and knows how to look after herself. She'll be all right. Now lets get on and get back into the camp before father returns from his hunting trip." Zuma's authoritative voice gave them all a little more confidence although no one was looking forward to seeing father.

In the meantime Nakita was inspecting the ground around the attack for any form of clue as to which way the animal had travelled. What she did find quite surprised her. It was the end of the big cat's tail, almost half a metre in length. As her machete had cut into the animal as it dived through the air it must have caught the tail end, which would have been quite rigid as most animals use their tails to help in their balance. She picked it up and stuck it into her belt. There was nothing else to see. No trail of blood and very few tell tale signs indicating which direction the animal had gone. After only a few minutes Nakita knew that she was wasting her time and made tracks to get back to the village before darkness fell. As she left the clearing she made a vow that she would return and kill the animal that had stolen her brother Zalai.

She got back to the village just as it was getting dark. There was a large fire burning brightly in the centre of the square around which sat the majority of the Indians from the village. No one was speaking, as it was the custom that when a life was lost the villagers would assemble in a sign of respect. Nakita's father was sat nearest to the fire on the left hand side of the oldest and wisest member of the council with the rest of the family sat behind him.

Nakita's entry into the square could not have been more dramatic. The shadows cast by the flickering of the flames from the fire danced over her body and made her look quite frightening for she was still covered with the blood of her brother, plus the grime from rushing through the thick undergrowth and fresh blood from her own body caused by sharp thorns. She went and knelt at her father's feet. Her father presented no form of recognition of her presence. He just stared into the glowing embers of the fire. Ever since she had known her father he had never shown her any form of affection at all. He only had time for his sons. She remained in that position until her father eventually spoke.

"What is it that you have hanging from your belt?" He said in a stern voice.

"It is the tail of the animal that attacked Zulai, father. It was cut off when my machete struck the animal. I will return soon and finish the job. Until it is killed Zulai's spirit will not move on." No one believed that would ever be achieved but it did seem to help relax the intense atmosphere.

The whole of the village stayed in the square until the last glow from the embers fizzled out and then returned to their huts to grieve privately.

The next day, Nakita's family stayed inside their hut. Villagers called each day and left food and water by the entrance and as a sign of respect picked bunches of brightly coloured flowers, which were placed in front of the porch. By the third week the family appeared to be back to normal. The only change from routine was that the children had been forbidden from entering the jungle.

Two months went by during which time Nakita spent every free moment planning the destruction of the animal that had taken her brother. She told no one of her plans and no one saw the meticulous shaping of the instrument that she hoped would be the downfall of the powerful aggressor. If it didn't work it would probably be the end of her too.

In her mind she had decided the animal would still remain in that vicinity. Most of the cat family, once they had established themselves in a specific area tended to stay there provided that the hunting remained good. They usually sprayed their urine around their territory as a warning to any visitors that if they entered their area they did so at their own risk.

Nakita had also spent her time questioning the elders of the tribe as to the hunting techniques of the black cat. She found out that it almost always attacked its prey from above. Anyone tracking such a monster should not only look at the ground for clues but also along solid branches where it would leave telltale scratches of the lichen from its huge claws. In the initial stages the animal would pick up the sound of a possible quarry long before it strayed into its domain so keen was its sense of hearing. Once put on the alert it would proceed to climb a suitable tree and work its way towards its prey. The unsuspecting animal would not be expecting an attack from above and all of its concentration would be focused on the area within its own proximity.

Nakita would be prepared for this and had devised a strategy that if successful would give the animal no second chance to attack once it had made its first aerial strike. She had designed a lance which was about two metres long and which was made of a very stout bamboo pole with a murderous looking blade attached to its end. At the other end she had made a ball of twine and fixed it firmly to the shaft. Her idea was to lay the lance on the floor next to her and when the animal struck she would raise the blade of the lance and leave the other end stuck firmly into the ground. As the ball of twine prevented the pole from sliding into the soft soil the animal's weight would impale its body down onto the shaft resulting in its death. That was the theory. Only someone extremely brave or foolhardy would dare put such a plan into action. Nakita had both such qualities.

It was during the ninth week that she decided that all her meticulous preparations were complete. The night before she was due to leave she hid all of her jungle clothing and weapons at the rear of the hut underneath grasses and leaves that she had previously collected. Deeper into the forest she had already hidden a small piglet in a cage made of bamboo which she had

31

hauled up into the forest branches away from any ground predators, hoping no snake would come along in the meantime and kill it. This small animal was to be the bait

The following morning she was up well before any member of the family had even begun to stir. By the time they did eventually get up Nakita had got into her hunting clothes, collected the piglet and was well into the forest. It took her almost a whole day to get to the area where the first encounter with the large cat had taken place. Most of the paths that they had previously forged into the jungle had become overgrown so Nakita had to hack her way through newly grown shoots and lianas, which was hard work but not as difficult as the first time they had cut their way through the virgin forest.

Nakita had hoped to be at the hunting grounds well before darkness in order to make her preparations. However the poor lighting prevented her from attempting this so she settled down to try to sleep until the following morning. The sounds of the forest life were far more unnerving than during the daytime and so Nakita only managed to get a few hours of sleep. She had taken the precaution of climbing up into the branches where the only dangers were the big cat and an odd snake.

As soon as there was enough light she climbed down from the branches feeling far less agile than when she went up.

She worked feverishly and within an hour the trap was set. The piglet was placed in the centre of the small clearing and Nakita lay to the side of it covered in small branches and grasses, the long spear at her side.

She lay there hour after hour making no movement at all. Occasionally a small animal would sneak into the clearing to investigate the noisy piglet but no animal of any significance came along.

Almost five hours had gone by when Nakita had the first inkling that something was amiss. She became aware how silent the jungle had become. Just like the time when she had been with her brothers. All animal noises had ceased. Only the sound of the wind in the high canopy was to be heard. It could only mean one thing. The inhabitants of the jungle sensed a presence.

Their main form of defence was concealment and silence. She tried to relax but the unnerving silence made her tense up. She took a firm grip of her lance, cut her breathing down to a bare minimum and waited. The first thing she noticed was that sounds were much louder to the east of her. She deduced from this that the black menace was approaching from this direction.

The piglet also seemed to have sensed that something was amiss and instead of quietening down did the complete opposite and began to squeal in a very high pitched note which echoed throughout the jungle. Perfect, thought Nakita, as it could not fail to attract the cat if it was a cat.

She distinctly heard the snapping of a twig some forty or so metres off to her left. She held her breath and listened intently. Another snap and then nothing. She thought she heard a branch move against another, again off to her left but much nearer this time. It could only be the animal getting ready for its kill. Nakita's heart was racing and its beating sounded like huge drums in her ears, so loud that she thought the stalker must be able to hear it. She noticed that the piglet had suddenly stopped squawking and had huddled into the corner nearest to her. So the attacker was coming in from the opposite corner to the piglet. Nakita slowly began moving her lance around so that the sharp bladed end faced the direction from which she expected the attack to occur. Instead of looking straightforward she looked up into the trees for a branch, which would be sturdy enough to hold the weight of a large cat. The only one within striking distance of the piglet was about four metres away and some three metres above the ground. One swift look around assured Nakita that this was the only sensible way for the cat to attack and so she prepared herself for the inevitable.

It happened in a split second just like the last time. There was no sound, only the sudden parting of the leaves at the end of the branch upon which Nakita was concentrating. She was ready this time however, and reacted just as fast as the large black cat. The animal had already commenced its aerial pursuit of the piglet when it caught sight of the forest floor suddenly moving and in the place of leaves and branches a form had appeared. The animal attempted to change the direction of its flight by a most amazing acrobatic manoeuvre. Had it continued on its original direction and gone for the piglet it would have survived but the change in flight took it directly in line with Nakita's lance. Death was instantaneous. The steel end of the lance went directly through its rib cage and into the left ventricle of the heart. As it brushed past Nakita she felt wetness across her face and down the length of her back. At the time the adrenalin was rushing through her body and the whole of her nervous system was focused on the animal and so she felt no pain whatsoever. The wetness was caused by the animal's left paw, which had glanced the side of Nakita's face and continued across her neck and down the entire length of her back.

Once the killing had been accomplished the pain set in. She forgot the animal for the moment as her wounds needed to be dealt with immediately, as in the present environment they would soon be susceptible to infection. She looked around for a suitable plant and found one whose leaves were used by the Indians as a cleanser and healer. The leaves were quite soft and by taking a large handful and squeezing them it was possible to obtain a small amount of juice which when rubbed into an open wound caused a great amount of pain but also killed almost any form of bacteria and stopped all bleeding. Once this process had taken place there was no need to even dress the wound. Nakita accomplished this ritual in half an hour and then returned to the clearing.

The large black beast took up almost the whole of the clearing. It was a magnificent looking animal and Nakita could not help feeling a little sorry for it even though it had killed her brother. The end of its tail was missing so she knew for certain that it was the same cat. The next hour she spent skinning the animal and then laid it out in the small sunlit area at the far end of the clearing. The residue of the body she took into the depths of the forest, as she did not want the scent of it attracting any of its friends. The sun was very strong and so dried the skin which was ready to be rolled up within half an hour. It was beginning to get dark so she hastily collected up all of her belongings, as she did not want to spend another sleepless night in the jungle and began the long journey back to her home.

By the time she got back the village was beginning to settle down for the night. The peace did not last very long.

"Nakita's back." It was Zuma who first saw her. He had been waiting on the outskirts of the village knowing that she would return within a few days of her disappearance. Deep down he knew that she had returned to the forest in the quest of her brother's killer and he was proved right when he saw the animal pelt hanging from her waist belt.

Within seconds the rest of the family appeared at the door of their hut and soon the other villagers began to assemble. Nakita's father then appeared from out of the large gathering and stood in front of his daughter. Nakita on seeing him walked forward and proceeded to unroll the animal skin at his feet.

"This was the animal that killed your son." And to prove the point she took the tail from her belt and placed it next to the animal's half tail. "Now Zalai's spirit may rest in peace."

There was absolute silence in the village. All were amazed at the size of the animal and the scars on Nakita's back.

Nakita's father looked at his daughter and for the first time in his life appreciated how courageous a little girl he had. Tears began to well up in his eyes as he stepped forward and took his daughter into his arms and gave her a long hug.

Nakita had never before experienced any form of love from her parents. It was a moment in her life that she would never forget.

From that day forward Nakita was allowed to go into the jungle whenever she wished and in time became the tribe's best hunter. Her skills were so good that she was able to catch enough food to feed all of the family. Her brothers had given up hunting once they had grown up and had laid down their hunting equipment and turned their skills to woodcarving, the wares they used to trade with the Incas.

Nakita had no time for the opposite sex, as she was extremely conscious of her hideous scar, so she spent all of her time hunting. Each time she would venture deeper into the jungle making sure that no one was following her especially on the day that she visited her very special place. She had stumbled across it by sheer chance when she was tracking a wild boar. The animal had somehow sensed that it was being hunted and had bolted through the thick undergrowth. Nakita had set off at a fast pace after it and had suddenly burst through the undergrowth to find herself in a clearing in the forest. It was a place which was abundant with the most colourful of flowers, many of which she had never seen before. Its floor was covered in a thick spongy moss, which soothed her weary feet. Running through it was a slow, meandering stream and at its centre was a large flat rock upon which she would often sit naked and allow the sun's rays to dry her off after having taken a cooling dip. She knew that there would be no prying eyes in this part of the jungle as it was supposed to be the haunt of the Jaguar that kept all other hunters away from the area. She would sit for hours watching the colourful butterflies in their courting manoeuvres and study the various species of birds which would come diving down from the branches high up in the canopy in order to bathe. It was during one of these visits to her paradise island that she met the person whom she would love for the rest of her life.

She had gone through her usual ritual of bathing in the steam and was lying completely naked on her flat rock. She was extremely relaxed and was finding the warmth of the sun beating down on her back very therapeutical. As she lay there looking up into the tops of the swaying trees she noticed a blue jay that was swooping down for its morning bathe. As it brushed past a low lying branch it dislodged a beautiful orchid that fell at the feet of Nakita. She picked it up and marvelled at its distinct and wonderful fragrance.

Suddenly for no accountable reason she became very alert. She had seen nothing move nor had heard any unusual sound, which often happened as numerous small animals frequently visited the clearing and yet she knew that something or someone was present. She slowly stood up and sensed that someone was looking at her from somewhere directly behind her. She paused for a moment trying to decide whether to quickly collect her knife and spear which were lying on the rock beside her and then to cross over the stream to collect her clothes, which she had left on the far side of the clearing, or to make a wild dash back into the jungle. She did neither of these things. Instead, she slowly stood up and turned to face her adversary. Motionless, she stared into the thick grasses ahead of her. After what seemed an eternity she saw a slight movement in the bushes at the top of a small knoll. As she continued to watch she noticed the grasses gradually move apart as the animal or person retreated.

Once the movement had ceased she grabbed her hunting equipment, leapt across the stream, collected her clothes and disappeared into the jungle. Whoever he was he would not get the better of her again, she thought, as she put her clothes back on. The next time that he dared venture into her now not so secret paradise she would be ready for him. No one got the better of Nakita in the jungle. He would be back, that she was sure.

He returned on three further occasions and each time she watched him take the same position as before lying quietly in the undergrowth at the top of the knoll. A person of habit she thought, which would prove his downfall.

She decided to take him on his next visit into her private world. She had made an assumption from his previous visits that he was some kind of hunter but not that good! From where she stood he looked quite athletic, with a pronounced muscular body and was very good-looking. She knew that she would have to be very careful tackling this prey.

He arrived almost dead on time and took up his usual position looking down into the clearing. He had now become so blasé that he made little attempt to look around for any intruders. Had he done so he may have noticed Nakita who was cleverly hidden by grasses only a matter of fifteen metres from where he lay.

Nakita was very pleased with the way things were going. Her well thought out plans were paying good dividends. She had placed a pile of spare clothes on the far side of the clearing indicating to the visitor that she was somewhere in the vicinity taking a swim in the stream. He had fallen for that ploy as all of his attention was focused on the pile of clothes.

37

It took Nikita well over ten minutes to slide along the ground to a place immediately behind her quarry. He was totally unaware of her presence. As she neared him she very slowly raised herself up onto her feet, quietly slid her knife from out of her belt, reached forward and proceeded to push the sharp point of steel into the softness of his throat. As the metal made contact with the skin she noticed that he froze like a statue. He was at her mercy, he knew it and she knew it. The two remained in that position neither saying anything. After quite a few seconds the Prince felt the pressure of the blade against his neck ease and he became aware that whoever had caught him unawares had moved away. He raised himself from the ground and slowly turned around to find himself facing the beautiful Indian who he had spied upon many weeks before. The girl had a large smile written all over her face. She was obviously elated by having caught him out and was even more pleased with herself on seeing the expression of sheer annoyance on his face.

Eventually he began to see the funny side of the situation that he had found himself in and began to smile. The smile turned into a subdued laugh and eventually the two were laughing almost uncontrollably. Initially they were both lost for words and stood staring at one another for what seemed an eternity. Eventually the Prince, presuming that the Indian girl would more than probably speak none of the Incan language at all, began to make simple sign language. As soon as he began to use his hands the girl began to laugh once more but allowed him to continue with his antics.

"Are you dumb?" she eventually said in perfect Inca.

The Prince was quite taken aback by her cultured voice and he began to feel even more foolish than when he had been caught out lying in the grass.

"Where did you learn our tongue?" he eventually managed to say. The beautiful eyes of the girl stared straight back at him and threw him once more off guard. He was unused to a woman looking him in the eye as it was forbidden by Inca law for anyone other than royalty to gaze upon the Prince.

"I am of the Andura Tribe. We supply your people with food

and merchandises from the jungle. I learnt your language from a very early age when I used to accompany my father into the big city in the mountains. I see that you are dressed in hunting clothes. Do you supply the city with food as well?"

The Prince decided that this moment was not the time to inform the Indian girl of his aristocratic position in the city. It was bad enough being a hunter caught by a mere Indian girl. He decided to play along as a commoner. As a commoner he would be able to look into the face of the Indian girl and not at the top of her head. Her face was too beautiful to be continually looking down on to the ground when she was in his presence.

"Yes, I live on the outskirts of the city and spend most of my time down here in the jungle, hunting. Strange that I have never come across you before?" A feeling of guilt swept over him as he had been brought up never to lie.

"Are you sure that you have never come across me before?" she said, slightly narrowing her eyes. She was not going to let him off of the hook that quickly, especially as he had been spying on her in her secret clearing.

"No. In fact I've never come across anyone in this area until I met you."

"Hm. Strange. I thought I saw you lying in these grasses on a number of times in the past. You must have a double?" She inwardly laughed to herself. One handsome hunter was difficult to deal with but two of them would be beyond her capabilities.

"Yes, I have to admit, I have been here more than once and yes, on the first occasion, I did see you."

"I would have thought that having seen me once and seen how badly scarred my body is that you would not have wished to see me again."

"I returned here as I did not believe my eyes on the first occasion. What I saw then was a very beautiful woman and seeing you once more has confirmed my initial impression. In actual fact you are even more beautiful now at closer range."

Nakita was not prepared for that response. No one of the opposite sex had ever made such remarks to her. The boys in the village had teased her over the years about her scars and she had been able to contend with that, but a complimentary remark from such a handsome person was extremely difficult to deal with.

"I would like to apologise for watching you in the past," the Prince continued, gaining his composure a little. "I should have retreated as soon as I had come across you in the clearing but your beauty caught me by surprise and human nature was stronger than the will to allow you to keep your privacy."

Nakita's face began to redden and she began to feel a little weak around her knees. She had had no experience of how to deal with such compliments. This was the first time in her life that someone from the opposite sex had said anything nice to her. She had often fantasised about meeting a handsome warrior and now it was for real she didn't know what to do. She was saved from further embarrassment when the Prince continued to address her.

"Well, do you forgive me, or should I jump off the nearest cliff and disappear for ever?"

The thought of never seeing him again greatly disturbed Nakita and without further thought on the matter said, " Yes, I forgive you, but do not make a habit of it."

They both smiled at each other not knowing what to say next. The Prince eventually cooked up courage and spoke.

"May I sit with you for a few moments on your favourite rock in the centre of the stream? I can't stay for very much longer as I have to be back in the city before dark."

For the next half an hour they sat and chatted about all manner of things including the beautiful marks on Nakita's body, which the Prince had assumed, were tribal markings. He was amazed when she told him the story of how a jaguar had killed her brother and how she had managed to kill it. No wonder he had not heard her creep up on him.

"Well it is time for me to leave." He almost asked if she would be safe going back to her village which would have been a complete insult to her after all that had happened during the last few hours. He held out his hand to help her up from her sitting position on the rock. Her strong and yet delicate hand slid into his and as he pulled her to her feet they both felt totally exhilarated. As she positioned herself in front of him her forearm for one brief moment caressed the well-developed muscles on his chest. This unintentional sensual experience sent a rush of electrical impulses throughout both of their nervous systems and within a split second in time had transferred the experience to the brain, which stored it in a very prominent position in the memory section where it would never be erased.

They stood there looking into each other's eyes and both knew that this would not be the last time that they would meet.

"May I see you again?" the Prince said in a very quiet voice.

"Only if you promise not to spy on me again!" A large smile spread over her face as she saw him once again squirm.

He gently squeezed her hand. "I look forward to the next time then. I will try to come here every tenth day. If I do miss one meeting then please forgive me. Please don't ever think that I would ever intentionally miss a chance of seeing you."

On that note they turned away from one another and began their way back to their homes both feeling extremely elated and already longing for the next ten days to pass by.

They met nine times after that and each time they became more intimate. It was during their sixth meeting that neither of them would ever forget. They had both been sitting on the rock holding hands and talking about things that had happened to each other over the past days. The sun's strong rays had been extremely hot so they had decided to cool down by dipping themselves in the stream. During the swim the Prince had dived under the water and grabbed hold of her slender legs and pulled her under the water where their bodies intertwined about one another. This experience of their bodies coming together was indescribable. On reaching the surface they both found it difficult to take in a breath of fresh air. Eventually they both let out a loud gasping noise as they sucked air into their lungs not really knowing whether the gasp was one of oxygen starvation or one of sheer delight.

Once their heartbeats were almost back to normal they began to slowly swim to the side of the flat rock. The Prince pulled himself up into a crouching position and held out both hands to the beautiful girl in front of him. With one powerful heave he pulled her straight out of the water. However, during the movement his wet feet began to slip on the smooth rock and he felt himself falling onto his back. He did not let go of his prize and as he fell onto his back she followed after him so that eventually they both lay fully stretched out on top of one another. Neither made any movement to get out of that position. They lay there looking into each other's eyes, their heart rates and breathing patterns increasing in intensity. She lowered her head towards his and in moments their moist lips were gently touching each other. It seemed quite natural for Nakita to slide the tip of her tongue under her captor's upper lip. They were now both fully aroused and with no feeling at all of being embarrassed, gently pulled the clothes from each other's wet bodies. Her silk-like skin slid over his tense body and soon they were making passionate love.

That moment in time when they gave their souls to one another they would remember for the rest of their lives.

For the next twenty minutes neither of them spoke. They just lay on the rock on their backs, holding each other's hands and gazed up into the jungle canopy. Neither wanted this blissful moment to end.

It was during this meeting that Nakita became aware who her handsome hunter actually was. Until this moment she had never seen him fully naked. It was as he turned onto his side in order to look into her face that she saw the markings of the Sun on the inside of his upper arm. She knew immediately of its significance. Only the Sun God or a Prince of the Inca Empire wore such a tattoo. Her hunter was in actual fact a Prince! She froze instinctively.

"What is that mark under your arm?" she asked inquisitively, knowing quite well what it meant.

The Prince looked straight into her eyes. This was the moment that he had dreaded. The truth had now to be told.

"I am the son of the Inca Sun God." Nakita immediately bowed her head much to the annoyance of the Prince. She was following the protocol of Inca law and he did not like to see her subservient to himself for she was his equal. The Prince took her head in his hands and raised it so that she once more looked him full in the eyes.

"I am sorry for not having told you, but I was afraid that if you knew you would not wish to see me any more. Whatever you decide to do, you must never bow your face in my presence ever again. It should be me who bows to you."

They both appreciated the position that the two of them were now in. They would never be able to see one another in public and they could never be as one. Nakita eventually spoke.

"I know how you must have been feeling over the past weeks knowing that we could never be together. I have those same feelings now. You know how strongly I feel about you and that I could never leave you. My love for you will never die. The only thing we can do is to continue as we have in the past knowing that one day we will have to stop seeing one another. Until that day arrives let us carry on loving one another."

The Prince knew there was nothing to add and stood there holding her hands. He looked into her eyes and noticed that they were full of tears. He pulled her towards him and held her tightly in his arms.

"Before you leave, I have a little present for you," she eventually said breaking the slightly embarrassing silence. "It's nothing splendid, not like you normally receive as a Prince, just something I came across in our stream." She reached across to her hunting bag and rifled around with her hand until she found it. "Hold out your hand," she said with a large smile across her face.

The Prince put out his right hand and felt something smooth drop into it. When he looked into the palm of his hand he saw what looked like a flat round pebble which had a jagged line running through it almost like a fork of lightening. It seemed to emit a strong glow when the sun's rays shone on it.

"That is the best present that I have ever had. I will have it made up with a clasp and I will wear it around my neck until my dying day. Now what can I give you in return?"

"Just a promise that you will never forget me."

Chapter Three

"Well, I've seen everything now," said one of the guards who was standing in the back row of the Royal Protectorate. The soldiers had been on parade in the heat for over an hour waiting to be inspected by the Prince. "Hope he doesn't come this far during his inspection," continued the man.

"Whoever is talking at the back will report to me at the end of this. Failure to do so will mean that every man present will continue to parade for the next two hours." The remark came from the Commandant who was in charge of the huge squad of some two hundred men.

The soldier wished he had not spoken out and knew he was in for big trouble when the men were dismissed.

It took the Prince a good half an hour to review the troops. He always stopped and spoke to as many of the men as possible, which they really appreciated even though the temperatures were up in the nineties. The soldier held his breath as the Prince worked his way along the line towards where he was standing. He actually stopped and spoke to the soldier next to him and then went on down the line. Fortunately for the soldier he did not look at his face for he would certainly have remembered him.

"Well, what have you got to say for yourself?" said the Commandant who was staring directly into the eyes of the lonely soldier who had been standing at attention all on his own for the past two hours. Sweat was running down his face. His whole outfit was saturated from perspiration and felt twice its normal weight.

"I'm sorry, sir, for speaking out of place, but the Royal Prince took me by surprise, as I have never seen him close range before."

"Are you trying to say that the Prince is some form of an ugly beast?"

The soldier desperately tried not to smile at the wisecrack from his superior officer.

"No sir. It's just that the only times that I've seen him in the past was when he was dressed in an old leather hunting oufit down on the lower approaches to the city. Seeing him now in all of his regalia was perplexing."

The Commander was very puzzled at the explanation from the soldier.

"Are you sure you could not have been mistaken? The Prince would never have been out of the city's perimeters without a Royal Guard and certainly not dressed as you have just described. You must have been mistaken."

"No sir, it was definitely him, as I recognised his voice when he spoke to my friend who was standing next to me on parade. You see, I actually told him off on one occasion for bumping into me and from then on whenever he went out hunting in the jungle I used to make him give me one of his catches."

Couldn't have been the Prince, thought the Commander, as the Prince would certainly have dealt with this man if he had demanded some of his catches. He had seen the Prince on numerous occasions in unarmed combat and no man ever got the better of him.

"If it was the Prince, how often does he venture down the trail?"

"Whenever I have been on duty he always passes me very early in the morning and returns just before sunset. He always keeps to the twentieth day."

The Commander pondered for a few moments. The Prince should not be leaving the city without an escort at any time and if he was it must be extremely important. He could go out hunting at any time with a small protection of soldiers, so why was he being so secretive?

"Have you mentioned this to any of your friends?"

"No sir. The only other person who knows is the soldier who was on duty with me on those occasions and he does not know it was the Prince."

"Good. What I want you to do from now on is to monitor whenever the Prince goes down into the jungle. I will arrange for you and the other soldier to be on duty in that area during that period. Once we have established his pattern I will arrange for him to have some sort of escort. We can't have the next Sun God venturing into the jungle unprotected. Well done, man. You can now return to your barracks. Tomorrow I will make sure that you have a very light day to make up for the extra hours that you have spent on the parade ground."

"Thank you, sir."

The Commandant watched the soldier walk across the parade ground. If the man had seen the Prince then what was he doing down in the jungle? This needed to be looked into. He decided there and then to have the Prince monitored when he took one of his trips into the jungle. Great care would be needed, for if the Prince ever found out that he was being spied upon it would mean certain death for all concerned. The least number of persons who knew of the affair the better, so the Commandant decided to use only one person. That person was his personal body guard who was not an Inca. He was an Indian from the jungles below who he had saved from execution many years previous. The Indian had been a member of a marauding tribe who had attacked an Inca garrison and in the skirmish had been captured. The Commander had found out that this Indian was one of the best trackers in this part of the jungle and so had spared his life so that he could track for his own soldiers. The Indian from that day swore his allegiance to his new master and over the course of the years had done many unsavoury things for the Commander, including assassinations.

Two months later a pattern had been established as to when the Prince ventured out of the city and the Commander decided that the next time he was due to go he would be tracked by his Indian.

The tracker could see by the way the Inca soldier was travelling through the jungle that he was no stranger to the problems that could arise in such dense vegetation. What did become clear to the Indian was that during the initial stages of the journey

46

the man was not set on hunting. He was certainly in a hurry and made little effort to check to see if he was being followed, so the task given by the Commander was not as difficult as he had anticipated.

It took the Prince about two hours to arrive at his usual rendezvous with his Indian love. The two then spent hours talking, laughing and eventually making love in their idyllic clearing not knowing that they were being watched. As soon as the light began to fade they embraced each other one more time and then went their separate ways. Again the Prince did not check to see if he was being followed and set off at a quick pace in order to be back in the city before dark. The one thing he did not forget in his haste was to catch a small animal for the guard who stood in his usual place halfway up the narrow path to the city. He seemed to be feeding this man more often as he was always on duty when he ventured down into the jungle. The Prince put it down to coincidence.

"Well, what have you got to tell me?" said the Commander hoping to find out what the Prince had been up to but in no way expecting the revelations that his tracker was about to relay to him.

"He met a beautiful Indian girl. They make love for many an hour."

The Commander was absolutely amazed. Only people of royal blood were allowed to have physical contact. It was forbidden for Royalty to mix with the lower classes. Anyone breaking this code was immediately put to death. What was the Prince thinking of? It was all right to copulate with the top echelon of the Inca population provided it was kept secret, but to fornicate with someone from the lower strata was unheard of. The commander needed to know more of this girl. He decided that the next time the Prince went off on one of his jaunts he would have his tracker follow the girl afterwards. Over the next few months he established where the Indian girl lived and using some of his most trusted spies found out almost everything about her. No one knew of the affair other than his trackers and himself. Anyone who began to get an inkling as to what was

47

happening was discreetly removed from the scene. The story given for their sudden disappearance was that they had been promoted and sent to defend the strongholds at the outer limits of the kingdom.

Nothing was recorded of the Prince's clandestine meetings in the jungle. The Commandant decided to keep it to himself just in case he could use it at a later date as a means of promoting himself, possibly into the Royal Circle. He never thought for a moment that in the near future the information would save his life.

Chapter Four

It was during an autumn evening that Juan Lopez was drinking in one of the many alehouses in Cadiz when he got into conversation with a sailor who was serving on a Spanish Galleon, which had put into port to replenish victuals. The sailor had had quite a bit to drink and was telling everyone within earshot that he was off to make a fortune during his next trip to sea. His ship was going to the New World in search of gold and silver and they had called into port for stores and to recruit men. By the end of the evening Juan was all fired up to join the expedition.

Juan Lopez was from a comfortable middle class family who had a sail repair business in Cadiz. The opportunity to see a New World and possibly establish trading ties was too great an opportunity to miss, so with his father's blessing he enrolled with the small flotilla.

The journey across the ocean was an horrendous affair for Juan who had never ventured outside the breakwater in his hometown. During the initial part of the journey one storm was followed by another storm with each one growing in ferocity. Soon salt water found it's way into the holds and contaminated the food and fresh water. For the remaining part of the trip the crew had to rely on dried food.

Juan became extremely weak as he was unable to keep any form of food in his stomach and at one time some of the more hardy sailors thought that he would not survive the voyage. When he did get his appetite back his first meal was of stale bread which when broken in half was filled with large white bloated maggots. He watched the professional sailors to see what they thought of the bread. He was amazed to see that no one complained. They just brushed aside the maggots and got on with their eating.

By the time they reached their destination on the north coast of Peru the whole of the ship's crew were in a very sorry state. All were extremely weak and many were suffering from scurvy due to the lack of fresh fruit.

They dropped anchor in a most beautiful cove that had lush tropical vegetation running right down to the shoreline. The initial landing party met no opposition, so the captain allowed most of the crew to go ashore where they soon found fresh water in which to bathe, and an abundant amount of exotic fruit and animals to hunt.

The leader of the army was Francisco Pizzaro. He was not a very well educated man but was a born leader. He could see that his men were in no shape to travel, so he decided to make camp along the beach and allow his men to swim in the sea, hunt in the dense forest and enjoy themselves.

Juan enjoyed those weeks on the beach. He was able to wash away the dreadful memories of the last few months aboard the ship full of horrible smells and poor food. Now he was in paradise. Each morning he would wake up and plunge into the crystal clear waters, which were abundant with fish. Pizzaro who knew that the salt water would clear up all the sores on his men's bodies had insisted that they all swam daily. He also insisted that after the bathe in the warm sea they had to jump in the much cooler waters of the river, which ran down from the mountains. The idea was that it would improve their body tone and make them alert for a hard day's training. During the rest periods Juan would walk along the beach well away from the rest of the group and lie on his back in the sand and watch the swaying of the tall palm trees. He had never been so relaxed.

By the end of three weeks they were back to their normal health and the camaraderie between the soldiers was at a high. It was now time to venture into the depths of the forest.

It didn't take long for the group to forget the relaxing times on the beach. The jungle was unbearable. It took hours of hacking away with machetes to cover a mere fifty metres, as there were no tracks at all, not even ones made by the animals. The profuse sweating caused by the heat and high humidity caused their unsuitable clothing to cut into their skin causing open sores, which soon became infected. Everything that was made of metal began to rust and great care had to be taken by the soldiers to make sure that their muskets did not seize up. Their shining armour had been reduced to dark brown in colour and they all sported long beards that were alive with lice and bugs. Their clothing was in shreds and stank, as they hadn't washed properly for months.

When they eventually emerged out of the jungle into the bright sunlight they looked a very motley crowd and were totally unprepared for what they saw. Unbeknown to them, they had been followed over their entire time in the jungle by Indian trackers who were employed by the Incas to report on any movements of strangers who entered their domain.

The Inca's method of sending messages throughout their kingdom was dependant upon incredible feats of endurance. Most of the lands of the Inca Empire consisted of deep valleys with steep sided mountains through which ran raging torrents of water. In order to overcome these obstacles the Incas had devised a relay team of hundreds of young, fit athletes who were trained to run barefooted along the very narrow paths carrying messages by word of mouth, as there were no forms of writing in those days. The runners would travel a distance of about five kilometres each and having passed on the message to the next runner would remain in that position until the next message came along. It was a most effective communication system.

During the first few days travelling out in the open the Spanish were amazed at the infrastructures built by the inhabitants whom they had assumed would have been a very primitive people. They marvelled at the steep-sided valleys that were lined in richly irrigated terraces. How the Indians managed to cross the swollen rivers by a feat of great ingenuity also amazed the Spanish. Whole villages of women folk and children would be used to gather the short dry grasses from the sun-baked sides of the steep valleys. These fine strands of grasses were then woven by hand into strands of string, which in turn were made into ropes. These ropes were then manhandled across the rivers when they were not in full flood, and eventually turned into suspension bridges that were strong enough to take the weight of a fully laden llama.

What worried the Spanish most of all were the huge fortresses that overlooked them in strategic places along the narrow paths that meandered up the steep rock faces. They found it very strange that no one appeared to mind that they were there. There was no sign of any form of an army that may have been stationed in any of these fortresses. It was when they got onto the higher plateaus that they first encountered the might of the Inca Empire.

They had just stopped to take a well-earned rest when the air was filled with thunder. Their initial reaction was to look up into the sky to see if there were any large cloud formations that might indicate the possibility of a downpour. When they found the sky completely devoid of anything that gave the slightest indication of a storm they began to look elsewhere for the source of such a deafening noise. They looked towards the unbroken skyline ahead and suddenly were petrified by what they witnessed. Over the brow of the hill as far as the eye could see came an army of thousands of heavily armed warriors. They came in at a run and stopped within two hundred metres of the Spanish contingent. None of the Spanish soldiers made any attempt to arm themselves in fear of antagonising the opposing warriors who could have finished them off in a matter of minutes due to their superior numbers. Suddenly the group of the warriors began to move apart and down through their centre came the at least two hundred warriors dressed in the most amazing uniforms. Their undergarments were of a turquoise material over which was worn a chest plate of what appeared to be made of real gold which glistened in the strong rays of the sun. On their heads they wore a leather hat, which was adorned with large white eagle feathers. They were the elite of the Inca army. They were in fact the Royal Guard. If the Spaniards thought that that was spectacular then they were in for an even bigger surprise.

Once the Royal Guard had taken up their positions between

their own army and that of the small Spanish band they knelt down on one knee. As soon as they had done that the thousands of other warriors followed suit. From the rear of the soldiers then appeared some kind of a litter that was being carried by twenty immensely strong-looking men who were dressed in an all gold uniform. They positioned themselves in front of the Spaniards and lowered the enshrouded litter to the ground. One of the entourage who had been walking alongside the litter then came forward and proceeded to pull back the gold silk curtains which adorned its sides. A splendid figure stepped out and the whole of the assembled warriors bowed their heads. All except one, who stood at the rear of the Royal Guard. Pizzaro noted that the soldier was dressed in a different uniform to anyone else. He looked straight into the eyes of Pizzaro and conveyed that he did not trust him. He was a man who Pizzaro would have to watch out for in the future.

The Spanish contingent stood aghast at the sight of the person descending from the litter. He must have been at least two metres tall and was covered from head to foot in golden regalia all of which had precious stones sewn in the patterns of the sun's rays. They were all in awe of the splendid figure of Atahualpa, the Sun God of the Inca Empire.

Pizzaro was the first of the Spanish group to kneel in front of what appeared to him to be the ruler of the Incas. He had decided to be subservient for the time being as they were totally outnumbered and had nothing to lose and everything to gain. His men on seeing him kneeling followed suite, which the Sun God seemed to appreciate, for he made a gesture for them to get up off their knees.

For the next half an hour polite conversation between the Sun God and Pizzaro took place between interpreters. Fortunately for the Spaniard he had recruited a number of Indians he had met whilst travelling through the jungle and had used them as guides. At about that time he had discovered that Juan Lopez had a talent for languages and put his skills to good use as his chief interpreter.

Once the initial meeting was over the adventurers were taken back to the Inca camp where they were amazed to see hundreds of acres of tentage. A sumptuous supper was prepared and enjoyed by everyone. By the end of the evening their stomachs were bloated with rich foods and their heads addled from the highly intoxicating brews. They would certainly sleep well that night which made Pizzaro feel very apprehensive. Had they been deliberately put at ease so as to make easy targets? If not, would this be an ideal time to take the initiative away from the Inca Sun God and for the Spanish to try to capture him? There would be no chance of that at any foreseeable time in the future as they were totally outnumbered. Pizzaro decided that they would make their move at first light on the following morning.

They had been placed in a small village nearby to the Inca encampment with no apparent guard. All that night Pizzaro made up his battle plans. He had been told that the Sun God would visit him in the square of the village during the morning. This suited Pizzaro as it would mean that only a small contingent of the Royal Guard would be at hand at any particular time, as the streets of the village were extremely narrow. Pizzaro arranged for his men to seal off certain areas so that there was no way to escape, once in the square, and there would be no way to bring in reinforcements. His whole strategy hinged on the fact that once he had the Sun God captured then the rest of the warriors would lay down their arms. He also had two major advantages on the opposition, muskets and horses, both of which the Inca warriors had never encountered before. And that was exactly how the battle was won.

As the sun arose the Spaniards were woken up by their night guard, given a breakfast and then sent out to their various posts and told not to make any noise at all. It was very eerie for the soldiers, most of whom were stationed on their own. The only sounds were those of the eagles which were soaring high up in the sky above their heads. Occasionally a small creature would scurry across the deserted square leaving a small cloud of dust in its wake.

At almost noon they heard the approach of the Inca warriors. First came the roar of thousands of bare feet pounding onto the sun-baked muddy road, and then the sound of drums. When the entourage reached the outskirts of the village all sounds ceased. Atahualpa's litter then appeared and was set down in front of the Royal Guard. As before, the whole members of the army knelt down, all except the one who had remained standing the previous day. Pizzaro was watching all of these procedures from an excellent vantage point to the rear of the village on a slightly higher area of land. He noted the soldier not kneeling and decided that he would be the one to watch out for when the fighting started.

Atahualpa was initially annoyed that no one had come out to greet him and put it down to the fact that they were all sleeping off the effects of the previous night's feastings. He decided to lead the way into the village, much to the delight of Pizzaro. The fly was indeed walking into the close-knit web. The Sun God was obviously getting annoyed as he began to shout to his elders. Annoyance soon changed to puzzlement. Had the visiting band of Spaniards left the village during the night? He decided to enter the village and look for himself. The warrior who had remained to the rear of the Royal Guard then came forward and took up his position next to his father. He did not like the situation of being in such confined spaces and pointed this out to his father. If there were some form of a trap they would be unable to bring in any reinforcements. His father dismissed him saying that no one would be so foolish as to attempt to attack the most formidable army ever created. The Sun God then started to make his way into the centre of the village still not encountering any form of life. They had indeed gone but would be easily found by his master trackers.

Suddenly there was a cry: "Santiago", came a loud shrill shout from the rear of the village. It was the war cry of Pizzaro. Immediately the hidden Spanish soldiers rushed out of their hiding places firing off their guns. The ear-splitting noises froze the Inca group in their tracks and within seconds most of the Royal Guard had been killed. The Prince was the only one who was not taken by surprise and he had already killed three soldiers in their initial rush at the Royal Party. On hearing the commotion the warriers outside the village made a rush for the nearest narrow street only to be confronted by four huge stallions in full armour. The stallions galloped into the Inca warriors who turned and fled.

The battle was over in ten minutes. All of the Incas who had entered the village initially had been killed or taken captive, except the Prince who was situated at the centre of the square and was still swinging his sword killing any Spaniard who happened to come his way. Fortunately for him he was eventually brought down by a musket ball that grazed his temple and momentarily knocked him to the ground. Immediately four soldiers jumped on him and pinned him to the ground. Another soldier was just about to thrust a sabre into his neck when a shout came from Pizzaaro.

"Stop. That's enough killing for today Tie him up and put him with the rest. We can deal with him later." Pizzaro then went over to the Sun God. "If you wish to live then I want you to send a message to your followers that all is well and that you will be returning to your city very soon. What we need is some of your wealth in return. Tell your people to bring their gold here to this village. When we have enough we will return to our country and you will be set free." And that is how the plunder of the Inca Empire began.

Six months later an incredible amount of gold and precious stones had been assembled in the village and no one had made any attempts to free the Sun God. The time came when Pizzaro decided that there was no point in collecting any more gold, as they would be unable to transport it back through the jungle.

One evening he called his council together. Over the months he had recruited a number of Inca soldiers and had promised them that when he returned to Spain he would leave them in charge of their Empire along with some of his own soldiers. These warriors were allowed to attend such meetings, as often they would come up with ideas on how to collect the gold and how to transport it through the forest.

Pizzaro faced the group of high-ranking soldiers assembled in front of him. He had to decide whether the time was ripe for him to move the gold and in doing so leave half of his men with the Inca deserters who would continue to rule the country until his return. His main concern was the Inca Prince who had shown no signs of submissiveness and who along with a small band of followers had been kept under lock and key.

"Welcome, gentlemen. My reason for calling you together is to inform you that the time has come to ship the gold back to Spain." There was a look of joy on the faces of the Spanish soldiers. At last they were going home and away from this hellhole. The Incas present were just as pleased for it meant that they would become the rulers of the country, even if it meant sharing the power with the remaining Spaniards.

"What I intend to do is to split our force, leaving one half to rule the country along with the help of our trusted Inca friends, and the other half will transport the gold to the coast. The only problem that I can envisage is what to do with the Prince. If we kill him or take him back to Spain it might cause a rebellion from the people." He paused for a moment to see if anyone could come up with a solution.

"I may be able to help." The group turned to see where the voice had come from. It was one of the Commanders of the Elite Guard. "The Prince has broken the laws of his Royal Peerage. If the people were to find out he would lose their following. I know of a way of breaking him in front of the Inca people."

Pizzzaro said "If that could be done it would solve all of our problems. The people would have no one to follow and it would be easy for you Incas to take over and rule the country as we see fit. Continue."

"Many months ago it was brought to my attention by one of my soldiers that the Prince was going out of the city disguised as a hunter. It is forbidden for any of the Royal Family to venture out of the city without the Royal Guard to protect them so I decided to have him followed to see what he was up to. It transpired that he was meeting an Indian girl with whom he was having an affair. This is totally forbidden, as no Royal blood should ever be mixed with that of a Commoner." He looked

57

around and was pleased to see that all were listening to him intently.

"My suggestion is that we bring this Indian girl to the city and make her a sacrificial offering to the Gods. This would take place before the whole of the city's inhabitants. We put the Prince on show in his full regalia and not inform him of what is about to take place. I think you all can imagine the response from him when he sees the girl and discovers what is about to happen to her." They all nodded in agreement.

"Excellent idea. Well done, Commander. I suggest that you send someone for the girl and in the meantime make all necessary arrangements. I look forward to the breaking of this proud Prince."

Chapter Five

"Wake up all of you pigs. Today we have a special treat for you. You're off to the pool house for a good wash." The guard threw open the door and waved his arms indicating for the Inca captives to follow him out into the open.

The oppressed looked at one another wondering if this was the last time that they would be together. As they emerged into the direct sunlight for the first time in over two months they could see very little through their squinting eyes. Eventually they became accustomed to the bright light and they were surprised to see that not only did Spanish soldiers surround them, but also their own Inca soldiers who had obviously changed sides once the conflict was over. During their captivity they had discussed the possibility of escape but there was no chance of that today.

They were ushered along to the washrooms and directed to strip off and get into a large vat-like bath, which had about a metre of water in it. The sensation of fresh, clean water caressing their stiff, filthy bodies was absolute bliss. They just lay there and made no attempt to talk. Eventually when the guards returned they were given clean clothing and a large breakfast and then told to sit in the courtyard outside and soak up the sun.

Some twenty minutes later one of the more senior members of the Spanish guard pointed to the Prince and told him to return to the washroom. Once inside he was told to strip off his clothes once more and then was presented with his full uniform of the Commander General of the Royal Guard. At first he refused to put it on but, when they told him that for each minute that he did not appear outside fully attired one of his fellow prisoners would be executed, he gave in.

When he eventually came out he looked immaculate, just as he used to on the parade ground when he inspected the troops. The small band of prisoners stood and bowed their heads in respect. That would soon finish, thought the Inca Commander who was watching from a distance. The Prince would soon lose respect from all of his followers.

They were all kept waiting for about half an hour when the main body of Spanish soldiers arrived. They formed up with the other group of soldiers and then began to march the Inca prisoners in the direction of the path that led up into the city. On entering the capital they were surprised to see that all of its inhabitants had been marshalled into the main square. There must have been well over a thousand people cramped into that area and all were quiet. Not one of them spoke. All looked at their Prince as he was marched through the main square and was then ushered up the hill to the cliff edge where sacrificial rituals were conducted. The small contingent of prisoners were stopped within ten metres of the cliff edge and then the Prince was led onto the smooth stone platform and made to stand within a metre of the sheer drop to the valley a thousand metres below.

As he stood there alone he could feel the warm air rising from the valley floor below. It brought back happy memories of his trips through his secret tunnel. He caught sight of an eagle that was using the thermal currents to glide peacefully above the gathering and wished he could fly away with it. Oh how he longed for his little clearing in the jungle below.

There was a commotion to his left. The throng of citizens was beginning to move apart to allow some form of procession to pass. The Prince could see that the Spanish Commander was leading the group followed by the Inca Council and behind them there seemed to be a group of women dressed in white. As the group neared the sacrificial stone Pizzaro held up his hand for them to stop. He continued on his way until he was standing next to the Prince. They looked into one another's eyes and Pizzaro smiled.

"You will remember this day for the rest of your life and it's all due to me." With that he raised his arm once more and from the far end of the group an armed soldier led one of the women towards them. The Prince froze. The woman was his Nakita who was attired in a flowing white silk dress. The guard brought her onto the stone square and made her stand so that she was in between Pizzaro and the Prince. Neither of them showed any form of recognition, which surprised the Spanish warlord. That would change in a few moments when the Prince fully appreciated what was going to happen.

The Prince and Nakita looked one another in the eyes. There was no need to speak, as they both fully understood what had to be done. It was as if they were both looking into one another's souls. They knew that this would be the last time that they would ever see one another in this life. A small tear formed in the corner of Nakita's eye and then began to run down her smooth cheek. Then a broad smile crossed her face and her eyes suddenly lit up. It was the look that she had given him on the first day that she caught him lying on his stomach in the grasses of the clearing. The Prince desperately wanted to step forward and take her once again in his arms but he knew that if he did so the Inca Empire would be lost forever. All he could do was to stand perfectly still and allow the proceedings to take their course.

Pizzaro again raised his hand and the guard who had accompanied Nakita stepped forward to take her by the arm. However, before he reached her she held out her hand in a gesture for him to stay where he was. He immediately stopped, not really knowing what to do next. Nakita then turned away from her Prince and slowly walked towards the edge of the cliff. It was now that Pizarro expected the Prince to make his move but he remained motionless much to the Spanish leader's annoyance.

As Nakita stood by the sheer drop a light breeze caught the strands of her long black hair and drew it across her face. A light mist began to drift up from the valley below giving the setting a ghostly effect. For a moment she paused, and then turned to directly face her Prince. Nakita knew that only he was able to see her face. She looked directly into his eyes and smiled.

"I will always love you." She whispered and then took one step backward and disappeared into the swirling mists.

There was a gasp from the watching crowd. Even Pizzaro was moved by the occasion. What a shame that such a beautiful woman had to die in the prime of her life, he thought. The only one who appeared not to show any feeling at all was the Prince who continued to stand at the edge like a statue. He was tempted to follow his loved one into the mist when he saw her step backwards but knew that she would not have wished for both of them to die. She had given her life so that his could be spared.

He took hold of the necklace that she had made for him and held the pebble tightly in the palm of his hand. Looking up into the clear blue sky he made a vow to himself that he would take revenge against the Spanish for the taking of her life. He then stepped forward so that he was right at the edge of the sheer drop. Pizaaro looked on hoping that he was going to follow the Indian girl as there was no way now of disgracing him. He was to be disappointed.

The Prince looked down into the swirling mist and whispered, "I will always love you till my dying day. We will meet again, Nakita."

As he turned away his eyes met Pizzaro's and they seemed to penetrate into the very soul of the Spaniard. A shiver went down the spine of his adversary who knew that he would have to have him killed before the Prince killed him.

That night Pizzaro called another meeting of his Council.

"Our plan did not work. You underestimated your Prince, Commander," said Pizzaro in a voice indicating that he was immensely annoyed with the man. "We will have to arrange for the Prince to have some sort of accident. I will leave those arrangements in your hands, Commander, and make sure that nothing goes wrong this time. I want him out of the way before I depart with the gold in three days time." Pizzaro then made plans for the removal and transportation of all of the gold and called the meeting to a close.

The following morning he was awakened very early by one of his soldiers.

"Sir. Sorry to disturb you but he has gone."

"Who's gone, man? Come on speak up?"

"The Prince and all of his men."

Pizzaro was enraged. He threw on his nearest clothes and rushed out into the square. The sight before him made his blood run cold. Along the side of the building in which the Inca prisoners had been kept, was a line of his own soldiers, each one lying face down on the dusty hard baked earth. From under each of them a trickle of blood meandered along the ground.

Pizzaro grabbed hold of the nearest corpse and turned it over. The man's throat had been cut.

"Did no one hear or see anything during the night?" No one spoke.

From that moment he knew that this was only the beginning. As long as the Prince lived then Pizzaro's life would be in danger. His best bet would be to place a large reward on the Prince's head and for him to leave quickly with the gold and return to Spain.

That night deep in the jungle the renegade band of Incas led by their Prince made camp. Someone managed to make a fire and others went out to find food and water. Within the next two hours they had filled themselves with succulent roast boar followed by a delicious fruit. They then sat around the fire and watched the flames flicker in the light breeze thinking about all that had happened to them over the last few years.

Without speaking the Prince suddenly got up and bent down by the fire watched by the rest of his followers. He proceeded to remove the stone that hung around his neck and using two long sticks put it into the red-hot embers of the fire. As they watched the stone changed from brown to red and then to a glowing hot white. What the Incas witnessed that evening they would tell their children who would in turn tell their children and so it would be passed on from generation to generation.

Once the stone could not possibly get any hotter the Prince proceeded to remove it from the fire using two long knives. He then held it up to the dark, clear sky as if showing it to the stars. Not allowing it to cool he then asked one of his men for their flat sword onto which he placed the red hot stone. Without flinching at all he then pressed the stone onto the upper part of his arm. His men shuddered as they witnessed his flesh burning. Not a sound came out of the Prince's mouth as he stared up at the stars. After a few moments he removed the stone from his arm, which now had a large swollen burn. It was only then that he said something softly to himself.

"I will never forget you, Nakita. One day in the distant future we will meet again."

The Prince then threw the stone into a nearby stream where it was quickly washed away.

Chapter Six

Snap. The sound of a breaking twig was like a cannon shot going off in the still jungle, which brought the grotesque figure, camouflaged in mud and leaves, back to reality. All thoughts of Nakita were pushed to the back of his mind. He was once again the formidable fighting machine whose sole aim in life was to avenge his lover's death.

He could now see the unsuspecting Spaniard slowly making his way through the dense forest towards where he lay in wait. The soldier appeared to have wandered away from the main group of Conquistadors whom the Prince had been tracking for the past two days. During that time three soldiers had disappeared without any trace and no matter how diligently the Indian trackers searched they could find no trace of any form of disturbances on the jungle floor. This had happened every time a group had ventured into the jungle in search of the outlawed Prince. He had become more feared than any of the jungle's predators. Everyone dreaded being selected to join such sorties.

Juan Lopez was now in fear of his life. This was his first venture into the jungle with a search-and-kill party and he was lost. He was given the position of end man, the worst place to be if someone was hunting you, that and the lead man. He had only stopped for a moment to relieve himself and when he looked up again the main party had disappeared. No matter how hard he searched for any form of track that the others should have left he found nothing. He dared not shout for fear of attracting any one else to his whereabouts. The only thing that was in his favour was his ability to memorise the smallest of things and all during this venture he had deliberately stored each directional turn they made just in case he did wander from the main group. This information was now about to be put into use. He knew that he could find his way back to base camp. There was no point in going on. He would return to the city and make up a story of being attacked by a small group of Indians from whom he managed to escape. There would be no way of substantiating his story and he might even come out of it with a little glory.

The Prince suddenly noticed that the soldier had stopped for a moment and then commenced to go back on his original tracks. If he was quick he should be able to reach a small clearing through which the soldier had previously passed about half an hour back. He could then lie in wait in the long grasses, which would allow him more manoeuvrability in his attack.

Brilliant, thought Juan, as he sat down in the clearing and allowed the sun's rays to absorb the sweat, which was running off of his body in small rivulets and forming small indentations in the dusty earth upon which he rested his weary body.

Suddenly without seeing or hearing any movement at all he was held in a vice-like grip. He knew that at any moment his neck was going to be twisted and broken and that would be the finish of him. All that he was capable of doing was to sit perfectly still and hope the end would be a painless one.

He must have sat in that position for over thirty seconds when the pressure began to ease and he was able to breath normally again. His attacker eventually let go of him so that he was able to slowly turn around and face his adversary. What he saw made him freeze, for towering in front of him was someone who was covered from head to foot in a thick matting of brown and green muddy slime which had proved to be the perfect camouflage for the present environment. Only the eyes could be seen and they were looking directly into his, making him feel extremely vulnerable. He knew immediately that he was facing the person who the entire force of the Conquistadors had been attempting to capture for the past two years. It was the Prince, the heir to the Inca Empire.

"Get up and place your hands behind you. If you make any attempt to escape it will be the last move that you will ever make."

Juan was no match for this man and did what was asked of

him. Within seconds his hands were firmly trussed up in some kind of thin vine that cut into his skin each time he tried to move his wrists around.

"Follow me closely and you will be perfectly safe," said the Prince in a reassuring voice.

For the next two hours Juan followed in the footsteps of the Prince who was following a path, which had been hacked out of the thick jungle some time ago as it was becoming overgrown again. As they walked they seemed to be gradually moving upwards and out of the valley. He could hear the sounds of running water near at hand and assumed that they were following the course of a river. Eventually the Prince stopped at the base of a steep cliff. He then turned to face the Spanish soldier, removed a large hunting knife from his waistband and proceeded to walk towards him. Juan immediately thought that this was the end for him and cowered away.

"Stop just where you are if you wish to live another day. I am not going to kill you. It is necessary to climb the rock face in front of you, which would be impossible with your hands tied behind your back. Now turn around."

Juan was relieved to feel the sharp knife cut through his bindings His hands by this time were almost numb and as the blood began to circulate more freely they began to ache profusely. He clenched his fist in order to relieve the pain and worked his fingers until they felt as if they belonged to him once more. He looked at the rock face and decided that there was no way that he would be able to climb it. That was until the Prince pulled back the climbing lianas that had attached themselves to the rock face to reveal steps that had been cut deeply into the solid rock.

"I will lead the way in case you fall which might mean you taking me with you in the process. Take it very slowly and stop for a rest whenever you wish."

It took over half an hour to climb the sheer face, and that included four stops. Juan dared not look down for he feared heights and he knew that they were quite high up. He was absolutely amazed at what he saw when he eventually reached the summit of his climb. As he pulled himself up over the brow of the cliff he was greeted by a hive of activity. There must have been well over two hundred people all busy carrying various forms of building material on their shoulders or working together in teams to move large stones from a rock face from where they were cut. These were then transported onto a plateau area where they were placed on top of each other to make buildings. Juan was witnessing the creation of a city. The inhabitants were of various races from what he could see, including light-skinned people, which he assumed were Incas.

"You are free to wander anywhere you wish. I suggest that you do not go too near the edge, though," the Prince said, and for the first time smiled. He had already assessed that his captor was not a trained soldier and did not enjoy living in his country.

"Someone will come and find you and make sure that you are well looked after." He then beckoned to one of the workers who was nearby and said something to him. The man then turned towards Juan and beckoned him to follow him. He was taken into a small store in which were piles of clothes and in the corner some form of a water tank.

"Take off your clothes, have a wash over there. You will find a bowl under the tank and then select some clothes from that pile. When you are clean come out and take a look at our city."

That night Juan sat down next to the Prince in some form of a communal building and ate a meal with the rest of the inhabitants of the new city. There was no form of hierarchy. No one seemed to sit in any form of a pecking order and there did not seem to be any gatherings of people who might have been the governing body.

"I'm letting you go tomorrow morning. You have been spared, as I want you to go back to your city, or I should say my city, and tell your leaders that if they leave us alone to get on with our own lives then they need not fear entering the jungle any more. If they make any attempt to seek us out they will all perish. I can see that you have not been trained in the art of warfare, and I think that you have a spark of intelligence about you, so try to make them listen," the Prince said with a large smile on his face. "I feel that I can trust you not to bring them back here," he added looking straight into the eyes of Juan.

"I will do just as you have requested, and yes, you can trust me."

Four days later Juan Lopez walked into the stronghold of the Spanish conquistadors and told them of his adventure. On the question of the possibility of finding the new city he informed them that at all times he had been blindfolded. He also made up a lie that there were thousands of warriors living in their newfound land and to try to get to them would mean the complete annihilation of the entire Spanish contingent. They took him at his word and from that day made no attempt to find the city.

Juan returned to Spain two months later and in time became a very successful businessman. Often during dinner parties he would reminisce about the terrible times that he had spent during his youth in the jungles of the Amazon and how savagely his compatriots had been in dealing with the Incas. He told of the heroics of the Inca Prince and of the beautiful Indian girl that he had fallen in love with and how she had met her death. The one thing that Juan never talked about was the city, which was hidden deep in the jungle. He felt that it should remain undetected so that the Inca people would never again be subjected to the terrible degradations that they had been put through by the Spanish Conquistadors.

Juan did wonder if he would one day return to see how the Prince and his followers had progressed and was worried that as time progressed he might forget the route that he had taken from the city. In order to help him remember how to retrace his steps back through the jungle, he made an etching showing the situation of the city in relation to the local features of rivers, valleys and mountains. He then had this etching attached to the base of a small statuette of a Spanish soldier who was riding a magnificent horse.

PART II

Chapter Seven

Mrs. Downing got up an hour earlier that morning even though she was not going to work. She had to make sure that she looked presentable, as she was going to see the headmaster of her son's school, and also to make sure that her son, Jason, looked his best.

At eight o'clock she went out from the kitchen to the bottom of the stairs and shouted up, " Jason, its time to get up. I want you down here, washed and dressed within the next fifteen minutes. Don't forget we have to be at your school before the bell at five to nine."

There was a loud grunt from the top of the stairs and then the sound of a creaking bed followed by the thud of the bathroom door. Mrs. Downing, on hearing that, went back into the kitchen and commenced to finish the dishes left over from the previous night. It should have been her son's job but he had arrived home from playing outside, late as usual.

Amazingly, Jason arrived in the kitchen almost dead on time. He knew that on this occasion his mother was serious so he had made a special effort.

"Good boy," said his mum, even though she didn't really mean it. She thought she had better humour him, as she wanted him to be in a good mood for his interview.

"Have you washed behind your ears and brushed your hair properly?" To her he looked as if he had got out of bed with his clothes on and come straight down to breakfast. His hair looked unruly, sticking out at the sides and falling over his eyes like an Old English sheep dog. She wished she had whisked him down to the barbers the night before. Never mind, a good combing down with a stiff brush would do the trick, she thought.

"There now. Get tucked into these eggs and bacon. I will put some toast on and get out the special strawberry jam." Jason thought that it must be his birthday but remembered that that had taken place only a month ago. "Before we leave make sure that you give your teeth a good clean."

After a final inspection and a hard grooming session from his mum, Jason set off in the direction of his school followed closely by his mum. They were at the school gates by ten to nine just as the last trickle of pupils filtered between the two prefects who were on late duty. They leered at Jason and made a joke just out of earshot of his mum but loud enough for him to get the jist of their comments about being accompanied by his mum.

They went up two flights of stairs, across a corridor carpeted in a red heavy duty material, to the main office windows, behind which sat a most officious looking secretary. On seeing them appear she pulled back the sliding glass window.

"Good morning," she said in a polite, welcoming manner. Jason could see nothing good about the whole affair. "And how can I be of assistance?"

"We have an appointment to see Dr. Jacobs. My name is Mrs. Downing."

The secretary looked at the appointment book on her desk.

"Ah, yes. You are due to see him at nine o'clock. He won't be long. He is taking Year Nine's assembly, which should be finishing about now." Just then the bell sounded for the first lesson and the school suddenly became a sea of movement and noise. It was over in a space of a few minutes and the school returned to a normal working day. Dr. Jacobs prided himself with having organised a school, which worked along very efficient lines and woe betide the person who interfered with this efficiency. Jason had done just such a thing!

"Mrs. Downing, Doctor Jacobs will see you now." She motioned Mrs Downing towards the door at the far end of the office, opening it to allow her and her son to enter. The room was quite imposing with leather seats each with colourful cushions. At the centre of the room was a long low coffee table on top of which stood an elegant vase full of daffodils. A rather distinguished man arose from out of one of the chairs and walked towards Mrs. Downing, hand outstretched.

"Good morning, Mrs Downing. So nice to meet you. And how are you this morning, young Jason?"

Jason was lost for words. He had only seen the headmaster from a distance during assemblies and occasionally in the corridors.

"Now that the pleasantries are out of the way let us deal with Jason and his problems. I have received a report from his Head of Year which does not make very good reading. The file contains numerous notes from members of staff complaining of Jason's lack of work and poor behaviour in lessons. Under normal circumstances the Head of Year would have dealt with this problem. However, as detentions and extra work have had little effect on Jason's behaviour the issue has been passed on to me. I see from reports from his previous school that this is not a new state of affairs, Mrs Downing?"

"No. He has had a few problems in the past. This was because he was picked on by his teachers. He's not very bright and they were expecting too much of him. I think he may be a little dilectic, which would account for his problems in the classroom."

"I think you mean dyslexic. Has he ever been to see an educational psychologist or his local doctor with regards to this problem?"

"Not as far as I can remember. I did once ask the doctor if he could be tested for a brain disorder. It was at the time when he was getting in trouble with the local policeman who would not accept that the boy was just growing up."

"Mrs. Downing, I would agree with you that your son does have something wrong with him. He's got we call in educational circles B.I.   Bone Idle! I have looked at the work that the teachers have been giving him and compared it with his CAT scores from the junior school, and these indicate that he is working far below expectations. For years he has been coasting and has managed to get away with his bogus disruptive attitude. This is going to stop as from today. If Jason does not improve his ways I will personally keep him in after school. If need be, every lunchtime and every evening after school. If I have to resort to such extreme methods I would expect your full co-operation by doing the same when he comes home. If this does not work we will have to expel him and arrange for him to have home tuition. This is a last resort and should that fail he might have to attend a boarding school."

The thought of the latter sent shudders through Jason's nervous system.

"I don't want him going off to a boarding school. Is there any chance of him being classed as one of these E.S.N's, sub-normal people? One of my friend's son is subnormal and he has some kind of minder who travels around the school with him and helps him with his lessons and keeps him out of trouble."

"Mrs. Downing, if there was anything at all wrong with your son we would have diagnosed it long before now. There are so many tests that children take nowadays from the age of five that it is almost impossible not to notice if anything is wrong with a student. He might be slow in certain subjects but he is as capable as most of the pupils in his sets. I suggest you take him home and have a long chat with him explaining the options that he has. He can return tomorrow morning and go to his lessons as normal. I will notify the staff to keep a special eye on him and give him as much help as possible." He looked Jason straight in the eyes." It's up to you now, lad. You have heard what may happen to you if you do not make any amends to your work and behaviour. This is your last chance in this school!"

That night Jason had a long lecture from his mum and then went to bed early. All through the night he kept dreaming of being taken away from home and put in a dark old building where the teachers taught in dark cloaks and covered their faces so they could be heard but not seen. Jason was glad when he finally woke up. He went to school the next day determined to behave himself and buckle down to work. That inspirational thought lasted until the first period when he went into French and almost fell asleep, as the teacher was so boring.

All through the day he was only just keeping out of trouble.

Mr. Browning the Technology teacher sat him in the corner for playing with the drilling machine instead of planning his project. In Art he managed to get paint on his friend's face, and in Physical Education he got a misdemeanour for kicking a volley-ball across the sports hall. Not bad for his first day back.

The following day he began the morning with one of the only subjects that seemed to inspire him for a short period of time. It was Geography and he liked Mr. Hankinson as he had a keen sense of humour. In actual fact Mr. Hankinson had given up with Jason years ago. He used to let Jason sit at the computer and browse through the Internet.

That morning, Jason had only been using the keyboard for about five minutes when the computer screen went blank. That usually meant that some clown of a pupil had pulled out a socket at the back of their computer, which in turn had crashed all of the computers along that corridor as they were wired in series. One down, all down seemed to be the motto along that floor of the building!

Jason was thoroughly fed up. He sat there for a few minutes gazing out of the window thinking of nothing in particular and soon got fed up with that. He put his hand into his pocket and pulled out a stick of gum, which he slid into his mouth whilst keeping a sharp eye on Mr. Hankinson. Once it had reached the pliable stage he took it out of his mouth and proceeded to squeeze it into the long golden hair of Emma, the girl in front of him, who was looked upon as Mr. Hankinson's pet pupil as she always did her work on time and got ten out of ten for her assignments.

Moments later Emma ran her hands through her hair and let out a loud squeal, which made everyone in the class jump, including Mr. Hankinson.

"What on earth is a matter with you, Emma?" By now the girl was in floods of tears.

"Someone has stuck chewing gum into my hair."

Immediately Mr. Hankinson knew who that someone would be and was justified in his assumptions when he saw where Jason was sitting in relationship to Emma.

"Right, you little blighter. Go and sit in the front desk and don't move from there until I tell you to move. Emma, you run along to reception and ask them if they can help you."

Once he had regained the attention of the class he set some written work from the white board and then went along to Reception to see how Emma was. He was relieved to see that the office staff had some form of liquid oil which they kept for removing gum from peoples' clothing and was applying it to Emma's hair with successful results. With a bit of luck he might be able to deal with the matter with minimal fuss. Damn child. Why did the boss allow him to return to school? He returned to his classroom just as the bell was sounding.

"Off you go," he said to his class. " That is except for you, Downing. Get your notebook and copy down the following homework, which I want brought to me tomorrow morning during registration." Mr. Hankinson then dictated some work about the Egyptians asking Jason to write notes and draw a few diagrams. Jason had never done any form of homework in the past and so Mr Hankinson didn't expect anything from him the following morning.

For the rest of the day Jason somehow managed to keep out of trouble. That night he was seen for the first time for many a year carrying a pile of books home with him. Mum was quite shocked when he walked through the door and placed them on the kitchen table. Dr. Jacobs must have made quite an impression on him, she thought to herself.

"I see you have some homework to do this evening," said his mum trying to not sound too overjoyed. "Sit down for a few minutes before you start your work and I will make you a round of bread and jam and a glass of milk."

Jason sat at the far end of the table and said nothing. This was the last thing he wanted at the moment as he really wished to go out with his friends. He decided however that it would be better to humour his mum as he did not wish her to ground him for another night. It didn't take him long to finish off two more rounds of bread and jam, and then he made his excuses that he wanted to get on with his work in his bedroom.

He sat on the edge of his bed and gazed out of the window where he could see his friends already playing football. The pile of books on his table seemed to have grown since he had put them down. He might as well make a start he thought, as there was no way of getting out of this other than handing in some form of work to Mr. Hankinson tomorrow morning.

The work he had been set was to look at the topography in a desert region and then explain the various causes for some of the features seen in the photographs. The first diagram was that of a rock that looked precariously top heavy. By reading the accompanying notes he found that the cause for such a phenomenon was small particles of sand that were blasted against the rock by strong winds. The sand ate away at the softer bands of rock at its base and left the upper sections almost intact. As he read he attempted to make a few simple notes. He had to admit to himself that he found the work reasonably interesting. He was amazed when he looked at his watch to see that a whole hour had passed by. That's enough, he thought. I'll go down to mum and see if she will let me out for a while.

"Mum, can I go out for a while and play with my pals?"

"Yes," came the unexpectedly reply which meant that for a change he could go out the front door and not have to sneak out the back and over the garden fence.

"Thanks mum, I will only be out for an hour at the most." He knew that was a lie and so did his mum, but for a change she did not mind as he had at last done some schoolwork.

It wasn't long before he was engrossed in a game of hide and seek, which was one of his favourite games, as he knew the best places in which to hide. He was into his third game and still had not been caught out. The game had moved into a different area from the one he was used to. They were playing in the High Street and the only places in which to hide were shop doorways. He found himself a well-darkened doorway of the travel agency. The interior of the offices was well lit so as to allow their advertising boards to be easily seen by passing trade. This glare on the eyes made the shop doorway appear to be very dark and obscured the presence of Jason. He must have been crouched in that corner for well over five minutes and he was beginning to get a little bored.

To break the monotony he started to look at the various photographs of the holidays on offer. The one in the top corner of one of the billboards caught his eye. He'd seen it before but could not place where. It was a photo of a large stone lion and in the background was a stone structure, triangular in shape. He decided to take a closer look even if it meant him being seen by the chaser. He slowly got up from the floor, and keeping in the dark as much as possible crawled across to the opposite window. He gazed up at the lion, which was lying in amongst some low sand dunes. Suddenly he remembered where he had seen similar statues. They were in the textbook that he had brought home from school. The advert also showed what appeared to be some form of a temple, which was covered in strange carvings.

He had now completely forgotten about the game of hide and seek. He was far more interested in the carvings. He pressed his nose up against the glass in an effort to get a closer look at the carvings, but the photograph had been taken too far away from the wall to be able to pick out any specific one in detail. The mechanisms of his brain cells began to delve into the area of inquisitiveness, which had lain quite dormant in Jason over the years. He was not used to this sensation and began to get a little irritated. He had to have a look at the carvings at a closer range. Perhaps his textbook contained a photograph of such a wall. After all, if it had one of the triangular buildings and one of the lion then there was a very good possibility of there being one of the carvings.

Forget the game, he thought. I will need to get home without being spotted by the rest my pals. He slunk out of the doorway making sure first that no one was in sight. He was in luck. Everyone appeared to have gone to another area in which to play.

"Hi, mum," he shouted as he came into the hallway.

"What's the matter? Have you hurt yourself, or have you got into trouble with the police again? You'll be the death of me, Jason."

"No, mum. I'm OK. Just thought I would come home a little

early to finish my work to hand in tomorrow."

"Yes. He was in trouble with the police," she thought. However, just in case she was wrong in her summation, she decided not to quiz him any further.

"I'll bring you up some supper in about half an hour, Jason. Now you get on with your work."

As soon as he got into his room he picked up the textbook, and sat on the corner of his bed flicking through the pages. He was in luck. There on page thirty-four was the lion which he read was a sphinx, and on the page opposite was an old wall upon which had been carved numerous drawings. The strange markings seemed to depict anything from animals, people and things. What did they mean?

He could grasp some of the meanings, or so he thought, by the way the animals seemed to be behaving. There was a drawing of a sphinx, followed by a fish, which was lying beside of two squiggly lines like snakes, which probably represented a river or stream. Next came an ear of a corn whose stalk had been broken causing it to droop over, and further on there was a group of men who were kneeling down in a praying position gazing into the sky. Jason remembered the dream of Joseph in the Bible and surmised from these drawings that there must have been some form of a drought, which had badly affected the animals and plant life.

He spent that night trying to interpret the picture writings. He read from the textbook that the carvings had been done by the Egyptians of those times and were called hieroglyphics.

Later that evening there was a knock on his bedroom door. It was his mother.

"Jason, are you aware of what the time is? It's almost eleven o'clock. You should finish your work now and get some sleep."

He was amazed that two hours had passed since he had returned from his game of hide and seek. It seemed that he had only been working for a short period of time!

"All right, I'll get to bed."

It took him ages to get to sleep that night. His mind would not move away from the writings on the Egyptian wall. He had managed to fathom out a lot of the meanings but had problems in certain areas. He was determined to translate as much as possible, so he decided the best place to go tomorrow morning would be the library. He would have to make sure that no one saw him, especially any of his friends. The best time to go would be first thing in the morning when most of his friends would be lying on in bed, so before turning off his light he shouted down to his mum and asked her to give him a call at about eight o'clock. His mum could not get over the amazing changes in her son over the past few days. Dr. Jacobs the headmaster certainly had had a profound effect on her son!

The following morning Jason was up, washed and changed before his mother gave him his requested early morning call. He had a quick breakfast and was out of the door by nine o'clock. He was relieved to see that none of his friends were out at such an early hour. It took him about ten minutes to get to the library and he was very disappointed to find it closed. The notice on the door stated that it would open at ten o'clock so he had to walk around the town centre for over half an hour.

He was the first one into the library that morning and went straight up to the lady librarian who was busy rearranging a pile of books, which had been returned the previous evening.

"Excuse me. Could I look at some books about the Egyptians, which shows their carvings on the walls?"

The woman looked up from her stacking and looked at the untidy boy standing in front of her.

"Are you a member?"

"What do you mean?" replied Jason.

"Have you never been into a library before, young man? In order to borrow a book you have to be a member. In order to become a member you have to fill out a card showing where you live and who will be responsible for any loss of books. I can give you a card to take home with you but you will be unable to take out any books until one of your parents has signed the card."

Jason was very disappointed at this piece of news. He wanted to look at the books now. Today was Saturday and he did not wish to wait until Monday.

The librarian noticed the disappointment in the boy's face. It was her responsibility to look after the books but it was also her responsibility to encourage people to read, especially young people.

"What you can do is to look at the books in here now, and then take the card home with you when you have finished and then the next time you come in you can borrow some of them."

That seemed a fair compromise to Jason and he actually smiled at the initially foreboding woman.

"Thank you very much," he said.

"If you sit down at that table over there I will look through the files and see what I can find for you on hieroglyphics. Is there any other type of book that you might be interested in?"

"No thank you"

She was back within the space of a few minutes with three books, which she placed upon the table in front of Jason.

"These should keep you occupied for a couple of hours," she said with an amused smile on her face.

For the next hour the librarian busied herself around the bookshelves rearranging books, many of which had been put back in the wrong places. From time to time she glanced at the untidy little boy who had not stirred from his seat and had not taken his head out of the books that she had given him. Eventually he got up and walked over to the counter.

"Excuse me. Do you have any other books which only have writings in?"

The librarian was puzzled at this request. She had noticed that he had been making some form of notes on a small piece of paper, so she had occasionally pretended to stack the shelves near him so as to make sure that he was not defacing any of the books. She had been surprised to see that his scribbling was drawings of the hieroglyphics.

"We do have some very old books in the reference library upstairs which are extremely valuable." She didn't really know what to say to him as such a request was usually only made by older distinguished professor-looking people. " If you bear with me for a moment I will call the reference library and see if they have anything which may be of interest to you." She left the untidy researcher and went to her office at the side of the lending library.

"Hello, is that Phil?"

"Yes and I know who you are. You're the most beautiful girl in the whole of the world and I want to marry you now." Phil was forty years older than her, married with four children and was always flattering the younger librarians. He was actually quite a harmless old man and safe to have a joke with.

"Yes, please. Why don't you go home now, pack a suitcase, get your passport and then go down to the bank and draw out all of your life savings. That should be enough for me to live on whilst you find a job in Barbados. I know you don't really mean it as you wont give up your daily reading of the *Financial Times* for me! Phil, I have a young boy in here who is interested in hieroglyphics. I have shown him the books that we have down here but he wishes to look at the subject in more depth. I was wondering if he could come up to you and spend some time looking at your reference books on this subject? I will warn you that he is not the type of student you would normally expect to want to study this area. In fact he has the appearance of a street urchin, if you understand what I mean."

"Send him up. Once he sees what we have on the subject he will either return to you straight away of go back onto the streets where he can play with the other street urchins! All the books that we have on that particular subject have no illustrations at all, just plain old hieroglyphics."

"Thanks, Phil. Give me a call when you have packed your case." She put the phone down and walked across to the little boy who was still sat at the table with his head in a book.

"You're in luck, my little friend. I have spoken to Mr.Yates who is on the floor above this one. He has a number of books on the subject that you are interested in. Go up the stairs immediately outside the door that you entered the library and on the first landing that you come to take the door on your left. At the desk just ask for Mr. Yates. He is expecting you."

"Thank you, miss." He picked up all of his notes and left the books on the desk for the librarian lady to put away. She smiled as he went out of the door and gave a little chuckle. She would love to see the expression on Mr. Yates' face when the unkempt youngster entered the reference library and asked for him in person.

Jason felt quite overawed by the whole affair. For the first time ever he had entered the library and actually had asked to see some books, and now he was going up the steps to meet some man who was expecting him and who was going to show him some very special books. He felt important for the first time in his life.

"Ah, you must be the young gentleman who has an interest in Egyptian hieroglyphics," said an old-looking man who was wearing a large pair of horned rimmed spectacles over the top of which poked two very bushy grey eyebrows. Jason thought that the librarian looked the part, rather like a Dickensian character, to be working in such surroundings.

"If you come over to this desk you will see that I have taken down a couple of books for you to look at. I am sorry if they appear to be a bit dusty but no one has asked to see them for many a year."

Jason nodded at the man. He didn't know how to address him, as he had not seen anyone quite like him before. He wondered if he lived in here with the books.

Jason sat down and was immediately amazed at the enormity of the books in front of him. They were very old, as they were bound in rather faded leather, which had dried up over the years. In places the leather was beginning to peel off. Even Jason could appreciate the value of such books and handled them with extreme care. He was not expecting the cover to be so heavy as he proceeded to open it and let it drop onto the desk. The noise vibrated throughout the entire silent area. Everyone, including the wizened old librarian, turned and looked in annoyance at the untidy little boy who had intruded into their solitude. Jason looked around the large auditorium and was embarrassed. He felt like crawling under the stiff cover of the book, which lay open in front of him. Perhaps this was not such a good idea after all to come into such a place.

After what seemed to be an eternity he was eventually

relieved to see the faces gradually return to their original positions. He wouldn't make that mistake again.

Almost an hour later Jason was still looking at his books and making copious notes much to the amazement of the old bespectacled librarian. During all of this time he had kept Jason under close surveillance, unsure of his motives.

Another half an hour passed following which the untidy boy got up from his desk and made his way towards the librarian.

"Excuse me mister, but is it possible to take these books home with me for a few days?"

The old man was most surprised. "Sorry, but this is not the lending part of the library. These books are for reference only. That means that they have to stay in this room at all times. The only ones that you are permitted to take home with you are the ones from downstairs where you were first thing this morning. Why don't you go back to there and ask the lady if she has any other ones that you have not seen which you could take home with you for the remainder of the weekend. I'll give her a phone call and let her know that you are on the way."

"Thanks, mister," said Jason and for the first time in this building he smiled.

"Hello, gorgeous. This is the handsome black stallion from upstairs. I'm pleased to report that the hieroglyphic whiz kid is on his way down to you. Wants to take home some of your prize possessions. I doubt if you will get them back in one piece, but you can't refuse a budding archaeologist in the making. Over and out." And with that he put the phone down and smiled to himself. There, young lady, sort that one out!

No sooner had she put the phone back on its hook than she heard the creak of the library door. She turned knowing that it would be the little boy with a mop of unruly hair. He looked wilder than before as he made his way towards her desk. She was sure he had a thin film of dust covering his face.

"Hello, miss. It's me again. Can I take home some of your books please?"

"Are you a member of this library? " she said remembering the words of old Mr Yates and not wanting to lose some of her books.

"No, but I will join now."

"I'm afraid that's impossible. You see you have to get an adult to sign your form. You will have to take home a form and get your mum or dad to sign it. Bring it back on Monday and then I will let you have some books."

"But I want to take some books home with me tonight as I have to do my homework for Monday morning."

"Sorry but rules are rules."

"Give me a form and I'll sign it for the boy," came a voice from behind one of the larger bookshelves. Jason looked towards a very smartly dressed gentleman who was smiling at him.

"I've been intrigued by your work. I've been watching you for most of the morning and I hope you don't mind but have been glancing over your shoulder from time to time to see what you have been writing. You are quite a dab hand at copying hieroglyphics. Fascinating language isn't it?" Jason nodded in agreement.

The man turned towards the lady librarian. "I know it's not the correct procedure Miss Rawlings, but I'm sure that you would be in the position to accept my signature on the boy's registration card?"

"Why certainly Mr Williamson. If you would be so kind as to sign here I'll do the rest for the young man," and with that she slid a white form across her desk. The gentleman signed and then turned to Jason.

"I'm sure that you will look after these books. This young lady is going to trust you with them so do not let her down. It makes a pleasant change to be surprised occasionally in this building, and you've just done that for me today. Thank you." He then walked out of the door leaving Jason with his mouth wide open.

"Who was that bloke?"

"That so called bloke is the senior curator for the whole of the county. It so happens that today he was on an official visit. I had no idea that he was going to call into here. This is your lucky day young lad. Now lets get down your particulars and then you can take home some books."

Ten minutes later Jason ran out of the library with his books under his arm and almost collided with Miss Browning his PE mistress.

"Jason Downing, watch where you are going."

"Sorry, Miss. Got to get home quickly to finish my geography homework."

"What did you say? You haven't done any homework since you have been at the school. I doubt if you know what homework is. What have you got under your arm," she enquired in her schoolteachers inquisitive voice.

"Books to help me with my homework. Can't stop, as I'm late. See you on Monday Miss", and with that he ran off in the direction of his home. Miss Browning made a mental note to question him about the books on Monday as soon as he came into school.

All day on Sunday Jason did not come out of his room. His mother was quite worried as usually he was out and about with his friends by ten o'clock. When she went up to his room to call him for breakfast, instead of him being hidden under the duvet fast asleep, he was already dressed and sitting at his bedside table reading his new library books. He told her that he had to get some very important work completed before going back to school on the Monday and that he was not to be disturbed. If any of his friends came to the door she was to tell them that he was not feeling very well. And so he remained in his room for the rest of the day, only coming out to be fed at lunch time and again around about five o'clock. His mum couldn't get over the transformation of her son since sitting in with the head teacher.

Monday morning was not a good one for Sarah Browning. She had gone out on the town with some of her colleagues on the Saturday night and spent Sunday recovering. Now it was Monday and she was off to school again. She knew her lessons were not properly prepared which usually meant that the students would become disinterested and probably start to misbehave. Stress, and a thumping headache were not the ideal combination to start the week, especially with an Ofsted Inspection looming. Beware any child who should happen to cross Miss Browning anytime before her mid-morning fix of caffeine.

"Why, Miss Browning, you do look a picture of health this morning. All ready to leap over a few boxes and swing through the air on one of your jungle ropes?"

"Oh, shut up, Bill. At least I feel healthy sometimes and don't have to resort to a stinking pipe to give me some form of sexual satisfaction. One of these days you'll catch that mop of shaggy hair alight and I won't help you to put it out."

"Now that's an interesting adjective, shaggy. Conjures up many an exciting picture. I can see a large black sea bird with wings spread open, drying in the morning mists."

"You can shut up too Mr. Phelps. Save your linguistic prowess for 1TH. Anyone else like to add to this stimulating conversation before I go and put my head into the washing machine with the boys muddy football shirts and smelly socks?"

"Whatever turns you on, baby," added the Latin teacher who was sat on the far side of the staff room. He was just about to add a few more words in order to get Miss Browning really going when in walked Dave Roberts the geography specialist not knowing that the grumpy Miss Browning was about to bombard him.

"Morning all. And how is everybody after a most relaxing and invigorating weekend? I see you're still on the old weed, Bill. Are you aware of the horrendous working conditions of the poor labourers who have to toil ten hours a day in order to pick the leaves that you puff at? You must know by now that it damages your lungs and at the same time damages mine by my passive smoking? Poor sods. If you gave up the habit there would be no need for them to harvest the crop in such atrocious conditions."

"Yeh, and then the poor sods could die of malnutrition as they would have no jobs," said another voice from across the room.

"I've got a bone to pick with you, Mr. Roberts. One of your little brats almost knocked me over on Saturday outside the library."

"Why, you have amazed me, Miss Browning. I was not aware that PE bods frequented the library. I thought you all spent your lives chasing each other around muddy playing fields battering each other with an assortment of sticks. Once covered in mud you all then dived into a large khaki bath and sung songs, whose words would never be printed in *The Times* Musical Supplement."

There was a small chuckle from across the staff room. Things were looking up so early in the week. With bit of luck, thought the old Latin teacher, Miss Browning was about to hang herself.

"I'll bash you with a hockey stick if you continue to be as rude as that."

"Begs second in the line for beating," chipped in the French teacher.

"No, I wasn't going into the library. It was Jason Downing who came running out with a pile of books under his arm and bashed into me." An ominous silence descended upon the staff room at the mention of that particular student. " He said he had the books to do a project for geography, in actual fact for you. I think he was in the process of pinching the books. You will be in the proverbial mire once the head hears of this." She looked around the staff room and smiled. Now they were not taking the rise out of her anymore.

"I feel there will be a simple explanation. I have Jason this morning period three. I'll see what he has to say on the matter. He might be a nuisance in class, but he is no thief. Leave it with me, Miss Browning." At that point the bell sounded for registration and one by one they slowly left the protection of the staff room and went to their individual battlegrounds.

Third period came around and Jason filed into the Geography room with the rest of the pupils. Mr. Roberts was already sitting at his desk in a sombre mood. You could always tell when he was in a mood by the way he held his hands. All of the pupils in the school had cottoned onto his quirks. They needed to, as no one got the better of this teacher. Watch for the hands. If held in a pointed pyramid shape, don't make any silly comments for the next fifty minutes! The hands were pointed. Silence descended in the Geography room long before it did in any of the other classes in the school.

"Right, get out your homework that I set you on Friday. If there is anyone who does not have it, then I suggest you stand up and explain your reasons to all of us."

Most of the class looked in the direction of Jason, including Mr. Roberts, as Jason always stood up. To the amazement of the class Jason remained seated.

"Some of you obviously were not listening to what I have just said. I'll repeat myself once again and if anyone fails to respond to my request they will certainly suffer. Now, whoever has not done their homework stand up."

No one stood!

"How about you, Jason?" The class knew that Mr. Roberts was annoyed by the sound of his voice and by his body language as he got up from his desk and made his way slowly between the desks towards Jason.

"I have done my homework sir," replied Jason in a somewhat cowering voice.

"Let's see it then, boy."

There was an ominous silence in the classroom as if an execution was about to take place. This usually took the form of a sharp smack behind the rear of the head followed by a jerk on the neck of the jumper and then a hoisting feeling as one was dragged to the front of the class for the final inquisition. No one particularly liked Jason but there was a unanimous feeling of sadness for what Jason was about to experience. Mr. Roberts took up his place behind Jason and looked over his shoulder at the opened books that were neatly spread across the desk in front of him. The writing certainly looked liked Jason's, untidy with badly formed looping, and not punctuated in the correct places. It was such a long time ago that Mr. Roberts had actually seen any written work by Jason that for the present moment he would have to give him the benefit of the doubt.

"Good. I will have a closer look at it tonight when I do my marking."

One could sense the feeling of relief come over the rest of the class when Jason did not receive his usual morning clout. The pupils remained quiet for the rest of the lesson, occasionally looking at Jason who was not looking out of the window as he usually did. In fact some of his classmates actually witnessed him doing some work. On one occasion he actually answered a question!

Mr. Roberts was most suspicious of Jason's antics. Perhaps Miss Browning was correct. Perhaps Jason had stolen those library books and was keeping a low profile until the police had been and gone. Well the problem would have to wait until he did his marking that night. His daily schedule that day was too tight to even contemplate reading just one page of the boy's work. All that day he could not forget Jason and as he drove home that evening after an exhausting day he was actually looking forward to his marking. This was quite unusual as marking was a chore, especially when linked with all the paper work required of today's teachers.

David Roberts lived on his own in a small terraced house out of the catchment area of the school. He had chosen that area for two reasons. One being that property was a little cheaper and the second was that he did not want many people to know that he was a teacher. He had decided that when he left school each day he would try to forget all about school and the problems related to it. He certainly did not want to discuss educational issues in his spare time. Once home he would pour a glass of red wine, prepare a light meal and sit down and read the *Financial Times* to check his investment shares. He would then spend about an hour doing his marking and then for the rest of the evening watch his favourite television programmes. This particular evening he changed his routine for the first time in many a year. It was Jason Downing's fault. That name had been distracting him all day long and so he had decided that he would do his marking first and get the damn boy out of the way.

He made a cup of strong tea, which he put down on his marking desk. He then went to the kitchen and got a chocolate biscuit out of the pantry, which he placed neatly alongside the steaming cup of tea and then proceeded to pile his pupils' books at the side of the desk from where he could easily reach them. Already placed at the top of the pile was Jason's book.

Little did Mr. Roberts suspect that this would be the only book that he marked that night and the chocolate biscuit would be his only meal.

The book at the top of the pile did not in any shape or form offer itself to the potential reader as an attractive proposition. It was not covered in brown paper like all of the other books, which had been the first assignment for the pupils. Jason was unable to find any brown paper and also he was too busy playing in the streets to tackle such a mundane task. The light green cover was discoloured with various greasy marks and scribblings. All four corners were turned up like dog ears and many of the pages were crumpled, some torn. This should not take too long to mark, thought Mr. Roberts, who handled the book with great care so as not to allow any of the grease marks to come in contact with his skin or his clothes. The work on the first two pages was just what he had expected. A very poor attempt to make almost illegible notes about the agriculture of the region accompanied by a few very rough diagrams.

It was the third page that caught him off guard. Instead of another page of scribblings he was presented with a page of the most beautiful Egyptian hieroglyphics that he had ever seen. It was obviously copied from the photograph in his textbook. But whereas the textbook picture was in black and white Jason's drawing was in colour. Mr. Roberts reached for the textbook in order to compare the text with this most colourful work of art. Initially Mr. Roberts had assumed that the boy had traced the hieroglyphics, but when he compared the two he noticed that Jason's drawings were slightly larger than the original. It must have taken him hours and hours of the most meticulous copying. Mr. Roberts was truly impressed at this exquisite piece of homework. It was at times like this that Mr. Roberts felt rewarded for the many hours he had spent encouraging students to love his subject. He was in for much bigger shock when he turned over to the next page. It was full of hieroglyphic words each individually accompanied by equal signs, which were followed by what he assumed to be their meanings. Where on earth had the boy gleaned such information? And then for the third and most amazing surprise of the evening. He finally turned to the next page. On the left-hand page was another copy of the hieroglyphics from the photograph and on the right-hand page was presumably its translation!

For the next two hours Mr. Roberts compared the two pages and from time to time turned back to the previous page. He was trying to fathom out how the boy had managed to complete the translation, if he had in fact done that, as there was no telling what he had managed to fathom out from his little scribblings on the previous page He could see some diagrams which were self-explanatory such as the sun and the moon and a wavy line which probably represented a river, but many of the other combinations were impossible to decipher. However had the boy managed to do this incredible piece of work? he thought. Eventually he glanced at the clock on the wall and was shocked to see that he had been sitting at his desk for over three hours with no thought at all about his tea and about marking the other books in the tall pile in front of him. He suddenly felt very drained and tired and decided to leave everything until the morning. Usually he got up at seven thirty but as he had not accomplished anything that night he decided to set the alarm for six o'clock and then attempt to get all the marking out of the way.

The following morning he had a shower, quick cup of tea and then commenced to mark. He completed the task within the hour and so was able to treat himself to a leisurely breakfast of cereal followed by toast and marmalade. By the end of breakfast he regained his equilibrium and headed off for school early.

He wasn't the first in that morning. The old CDT teacher was already making the staff tea and Miss O'Brien was hovering over the photocopier.

"Morning all," he said. Miss O'Brien looked up and smiled and old Howard grunted and began to pour himself a mug of tea. Soon staff began to drift in and within fifteen minutes the room was almost full of bodies. Mr. Roberts took a seat in the corner of the room and watched the various members of staff going about their morning rituals before the dreaded bell.

"Well, Robo, did he steal those books from the library?" It was Miss Browning.

"I'm not sure at the moment. I intend to speak to Jason during my free period at ten o'clock. I'll get to the bottom of it and let you know during the lunch recess."

"Are you talking about Jason Downing of 3PH?" came a voice from the other side of the room. It was the relatively new mathematics teacher. "What a dramatic change has come over the boy during the last few days. During the last few lessons he actually did some calculations and amazingly got them correct."

"That's interesting as he did some work for me for a change without me having to threaten him with a detention. Someone try to find out what he is on and then see if you can get some for us," added another voice.

At 10.00 a.m. Jason appeared outside the staff room and asked for Mr. Roberts who was already waiting for him.

"Ah, Jason. You obviously got my message from your form teacher. Let's go along to the prep room where it is a little quieter. I want to talk to you about your assignment that you handed in yesterday."

Once in the prep room Mr. Roberts took Jason's work from out of his brief case and laid it on the desk in front of him. "Now Jason, can you honestly say that this is all your own work, or did you have some guidance from someone else?"

"No sir, it's all of my work. No one gave me any help. I did most of it in the library on Saturday and the rest at home on Sunday."

"Mm. I don't see how you managed to translate all of these from the notes that you have on the previous page." He pointed at the work on the left-hand side of the book.

"Well sir, I got almost all of the information that I needed from the Papyrus of Anhai. You probably know that it was found at Devel-bahara, which as a geographer you will know is situated on the western banks of the Nile opposite the site of the ancient city of Thebes. There were a few areas where I got stuck. However, by spending some time studying the Papyrus of

Hunefer, which was also found at Thebes I was able to work out all of the translation. The original was bought by the British Museum. One day I will go and see it."

"Well done, boy." At that particular moment those were the only words that Mr. Roberts could think of. He was absolutely dumbfounded and for once in his life felt uncomfortable in the presence of a pupil. The boy appeared to be a genius. Dave Roberts was almost ashamed that he had not recognised Jason's talent earlier.

"Jason, this piece of work of yours has really impressed me. It's worth at least two commendations. I will write them out later and pass them on to your form tutor. Now run along and try to do as good in all of your other lessons."

Jason went out of the room feeling really great as no one had ever praised him like that before, and he had never been given a commendation for anything. For the rest of the day he set out to impress all of the teachers he came in contact with. He soon became the talking point of the staff room. Mr. Roberts did not join in the conversations about Jason. He was still trying to get his mind around the piece of work that he had had the privilege of marking the evening before. Even at the end of the day he was still thinking of the script so much that he decided to take it home with him that night.

By eight o'clock he had finished all of his marking and then sat down in his old leather armchair and once more read through Jason's work. The more he read it the more intrigued he became. At nine thirty he knew what he had to do. He needed to get in contact with someone who dealt with hieroglyphics on a professional level, and he knew just the very man, Professor David Hislop.

Professor Hislop had been his lecturer when he was at university and since then had been appointed assistant director of the British Museum. He had been in contact with him only once since leaving university and that was to congratulate him on his new post. He flicked through his address book and eventually found the home number of the professor. He wasn't sure what he would say but decided to phone in any case.

"Hello, is that Professor Hislop?"

"Yes." The tone of the voice was gruff. The professor had actually been dozing on his settee and did not like to be disturbed after nine o'clock any night of the week.

"Sorry to interrupt your evening, sir. I don't know if you remember me. My name is David Roberts and I used to attend some of your history seminars when you lectured at Exeter University."

"Why of course I remember you." The voice had somewhat mellowed. "What can I do for you, old chap?"

"Well, I need your advice on one of my students." He then went on to relay to the professor all that had happened during the last couple of days. When Mr. Roberts had finished his account there was a slight pause before the professor replied.

"I am intrigued by what you have told me. What I find most interesting is the reference to the Papyrus of Anhai and the Papyrus of Hunefer. The only people who would normally be dealing with these old parchments would be professors who are looking into the history of the Pharaohs when new archeological finds are made and which might require a translation, or only my very best students who are studying for their Doctorates. Most strange. What's the child's background? Does he have any brothers or sisters who have the same gifts?"

"No. He is the only child. One parent family. Mother not very bright from what I have seen of her."

"David. Is there any chance of you bringing the boy along to us here in the Museum?"

"I don't see why not. I could get in contact with his mother tomorrow and see what she has to say."

"OK. When you have any more news about the boy give me a call. I'll give you my private line into the Museum. Very interesting. Look forward to hearing from you in the near future. Thanks for phoning me."

Mr. Roberts put the phone down. So he might have some form of a genius in his class after all, otherwise the professor would not be wasting his valuable time wanting to see Jason at the Museum.

The following morning Mr. Roberts sent a message requesting Jason to come to the Geography Department at break time. In the past Jason would not have adhered to such a request from any member of staff. He was there dead on time on this occasion.

"Good morning, Jason. I had another look at your work last night and decided to have a chat with one of my old professors from my university days. I thought he might be interested in it, and he was. He asked if you would be prepared to go along to the Natural History Museum to have a look at some of the original manuscripts on hieroglyphics. Would you be interested?"

"Yes please, sir."

"OK. I will have to have a word with your mother and get her permission. I would prefer to speak to her in person if you don't mind: how about you speaking with her tonight and arrange for me to see her after school tomorrow? I could give you a lift home."

"I'll ask her as soon as I get home," he said in a most enthusiastic voice, which was not at all like him. Mr. Roberts could still not get over the changes he had seen in this boy's personality during the last few days.

When Jason got home that night he burst through the door and almost knocked over the ironing-board. Mum was holding the iron at the time and almost dropped it on the floor.

"Mum. Can Mr. Roberts come in and speak to you tomorrow evening on his way home from school? He said he would give me a lift home."

"Oh no. And you were doing so well at school during these last few days. What have you been up to?"

"No, it's all right, Mum. He wants to ask you if I would be allowed to go along to some museum to see the hieroglyphics."

"Well I suppose it would be allright. What are these glyphic things?"

Jason tried to explain to his mum but gave up after only a few moments. Such things were well beyond his mum.

The following evening after school Jason arrived home earlier than usual as he was given his promised lift with Mr. Roberts.

"Mum. This is Mr. Roberts, my geography teacher." Mrs. Downing held out her hand.

"Pleased to meet you, Sir" she said quite sheepishly, as she was not used to being in the company of professional people.

"And I'm very pleased to meet you, Mrs. Downing," he said with a warm smile on his face. " I believe Jason has already mentioned that I would like to take him along to the Natural History Museum. Jason, I wonder if I could have a word with your mum on her own for a few moments?"

"Jason, I know what you can do whilst I am talking to Mr. Roberts. Nip down to the shop on the corner and get some chocolate biscuits so that we can have them with our cup of tea." She gave Jason a pound coin and off he went to the shop.

"Mrs. Downing no doubt you are a little intrigued as to why I want to take your son to the museum. An old friend of mine there would like to meet Jason. You see, we both feel that your son may possess quite an extraordinary gift for translating an old Egyptian language. We could both be wrong but we would like to give him a few tests. Would this Saturday be OK? You are more than welcome to come along if you so wish."

"I can't do that. I work part time on Saturday mornings in the supermarket. I can't see any reason why he can't go with you, though. That's very kind of you, Mr. Roberts. I will make sure that he has money with him for the tube and buses."

"That won't be necessary as I thought I would take my car."

When Jason returned from the shop Mrs. Downing made them all a cup of tea and then they set about making the necessary arrangements for the following weekend.

That week passed very slowly for Jason, as he was extremely excited about his forthcoming visit to the museum. Eventually the day arrived and he was picked up outside his house at nine thirty and by ten fifteen they were standing outside the tall impressive façade of the Natural History Museum. Jason stood agog at the immensity of the building and of all the people of different nationalities who were queuing to go in. He felt very important as Mr. Roberts went to the very front of the queue and showed a special pass to one of the ticket men who let them straight in. Someone else directed them to an office half way up a flight of stairs. On the door of the office was the name 'Professor William Hislop M.B.E.' Mr. Roberts knocked on the door and the professor came out.

"How nice to see you, David, and this must be Jason." He held out his hand to Jason and they shook hands. "I've heard a lot about you, young man. Before we have a chat I would like to spend a few moments with your teacher. What I suggest you do is to go along and have a look at a very special stone, which I think will be of interest to you. John, would you escort this young man along to the Rosetta Stone and let him have a look at it. I will come along in a few moments and collect him from you." The man he spoke to was dressed in a green uniform.

"Right, lad. You follow along behind me. It will get a little crowded when we get in the vicinity of the stone so keep an eye on me." Jason had no intention of losing this man in the crowds and followed him almost as if he was part of the man. They went up a flight of smooth marble steps, across a long room, which was full of Egyptian artefacts and eventually reached the room, which housed the Rosetta Stone. There was a small crowd standing around something that was raised up on some form of a dais. Jason could not see very well as he was by far the shortest person in that room. The man in the green uniform led him around to the back of the stone, which was surrounded by a large loosely hanging rope, and which he unhooked and beckoned Jason to step inside. He then rehooked the rope and moved Jason around to the front of the stone and suggested he sit down on the floor so that he would not block out the view of the stone from the people who had already assembled at the front. They were just in time to catch the beginning of a talk by one of the official guides of the museum.

"The Rosetta Stone was one of the greatest archaeological finds of its time. Until it's discovery the writings of hieroglyphics were undecipherable. In 1799 during Napoleon's Egyptian expedition this block of basalt was discovered at a place called Rashid. At the time no one understood its significance. It has three different scripts on it, Lier, the derived demonic script and Greek. The writings commemorate the accession of Ptolemy V Epiphanies 205-180 BC. By studying the three languages scholars were able to decipher hieroglyphics. The word hieroglyphics incidentally comes from the Greek 'sacred carving' because of its prominent usage in temples and tombs. It is written from right to left." The guide went on to talk a little about the history of the Egyptians but Jason had stopped listening as he was intrigued by the writings on the stone.

Jason must have been sitting there for well over twenty minutes when the professor accompanied by Mr. Roberts, appeared. They squeezed their way to the front of a large tourist group and spoke to Jason.

"Jason. Sorry to be late. Climb under the rope and we will go along to my office," said the professor.

"There's a mistake in the stone," said Jason much to the amusement of three young classical students who were standing at the front of a large group of American tourists. The professor was a little embarrassed when people began to look at him as he was wearing his official pass around his neck. They were already beginning to wonder about the little boy sat in front of the stone and inside the official viewing area.

"Come along Jason, we'll talk about that in a minute."

"But there is a mistake in the thirty-third line. Look just here." Jason went as if to touch the stone with his finger.

"Don't touch," came a stern voice to the left hand side of Jason. It was the man in the green uniform who had been designated to look after him. Jason froze at the command.

"It's all right John," said the professor. "I don't think he meant to actually touch the stone."

"Why not let him show you where the stone is wrong professor?" said one of the three students who were now really amused by the happenings

The professor did not want to cause any embarrassment for Jason and would have preferred to have led him away to his office but now the challenging comment from one of the bystanders had highlighted his and Jason's presence and people were beginning to sense that there was something going on. He thought the easiest way to defuse the situation would be for Jason to point out where he thought the mistake was and then hurriedly lead him away from the scene.

"OK, Jason. Put your finger over the place where you think it is wrong and we will follow it up later."

Jason went over to the stone and peered at it for a few moments. "There, just above those two squiggly lines. That symbol there should be one of those upturned half-moon shapes like that one there and on top of it should be two stalks of wheat."

The professor peered at the place where Jason was pointing. The three students had now stopped smiling and had moved nearer to get a better look at the spot that Jason had just high-lighted. They could see that the professor was deep in thought. He eventually turned to Mr. Roberts.

"David. I wonder if you would mind taking Jason down to the cafeteria. The poor boy must be absolutely famished by now. Come back to my office in half an hour." Mr. Roberts nodded and escorted Jason out through the group, which had now swollen in size. The professor turned to the Jason's minder.

"John. Would you extend the rope back from the stone by about a meter as I will need a little more space here in about five minutes' time. I'll send over some help for you as you will need someone to move the group back." The size of the group had now almost doubled in numbers. The professor left the museum official and returned to his office where he went straight to the phone and made a call to the central offices.

"Hello, is that Jayne? Good. Jayne can you put out a call for Professor Jacks and Professor Tookey. Ask them to meet me in front of the Rosetta Stone in five minutes' time. Tell them it's very important." It must be very important for those two pro-fessors to be called from their work at such short notice, thought Jayne. They won't be at all happy. How right she was as two stern looking professors appeared at the stone five minutes later.

"Ah, there you are. I want you to take a look at this line here and see if you can see anything possibly out of place." The two professors looked at one another, decided not to say anything and peered at the stone. The three American students were still there right at the front of the group and enjoying every moment.

"Nothing wrong here," said one of the professors after a few moments. The other one nodded in agreement.

"Look here," said Professor Hislop. "Take a closer look at that symbol there. Shouldn't it be the same as that one?" He pointed to a marking three lines below. The other two professors looked to where he was pointing and back to the original place. They pondered for well over five minutes and then one of them spoke.

"You clever old chap. How on earth did you discover this spelling mistake? The number of times this stone has been studied by the world's most leading archaeologists and they didn't find anything wrong with it, and now you suddenly discover this. How on earth did you do it?" Professor Hislop had no intention of explaining the last two hours to these two professors.

"Thank you very much for your help, gentlemen. I will let you know more about this in a few days' time." He then moved out from the roped-off cordon and made his way back to his office. The three American students were totally amazed as to what they had witnessed in that last hour. It was the highlight of their entire visit to the UK.

Jason and Mr. Roberts arrived back in the professor's office five minutes later.

"No time to sit down. I have a special treat for Jason. If you don't mind waiting here for a few moments, David, I would like to take Jason down into the archives. I intend leaving him there for a while, if he so wishes. He will be under the close eye of one of the research students so should be all right. Come on then, Jason," and with that they both went out and left Mr. Roberts relaxing in the spacious office.

Jason was led down four flights of stairs and into some form of a waiting room where there were white overalls hanging up on hooks.

"Now lets see. Look for a pair of these cover suits, which is nearest to your size. They will all be too large for you but it doesn't matter what you look like. Also you will need one of these masks and a pair of plastic gloves. There you are." Jason looked at himself in the mirror that was hanging on the opposite wall. He resembled an alien! "The reason for all of this clothing is because I am about to take you into a restricted zone which houses some of the rarest of all our historical treasures. They are so precious that we dare not let any form of moisture get onto to them. Even the water vapour from your breathing could damage them."

Once dressed, they proceeded into the inner room which had nothing but large desks and a few chairs within it. All around the walls were large filing cabinets one of which the professor approached and proceeded to pull out one of its shallow drawers. From it he very carefully removed a large plastic envelope and placed it on one of the desks. He then proceed to open the envelope and lay it's contents on a sheet of white paper which had been put on an adjacent desk by one of the research students who was assisting the professor.

"Jason, you are now looking at a parchment which was removed from one of the pyramids in Egypt. It is thousands of years old so you can no doubt appreciate why we go through the procedure of wearing all of these garments. I'm going to leave you with Bernard here who will show you more of our archaeological finds. Take as long as you like. I am going back to keep Mr. Roberts company. Bernard here will give me a phone call when you are ready to return."

It was as if some one had left a four-year-old in Willy Wonkers Chocolate Factory and asked him to eat as much chocolate as he wished. Jason was astounded at the beauty of the manuscript that was before him. This was followed by many more from different countries and of different centuries. He could have spent his whole school holidays in here and he would never have got bored.

Back in the office the Professor and Mr. Roberts were deep in conversation. The Professor had just related the incident at the Rosetta Stone. "So you see, David, we have some form of a genius in our midst. We are going to have to look after this little fellow as if he were made of gold. If he is happy to do so, I suggest in the initial stages we allow him to come along to the museum whenever he wishes. We will obviously arrange for him to be transported by taxi each time. We will have a word with him now and later in the week get in contact with his next of kin."

The rest of the afternoon Jason was shown around the museum and eventually finished up where he had started that morning outside Professor Hislop's office.

"Well, Jason, I hope you have enjoyed your visit here as much as we have enjoyed having you. And look here," he turned and pointed to the sign on his door.

"One day your name might be on this door in place of mine."

Twenty-five years later the name of "Professor Jason Downing" was placed on that very door.

Chapter Eight

"Hurry up, darling, the taxi will be arriving at any moment and we only have ten minutes to spare before the coach arrives." Angela Bryant had been ready for the past fifteen minutes, as was usual, and her husband Brian was still getting dressed. Brian put paid to the myth that the woman always took longer to get ready. Angela had prepared everything for the holiday in Bournemouth. She set the clothes in neat piles on the bed in the spare room days ago, making sure that they all were colour coordinated All of that week she had kept ahead of the washing pile and ironed as soon as the clothes had come out of the washing machine. All the money and various tickets had been checked and double-checked. Notes had been given to the various delivery men a week before, as she did not want to come home to a pile of newspapers and a row of sour milk bottles lined neatly along the doorstep. That had happened during their last holiday when her husband had forgotten to do the only thing that his wife had asked of him and that was to put out the note for the milkman.

"Ready, darling. Just have to shut the bathroom window and I'll be straight down." She waited until she heard the window shut, at least that was one thing that she could cross off her checklist.

Eventually Brian appeared at the foot of the stairs, just as the taxi pulled up at the front of the house. "There, how is that for perfect timing, darling?" His wife smiled in a lovingly way, for although he was a test of her patience at times, he had qualities that had endeared him to her for the past sixty years of a wonderful marriage.

It was early September. The country's children had returned to their schools and the hotels had dropped their prices dramatically to ensure a busy autumn. It had been a bad summer for weather with only an odd few days of sunshine and the rest either cloudy or drizzle. Now, however, a high weather front had come in and the long-range weather forecast was a possible late Indian summer. That would be ideal for Bournemouth because one could either sit on the golden sandy beach or walk across the promenade into the park where there was an abundance of tall shady trees under which to shelter from the sun's rays.

The taxi only took ten minutes to deliver them at the local bus station where the coach was already loading with passengers and their baggage. Angela noticed a few faces from past holidays and gave them a wave. The Bryants were a very popular couple as they mixed well with all types of folk. Neither was extrovert but both liked to join in the fun, especially after a few drinks.

"Hello, Brian," said a rather rounded man who was sat near the rear of the bus.

"Are you staying at the same hotel as last year?" Brian recognised him as the one who had fallen off the bar stool on the last night and broken his wrist. Fortunately for him at the time he was absolutely filled with alcohol and on hitting the floor was completely relaxed. Had he been sober he would have probably broken his collarbone as well as his wrist.

"Yes, The Palm Court where we have stayed for the past twenty years. Wouldn't go anywhere else."

Angela certainly knew that. Although she liked the hotel there were times when she would have preferred a change in scenery. She had not pushed the point, as she knew that Brian loved it. She had noticed too, that recently he had become somewhat forgetful, which he found rather disconcerting. At least if he got lost in the town he would be able to find his way back to the hotel.

The coach arrived at its destination half an hour before dinner was due to be served so there was no time to unpack, just enough to have a quick wash and change of clothing. By the time Angela had got Brian sorted out and gone down to the dining-room the first course was being served. They were sat with a couple who said they remembered them from ten years ago and who had not been back again until this year. After a bottle of house red wine and two courses of the meal had been consumed the conversation was flowing. After the meal they all went to the bar and soon met up with numerous other people whom they had met over the years. Perhaps it would be a mistake to go to a different hotel each year, thought Angela, as they had made so many wonderful friends. This was going to be another blissful holiday just as all the others had been. She didn't realise that this was to be her last.

Angela and Brian had a routine for their week's holiday. Each day they would go down for breakfast at eight thirty and order a full English fry up. They would then venture down into the town where Angela would buy a few post cards and Brian a newspaper. After a browse around the shops they would then order a pot of coffee from the small café at the end of the High Street, and then sit and read the papers and write their cards. By that time the sun would be well up in the sky, which meant making for the promenade to get their usual place and deck chairs.

Lunch was taken in the restaurant on the pier and then afterwards they would make their way to the park to listen to the brass band, which was a daily feature of Bournemouth life. At about four o'clock they would slowly walk back up the main street glancing in the shops as they went. At the end of the street, just before they turned to go up a steep hill to their hotel, was an old antique shop where Brian always insisted on stopping for a few minutes. He never entered into the shop saying that it was far too expensive for them, but would look admiringly at the old curios on the dusty shelves. One of his favourite antiques was of a warrior on the back of a horse, which was rearing up. The rider wore some form of body armour and held the reigns of the horse in one hand and a long lance in the other. The base of the statuette appeared to be made of some form of metal. Angela had often tried to make her husband go in and buy it, but he always made some form of an excuse not to do so.

On Wednesday the Bryants got up at the usual time and went down for breakfast just as the bell sounded. The sun was shining in through the dining-room's French windows, which helped to put both of them in a very happy mood. By ten o'clock they were on their way down to the town centre and were soon following their daily routine. Everything went smoothly until about two-thirty in the afternoon. They had just had a really nice lunch in the restaurant on the pier and were walking along the High Street towards the old antique shop on the corner when Angela suddenly stopped in her tracks.

"What's the matter, darling," said Brian with a worried look on his face.

"I have a horrible feeling that I may have left my purse on the table back in the restaurant." She then opened her bag and began to search for her purse amongst the many items which had accumulated over the past few months. She wished that she had spent a little time before coming on this holiday sorting it out.

"It's not here, Brian. Would you be a dear and go back to the restaurant and see if anyone has handed it in? I will do some shopping in these shops and then meet you outside the antique shop on the corner. Let's say in half an hour. That will give you plenty of time to go back to the pier and you won't have to rush up the hill afterwards."

"All right, darling. Don't worry as I know it will be where you left it." Angela was not at all worried as her purse was in its usual pocket in the side of her handbag!

As soon as Brian was out of sight, Angela made her way to the old antique shop on the corner of the High Street and quietly let herself in through a sturdy oak front door, which had ornate coloured glasses at its centre in the shape of a ship's wheel. There was no doorbell to indicate that anyone had entered the premises and there did not appear to be anyone inside of the shop. Angela stood still for a few moments in order to allow her eyes to get accustomed to the gloom. As she looked around she became aware of how cluttered the shop was. Every conceivable space on the floor to ceiling shelving was filled with curios from all over the world. Even the floor had little space left in which to store anything.

"Good afternoon, Madam" came a soft voice from the rear of the shop. Angela looked in the direction from where the sound had emanated and noticed an old man who was sittiing in a very ornate rocking chair. "I know why you have come in here. You would like to know how much the statue of the man on horseback costs. The one, which is in the middle of the shelf in the front window."

Angela was lost for words. How on earth did the shop owner know that? Before she could ask the question he continued to speak.

"How do I know that?" he smiled at her. "For the past number of years I have seen you stop outside of my shop with your husband at about the same time each day. I've watched his expression as he's gazed along the shelves at the window and noticed that he particularly focused on the knight on horseback."

"That was very astute of you," said Angela. "I've tried for years to get him to come in and purchase it but he thought that it would be too expensive. We have our wedding anniversary coming up in a few months' time so I thought I would give him a really big surprise. Can you tell me how much it is, please?"

The old man scratched his head in deep thought for a few moments. The statue was a very rare one and commanded a high price, which was the main reason why it had remained on his shelf for so many years. What was the point of keeping it any longer, thought the shop owner? He assumed that it would probably be out of the price range of the lady but having seen the expression on her husband's face each time he looked at it he knew that if he sold it to them it would at least be going to a caring home.

"Eighteen pounds and fifty pence," the old man said with a little smile on his face.

"That seems to be reasonable. I'll take it. Now I am after a favour of you. I can't take it with me at the present moment as my husband will see it and I want it as a surprise. Would you be so kind as to put it in the back of your shop and I will pick it up in a few days' time?"

"No problem, Madam. I will give you a receipt in case someone else is manning the shop when you come in. Your husband will be really pleased with your present. What I will do is to wrap it in straw as it is quite fragile and place it in a box until you call in the next time." The old men went to the window and carefully removed the statue from the centre display shelf and placed it on a leather-topped cabinet. He then took a small blue book from out of his office desk and commenced to write out a receipt.

"Thank you very much," said Angela feeling really pleased with herself as she handed over the correct money. "I must go now as my husband is due to arrive outside of your shop at any moment."

"It's a pleasure to do business with you, Madam. See you in a few days' time." He then went to the door and held it open for Angela.

No sooner had Angela got outside of the shop when she noticed Brian coming along the High Street. He had a worried look on his face.

"Before you say anything, darling, I've found my purse. It was in my handbag all of the time hidden behind the programme which I purchased at the theatre last night. I'm really sorry to have made you walk all that way back to the restaurant for nothing." A look of relief spread over Brian's face.

"No need to apologise, love, I needed the extra bit of exercise." They both laughed at the same time and then went on their way holding hands. The old man in the shop watched them and felt very pleased with himself even though he had sold the statue at a loss.

It was Thursday morning at about three a.m. when Brian knew that something was wrong. Angela had been tossing and turning for the past hour which was very unusual for her as she was normally a very sound sleeper. The bed seemed extremely hot and Brian put it initially down to the fact that the previous day had been exceptionally warm and they had both caught the sun, even though they had both used a high factor sun cream. He got up and went to the window to open it at its widest point. He looked outside and was surprised to be able to clearly pick out the outlines of the adjacent buildings as it was a full moon and the sky was cloudless. It was going to be another blistering day, he thought. Just at that moment he heard his wife murmur in her sleep.

"Are you all right darling?" he whispered quietly, just in case she was still asleep. She turned and faced him.

"Brian, I don't want you to worry, but I am not feeling too well. Would you be a pet and make me a nice cup of tea."

Brian walked over to the bed, sat down on its edge and took hold of wife's hand.

"You don't look too good, but that is quite normal for you in the morning." His little joke was an effort to ease the apprehension that he and his wife were both feeling at that moment. She was never ill, and when she did have anything wrong with her she never mentioned it to him, as she knew that he would worry. He got up from the bed and made his way across the room to the dressing table on which stood the electric kettle plus the various sugars and milks.

"I'll put the tea-maker on and we'll have a soothing cup of tea." He pulled the socket from the back of the kettle, placed it back on the surface of the dressing table, and then went to the tap and half filled the kettle. His wife watched his movements and smiled at the way he stood hovering above the kettle as he normally did, impatiently waiting for it to boil. He would never get out of that habit. She used to say that if he watched for the steam it would take twice as long to appear. Although at times it used to annoy her she would not like him to change in his ways.

Brian turned to look at his wife and she gave him a reassuring smile. She looked so lovely lying back on the pillow, just like she had done on their first night together. It didn't seem that long ago, although it had been almost sixty years. Next year would be their Diamond Wedding Anniversary. His mind began to scan back over some of the most memorable moments they had had together. They had had such a wonderful life.

The hissing of the kettle brought him back to his senses. He flicked off the switch and poured the hot contents into two cups, which already had their tea bags and spoonful of sugar inside them, which he had prepared the previous night. Once the milk had been added he stirred the contents quite vigorously in order to get the full strength of the tea from out of its perforated bags.

"There, one nice cup of tea as ordered by the doctor," he said as he turned to face the bed. Angela had moved her head and was facing the other way and did not respond to his voice. He placed the two cups of tea on the small table beside of the bed and touched his wife's shoulder. She slowly turned and looked into his eyes.

"Brian, if I don't feel very well tomorrow would you run along to the antique shop on the corner of the high street and ask the old man in there for the box that I left there?" At that moment in time Angela knew that she would not be going out into the town tomorrow.

What a strange request, thought Brian. Why on earth had Angela gone into the antique shop? He shook his head. He wasn't going to question her at that moment when he knew she was not feeling too well. He would do that later when they were sitting in the café writing their cards.

He turned away for a moment and reached over for her cup of tea. As he turned back he looked at her face and knew that she had left him forever. The smile was still on her face but her eyes were closed. Brian stood for what seemed an eternity just looking at his wife. Tears began to well up in his eyes. He put the cup down on the table, reached across and gently stroked the side of her face with his hand hoping that she would suddenly open her eyes but knowing that she would never speak to him again. He sat there for what seemed an eternity, not wanting to notify the hotel staff as that would mean that she would be taken away from him forever.

He eventually got up from the bed, went over to the phone and spoke to the young man who was manning the switchboard. Within minutes the tranquillity of the hotel was broken. People came rushing up the stairs. Frantic phone calls were made to the local doctor's surgery in order to get the emergency number for night visits, and someone called for an ambulance just in case something could be done for the old lady in room number forty two, not knowing that she had already passed away.

That morning the atmosphere in the breakfast-room was very subdued. Many could not believe that Angela had passed away. It seemed only a few hours ago that she was sat in her seat having her dinner with her husband, laughing at a joke that

George had made at the table adjacent to her. Now their table was empty.

Everyone was brilliant in the hotel when it came to looking after Brian. He had been an extremely popular resident and had got to know most of the staff by their Christian names. He knew all about their private lives and always asked how their parents and children were. If they had any ailments he always sympathised with them and tried to offer some form of a remedy. He knew quite a lot about the old country ways of dealing with illnesses and never failed to amaze his listeners with unusual remedies.

All that day Brian had to spend filling out various forms with the aid of the manager, who also had to deal with an extra amount of paper work. It wasn't the norm to have somebody pass away at the hotel. By evening time both were physically and mentally exhausted. Brian did not want to return to his room at that present moment as he could still visualise his wife lying on the bed. He decided to go down into the park where the brass band would be playing and where he could try to relax under the shade of a tree, with no one to bother him. He found a suitable spot where there was a vacant deck chair and moved it slightly so that it was entirely in the shade. Five minutes later he appeared to be fast asleep but inside the shell of his body he was in absolute turmoil. He just could not let his wife go even though he knew in his dream that she was dead. He hoped that it was some form of a nasty nightmare and soon he would awake from his sleep to find her next to him, writing her cards.

Eventually he awoke and began to feel a little better. Memories came flooding back of the marvellous times they had spent together. He remembered her saying that the time would come when one of them would go to the Promised Land, but he did not expect that she would be the first. He was sure of that, having seen various statistics on the expected length of life of the two sexes and that a woman usually outlived a man by some ten years. With that little piece of useful information, he had not had the need to think out the logistics of how he would manage on his own. Both had promised one another that whoever was the surviving half of the marriage, that that one would not spend time grieving. This, Brian found extremely difficult to achieve although he was determined not to let his wife down. He decided there and then to make a very conscious effort to be positive about his future life. He would remember all of the good times that he had spent with Angela and use them to give him strength. He knew that this would probably be the last time that he would ever visit Bournemouth so he decided that he would still go through the usual routine of the day, as Angela would have wished that.

Brian got up from the deck chair already feeling a little better, folded it in half and rested it against the tree so that it would be easy for the attendant to pick it up on his last rounds of the park. He slowly walked out of the park, turned left and made his way up the High Street. As he neared the corner where the antique shop was he suddenly remembered Angela's conversation about her having left a box there. He looked into the window and was disappointed to notice that his favourite statue was no longer standing in its place in the centre of the shelf.

The door of the shop had a wrought iron grill across it's front, partly to protect the beautifully inlaid coloured glasses and partly to prevent unwanted visitors at night. Brian pushed it open and walked in. It was quite dark. He had just a few minutes ago been standing in bright sunlight, so he paused to allow his eyes to become accustomed to the dim lighting.

All around the room were shelf upon shelf of antiques. Even all the available floor space was stacked high with old pieces of furniture, pictures and statuettes. Brian was aware that when he entered the shop there was no form of bell or buzzer to indicate that someone had entered the premises so how did the owner or the manager know when someone needed serving? The question was soon answered when a voice came from the far side of the shop.

"Good afternoon. I assume that you have called in for your box, the one that your wife left here yesterday."

Brain looked to where the voice had come from and witnessed a large old leather seat swivel around from its initial position facing the window to exhibit a wizened old man with quite long white hair looking at him. The old man stood up and immediately looked much younger. He was dressed in a rather smart pin-striped suit, which made him look very business-like. He made his way across the room and stood in front of Brian with his right hand held out obviously wanting to shake hands. The man had a very strong, positive handshake.

"I was wondering when you would eventually come into my little shop. It must be all of twenty years that you have positioned yourself on the pavement out there and enviously looked at the statuette of the warrior on the back of the horse." Brian was amazed that this old man had noticed him looking in the window let alone at the statue.

"I could almost have set my watch by your visits" he continued in a softer voice. "Always the same time each year and at the same time each day, and now you are here to collect your prize which your wife asked me to wrap up. I'll go and get it in a few moments once I've told you a little bit about its history.

"I think the statuette was probably made in Spain during the time of the Spanish Inquisition of Southern America. The warrior is very similar to the soldiers who used to accompany ships, which went off to explore the oceans for new lands. If you take a close look at his armour you will notice that he has a cross on his breastplate. Soldiers who fought the holy wars wore such an outfit. They were not the usual soldiers who protected the homeland from intruders. It's beautifully carved from a black hardwood, which more than likely indicates that its origin was probably from the tropical forests of the Amazon basin. The Spanish did a lot of exploration in that part of the world. So there. You are now the proud owner of a Spanish warrior. I will go out to the back of the shop now and collect it for you. It's already safely wrapped up and boxed. I should get it insured as it quite a rare piece."

When the old man returned with the box Brian thanked him once more, shook hands and smiled as the old man opened the door for him. That was the last time they met as Brian never went back to Bournemouth again because the memories of his wife were too sad for him to bear.

The statuette now stands in the middle of the mantelpiece in the front room and is often the subject of conversation when Brian has visitors. It had a slight accident a few years ago whilst Brian was doing his weekly dust around the house. The end of his duster caught the point of the lance that the soldier was holding and as Brian turned, the statuette was pulled from its resting place onto the floor. At first Brian had thought he had broken it, as the plinth on which the horse stood seemed to break in half and the end of the lance was bent over almost at right angles. On closer examination he was pleased to see that the lance could be straightened out, as it was made of some form of metal, which he did there and then. The base was not broken. In fact it was meant to split in half. Brian had not noticed the very fine join that ran the whole way around the middle of the plinth, so fine was the fit.

The base was actually hollow, and on the piece that had fallen off of the bottom he could see some form of an engraving. It looked like a map, showing various rivers and markings, which were very similar to the ones that he had seen on Ordnance Survey maps, depicting hills and valleys. There were also the names of villages or towns sprinkled along the rivers and valleys, none of which he recognised.

At the very bottom of the drawing was the signature of probably the artist, Don Martinez. It was amazing how much this man had been able to intricately etch in such a small place. Brian wondered who the man was and what period in time he had lived. He made a mental note to take it with him the next time he went to Bournemouth, which he never did.

The years continued to fly by for Brian during which time he tended to forget the etching on the plinth of his statue. Then one day quite out of the blue he was jolted into remembering.

It was a Tuesday morning in September, and he was taking his walk up to the garage, which was at the end of his street, in order to buy his daily newspaper before having breakfast. It was his usual morning ritual, as he liked to have his toast and coffee whilst catching up with the world's news. It was during his second cup of coffee when he made his startling find: he had just finished reading the sports pages, and was about to turn to the business section to check the current prices of his few windfall shares in the Halifax Building Society, when he caught the sight of a photograph of a ruined city on top of a mountain. He began to read the article, which was about a professor who had just returned from Peru where he had been studying the history of the Inca civilisation. The professor had spent much of his time at the famous ruins of Machu Picchu studying the writings of the Incas, which was in the form of a type of hieroglyphics. Then the article went on to say that the professor was the first person to be able to decipher the writings and that he was working on some new findings which described the times during the occupation of the Spanish Conquistadors. The professor had also spent some time in the archives of various Spanish museums and had come across some writings by a young scholar who had reputedly been to Peru with the first explorers, the most famous of them being Francisco Pizzaro.

In one of the articles the scholar told the story of a warlike Inca Prince who had abducted him and taken him into the mountains to probably the last stronghold of the Inca Empire. He then went on to tell of how he had been set free in order to tell the authorities that the war between the Incas and the Spanish was over and how he had attempted to keep a record of his journey so that one day he might retrace his steps. The professor then added that it was a great pity that the scholar, Don Martinez, had not kept his records of the trip into the mountains with the Inca Prince, as it would once and for all prove if there was such a place as the Lost City of the Incas

On seeing the name Don Martinez, Brian's brain immediately began searching the millions of memories that it had stored over the years. The search took a mere hundredth of a second and Brian was reminded of the name on the bottom of the statuette, which was standing at the centre of his mantle piece in the very room, that he was sitting in at that present moment. He put down the paper, got up from his chair and reached for the statuette. Was this a sheer coincidence or was he the owner of a very rarefied antique? If this were the same person it would make his antique over four hundred years old!

He removed the bottom of the plinth and looked at the finely etched map inside which had the name Don Martinez signed clearly at the bottom. His mouth suddenly became quite dry and he could feel his heart start to race as he became more and more excited at the prospect that his Martinez could be the same person. He sat back once again in his chair and tried to formulate in his mind as to what he should do next. After a few minutes he decided he would attempt to get in contact with this professor and see if he would be at all interested in seeing his statuette. He looked at the article again to ascertain the name of the professor, Professor Jason Downing who had an office in the British Museum. That afternoon Brian phoned the museum and was put onto the main switchboard.

"Good afternoon, and how can I help you?" came a pleasant voice down the line and into Brian's living room.

"Yes, I would like to talk to Professor Jason Downing, please."

"You must be the hundredth person who has asked to speak to the professor during the last four hours ever since his press release in *The Times*. All I can do is to take your name and telephone number and get back to you within the next week if possible, and let you know when it may be possible to speak to the professor. Presumably it is about his works in Peru?"

"Yes. I did really want to speak to him but can appreciate that he is a very sought-after man. I think I will leave it for now and phone back later next week. Thank you for your time." He then put the phone down but had no intention of leaving the matter until next week. He decided there and then that he would go to the museum tomorrow morning. There would be little chance of seeing the professor in person, so he would have to work out a plan, which would capture the attention of the man.

The next day Brian got up at the crack of dawn, had an early breakfast and travelled up to London in the rush hour, which he had sworn never to do again once he had retired. However this was something special and he was sure that the professor would be interested in his find.

He arrived at the museum just as they were opening the doors to the public. Even at that time in the morning there was quite a long queue and it took Brian a good fifteen minutes to get through the impressive doors of the museum. Once inside he went straight to the enquiry desk and asked for the office of Professor Downing and was guided to the second floor. The office was about half way along a most impressive colonnade which had large glass cases down either side in which were housed various specimens from all four corners of the globe.

On reaching the office he noticed that there was an outer office, in which sat a secretary, and behind her he could see the door of another office, which he assumed, would be that of the professor. He had already decided that the secretary would not let him get anywhere near to the professor so he had written a short note, which he hoped to be able to slip under the door of the professor's office. The problem was how to get past the secretary. He decided to be very audacious and went into the office and stood in front of the desk at which the secretary was working.

"Sorry to disturb you but there appears to be some form of an emergency at the far end of the corridor. I think an old lady has been taken ill. You were the first person I saw that I thought would be able to give assistance or who would know whom to contact."

The young girl immediately got up from her desk and made for the door.

"Which end of the corridor?" she asked as she hurriedly brushed past Brian.

"Turn right as you get out of the door," replied Brian, who was very pleased to see that his plan was beginning to work.

The girl was gone in seconds and as soon as she was out of sight he made for the door at the rear of the office upon which was a white plastic name tab, "Professor Jason Downing."

Brian took an envelope from the inside pocket of his jacket and slipped it under the door of the office. He then quickly turned and made for the outer office door before the girl returned, as he knew that she would be furious with him. Sure enough, she returned within the space of two minutes in a very bad mood looking for the man who had sent her on a wild goose chase, but by this time Brian was making his way down the stairs to the restaurant, where he ordered a cooked breakfast and settled down for an expectedly long wait.

Half an hour later Professor Downing arrived at his office hoping to have a normal working day after an evening of being continually disturbed both at the office and at home. Everyone seemed to want to interview him about his latest works. Even the television presenters wanted to talk to him. He did not enjoy being in the limelight.

"Morning, Natalie. Anything exciting for me today, and before you answer that say 'no' and put it in the in file for a later day? I need a day to myself, totally undisturbed. If anyone wants me just say that I am indisposed," and without waiting for a reply he went straight into his office.

He hung his coat on the coat stand beside of the door and then went across to his leather seat and flaked out. He was tired already, and he hadn't even started work yet! The ride up in the tube had been an unpleasant one as the weather was bad and no one seemed to want to walk anywhere on that day. The tube was jammed with people all of whom wore wet, soggy raincoats, which tended to smell of rotting vegetables. He was glad to get out at his stop and quickly get into the sanctuary of his office.

He swivelled around on his chair and eventually noticed the white envelope lying by the door that he had just come through. He got up from the comfort of his chair, went over to the envelope and picked it up from the floor. It was addressed to him in a neat handwriting but had no stamp on it. Strange, he thought, as his secretary was so meticulous with his mail and wouldn't have dropped the letter without noticing it on going out of the office. He reached over to the glass jar on his desk and selected a sharp paper knife from amongst the collection of pens and pencils. The blade of the knife slid efficiently across the inside of the letter. The professor placed the knife back into the glass and proceeded to slide the enclosed letter carefully out

119

of the envelope and laid it in front of him on his desk. He was always careful in handling all forms of paper, which came from his occupation in dealing with delicate and extremely rare works from centuries past. He studied the handwriting before he actually read the words and decided it had been written by someone who was quite meticulous. He then began to read its contents.

"Dear Professor Downing,

I read with much interest your recent article in *The Times* about the Inca civilisation and found it very fascinating. In your article you mentioned a Spanish scribe called Don Martinez and wished that he had written more information about his ventures into the jungle with one of the last of the Inca Princes. As it so happens I am in the possession of a carved warrior on horseback, who stands on a metal base plate. Recently I dropped the ornament onto the floor and the base split into two to reveal some form of a map, which was etched onto the base plate. It shows various names of what I assume to be towns or villages none of which I can identify from maps of Peru and the adjacent countries. The interesting thing is, that at the bottom of the sketch is the signature Don Martinez. Whether this is the same Martinez as your scholar or whether it is some form of a hoax only someone of your expertise will be able to decide. If you are interested in the statuette, I have it with me. At the present moment I am down in the restaurant. I will remain here for the next two hours. If you are too busy to come down then my address is at the top of this letter along with my phone number.

Yours sincerely,

Brian Bryant."

The professor sat back in his chair and read the letter once again. Was it some form of a hoax or was it a genuine letter and did the writer actually have such a statuette? He reached over to his telephone and pressed the button in order to contact his secretary.

"Natalie, would you come in here for a few moments' please." His secretary put down the script that she was working on, knocked on the Professor's door and entered.

"Natalie do you know anything of this letter which you must

have dropped on the floor when you came into the office earlier on?"

"I haven't been in here this morning, and there was no delivery of mail for you when I came in at nine o'clock," she said in a slightly puzzled voice.

"Well how did it get by the door of my office? It wasn't there last night when I left."

Natalie thought for a few moments and then said,

"The only unusual thing that happened this morning was when an older man came into the office and said that there was an emergency further down the corridor. I went out to see and found nothing. I was only gone for a matter of moments and by the time I got back to the office the man had disappeared. I suppose he would have had time to slip an envelope under the door."

"That could very well explain it, Natalie. I will be going down to the cafeteria for a few moments. If anyone wishes to see me tell him or her that I will be back in the office in about fifteen minutes. At the moment I only want to deal with people within the museum."

The restaurant was about half full. The professor had not thought of asking his secretary what the man had been wearing so he stood back by the door and surveyed the room. There were only three men sitting on their own so he studied each of them. He looked for a bag in which the statue might have been placed. Only one of the men had such a bag and that was a plastic bag similar to the ones that are given out at the supermarkets. He decided that that was the man who had come into his office, so he went across the restaurant weaving between the individual tables which were far too close to one another. He made a mental note to bring it up at the next committee meeting.

"Excuse me but are you Mr. Bryant?" The man nodded in acknowledgement, which made the professor feel a little less apprehensive. " I read your letter a few moments ago and found it rather intriguing. If you have finished your coffee perhaps you would come back up to my office where we can discuss your find?"

Brian stood up.

"Yes, that would be ideal as it is a little noisy for me down here. Not used to children anymore."

They made their way to the lift, which took them almost directly opposite the professor's office. As they entered Brian could not help noticing the expression on the face of the secretary who immediately recognised him as the man who had sent her on the wild goose chase. She didn't say anything. There was no need to, as her face said everything. Brian was very relieved when he heard the professor shut the door behind them thus blocking off the secretary's stare.

"Please sit down there," the professor pointed to his own seat and then went to the other side of the room and brought across an uncomfortable upright office chair upon which he sat.

"I'm dying to see your statuette. May I?" he pointed towards the plastic bag which Brian had placed on the floor next to him.

"Certainly. I hope it does not prove to be a big disappointment for you." He lifted the bag onto the small table in front of him and proceeded to unwrap the statuette and then placed it on the table in front of the professor.

"Exquisite carving. I like how the horse seems about to charge and how the soldier looks in complete charge of the stallion." The Professor lifted it off the table and proceeded to examine the base plate, which after a few twists came apart in his hands. He did the process very carefully so as not to damage any part of the statuette, especially the delicate looking lance that was protruding well out in the front of the horse. He then turned it upside down and began looking at the etchings inside the base plate.

After many minutes he said, "Very interesting. I think you may have discovered something of great importance. I'm going to call in one of my colleagues if you don't mind who may be able to give us a better opinion as to the authenticity of the statue."

The professor pressed a button on the telephone on his desk. "Natalie, could you see if you can get in contact with Professor Billings of the Spanish Antiques section and also George Arnold who is probably down in the bowels of the museum helping to unpack a new shipment from India. Ask them to come up to my office for a few moments, please."

The two new professors arrived five minutes later both at the same time and were shown into the office.

"Gentlemen, I want to introduce you to Mr. Bryant who may have something of interest for you to see. We would like your opinion as to whether it is genuine or a very clever fake."

The two men looked at the statue for over five minutes and then looked at one another and nodded in unison.

"I believe that you have the genuine article here dating back to the times of the Spanish Inquisition, wouldn't you agree Phil?" said Professor Billings.

"Yes, I would agree with that statement. What interests me most about the statue are the markings inside the base plate. It appears to be some form of a map. Any ideas as to which part of the globe it might be? I don't recognise any of the names. Do you?"

"No, but I know how we could find out. I have a friend over in the Science Museum and he was telling me of a new addition they have just been given from NASA. It's a computer, which has all the topography of the world taken from satellite photos and programmed into the computer. When one puts anything from a river, hill, valley or even a road into the computer it scans it's memory banks and attempts to find a match. Hang on a minute and I'll give him a phone. This finding is too good to wait until tomorrow." He went off in the direction of the outer office and asked the secretary to get in touch with the British Museum and ask for Frank Jasper. One hour later, after all four had jumped into a taxi and made the short journey to the Science Museum they were standing in quite a large room which housed numerous complicated machines.

"Must be one hell of an important find to get you all to come over here at such short notice. What is it all about then?" Frank asked his pal.

"Not quite sure at the moment, Frank, but when we do put all the pieces together you will be the first to know, seeing how co-operative you have been. Might have to dig into my pocket and buy you a pint."

"Then it must be important for you to offer to buy a pint. The last time you did that was when I discovered the tomb of that Egyptian bloke Tutan something for you." They all laughed at that. "OK lets get the show on the move. If you place the base of the statue on this glass screen I will get the computer to scan it into the memory banks." The professor carefully balanced the statuette on the glass surface making sure that it did not scratch it. It was a toughened glass and would take most things sliding over its surface without incurring any marks.

They were all transfixed at what happened next. The etchings suddenly appeared on the wall opposite them, which was in actual fact the screen for the computer. Frank touched a few small buttons on his control panel and the lines of the etchings gradually became more distinct. The bottom of the base of the statue was being magnified a hundred times. Frank touched the control panel again and this time maps began to slide across the screen to superimpose themselves over the markings from the statue base. There were some forty maps all of which bore some resemblance to the etchings but none of them made a good match much to the disappointment of the gathered professors.

"Well, it was worth a try. Thanks for putting yourself out for us, Frank. It was well worth a pint."

"Hang on a minute. I haven't finished yet. I don't give up that easily. How old would you say these etchings are?"

"We think they date back over four hundred years," said Professor Downing.

"OK, during that time the contours of the valleys would have changed a lot due to erosion caused by the natural weathering from rainfall which would also have had a profound effect on the directions of the rivers. In various parts of the world what were once raging torrents are now dried up riverbeds whose banks have almost disappeared from wind erosion.

"Now one of the most interesting features of this computer is that it has the ability of showing the topography of the world, as it was hundreds or thousands of years ago. It has been programmed with past climatical changes over the centuries, which then makes allowances for such things as the cutting power of the rivers and how they would have effected the shape of the valleys. So, what I have to do is to feed in the approximate year and then see if there are any nearer matches to our sketch."

He then proceeded to tap the information into the computer and then the party sat back and waited. New maps began to slide across the screen to disappear on the far side of the wall. They had been studying about twenty of these maps when one appeared which caught all of their eyes, as they knew they had seen it before. As it slid slowly across the screen they could see that it was going to be a reasonable match. What they did not expect was for it to be almost identical to the one on the base plate.

"Stop." They almost all called out in unison. Then there was a complete silence as they studied the new map. Frank was the first one to speak.

"Absolutely amazing. What I will do now is to bring up onto the screen the present day map of the area and then we will be able to distinguish where in the world it is."

Immediately it came up on the screen Professor Downing spoke in a very excited voice. He went out to the large screen and pointed to a mark on the map, which had a name next to it.

"That there, gentlemen, is Machu Picchu! I recognise it by the contours of the rivers. I was there only a matter of a few months ago. This is absolutely staggering. If this is the genuine article, which it must be as no one would have been able to draw this map unless they had had the use of this computer programme, then we could be at the brink of possibly finding the last of the Inca strongholds."

There was another lengthy silence as the professor's statement gradually sank in. If they had found the map, which would take them to the lost city, then they were on the brink of solving one of the most baffling mysteries since historical records were kept. There had always been talk and scepticism of a Lost Empire. Numerous people over the centuries had come forward with tales of sightings in the jungle of carved stone eagles. Some natives were even supposed to have bartered for golden trinkets with nomadic tribes that roamed the forests of the Amazon Basin. Now there was a possibility of proving once and for all that the lost city of the Incas did exist.

It was Professor Downing who eventually broke the silence.

"Well gentlemen, we need to call a meeting with the committee as soon as possible and show them what we, or I should say, Mr. Bryant, has found." The group looked towards Mr. Bryant and nodded, making him feel very important indeed. "Mr. Bryant we are indebted to you. May we have your permission to keep the statuette for a few weeks so that we may make some copies of the etchings? I would then suggest for the time being that we put it in a safe place for if word gets out about the discovery before we have had the time to plan a sortie into the forest every Tom, Dick and Harry who specialises in plundering archaeological sites will be scouring the jungle and invading your privacy, Mr. Bryant, especially if there is the slightest possibility of gold at the end of the trail."

"I would be most honoured for you to keep the statuette for the moment. Perhaps in the future if it is so important I may present it to the museum so that it can be put on display. I could then have a season ticket which would allow me to come into the museum from time to time and look at my statuette?"

They all smiled at the unassuming old man and nodded in appreciation for what he had just said.

"There then, gentlemen. I will arrange for my secretary to give you all a call when a meeting has been scheduled with the powers above which I hope will be within the week. In the meantime I will arrange for some of our geographical historians to take a look at our map and try to come up with ideas as to where we might begin our search. Mr. Bryant, I hope that you will be available to attend some of the meetings?"

"Yes, that would be very nice, thank you."

The meeting was then called to a close and they gradually sauntered off to their various departments all with exciting thoughts in their minds.

Chapter Nine

The expedition got off to an excellent start due to the tumultuous efforts of Jeremy Billington. He had been assigned to the task of purchasing all of the necessary equipment from Landrovers right down to toilet rolls. The British Museum had used him on a number of previous occasions and he had never let them down.

The expedition consisted of two mechanics whose sole jobs were to keep the four-wheeled vehicles on the road. This would be no easy task as there were no tarmac road surfaces, all going would be over mud baked terrain which could change without any warning into boggy mud, caused from torrential rains higher up in the mountains. Often these downpours would cut through the tracks leaving deep scars.

There were six professors specialising in different areas of the Inca civilisation and ten Sherpas whose jobs were to cook, set up camp and repair the holes in the road.

For four days the expedition criss-crossed the narrow gorges and eventually arrived at their base camp. They had chosen a small village at the base of the mountains, which was inhabited by only a few Indian peasants. The reason for choosing this village was because it appeared to be the one that was at the epicentre of Juan Lopez's Mixxatii.

During the preliminary planning stages back in London, the party had decided to start exploring from this village using the latest satellite navigational instruments to make sure that they covered every inch of the territory and in doing so did not go back over their tracks.

The actual base camp consisted of a row of tents, which had been pitched on the outskirts of the village, just far enough away from the inhabitants so as not to invade their privacy.

Each night whilst the Sherpas were preparing the evening meal the professors would sit out in their collapsible chairs and plot on the map the areas that they had explored and discuss any findings that they had made. At first the atmosphere of the debates was one of excitement, but as time progressed and nothing was discovered, the whole group became quite despondent. Even Professor Downing was beginning to doubt the authenticity of his map.

It was during one of these evenings that the professor decided to get away from his colleagues and go down into the village. As he walked towards the simple designed buildings, he began to feel a little guilty that he had never tried to make any form of contact with its inhabitants and neither had any one else in the party. In fact he had never seen anyone in the village other than an old lady who used to come out every evening just before it got dark and sweep the ground in front of her house. Once this had been accomplished she appeared to make some form of an etching with the broom handle on the ground in front of her house. She would then retire to her porch where she would sit and watch the sun disappear over the top of the mountain range.

On nearing the first building he noticed that the old lady had finished her chores and was already in her seat.

"Good evening, mam," the professor said in the native dialect. "Lovely evening. I was wondering if you could tell me something about this village. I would be quite interested to know why it was built here?"

The old lady did not speak for a few moments. She looked at the professor, which made him feel a little uncomfortable as he began to wonder if the old lady had understood his words, or perhaps she was suffering from some kind of dementia.

"Please come and sit yourself down here." She pointed to the ground next to her chair. "I have lived in this village all of my life and during that time have seen many changes. In my youth this was a thriving town, the centre of commerce for the whole of the region. The Indians from the jungles below used to bring in their wares and then would barter with the businessmen from the city way down in the valley. Many of the village's inhabitants worked in the fields on the side of the mountain where they cultivated wheat and vegetables. As time went on, however, the younger folk became dissatisfied when they came in contact with people from the city and heard of the exciting things that were happening there compared to their lives of working in the fields. Soon they began to leave and now there are only sixteen of us remaining."

For the next twenty or so minutes they chatted about what was happening in the outside world and how life in her village had changed so drastically. She was a lovely old lady and reminded the professor of his own grandmother. She had spent her entire life in this village and as far as the professor could see had not suffered from not being exposed to the outside world.

It was now beginning to get quite dark and so the professor decided it was time to get back to the camp in case the others were wondering where he had disappeared.

"Well, I must get back to my work. It was very interesting to talk to you. May I come back another night?" The old lady nodded and smiled. As the professor turned to leave, he glanced over to the area where she normally stood each night and swept the road and what met his eyes momentarily stopped him in his tracks. On the floor in front of the house was a drawing of the stone, which was identical to the etchings produced by Juan Lopez! He turned to her once again.

"That drawing there, the one which you do every evening. Have you seen it somewhere before?"

"It is the sign of the Inca Prince. It is carved on a large flat stone in the jungle next to the steep cliff face into which are carved many steps. Come I will show you." The mention of a carving and stone steps made the professor's heart miss a beat. Had she discovered the lost city? She proceeded to walk around the side of her house and made towards the jungle. The professor quickly followed in her footsteps and soon they were travelling up a narrow, dark path that meandered between the tall forest trees and dense undergrowth.

It took fifteen minutes to reach the overgrown cliff face

where the old lady stopped and then commenced to pull at the thick mosses, which covered the floor of the clearing. As the mosses came away they revealed a stone surface upon which was carved the marking of an almost circular stone which had a jagged line gouged through it's centre, which resembled a fork of lightening. The professor knew then that the lost city was about to be discovered.

The old lady beckoned him over to the rock face and pointed out to him the carved footsteps. It was up there, thought the professor. No wonder they hadn't discovered it before as it was so well camouflaged and would not have shown up on any satellite surveys. He turned and gave the old lady a hug.

"I must get back and tell my friends about your discovery. I know that this is a very special place for you so I would like your permission to bring my friends back here."

The old lady nodded her approval and then the professor quickly made his way back to the camp. He arrived just in time to prevent a small party from leaving to go in search of him.

"Where the hell have you been, Professor? You know the rule. Anyone leaving the site at any time should inform someone else. We have been worried sick in case you had got lost in the jungle." fumed Jeremy Billington who was overall responsible for the party's safety.

"I have found the Lost City!" said the professor in an excited voice.

The following day they climbed the rock face and on the plateau above found the remains of stone buildings amongst the thick undergrowth. They had indeed found the Lost City of the Incas.

Chapter Ten

Claire Axworthy was born in an old Folkestone terraced house in one of the less salubrious areas of Plymouth. Ker Street in its hey day was a very upmarket place in which to live. At the top of the road was an imposing building called the Guildhall, whose architectural features were modelled on the Parthenon with its four large pillars supporting a triangular roof which had at its apex a statue of Britannia in her full regalia.

Adjacent to this Roman building was Ker Street Primary School where Claire had spent her early days being educated in a very regimented fashion. A few doors down from the school was another fine old building which was modelled on an Egyptian Temple and where the Odd Fellows Organisation met, hence it being sometimes called the Odd Fellows Hall.

The children of those days did not appreciate the significance of the architectural features of their street but did appreciate the wonderful opportunities they presented for hiding away from one another. Claire's favourite building was the Egyptian one, as it had small spaces between its pillars and surrounding walls just barely wide enough to squeeze between. Only the smaller children could get through these gaps much to the annoyance of the older teenagers. Often Claire would arrive home with the fronts of her shoes badly grazed, which was always rewarded with a harsh telling off from her mum.

Claire's mum had had a hard life. She had conceived Claire at the tender age of twenty. Claire's father was a Chief Petty Officer who had little bearing on the upbringing of Claire, as he was either serving on board one of Her Majesty's Ships or drinking with his shipmates in the notorious Union Street, which boasted some twenty pubs in the space of one mile. Fortunately or unfortunately depending how one looked at it, he died in a motor accident when Claire was only four years old. Claire therefore had little recollections of her father and looked upon her uncle George as her real father.

Claire's earliest memories of living in Devonport were when she used to play with her friends in the derelict buildings left over from the aftermath of the Second World War when Germany sent over bombers in an attempt to blitz the dockyard.

The bombers used to fly in over Plymouth Sound, lining themselves up with the lighthouse at the end of the Breakwater, and then jettisoning their bombs onto Devonport. On numerous occasions they missed their targets and in doing so devastated much of the civilian buildings in the city. The only good feature that came out of these bombings was that the city planners were able to construct a whole new city centre to make it one of the most modern cities of its time. The King and Queen came down to see the devastation and in later years returned for the official opening of the new town centre. Many people felt that the city lost its heart during the blitz and had never recovered from it.

Claire could remember the day when the largest new shop in the city centre, Dingles, was opened. She and many of her friends were amazed at the moving staircase inside it. They spent many a time travelling up the staircase and coming down the lift, until the store detective chased them out.

In her home in Ker Street, one of Claire's favourite hiding places was the old corrugated tin air raid shelter that was situated at the bottom of her garden. They were one of the more fortunate families in the street, as they possessed their own shelter. Most people used the communal one at the bottom of Cumberland Gardens. During one evening's raid the bombers used land mines attached to parachutes, which slowed down their descent so that when they made contact with the ground the blast went sideways instead of into the ground, causing maximum damage to the surrounding buildings. On that night over sixty people from Ker Street perished when the air raid shelter received a direct hit. Claire lost three of her closest friends that night.

The ruins left by the bombings produced magnificent play areas for the children of this neighbourhood. There were no such things as health and safety measures in those days. None of the ruins were fenced off. In some buildings one could climb three flights of stairs to eventually be confronted by a sheer drop. The old market, which was littered with glass fragments, had a whole labyrinth of small tunnels in which one could lose the chasing opposition. Claire certainly had an exciting and dangerous upbringing.

Times were hard just after the war. Their house was over a hundred years old and was built in the days of the Window Tax so some of the windows in the house were bricked over to soften the payment of the tax burden.

There were five sets of people living in Claire's four-story house. On the ground floor lived her grandmother, in the basement was a lodger, who had been brought home one day by her grandfather who had felt sorry for him, and on the first floor was Claire's bedroom. Adjacent to her room was the lounge of another lodger called Mabel, who was partially blind, and on the top floor was the living accommodation of Claire's mum. Then at the very top of the house in the attic were the two bedrooms belonging to Mabel and her aunty and uncle. Quite a little community.

The basement had a slate floor and it was here that all the washing of clothes and bathing was done. There was a small copper in the corner, which was used for heating the water by placing kindling wood underneath it. On bath days, which were usually at the end of the week, Claire being the youngest went in first. The bath was a tin one which meant that one's bottom got extremely cold next to the slate floor. During the winter periods there often used to be a thick fog that seemed to hover above the bath, and when one spoke, a steady stream of fine water vapour came out of one's mouth. Claire would always remember those cold, damp, bath days.

One thing she did look forward to at the weekends was when her grandmother used to give her the ration book to go to the corner shop and buy a quarter pound of sweets.

School was not an enjoyable time for Claire as she was often the recipient of bullying. There were two particular girls called Sarah and Margaret who used to push into her in the playground and call her names during the lunch hours and at playtimes.

Often they would take her sweets away from her, knowing that Claire would not retaliate and would not inform the teachers.

Weekends were her favourite times for it meant either playing in the streets or on the bomb ruins with her friends and in the summer the family would go out on day trips. The best trip was when they went to Mount Edgcumbe Park.

Her mum used to pack up a picnic and then Uncle George would appear always on time at nine thirty and help carry the bags down to Mutton Cove, where they used to wait for the first rowing boat to take them across the river Tamar to Cremyll, which was on the Cornish side of the river.

There was one special weekend that Claire will never forget. It was a glorious Sunday morning and they had set out especially early to make sure that they were the first in the queue for the ferry. When they arrived at the jetty, Bill, who was the ferryman, was only just casting off his old rowing boat from its moorings in the small harbour. Claire climbed up onto the low wall and shouted down to the old man.

"Hurry up, Bill, you are late this morning."

Bill didn't need to look up to see who it was. He knew that lovely little voice belonged to the little girl who always had a smile on her face.

"Won't be a moment, my darling. You come down the steps and then you can help me tie up when I come alongside. Just remember what I told you about keeping your fingers away from the wall and the side of the boat. Got to watch out for those nasty little barnacles on the wall."

Claire knew what he meant. The barnacles were more the size of limpets, which seemed to spend their whole lives in the same place. The only time they made any form of movement was if you touched them and then they would cling tightly to the wall. What a boring life they led, thought Claire. She jumped down from the wall and carefully made her way down the slimy green steps to the waters' edge. She waited quietly and eventually she could hear the sound of leather against wood as Bill pulled on the oars of the heavy wooden boat. The bows suddenly appeared around the corner of the pier. Bill skilfully manoeuvred it into the side of the steps and Claire was able to

134

reach into the boat and grasp the neatly coiled rope in the bows.

"Make us fast," shouted Bill, "otherwise I will skin you alive!" Claire loved it when Bill went into his pirate charade. She jumped into the centre of the boat so as not to make it rock and gave the old man a big hug. "Careful, young lady. You are getting so strong that you are beginning to knock the wind out of my sails. If you keep that up I may not have the energy to row you across the river. There is a strong tide running this morning, which may take us out to sea where Blackbeard the scourge of the Seven Seas is laying in wait. Avast ye there. Go and get the rest of the family and we'll be off."

Claire jumped out of the boat and climbed up the steep steps. She was pleased to see that they were the only passengers for this first trip, which meant that she could sit in the bows of the boat.

Her uncle eventually pushed them out and soon they were edging into the strong tide and almost going across the river sideways. Although the distance didn't appear to be very far across the river it was a good three quarters of a mile. Bill knew all the tides and winds that came up and down the estuary and at times, when wind was against tide, he knew to expect quite large waves. He was also very particular to look at the briefings given out by the navy with regards to the movement of shipping in the Hamoaze. Large ships were usually accompanied by at least two tugs whose powerful engines always set up a large bow wave, which never failed to alarm his passengers.

This day the fairly strong breeze had whipped up moderately sized waves which beat against the bows of the sturdy rowing boat and sent fine clouds of spray up into the air and onto Claire's face. The river was already filling up with small craft. A few small fishing boats were heading out together probably off to the Eddystone Reef in search of pollack and a few evil looking congers. Claire waved to the sightseers who were going up stream in one of the small ferries, which ran trips to see the warships and the dockyard.

The crossing in the rowing boat took a little longer than usual as the tide was running quite fast. There had been a full moon recently, which always meant high tides. By the time they reached the other side of the river Claire was quite wet but did not mind, as she knew that she would soon dry off in the sun.

The boat ran up onto the steep pebbly beach and as it grounded Uncle George jumped off with the bow rope, which was attached to an anchor which had large evil-looking claws radiating out from its base, and which he stuck into the beach. He then held out his hand, firstly helping out Claire and then her mother. He then gave old Bill the fare, picked up the anchor, which he placed back in the front of the boat, and then gave the bows a firm push off the beach.

"Don't forget that the last crossing is at seven o'clock tonight," shouted Bill as he pulled on one oar in order to turn his boat once more into the tide. Claire gave him a wave and then ran up the beach to the private turnstile where an old lady sat. The beach was a private one and the landing fee was one penny per person. The lady let Claire crawl underneath the metal barrier as she was only small and not worth a penny, so the old lady used to say.

Once they were all through the turnstile they made their way past the old pub where they usually had a small shandy whilst waiting for the boat on the return journey, and into the entrance of the park. It was a very impressive point of entry via a very large ornate metal gate, which stood at the end of a long drive which led up to the stately house of the Mount Edgcumbe family.

Just inside the gate they turned left and walked through a gatehouse, and into an elegant orangery. It was now used as a café and still contained its famous orange trees, which gave fruit in the summer. This was always their first stop. Mum and uncle had their usual cup of tea and some form of a bun, and Claire always had an ice cream. The building had large high windows through which the sun streamed in. In the neat gardens in front of the building were statutes of Roman figures in various poses. The combination of the building and grounds were so aesthetically beautiful, that Claire had already decided that when she got married she would have her reception there.

The next part of the walk followed a path, which on one side had the river, and on the other tall trees, many of them not normally found in this part of the world. One of the previous Earls had been a bit of an explorer and had sent back many different types of trees and bushes from all over the world. Most of these specimens had been expected to perish due to the change in climatic conditions. However, the park had it's own little microclimate and most had survived.

Claire's favourite tree was the cork tree as the bark was very spongy to the touch. Once past the little guardhouse, which housed fully armoured soldiers during the times of the Roundheads and the Royalists, Claire was allowed to make a small detour on her own. She used to venture into a little wooded area in which was a dogs' cemetery, where all the pets of the Earl were buried. This was somewhere quite sacred for Claire.

When she used to come out of there she always used to tell her uncle that she had touched the face of god. Her uncle could never find it when he was permitted to enter, even though on occasions he was standing right next to it. It's even there to this day.

The next part of the walk Claire did not like, as she had to climb up two very steep grassy banks to the Folly. The Folly was built in the days when it was very fashionable to have small historical buildings, or old partly built ruins, constructed in places of interest within the grounds of large estates. On the Edgcumbe estate there were numerous examples of this phenomena.

Once at the Folly, she used to climb to the top of the old building and survey the amazing panoramic view of Plymouth Sound. Many people have said that this was one of the most beautiful views they have ever come across and have donated seats with their names printed on them on little brass plaques. Claire used to read the inscriptions and try to envisage whom the people were. She decided that one day she would make a thorough search of the park and make a list of all of the plaques.

The last part of the walk followed a path through the dense trees high above the sea. In places there were sheer drops down onto razor-sharp rocks. It was in such places that her uncle used to insist that he held her hand, as he was afraid that Claire might slip on the wet mosses that bordered the well-worn path. Eventually the path opened out onto a large field from where one had a grand view of the little fishing village of Cawsands.

Some two hundred yards down over the field was a small

opening, which led to a steep set of steps that led down to the tiny, almost unknown beach of Sandway. Few people ever ventured to this sheltered little beach as the majority of Plymouth folk preferred the open expanses of Whitsand Bay. This bay was ideal for safe swimming as it was almost entirely surrounded by rocks, which helped protect the swimmer from the swell and waves caused by the tides and passing powerboats.

When the tide was at its highest, it surrounded a small jetty which was about ten metres off the beach and which was within the swimming capabilities of Claire. She used to look upon the jetty as her own little castle which had its own surrounding moat.

Usually on arrival at the beach Claire's uncle used to insist that they all went for a quick dip into the sea so as to work up an appetite before lunch. Mum would then lay out a chequered tablecloth on a special flat rock and proceed to put out a picnic for the three of them to nibble at. Once the meal was over no one was allowed to do any physical activities until the food had been digested. This took about half an hour after which uncle George would walk Claire into Cawsand so that her mum could have a little snooze in the sun.

The walk was over a wave cut platform, which had been formed by a lava flow thousands of years ago. Half way along the walk was an old building, which uncle George said had been the local herring factory. Once in Cawsand the two of them made for the clock tower, opposite which was a small tearoom which sold the most delicious ice creams.

The village of Cawsand is steeped in history The Smugglers Inn, which is situated in the village square, is supposedly to have tunnels underneath it where the village folk used to hide their contraband of brandy. The men of Cawsand used to row across the Channel to Brittany and then smuggle back various fine wines. The Customs and Excise boats never managed to catch them due to their lack of manoeuvrability. The excise boats were powered by sails and so had to tack when the winds changed whereas the rowing boats from Cawsand could continue in a straight line. By the time the authorities had landed on the beach the contraband had been distributed around the village and hidden in the labyrinth of tunnels.

On this particular day Claire chose a toffee ice which dripped all down her arm by the time they had walked half way back, as the midday sun was extremely strong and hot. She was made to wash in the sea before returning to her mum, as her uncle did not wish to be told off for spoiling Claire. Her mother always knew, however, that she had had an ice cream, but never mentioned it.

Once back on the beach Claire played for a while in her hide-away in the rocks and then went down to the waters edge to sit and watch the patterns of the waves as the incoming tide pushed them up over the small banks of warm pebbles. The beach in that particular area was made up of small shingle with a smattering of sand and broken seashells. The flow of the water was across the beach in the direction of Cawsands, which made it roughly east to west. The sun was quite dazzling on the water and made it shimmer in various shades of blues and greens. Small pebbles were being dragged along the beach with each thrust of a wave leaving small long indentations in the loose sand.

Claire must have been sitting there for quite a long time as her mother shouted across to her that they would be leaving in the next half an hour and that she must soon come up from the water and dry her feet. Rather than go for a final walk along the beach Claire decided to remain seated and continued to watch the patterns of the pebbles. As she sat there she noticed a slight change in the direction of the waves. Instead of travelling across the beach they were now moving directly in towards her and bringing an array of small pebbles, which they lined up in front of her, as if for her to inspect. One pebble caught her eye, as it was moving faster than the rest and due to its speed finished up out of the water adjacent to her little toe. This was no ordinary pebble, as it sparkled in the sun's rays almost like a diamond. Claire bent forward and grasped it in her hand in case the next wave washed it back into the sea. Her initial reaction was to drop it back into the water as she was expecting it to be quite cold. Instead it appeared to be very hot. She left it for a moment and then made another lunge for it. This time it seemed to have cooled a little. It felt very smooth and was almost clear. It was about the size of a ten pence piece and had a jagged line running through it, almost like a fork of lightning.

In her excitement she completely forgot the safety aspects involved in travelling across a rocky area. Each time the family visited the beach Claire's mother would remind her not to run across the rocks and to be very wary of patches of wet seaweed, especially the light green weed which looked like long strands of hair and which was absolutely lethal underfoot when wet. Without thinking, Claire ran across the rocks towards her mother, holding the stone tightly in her fist. Suddenly her feet went sideways as they made contact with a patch of wet weed and she found herself tumbling down the side of a steep outcrop of rock. Clinging to the sides of the rock were numerous sharp edged limpets. As she fell, her face came into contact with three of the shells that gouged large pieces of flesh out of her soft cheek and as she rolled over another set of shells dug deeply into her back. It was amazing that she felt no pain at all. Luckily her fall ended in a soft patch of sand and by the time she had picked herself up and brushed off all of the sand, blood was freely running down her face and back.

"My goodness, Claire, what on earth has happened to you? Quick, Uncle George, get out the first aid kit and find some plasters for Claire's face and back."

"Look what I have found. A precious stone. See how it sparkles." Mum and uncle paid little notice to the dull looking pebble in Claire's hand, as they were too busy patching up her wounds.

"Uncle. Do you think that you would be able to drill a hole through it so that I could wear it as a necklace?"

"I will certainly have a go at it during next week when I return to work. We have some diamond drills in the workshop which will go through anything. However, there is the slight chance that the drill might split the stone into fragments. If you are willing to take that chance I will have a try during one of my lunch breaks?"

"It won't split as it is a very special stone," said Claire in a very excited voice.

Claire did not notice the usually arduous walk back through the park as she was absolutely mesmerised by her stone. She had it clenched in her hand the whole of the way home. It seemed to give her added strength when it came to climb the steep grassy banks. Normally she would request a stop at the Folly, which was about half way back to Cremyll, but much to the amazement of her Uncle and Mother, insisted that they get back to the ferry as quickly as possible. She didn't even want to stop for the usual half of shandy in the Edgcumbe Arms.

She was soon on the beach and waiting for old Bill to row across the river. She could see him about half way across the river making in their direction. There were no other passengers on board, so he would only take about five more minutes to beach his craft. That seemed too long for Claire, as she wanted to get home on this particular day as soon as possible.

"Ahoy there, my hearties, "called Bill just before reaching the shore. Uncle George stood right at the waters' edge, not afraid of getting his feet a little wet, and caught the line as it uncoiled its way through the air. He pulled tightly on it until the rowing boat was firmly on the beach. Claire ran forward and was the first to jump into the boat.

"Someone's been in the wars. What happened to you young lady? Had a fight with a jellyfish?"

Claire smiled and then took her usual place in the bows of the boat. Her mother preferred to sit in the rear of the boat, as she did not like to be caught by the salty spray. Again they were the only passengers, so after waiting for five minutes Bill decided to cast off. He was beginning to feel quite tired as it had been spring tides that day and the amount of water flowing between the banks of the River Tamar seemed to be much more than the usual highs for this time of year. He was also wondering whether it was about time he gave up these weekend pulls across the river. There was no one left to take over the licence, which had been handed down through the generations from father to son. Bill had not had any children and so when he did eventually give up the license it would go up for open tender. His wife had passed away a few years ago, and since that time he had found it very difficult to live on his own. The weekend trips helped him to forget his sadness. He had in actual fact become a bit of a recluse. When his wife was alive, he used to frequent the local Crown and Column Pub before Sunday lunch, where he used to reminisce about old times with some of his friends. Since his wife's death, however, he was unable to visit his old haunts without feeling very sad. He didn't even stay on in the harbour when he had tied up his boat to have a chat with the other boat owners.

They were about half-way across the river and Claire was watching the strong forearms of Bill, which were decorated with tattoos of anchors and ladies' names. The veins of his arms stood out as he powerfully gripped the long slender oars, which were very old as they had quite deep ridges in them, which was caused by the continuous rubbing against the rowlocks. Claire also noticed that the old sailor had been watching her hand as soon as she had got into the boat and had kept his eyes on it during the entire journey across the river.

"Claire, what is that, that is shining so brightly in your hand?" remarked Bill. "I noticed it as soon as you got into the boat."

"Oh, it's my precious stone that I found on the beach at Sandway." She held out her hand to show Bill the pebble with the jagged line running through it.

"It looks extremely valuable to me and I'm no expert on gem stones. It is a most unusual stone. If I were you I would get it insured. It must have come off of an old wreck," he said smiling at Claire.

Her mum looked at Bill and smiled. He certainly knew how to play her daughter along with his old tales. Strange though, she thought, for how could he have noticed the dull old pebble in Claire's hand as she had held onto it tightly in the palm of her hand, which totally obscured it? She looked at Bill once more and was sure that she could see a difference in the old man. He seemed to have lost some of the deep furrows across his forehead, which made him look much younger. A form of tranquillity had come over him.

Bill continued to look at the little girl. She was so full of life, continually moving about the boat, always with a broad smile on her face, which was even broader now that she had her precious stone. Bill began to feel less tired and as he made progress against the strong tide he began to feel as if a weight had been taken off of his shoulders. His strength had returned to his body and he increased his rate of stroke until he was moving the boat along as he used to in his youth.

"What's the hurry, Bill?" said George, " Have you got a train to catch? I have never seen you row so fast." Bill nodded with a smile. He felt really good. That evening when he had tied up his boat, instead of going straight home he wandered over to the tin boathouses where the owners kept their spare engine parts, and where they often sat outside in the late evening sun. He positioned himself on the low parapet wall and had a long chat with some of the older ones who were there. He got home quite late that evening and once he had made himself a meal and done the washing up he made his way down to the Crown and Column for a pint of beer, much to the surprise of his old mates who were really pleased to see him once again. They were all amazed when Bill bought a round of drinks and then began reminiscing of the good old days when he used to take his wife for a romantic walk around Richmond Walk, followed by a drink in this very pub, afterwards. When he finally went home the conversation in the pub that night was what could have happened to Bill that day to have changed his outlook on life so dramatically.

For the first time in years when Bill went to bed and saw the pictures of his wife on the bedside cabinet he did not feel any sadness as he smiled at her, and just before he nodded off he remembered the brightly shining stone that the little girl had held so tightly in her hand

Claire got home just as her granny was putting out the note in the bottle for the milkman. Her granny noticed how excited Claire looked but decided to say nothing, as it was getting quite late and she could sense that her daughter wanted to get her off to bed. Before Claire went to her bedroom she reminded her uncle that he had promised to make her stone into a necklace. Her uncle suggested that she gave it to him so that he could take it into work the following day, but Claire did not wish to part with it so early after her find and said he could have it tomorrow. That night Claire placed the stone next to her on her pillow and was amazed how it glowed in the dark. It took her ages to get to sleep that night.

Two mornings later Claire's uncle was given permission to take the stone to work so that he could drill a hole in it. He carefully wrapped it in front of Claire to show that he appreciated how valuable it was, much to her delight, and then put it into his pocket. His plan was to drill it during his tea break. It should only take a few minutes and he would still have time for a cup of tea.

When he arrived at work he looked at his work schedule for the day and found it to be quite a difficult one. A new set of plans for a transformer had been sent down from central office and the engineers in George's shop had to make up a set of industrial clamps to hold the machine on a base plate to keep it in a firm position whilst it was being worked upon. George gave a short sigh when he saw the rota for the day. One of his work mates noticed this.

"What's up George, getting too old for the job?"

George smiled. " I promised my niece that I would drill a hole through a pebble that she found on the beach a few days ago. She wants to make it into a necklace. She has set her heart on it and if I go home tonight not having completed the task she will be very disappointed. The schedule that I have today will probably not give me any spare time, even though it will only take a few minutes."

"Let me have a look at it. I have to do a job in the drilling shop this afternoon and I might be able to do it for you." George took the pebble out of his pocket, unwrapped the paper around it and gave it to his friend.

"That looks pretty straight forward. I'll bring it back during this afternoon's tea break."

"That's really good of you, Dave. I'll pay for your tea and if you can scrounge a piece of leather twine from the upholstery department I may even treat you to a bun."

When Dave entered the workshop he glanced around to see who was on the duty shift with him. There were seven others at their various stations all busily working away. He knew all of them and knew that none would be paying much attention to him. The only one he had to keep an eye open for, was the charge-hand who supervised the smooth running of the shop. His job was to be on call in case anyone needed any help or extra information.

Today's charge-hand was John Fletcher who rarely walked

around the shop, as he preferred to help out with the work and so spent most of his time at his bench. Dave took one extra look around the workshop and then set about fixing the stone into a clamp, which he then put into the vice and from the cupboard on the wall adjacent to his work bench he removed a box of masonry bits which were tempered to drill through concrete. He placed the tip of the bit onto the stone, selected a slow drill speed and commenced to drill. After a few minutes he shut off the drill and looked at the results. Nothing. No sign of a hole. Not even a scratch on the stone. Must be a blunt bit, he thought, so he went to the store cupboard and removed a new box of drill pieces and selected a medium cut one. This one he used for a longer period only to see it get red hot. When he inspected the end of the bit he saw that the cutting edges had begun to melt at the tip. Once again there was no impression on the stone. He was amazed at the resilience of the pebble. His only other alternative was to use one of the expensive diamond drills whose usage had to be logged in a diary, as they were only used for specialist drillings where accuracy was tantamount. He knew that for this job he would have been given no clearance at all. He didn't wish to disappoint his friend George, or the little girl, so he decided to do the drilling and not log it in the book.

He glanced around the workshop to make sure there were no prying eyes, removed the expensive drill from its sheath, fixed it into the drill and commenced to drill into the stone. He was dumfounded when he removed the bit for inspection. No mark whatsoever! He gave it one more go and still nothing. He quickly glanced around once more, placed the bit back into its container and casually walked out of the shop.

As he walked back to the canteen with the stone held firmly in his hand he couldn't help wondering what the little girl had found. The diamond bit was the toughest form of a drill developed by man and should have made some impression on the pebble and yet it had failed, so what had this little girl found?

During the afternoon tea break he sat at the corner table so that no one would hear their conversation. He ordered two cups of tea, knowing that George would be appearing at any moment. Sure enough he arrived just as Dave was taking his seat.

"I said I would buy the teas and a cake," said George. "Got the stone, or should I say pebble?"

Dave nodded for him to sit down and said in a low voice in case someone overheard.

"Got a slight problem, George. I was unable to drill a hole into the stone. I first of all tried masonry bits, new ones at that, and they had no effect on the blighter. I then tried a diamond bit and that didn't even make a mark. What you have here George is some kind of stone. I have never come across anything like it. I don't know how long it has been rolling around the bottom of the sea but it could have continued for hundreds even thousands of years and it would still look as good as new."

"I don't know what I will say to Claire," said George, totally oblivious to the physical properties of the stone. All he wanted was a hole to be drilled through it. "Oh, well. Thanks for trying. I will still buy you a bun and tea at tomorrow's break for the effort that you have made."

"There is one other avenue we could try, George. I know one of the boffins over in the research centre. We used to play together in the local soccer team. He used to tell me about some of the latest machines and computers that they use in the labs. One of the machines was a laser, which was used for piercing holes into hardened steel that was used for the armouring of tanks. Perhaps he can help. I'm due to go down to the soccer club tomorrow evening for a committee meeting and he should be down there. Can I keep the stone until then?"

"That's really good of you, Dave. I'm sure Claire won't mind waiting for a few more days. I'll leave it with you, then. Got to fly, as we have a lot of work on in the shed at the moment. Probably enough for some overtime. See you tomorrow."

The following day Dave attended the meeting in the director's room and afterwards went into the bar where saw his friend Pete who was chatting to a group of past players.

"Thought you had hung up your boots, Pete. Don't mind me saying, but you have put on a little weight around the midriff, which will get in the way when you attempt to tie up your laces. If I were you I would stay home with the Mrs. and watch a game on the box."

"You cheeky old devil. I could run rings around you with my eyes shut and with one leg in a sling. Let me buy you a pint. You look as if you need one now that you are on the committee and making all of those diabolical decisions about how to run a successful football team. Any chance of winning a game this season?"

Dave smiled and went towards the bar with Pete. After a chat about past playing days and how the families were getting along, Dave brought up the topic of the stone.

"Pete, I remember you once saying that in the lab in which you work you sometimes used a laser for cutting into steel. I was wondering if you would do me a small favour. Take a look at this stone. It belongs to a little girl who found it on a local beach and she wants it turned into a necklace. A friend gave it to me to drill a hole through it in the workshop. I first used a masonry bit with no success. In actual fact the stone caused the ends of the bit to melt. I then tried a diamond drill and still not a mark on it."

Pete held the pebble in the palm of his hand and turned it over a few times.

"Have you been leaning against a radiator, or are you on heat? This thing is quite hot. Don't tell me it's retaining the heat from your drillings. Looks like ordinary sandstone, which would fit the picture as it was found on the Rame Peninsula, which is a sandstone area. There is also some basalt there. You can see remnants of a lava outflow near to Cawsands. That might help explain the hardness of the stone as it may have changed its molecular structure under extreme heat. You were right about the laser machine. I'll give it a try tomorrow."

For the remainder of the evening they chatted about their own personal lives. It was a very pleasant evening for the both of them as, although they were both members of the same club, they hardly ever crossed paths and when they did it was only for a few fleeting moments.

At about two-thirty the following day the laser was not being used, so Pete logged in the recording book that he was trying an experimental pulse on a stone that had possible unusual properties. He had decided to make it semi-official in case one of the big wigs happened to drop into the lab with a group of visitors, as they always wanted to see the laser at work because it was so spectacular. When in use one witnessed a thin deep red beam soundlessly cutting into a hard substance. To make it more spectacular the lab assistants used to spray a fine film of white dust across the beam, which made it glow a florescent purple.

Pete got an adjustable vice grip from one of the bench drawers underneath the drilling table and placed the stone in it. Once fixed firmly he placed it underneath the lens of the laser and looked through the focusing viewer. Strange he thought, as the stone appeared to be glowing. Once in focus he stood behind the safety screen and switched on the machine. He was not prepared for what happened next and neither were the other laboratory assistants and chemists. As the first ray of the laser made contact with the stone there was an explosion of the most amazing display, sparks displaying all the colours of the rainbow. Far more spectacular than the Sydney Bridge Millennium display.

"What the bloody hell are you doing, Peter?" cried a voice from the far end of the lab.

"You silly sod. You could have killed us," shouted another person who had thrown himself onto the ground. Peter could not see anything for some thirty seconds due to the brightness of the display. When he did get his vision back he could see no damage at all. Everything seemed to be in place except for the staff that started appearing from different hiding places.

"Whatever you were working on you can take it straight out of this lab and don't ever bring it back in." It was one of the more senior technicians. Peter did as he was told and quickly removed the stone from its mount and went sheepishly out of the lab. He didn't even inspect the stone, as he wanted to get as far away from that area as quickly as possible. As he made his way to the washrooms he decided that he would never do anyone such a favour again.

At four-thirty Peter picked up the phone and gave his friend Dave a tinkle to say that they should meet as soon as possible so that he could return the stone. They arranged to meet after work in a nearby café.

"Hiya, Pete. You look worn out. Had a tiring day?" Pete grimaced and then began to tell of his horrendous experience in the lab. By the end of his graphic description of happenings in the lab Peter felt very guilty.

"I hope you are not going to get into any trouble, Dave. All that for one little old pebble. Better let me have it back. I will explain to George that we were unable to get into the lab. No need to worry him. I owe you a big favour. Call on me at any time, Dave." Dave put his hand into his pocket and took out the stone and placed it into Peter's palm. It still felt hot to the touch. Peter looked at the stone.

"Absolutely incredible that the laser didn't even affect the stone. As you have already said, although the beam was only on it for a fraction of a second it should have made some form of an impression upon it, and yet there is not a single mark. I have already decided what to do next. When I get home tonight, I will get my girlfriend to make up a clasp for it. She attends evening classes in jewellery design. Don't want to disappoint the little girl."

Eventually the stone was returned to Claire who immediately placed it around her neck. She went to bed that night very excited and looked forward to the morning when she could show her friends at school her new jewel.

Breakfast over, Claire collected her school bag, gave her Mum a big hug and ran across the road to the school with her necklace swinging around her neck. When she arrived in the playground she gathered her friends around her and began to tell them about her adventure on the beach at Sandway and how she had found the stone. The small gathering unfortunately caught the eye of two girls who often took sweets and money away from Claire.

"What have you got there, ugly face?" the older of the two girls said looking at the red puffy scratches down the right hand side of Claire's face. "Let me see. Why it's an old pebble. I'll have that."

The other children moved aside not wanting to get involved with the two nasty, older girls. The girl put out her hand to snatch it off Claire's neck. Instead of feeling frightened Claire suddenly felt enraged. No one would ever take her precious stone away from her. Claire grabbed the girl's hand and very fiercely twisted it around with such a force that the girl fell to the ground grasping her wrist in agony. The other girl just looked on and made no effort to help her friend. She was actually afraid of Claire. The older girl eventually got up from the ground and without looking at Claire walked to the far side of the playground and remained there until the bell sounded. Claire never had any trouble from those two girls again.

Since that day Claire seemed to blossom out. Her teachers noticed an amazing improvement both in her work and her self-esteem. As the years went on she improved to such an extent that when she sat the Eleven Plus Examination she finished in the top ten percent and was awarded a place in a grammar school. She spent an enjoyable five years there and at the end gained eight O Levels in the National Examinations. She should have continued with her education, which would have enabled her to go on to university. Her teachers were extremely disappointed when she decided to leave school and apply for a job with the local council. They had destined her for either Oxford or Cambridge! She was accepted for a post with the planning department where she remained until the present day. She enjoyed the work and found the other office staff very good company.

Her reason for not going on to higher education was that she did not want to leave her mother who had struggled to look after her over the years. As a single parent her mother had had little money to spare and any excess that she managed to save she spent on Claire, so Claire had made the decision to remain at home and care for her mother.

Chapter Eleven

Surgery was always busy on a Friday. It was as if his patients had been saving their illnesses for the weekend. Doctor Bradden knew better. His practice was in Devonport, which was one of the poorest areas of Plymouth. The area actually ranked in the top five in the country for poverty and deprivation. Families tended to be large with many of them claiming huge amounts of supplementary benefits. This coupled with the lack of job prospects, one would have assumed that the area would have been the ideal breeding ground for crime and the misuse of drugs. However, quite the opposite prevailed. Families not only looked after their own siblings, but also when the occasion arose would willingly look after other people's children. There was a great feeling of camaraderie within the community. If anyone came upon hard times there would always be someone near at hand to lend a listening ear, or even help financially even though they may have been poor themselves. It was the unwritten code that people always paid their debts in kindness or by financial means. This was the main reason why Doctor Bradden had remained in that area on becoming a qualified doctor.

Doctor Bradden had arrived in Devonport some thirty years before, after qualifying at the London School of Medicine. His lecturers had noted from his first dissertation that he was destined for great things in the medical profession. He qualified with a First Class Honours with Distinction. The University offered him a two-year post in one of their prestigious research programmes but he declined and instead served for four arduous years in the wards of a nearby hospital. He managed to survive the long hours of work and the near poverty conditions of his bed-sit with the help of Madeline.

Madeline had been a nurse on one of the child wards in the hospital. He had noticed her on a few occasions when visiting the wards but did not make any form of contact other than in a professional manner. It was not until a year after he had arrived at the hospital, when he was attending a Christmas party for the nurses, that he actually spoke to Madeline socially. He was at the bar when he noticed her standing next to him. He offered to buy her a drink and from that meeting a romance began to flourish which was eventually sealed a year later in their marriage.

One of the promises Barry Bradden had made on that day was that when his time was completed at the hospital he would seek out a practice in a pleasant rural community where they would raise a large family. Sadly they discovered a year after their marriage that Madeline was unable to have children and instead of ending up in the country they eventually came to settle in Plymouth.

Surgery usually finished at 6 p.m. on a Friday. Dr Braddon looked at his watch, which indicated that he only had fifteen minutes to go before shutting up the surgery for the weekend. On his appointment list he had two more patients to see. The first was a Mrs Fowler who was an old lady in her mid 80's and who attended the practice at least once every two weeks. With each visit she seemed to have contracted a different illness to the one she had had on the previous visit.

The doctor had diagnosed her problem early on in her initial visits. It was simply loneliness, which the doctor appreciated was one of life's most difficult things to cope with. He therefore spent a little more of his precious time with Mrs Fowler than he should have done. His secretary constantly reminded him of this which he tended to ignore. He had a wonderful way of dealing with the illnesses of this old lady. If more practitioners followed his ways the country would spend less on drugs in the National Health Service.

He would get his secretary to make the two of them a cup of tea and also add some digestive biscuits. The biscuits he used to dunk into his cup and deliberately leave them in too long, so that when he lifted them out of the cup towards his lips they used to drop onto his desk or into the saucer. This act never failed to amuse Mrs Fowler who would take much pleasure in rebuking him for his poor eating habits. By the end of drinking the tea and eating the biscuits Mrs Fowler had almost forgotten why she had come into the surgery.

One contented patient dealt with and now for the last one of the day. He looked at his appointment list and saw the name Claire Axworthy. Strange, he thought, for he had not had to deal with Claire since she was a young child. She was a lovely girl. He had been at her mother's bedside when she had given birth to Claire. He had seen her grow into a bonny lass who was always full of fun and vigour. He had in the past seen her for the odd bout of flu and for various vaccinations but for little else. Recently however, he had seen her when visiting her Mum who had been very ill at the time.

Claire had never got married and had lived with her Mum for the whole of her life. She was devoted to her Mum, and when her mum was invalided with a stroke when Claire was twenty-three years old, she had spent the next ten years of her life looking after her. She never had the time to go out for an evening and the question of a holiday for her never arose. Dr Bradden had become more concerned for her than for her mother, as Claire had become a bit of a recluse.

Claire did have a job working in an office in the Civic Centre for Plymouth City Council, which got her out of the house during the day and which actually helped take her mind off the ordeal with her mother. She was a very popular girl at work as she always put others before herself. She was loved by her neighbours who appreciated the sacrifices that she had made for her mother and through all of that she still had time to help them in their hour of need.

Eventually her mother died and Claire was left all on her own. She had no relations and no close friends. The neighbours and her work mates rallied around to try to help her, but with little success. One day one of her neighbours, a Mrs Brookenshaw, decided enough was enough and actually made an appointment for her at the doctors. She did that before notifying her, as she knew that Claire would not have gone of her own accord. As the appointment was with Dr Braddon, whom she was very fond of, she made no fuss and attended the surgery at the appointed time.

The waiting-room had changed little over the years. Same old decor, light grey walls with a dark blue dado rail running the entire length around it. The major change was the children's area in the corner which consisted of a small desk upon which were scattered reading books for various ages and a box of Lego. The lighting was upgraded from one dull light in the middle of the room to three sets of spotlights. She could remember it being quite dark and not at all uplifting for the ill patients. This was a vast improvement. There was even a large potted rubber plant in the opposite corner to where she was sitting.

"Claire, the doctor is ready to see you now." A smartly dressed, young receptionist had appeared from around the corner of the waiting-room without making any noise, which made Claire jump. She opened the door opposite and beckoned Claire to follow her.

Dr Bradden's office had not changed at all from what Claire could see at her first glance. The familiar picture of a large stag hung on the adjacent wall to where she had entered and slightly to its left was a photo of a rough-haired terrier. A few large charts were pinned to another wall depicting the various anatomical parts of the human body. Their corners were curled up to indicate their age along with the dust that they had collected. On the old green leather topped desk was a smoothly polished piece of oak which had as its centre a brass ink well and standing either side of it were two elegant quill pens. When she was quite young, Claire used to try to guess from which bird they had come from but she was too shy to ask the doctor. There was one major change however, on the desk. In place of the usual pile of papers stood a computer and monitor. Dr Bradden had entered the modern age of technology, she thought, not that he needed any of that as he was a brilliant doctor and everyone in the area knew it.

"It's so nice to see you again, Claire," he said, as she entered the room. He stood up from behind his desk and came around and took hold of her hand. The last time he had seen her was when he had the unfortunate duty of coming to her house to sign the death certificate of her mother.

"Do take a seat. As you may have noticed I have been spending some of my savings on new seats for my patients. Must make the poor people feel a little more comfortable in my presence," he said with a little chuckle. "I may have to put back the old ones however, as people are tending to stay too long for their appointments. Only joking, Claire, as I would hate for you to leave too quickly. Please stay as long as you like. You are a breath of fresh air in my office."

As he spoke he studied her face and noted how tired she looked around the eyes. Her complexion was quite sallow and she had lost a fair bit of weight. The sparkle in her personality had disappeared. Considering the events that she had had to deal with over the past two years this was not at all surprising.

"Now young lady, what seems to be the matter with you? Why aren't you out jumping around in one of those confounded noisy dances being shouted at by some jumped-up little fellow called a disk jockey? Never could understand the logic in calling them jockeys. I bet they have never been within ten hands of a horse in their lives! By the time I've finished with you, you will be jumping around and making so much noise that those jockeys will have to turn their confounded music up to full blast." Claire laughed and Dr Bradden could just pick out a glimmer of the young Claire he used to know. All was not lost yet.

"I'm not feeling too good, doctor. I am having difficulty in sleeping and during the day I have been finding it very difficult to concentrate on my work."

"Claire, what has happened to you is quite a common phenomena. We both know how close you were to your mother and what a terrible loss it was to you when she passed away. Also over the past few years you were so intent on looking after her that you were unaware of the stress it was having on yourself. Quite simply, you have drained your body of all of its energies. You can compare yourself to a car using up all of its petrol and with its battery totally drained. You probably need only a good strong tonic. However, just as a safeguard we will give you a thorough examination. Have you ever given a blood sample?"

Claire shook her head.

"Good. I like taking a few pints of blood out of my patients as it hurts a lot and I like to hear them scream." Claire laughed. He was a lovely old man and liked to joke with his patients. He always said that laughter was one of the best and cheapest medicines known to mankind and that it was not used enough.

He went to the door and called in his secretary and explained that he would like to give Claire a thorough examination and would she mind remaining in the room until he had finished. Dr Bradden explained that it would mean his secretary would be a little late going home that night, but the girl didn't mind at all as he was always generous when extra time was given to the practice.

The examination took about fifteen minutes and by the end of it Dr Braddon was beginning to feel a little relieved. Claire's blood pressure was fine and her pulse beat per minute was that of a normal person.

"Claire, I am going to sign you off from work for two weeks and in that time I want you to promise me to get out of the house and go and visit some of your friends. Get to the cinema, as there are some really good films out at the present moment. I hear that some of the films have talking characters in them now. Can't be much of a challenge now you don't have to lip-read and keep up with the action at the same time. They will soon have the noises of the galloping horses in the cowboy films. Once that happens my surgery will be jam-packed. Now go away and come back in a few weeks looking like you used to look when you were three. By that time we would have had the results of your blood test," and with that he ushered her out of his surgery.

Claire left the surgery feeling a little better as she knew that if anyone could cure her problems she could find no one better than Dr. Bradden To cheer herself up a little more she stopped off at Robbie's the tobacconist and treated herself to a large bar of Cadbury's fruit and nut chocolate.

It was quite late on a Wednesday evening, 10.40 p.m. to be

more precise. Dr Bradden had just had his nightcap of a cup of Ovaltine and a small brandy, which always helped him sleep. The phone rang, which usually was not uncommon if it was his week on standby for the practice. However, this was his week off, so he was a little puzzled. It could not be one of his patients as his phone number was not on this week's recorded message and it was a little late for friends to be making a social call. It must be one of his collegues probably asking for a second opinion.

His wife took the call. She was his first line of defence and she would attempt to pass it on to one of the junior members of the practice.

"David, there is a call for you from a Mr Whitting. Would you like to take it in the sitting-room or down here in the hallway?"

"I'll take it up here, darling. Give me a moment to put on my slippers" He knew the floor would be cold in the hallway and so he slipped on his old battered but extremely comfortable slippers and went into the sitting-room and lifted the phone. He put his hand over the mouthpiece and shouted down for his wife to come off of the extension.

"Good evening. This is Dr Bradden speaking. How can I help you?" A strong Scottish accent came down the line.

"Hello, Dr Bradden. Do accept my profound apologies for phoning you at such a late hour but I wanted to make contact with you personally, and knowing how busy you practitioners are at the chalk face I knew that if I waited until tomorrow morning whilst you were in your surgery you would probably have had your secretary take a message.

I specialise in Tropical Disease for the National Health Department. A few days ago a junior assistant of mine was doing a routine blood test on a sample that was sent from your practice. Nothing unusual was noticed in the initial tests. In fact the tests were almost over when he was called away for a few moments. The blood sample was under a standard microscope, which is used for simple testing. As I previously stated nothing was at all irregular and when he came back he was going to remove the slide and write on it that all was OK. Fortunately, he decided to take one last look and was amazed at what he saw. The whole configuration of blood cells had changed. He was now witnessing a battlefield be-tween white blood cells and the red ones, which is an almost un-heard of phenomenon. As you will appreciate from your medical knowledge the white cells only attack foreign bodies. The young technician was extremely perturbed for he had noticed nothing in his initial tests and now all of a sudden all hell was breaking loose before his eyes. The only thing he could put it down to was that the specimens of blood had slightly warmed up and in the same process had picked up a foreign body from the surrounding atmosphere. Not an uncommon occurrence in hospitals of today. We are often reading in the newspapers of hospitals being the breeding grounds of the so-called super bugs. As he continued to watch, the white cells managed to kill a tenth of the red cells before they in turn perished from what appeared to be fatigue."

Dr Bradden was now fully awake and very worried as he began to realise that the sample of blood could only be that of his patient Claire.

"The young assistant biologist didn't quite know what to do next. The normal procedure was to put the sample into an airtight container and label it for a further analysis in a more sophisticated lab that was on the next floor. He knew that it could be a matter of weeks before the sample was looked at again, due to the pressures on that department. In exceptional cases there was a number to call, and that was to my department. And that, fortunately, was what he did.

When he explained what he had just seen the receptionist who was a fully qualified biologist decided to contact me in person even though I was at a meeting. After spending a few minutes on the phone talking to the junior biologist I decided to go to his lab rather than him sending the sample to me. I wanted to see not only the sample but also the lab in which the experiments had been conducted. Also as a safeguard I notified security to shut off the floor and prevent anyone entering or leaving the lab area. I have seen some very nasty viruses in my time and I did wish to take any chances at all. You can imagine how the young biologist was now feeling knowing that I was about to descend upon him, and also seeing security suddenly appear at the door of his lab.

When I arrived at the lab I immediately picked out the poor fellow for he was looking quite pale, almost in a state of shock. I first put him at ease with a smile and said he had done the correct thing in notifying my laboratory.

The sample was still under the microscope and just one glance sent a cold shiver down my spine. It had all the hallmarks of Daimler's Fever. Daimler was a German scientist who did most of his research in the Amazon Basin and had discovered a number of deadly viruses unknown to man at that time. Fortunately for us all, as he discovered a new virus he spent his time developing an antidote for most of them. The ones he left were the ones that could only be spread by insects living in that particular area and which never left their natural habitat. He spent his time dealing with the ones that could be passed from one human being to another via inhalation or physical contact.

My initial diagnosis of Daimler's Fever was ratified when I placed a new sample of blood under the microscope. The cells initially behaved in the manner that Dr. Daimler's notes had indicated with the white cells being attacked by the virus. It was when the white cells were victorious that they in turn started attacking their allies, the red blood cells who were not equipped for any form of retaliation. After a prolonged fight they eventually appeared to tire and eventually die. If this process were to continue over a period of time there would be a deficiency in the process of the red blood cells being able to transport oxygen and nutritions to the muscles and organs of the body. This would result in a patient becoming very lethargic and in time being confined to a wheel-chair waiting for a new virus to attack with little if any defence being offered by the already depleted white cells.

To cut a long story short, your patient has somehow contracted a strand of the fever, which fortunately for us is not transmitted from one human being to another. She must have at some time come into contact with the insect, which carries the virus. What we, or I should say you, have to do is to track down when your patient was in South America so that we can understand a little more about the incubation period of the virus The sad thing I have to tell you is that there is no known cure. Your patient will eventually die."

There was a ghostly silence for a few moments as Dr Bradden digested the horrible facts. Poor Claire.

"Dr Bradden, are you still there?"

"Yes. I am very sorry, but the information that you have just given me has come as quite a shock. My patient is a middle aged lady who does not deserve such an ending to her life. Tell me. What is the next stage in the procedure? Will she have to be kept in any form of quarantine?"

"Fortunately no, is the answer to that question. As I previously stated, as she cannot transmit the disease she can continue with her life as she is doing at the present moment. You will have to interview her and then send on the details to myself. The main problem at your end is for you to help the unfortunate lady to make preparations for her eventual paralysis. We are unable to help in diagnosing how long this will take. It could be a few months or even a few years. Only time will tell. Sorry I have to leave you with such an open-ended problem. Please give me a ring as soon as possible. Bye for now." And with that he rang off.

Dr Bradden slumped back into his chair. He was mentally and physically drained. The poor girl. What a dreadful thing to have to face up to so near to the death of her mother. It was not going to be at all easy for him to break the news to her, as he knew her so well. Life can be so mean.

He eventually went into the lounge and proceeded to put on his old checked slippers with the braiding peeling off of one side. He refused to have new ones as these had taken many hundreds of miles pacing over the fitted carpets and wooden floors to make them fit snugly onto his size eight feet. No way would he trade these in for a new model, which would mean many months of tedious running in.

His wife was worried to see how tired he looked. He always looked tired after a day in the surgery but this evening he looked even more so. The details of the telephone conversation were soon explained to his wife after which they both sat in silence for a number of minutes.

In order to break the tension Mrs. Bradden went to the sideboard, took two cut glass tumblers off the shelf and proceeded to pour two very large scotches. Usually she tried to persuade her husband from having a small tipple when he was a little fatigued, as the medical profession was littered with alcoholic doctors. However, this was an exceptional occasion. For the remainder of that evening they sat in silence.

Before dropping off to sleep Dr. Bradden made a short scribble on his note pad, which rested on a small table next to his bed, "important to contact Claire first thing in the morning."

The next day the doctor was in his surgery before his receptionist. He had to make sure that there was plenty of time to spend with Claire. When his receptionist eventually arrived on time at eight-forty five a.m. he ushered her into his office.

"Margaret, I want you to get in contact with my patient Claire and tell her that I would like to see her as soon as possible. It is imperative that I see her today, so change any of my previous booked appointments as is necessary."

The receptionist was quite taken aback as the doctor was a stickler for keeping to his appointment lists and only a dire emergency would cause him to make any form of rescheduling.

"Oh, and when she comes into the surgery I want you to accompany her into my office and remain with me for the first few minutes."

"Certainly, Dr Bradden, I will get onto it immediately. Is there anything else you would like me to do before I set out today's schedule? " The doctor nodded no. She went quietly out into the outer office, sat down at her desk and proceeded to make the appropriate phone calls.

It took almost two hours to track down Claire, as she had not gone into her work that morning because she was not feeling too well. Because Claire did not have a telephone the receptionist had to look through her files to see if any of the doctor's patients lived in the close vicinity of Claire. Fortunately a Mrs Pearson lived only a few doors away and it so happened that she was in that morning.

"Hello, is that Mrs Pearson? This is Dr Bradden's receptionist.

I am phoning from the surgery. There is no need to worry. We are going to ask a favour of you. I believe that from our records that Claire Axworthy lives a few doors away from you. We need to get in contact with her and were wondering if you could help us out by calling down to see if she was in and to ask her to give us a call?"

"Why certainly, young lady. Give me about ten minutes and I will try to get her to come back with me and make a call on my phone. She doesn't have a phone of her own and we do not want her to have to walk to the bottom of the street to the public call box. I will hang up now."

She was around to Claire's house within three minutes. She didn't even bother to put a coat on as the circumstances seemed to indicate that time was of the essence. There was no doorbell, only an old rusty knocker that didn't have seemed to have been used for years, as it was extremely stiff. Mrs Pearson lifted it up and forced it down so that it made a dull clang, which seemed to echo throughout the darkly lit house. She had to repeat the exercise three more times before there was any response. The door eventually opened and a tired looking Claire came to the door.

"Why, hello, Mrs Pearson, I haven't seen you for a while. Must be very important for you to be out on such a cold morning with no coat on."

"Ah, Claire, I have just received a call from Dr Bradden's receptionist. They have been trying to contact you all morning. They would like you to give them a call as soon as possible. You can come back with me and call them from my house, which will save you from going down to the phone box. Make sure you dress up in a thick warm coat before you come out. We don't want you to catch the death of cold! Come over as soon as you are ready."

Claire had not been having a very good day. She had not slept very well the previous night and she had been dozing in the lounge chair when the knocker had sounded. The sound had made her jump up with a jolt, which in turn had given her a slight headache, so all in all she felt pretty dreadful. However, she could still manage a small smile when she recalled Mrs Pearson's farewell sentence "We do not want you to catch your death of cold." At that present moment in time she felt as if she had already reached that stage.

It took Claire much longer than normal to get ready, as she was feeling quite run down and all the time she was wondering why the doctor had the need to get in touch with her in such an urgent way. She could not comprehend why she had not been called to the surgery in the normal way, i.e. a card sent through the post.

Claire knocked at the door of Mrs Pearson who must have been standing inside waiting for her arrival as the door seemed to fly open almost as her knuckles made contact with the wood of the door.

"Come in, Claire. Would you like a cup of tea? The pot has just come to the boil. I was about to make one for myself. Whilst you are making your phone call I will add the tea to the pot and find a few digestive biscuits."

Claire went into the hallway, which was cluttered with piles of newspapers and cardboard boxes, which were probably ready to put out for the dustmen who were due the following morning. Mrs. Pearson then led her into the lounge, which she could only recall having visited when her mother was alive many years ago. It was quite a pleasant room with light cream wallpaper, dark green carpet and a light autumnal suite of furniture.

Claire sat down on the settee and picked up the phone whilst Mrs Pearson went into the kitchen to make the tea. She had brought the telephone number of the surgery with her on a small piece of paper in case there was no directory at hand. She noticed that there were several under the nearby coffee table. Fortunately the line was free and she was soon talking to the receptionist.

"Good morning. How can we be of any assistance for you."

"Ah, hello my name is Claire Axworthy. I was asked to get in contact with you via Mrs. Pearson."

"Oh, hello, Claire. That was quick work. We did not expect to hear from you so soon. Doctor Bradden would like to see you as soon as possible. He told me to say that it was nothing to get worried about. When would you be able to come in? I have been told to make an appointment for you at any time.

Could you come in today? How about this afternoon at about two o'clock when the afternoon surgery begins? Would that be interfering with your arrangements for today?"

"No, that's fine by me. I have nothing to do for the rest of the day. In actual fact I was going to phone you to make an appointment, so that works out perfectly. I will be there at two o'clock then. Thank you very much."

By this time Mrs Pearson had returned from the kitchen with a tray full of ornate crockery, bone china cups and saucers and a most beautiful silver teapot with a matching sugar bowl. Claire felt quite important. She could remember her mother doing a similar thing when the doctor used to call or when the insurance man from Pearl came in to give the yearly bonus.

"I hope everything is all right, Claire. I couldn't help hearing that you had to go to the surgery at two o'clock today. I'm sure there is nothing wrong with you. This cup of tea will help perk you up." She proceeded to pour two very strong cups of tea and on the saucer of each one placed a digestive biscuit.

The next twenty minutes was spent chattering about what had happened in the neighbourhood over the last few months. After another cup of tea, which had slightly diluted with the adding of some more hot water, Claire made her excuses to leave. She thanked Mrs Pearson for the lovely cup of tea, which had made her feel much better, and then went out into the cluttered hallway and then out into the street. The next few hours were spent catching up with her washing and ironing and then it was time to go for her appointment.

Claire thought that it was rather strange when she entered the office of Dr Bradden as he was standing right next to the door and his receptionist remained in the room instead of retiring into the outer office as she usually did. Dr. Bradden also did the unusual gesture of holding her by the hand.

"Do come in, Claire. Come and sit here." He led her to the side of the office where two chairs had been previously placed adjacent to one another. He remained holding her hand as they sat down and the receptionist remained standing and tried to position herself so as not to look too intrusive under the circumstances.

"I do apologise for the intrusion on your day, but I needed to speak to you quite urgently." The word urgent found a nerve within Claire and for the first time in a long time she began to feel quite anxious. This was going to be no ordinary consultation. She should have realised that from the beginning when Mrs Pearson had suddenly appeared at her door. Dr Bradden continued in a very soft voice.

"I have known you since you were born and have seen you experience many a major trauma in your life. During that time I have witnessed what a very brave young lady you have become and finally with your mother's passing away I was hoping that you would at last have a well-earned rest."

His grip on Claire's hand increased in pressure as he made the last comment. She looked into his eyes and for a moment she thought she could see them filling up. The receptionist changed her position in a notably uncomfortable manner for she knew what was coming next.

"Claire, I will not 'beat about the bush'. Do you recall that during your last visit I mentioned that I was going to send a specimen of your blood to the labs just as a safety precaution, as I felt my initial diagnosis needed a second opinion? The results came back a few days ago." Dr Bradden had decided previously not to mention the conversation with laboratories. "The results seem to indicate that you have somehow contracted some form of a rare tropical disease. Have you been abroad during the last few years?" The receptionist awkwardly shifted her stance.

"No. The only holiday that I had during the last ten years was when I visited a relation with Mum about four years ago. I have never been abroad."

"I have to ask you a more delicate question, Claire. Please forgive me for enquiring about your personal life but the laboratories have requested that I do so. Have you been in physical contact with any person who may have been abroad recently?" The doctor was very careful how he phrased the question as he did not wish to embarrass the poor girl and yet he needed to know the origin of the illness. He knew from his conversations with the laboratories that it was not contagious but he needed

165

to know if there was some other way of contracting the disease, which perhaps they may not have come across as the experiments in this area were in their early stages. As she had not been abroad there had to be some other explanation.

"I'm sorry, doctor, but I can't be of any help. If you were referring to sexual contact I haven't had the opportunity especially the way I have felt over the past few years. Also none of my friends have been out of the country recently and when they have been away they have only hopped over to the continent." Claire looked a little flushed. "What must I do to get over this illness?" she continued in a very quiet, soft voice.

At this point Dr Bradden reached across and took her other hand and held the both of them in his hands. The receptionist moved once more sensing that this would be the moment when the doctor would have to give the devastating news to Claire.

"Claire, I am afraid that somehow you have contracted an extremely rare form of virus for which there is no known cure. The report from the laboratories stated that it was only to be found in a rather small area in South America, somewhere in the Amazon basin. The virus cannot be passed from one human being to another and can only be contracted from an insect bite so you can see why I questioned you about your travels. My other questions were a shot in the dark."

"How long do I have to live?" The question was asked in an amazingly controlled voice. There was no hint whatsoever of any anxiety. What an incredibly brave young woman, thought the receptionist. This was a whole new ball game for her, as she was never allowed to witness any form of interaction between a patient and a doctor. She began to understand why the doctor had requested her presence during Claire's visit.

"That I am afraid I cannot tell you. There have been so few of these cases that there is no pattern. It could be a matter of months or even years. Claire, I have known you since you were a tiny baby and since those days you have proved to be a pillar of strength for numerous people around you. You have had to endure many hardships and at a time in your life when you should be free from all of that you are presented with this devastating news. Claire, don't consider what may happen during the next few months or years. I'm not going to advise you what you should do. I am going to tell you what you will do." The last sentence was said with so much conviction that all within the room were astounded. Before anyone else could make any comment the doctor continued "You have spent the whole of your life thinking of others. Now you will think of yourself. What you will do is to take yourself away on the holiday of a lifetime. Forget the expense of it. If you spend all of your savings the country will look after you. Look how much you have paid in taxes over the years. When you walk out of this office start making plans even as you walk home as to where you might venture and what you will need in the form of clothes etc. and then go out and spend. You can't take it with you. Now be on your way, young lady, and make sure you send us lots of postcards to keep us in touch with your travels."

He stood up and gently pulled Claire to her feet, led her to the door and before opening it he turned momentarily to face her.

"I know that this is totally unprofessional but I want to hold you for a moment like your mother and father would have done", and with that he took her in his arms and gave her a long hug. The receptionist noticed a tear had formed in the corner of the old man's eye, which matched the two that had formed in hers. "I have noticed one major change that you have made in your appearance, Claire. I see that you have replaced the pebble around your neck which you always wore as a child for a spectacularly shining stone," he added.

Claire did not have time to respond to the conversation as she was whisked to the outer of the door of the surgery and ushered out before the doctor and the receptionist totally broke down. Strange, she thought, as the stone had always shone brightly!

Claire was absolutely numb as she stood in the street outside. What an amazing fifteen minutes. One minute she had been feeling quite ill and now she felt no pain or illness at all but knew that she was going to die. None of it seemed real. She turned to her left and proceeded down the hill towards Mount Wise Park. She needed time to think and she always thought

167

better in the open air.

Within minutes she was standing next to Sir Walter Scott's Memorial. The view was spectacular with the setting of Mount Edgecumbe Park in the background and the River Tamar in the foreground. The sun was shining quite brightly sending an array of bouncing light shows across the choppy water. She sat down on one of the park benches and let the fingers of the sun caress her pale face. The warmth made her feel slightly better and she began to relax a little.

From her vantage point she could see the beach on the Cornish side of the river where the rowing boat used to land her when she was a child, and directly opposite her she could see the stately drive that led up to Mount Edgecumbe House. It seemed so long ago that she used to walk those paths with her Mum and Uncle. The memories came flooding back.

A dog barked to her left as it chased after a stick, which had been thrown by its owner. It brought her back to her senses and so she started to recall what Dr Bradden had told her to do. "Go away on a holiday." Where? she thought. If she were to go off on a trip she would have to consider her finances. She tried to remember how much she had in her savings. Probably at a guess somewhere in the region of a thousand pounds. She also had some money invested in a building society which should account for another three hundred pounds so in all she had enough to even go on the continent! There was also the house in which she lived. It was a small terraced house, which would be worth in the region of £12000. She immediately dismissed this thought, as she would need somewhere to live on returning from her holiday. She could sell and live in rented accommodation but that seemed too drastic a move for her. It was bad enough trying to pluck up the courage to take a holiday.

She must have been sitting on the seat for a long time as she began to feel a chill. The sun had set in the uppermost parts of the trees in the park opposite and long finger-like shadows were beginning to creep across the grassy slopes towards her. She decided she should get home before dark, as there was much to do. At no time in her thoughts had she dwelled upon actually dying. She went home via the footpath around Richmond Walk, which took her past the swimming pools and around by the boats, which she used to dive under when playing "hit" with the boys.

By the time she arrived at the front door of her house it was quite dark. She pushed the key into the old lock and forced the door open as it had slightly warped with all of the rain that they had recently experienced and was beginning to jamb at its bottom. Inside on the doormat was a note. It was from Mrs Pearson hoping that all had gone well at the doctors. Nice thought. Claire made a mental note to go in and see her tomorrow morning.

Claire was not at all hungry but she made a round of cheese on toast and a cup of coffee before sitting down at her desk with a sheet of paper and pen to make notes on her finances. She also made a list of possible destinations for a short holiday and the preparations that she would have to do such as inform the neighbours, stop the papers, tell the milkman. There were so many things to do that she began to think that the effort was not worth it.

By nine o'clock she was mentally and physically exhausted so she decided to have an early night and continue with her notes the following morning before going in to see Mrs. Pearson.

She had a very restless night's sleep and felt just as drained of energy as she had felt the previous night. However she was not perturbed and by three o'clock she had decided what she would do. She had dismissed going abroad as she felt that that was far too extravagant and she would also have to cope with a foreign language. She settled for London.

The next morning she caught the nine o'clock number four bus into the city centre and went into the first travel agency she could find. By lunchtime her holiday was settled, including all travel and accommodation arrangements. All that she needed to do now was to buy some new clothes, not too many and not too expensive for if she only lived for a few more months that would be such a waste of money. Mind you, she thought with a smile, at least she would look very smart at her own funeral.

Chapter Twelve

The taxi came for Claire at the prearranged time of six thirty in the morning. It was dry and the air had a slight bite to it. There was a light covering of frost on the windscreens of parked cars and the only other person in sight was the milkman on his early rounds. He didn't bother to stop at Claire's door as he could see the note in the milk bottle and automatically assumed that she was off on holiday. Strange though, he thought, as Claire never went away for more than a day and she had not stopped her milk as far back as he could remember. He made a mental note to collect it on the way back up the street. One did not wish to advertise the fact that someone in the street was away on holiday. It might invite unwanted visitors.

The ten minutes' journey into the bus station went without any interruptions by traffic. There were the odd few people travelling into the dockyard. Years ago there would have been hundreds of men travelling along this route into Devonport Dockyard. Those were the days when we had a fleet and not just a few frigates. Claire could even remember seeing an aircraft carrier being launched into the Hamoaze when she was very young.

The bus station was a grim old place. Paint was peeling off the walls and the smell of urine lingered from the late night revellers who had walked up from the clubs in Union Street hoping to catch the last bus. No toilets were open at this time of night and so they used to relieve themselves of their excess amounts of alcohol in any dark corner they could find. She was pleased to see that the bus was already there which meant that she did not have to wait in this most unpleasant environment.

As she made her way towards the bus she became aware of a bundle of clothes that had been dumped on one of the seats used for waiting passengers to rest their weary feet. She momentarily jumped as the clothes suddenly moved and drew apart to reveal an old bearded man who had been sleeping rough. Had she had the time, Claire would have bought him a nice warm cup of tea and a sandwich. Poor old chap, she thought.

The coach was a double-decker and Claire made for the upstairs from where she hoped she would get a really good view of the beautiful English countryside. She was not in the least disappointed. As the coach drove through the early hours of the morning out of the city and into the rolling landscape of Devon she could pick out the early morning hunters. She saw two foxes running across the undulating fields and diving into the bushes in chase of their quarries. She also witnessed a large hawk dive down and catch a small animal in its talons and then swoop off to some quiet spot to devour it.

Claire had never travelled by coach before and was mildly surprised at the comfort of the seats and the attention given by the stewardess to her passengers. She was able to purchase hot drinks and sandwiches throughout the entire journey, which helped to pass the time.

London was an exciting place. Claire loved the invigorating atmosphere of the city when comparing it with her quieter Plymouth. Everything seemed to move at double the pace.

During the first day of her visit to the capital she had decided not to visit any of the major tourist attractions. Instead she would hail a taxi just like they did in the films that she had seen on television and make for the nearest underground station.

She was staying in a small bed and breakfast hotel near Earls Court and was unaware how close the nearest Underground station was. It took only what seemed a few seconds to get a cab and she was most embarrassed to be dropped a minute later at a tube which was only around the corner from her hotel. She half expected the taxi driver to be annoyed by the shortness of the drive and decided to tip him well.

She looked at the meter on the dashboard of the cab and saw it finally register one pound and five pence. She pressed two pounds into his hand and said, "Keep the change"

She was truly amazed when the driver turned to her and said,

"You are too kind. Never tip more than fifty pence on such a short trip. That's my tip for you for today. Here you are," and with that he pressed fifty pence back into the palm of her hand. He also gave her one of the mints that he was chewing.

"Have a nice day, lady," and with that he drove off into the heavy traffic.

What a nice man, Claire thought. So much for the unfriendly city she had read about so many times in the local tabloids. Now for the ride on the Underground! She knew that she had to pay particular attention to the direction in which she had to travel. She had read in the guidebooks not to jump on the first tube that came into the station. There would be a tube coming in every few minutes so if you miss one, another would soon follow. "Don't panic," the book had said. "If need be ask someone the way if one is unable to read the complicated tube map." Complicated was not an exaggeration.

The taxi driver had dropped her outside Gloucester Road Station where there were three tube lines. Claire purchased a daily runabout ticket, which would enable her to use the tubes within a certain radius of the centre of the city and also the bus system. Excellent value, she thought.

Claire was absolutely lost when confronted with all of the numerous lines shown in their various colours and the hundreds of stations shown by black circles interspaced on them. Take it calmly, she said to herself. Remember what the guidebook had said. She took a small step back from the map and eventually decided that she would need the blue Piccadilly Line, which would get her up into the city.

"Having trouble?" came a voice over her left shoulder. She turned and was confronted by a very dark skinned gentleman in a dark navy blue uniform which had some form of an emblem on its breast pocket. He also wore a peaked hat which he touched as he spoke to her. What a gentlemanly gesture, Claire thought. People didn't do that in her hometown, although she vaguely recalled someone doing that to her mum back in Devonport. He was an old man in a tweed jacket. Funny how the mind can suddenly shoot back into the past and pick out irrelevant trivia.

"You seem to be lost," he said. "Tell me where you are making for and I will show you the easiest route."

"Well, I would like to get up to the centre of the City where I want to visit the shops. I would like to see Covent Gardens first, before I get too tired"

"Right. Your best bet is to jump on the Piccadilly Line just there." He placed his large thumb on the spot where they were at present and then traced the line through to Piccadilly Circus and then on to Leicester Square and eventually Covent Garden.

"There is another way by jumping on the Circle Line and making a change on route to a third line. However, as it would appear that you are a stranger to our service I would suggest that you take the Piccadilly Line, which will mean no changes in which to get lost. It will mean an extra five minutes on your journey, however."

Claire smiled. "That's very kind of you to explain which line to take" and with that she said goodbye, walked down the platform and got onto the wrong train!

Claire eventually got to her destination after making three changes, each time laughing inwardly to herself.

It was great to get out into the fresh air even if it was polluted by the carbon monoxide fumes from the never-ending stream of traffic that confronted her. Somehow she would have to find a way of getting to the other side of the road. She looked to her right and saw a group of people standing next to the kerb and assumed they were waiting for the lights to change in order to cross the road. She made her way slowly through the tide of people coming towards her. She dreaded the thought of the rush hour. How would it be possible to get twice as many people into this amount of space in safety? She made a mental note not to travel in the rush hour!

She eventually reached the group of people that had now grown in size. She could not see anywhere to cross over which seemed strange. What on earth were they doing? Perhaps someone had been taken ill. She managed to squeeze into a gap and could see a man kneeling down on the floor with an open suite case. Money was changing hands and things were being taken out of the case and handed to the buyers. It must be one the illegal street traders that she had read about in one of the London guide books that she had borrowed from the library. He was selling perfume that had leading brand names on their labels. The guidebook had hinted that these bottles were not "off the back of a lorry" i.e. not stolen, but were cheap counterfeit replicas. Like everyone else in the crowd however, she fell for the smooth talk of the vendor and ended up buying two bottles of Allure.

Suddenly without saying another word the vendor shut up his case. Someone else in the crowd picked it up and they both went off in different directions. It was then that Claire noticed two London Bobbies walking briskly towards the gathered throng of people. She felt a twinge of guilt and moved off with the quickly dispersing crowd. She didn't want to be caught with stolen goods and have to appear in front of a magistrate!

Covent Garden is an amazing place. It still has the old market buildings where My Fair Lady was filmed, but these have now been transformed into quite exclusive shops. In front of the shops was a hive of activity. Jugglers were throwing flaming clubs into the air whilst two people were balancing on each other's hands and walking underneath the archway of flames. Very spectacular, she thought. In another area she came upon a quartet of what seemed to be young students playing classical music. She stopped there for over five minutes enjoying the professional sounds from their instruments. As she left them she dropped a pound coin in a hat, which had been placed strategically in front of the group. By this time she was beginning to feel quite tired. Her feet were getting sore so she decided it was time for a cup of good old English tea.

She searched around for a few minutes and found a delightful eating-place within the covered area of the main market and sunken down below ground level. It had a very relaxing atmosphere about it, almost giving the impression of travelling back in time, as everything about it was old. The wooden tables were not covered in a cloth and so one could see the smoothness of the knotted joints that had been worn down over the years by plates and saucers continually being slid across their surfaces.

The chairs were not particularly comfortable but were in keeping with the tables. They were of the folding type with rusty old frameworks and wooden slatted backs .The people serving wore black shirts and trousers, and tied around their waists they had black and white striped pinafores. Occasionally a sparrow or pigeon would descend from the overhead rafters in an attempt to devour any food that had dropped from the plates.

Initially Claire felt quite embarrassed because above the sunken area there was a rail which ran around the whole cir-cumference of the café and which was used as a resting place for many of the visitors. They all seemed to be looking down on her. However as her self-confidence grew she gradually looked up into their faces and saw that none were looking at her. Some were having a quiet cigarette and others were just chatting away to one another.

She ordered a pot of tea and a toasted teacake and sat there soaking up the vibrant atmosphere and thinking how lucky she was to be there. Everyone around her seemed to be in a happy mood. It was a very sunny day, which always seemed to bring the best out in people. Her mind drifted back over the morning and the people that she had met. It was strange to think that she would probably never see any of them again, even if she man-aged to live to a ripe old age! No chance of that now, she thought. A smile came over her face. She had come to terms with that little problem and was now really enjoying herself.

The warmth of the tea seemed to flow to all parts of her body, much like the Carling Black Label Lager in the adverts. That, combined with the added energy from the glucose and carbohydrates in the toasted teacake, had a refreshing effect upon her. She left a small tip on the table and proceeded to climb the circular staircase to the floor above.

During her little tea break she had read the information in the London guidebook about the history of the area in which she now stood. How strange to think that years ago in this very same place there was a thriving fruit market which operated throughout the night and which supplied not only the whole of London but also the surrounding counties. Vegetables came as far afield as the outer extremities of Cornwall and even came across from Brittany on the Roscoff ferry into her hometown of Plymouth. The area was never asleep. As the market prepared for the next influx of lorries so the tramps and down and outs assembled around their open fires to keep warm during the cold winter nights.

The most bizarre feature of these evenings was to see gentlemen in their dress suits and bow ties escorting ladies adorned in the most exquisite ball gowns and glistening in exotic jewellery intermingling with the scruffy looking tramps. These well-heeled upper crust members of the elite society of London were off to the Royal Opera House.

Claire's next visit had to be the Opera House. She walked along the majestic arcade that enclosed some of London's most opulent shops and entered the rear entrance to the Opera House. A short slope took her up to the booking area for tickets to the various performances that were being staged during the next three months. She looked longingly at the poster advertising the Royal Ballet that was to perform Swan Lake. Ever since a child she had longed to see a ballet but never had had the opportunity of going to a show even though travelling troupes sometimes came as far as Plymouth, and when they did the tickets were far too expensive for Claire to purchase.

She stood in the auditorium and savoured the wonderful atmosphere produced by the beautiful architecture of the building and the elegance of the well-dressed people who seemed to glide through the building with their heads held high as they went about their daily jobs.

In the main entrance were costumes encased in shiny glass boxes that had been used in past operas. In one of them was a beautiful costume, which commemorated the fiftieth anniversary of when Maria Callas had sung Tosca. In another case were four of the original costumes which were used in the 1956 production of Noctambules. She knew that this visit would be placed high on her list of London memories when she returned home. A sign at the bottom of a regal staircase caught her eye. There was an arrow pointing upwards to a gazebo bar. As she ascended the thickly carpeted staircase she wondered how many Royal Princes had gone before her. She closed her eyes momentarily and tried to imagine what it must be like to be at the opening night of a famous ballet. Although she would never have the opportunity of witnessing such an occasion at least she was actually standing where it took place and she was enjoying the feeling of being there probably more so than the people on the actual night who had had to pay a huge sum of money.

At the top of the stairs she found herself in a very large open room, which had a semi circular glass roof, which gave it the effect of actually being out in the open. At its centre was a circular bar, which appeared only to serve champagne, and around the outside of the room tables had been laid for the evenings' performance. She thought initially that she was the only one present but then noticed someone crouching down inside the circular bar removing a box of slender looking glasses, which Claire assumed were for the champagne.

"Can I be of any assistance, Madame?" said the gentleman as he stood up from behind the bar. "I am afraid we are not open at the present moment. Perhaps if Madame would venture down to the lower level you will find a coffee bar which serves alcoholic beverages if one should need it."

Claire smiled at the man. "I was enjoying the atmosphere of your beautiful building and I doubt very much if I could afford to purchase a drink in here." There was a slight pause in the conversation and Claire felt a little guilty at her last comment. The poor man had probably never had anyone speak of prices within his establishment.

"I couldn't agree more with you, young lady. Why, I even find these prices extortionate and I am the manager of the restaurant and it is I who set the prices." A smile gradually spread across his well-proportioned face. "You're from the West Country. I can tell by the way you elongate your endings. It makes a very pleasant ring to the ears. Quite a change to the accents I hear in here during the evening performances. You have brought a moment of joy to my usual boring afternoon. As a token of thanks you must join me in a taste of a new brand of champagne we are trying out on the locals this evening. It is only £5 a glass and a bottle would set you back one week's wages. Don't worry, as it is on the house. I never thought I would ever utter that phrase in this establishment," and with that he took a large gleaming bottle from out of a glass fronted cooler, pulled the cork without spilling a drop and gently poured the bubbling liquid into two long slender glasses.

"There you are, Madame. It is of a very good year. Watch out for the bubbles up your nose." Yet another phrase that he would not dared have used with his normal clientele. He was quite enjoying himself. The young lady had an air about her that made him feel quite at ease. Not a feeling that he experienced very often.

"So is this your first time to the Gardens?"

"Yes, and it is the first time that I have been to London. All very exciting and the people are so friendly." The gentleman nearly choked on his drink when he heard that last remark. This lady could have only have been in London for only a few moments. No one is friendly in London, he thought, especially when comparing it with the West Country. The more he talked to her the more he liked her. She had no airs and graces like many of the people he had to deal with in the course of his job. She was one of the most enchanting ladies he had ever had the pleasure of meeting.

They talked for about a quarter of an hour and then the gentleman apologised that he would have to return to his mundane duties otherwise he would receive many complaints that evening if things were not ready. With that they shook hands and Claire slowly walked down the stairs looking at the paintings on the walls of past famous singers and dancers. On reaching the bottom of the stairs she turned to her right, walked past the booking desks for ticket sales and made for the door. Just as she was about to walk into the revolving door to go out into the square a voice drifted down the corridor.

"Excuse me, Madame, but you have forgotten to collect your ticket for tonight's performance."

As this did not apply to her, Claire continued to enter the revolving door and the next minute she was out into the busy thoroughfare of the square, once again mixing with the hundreds of tourists. She had only taken a few steps when someone touched her on the shoulder from behind.

"I hope I didn't startle you, Madame." She recognised the voice as the one who had beckoned to someone in the theatre with regards to tickets. "I have your ticket here for tonight's performance" The man held out a white envelope.

"There must be some mistake," Claire said." I have not paid for any tickets whilst in the Opera House. It must be for someone else."

"I'm sure it's for you. You are the lady from the West Country judging by your accent, and the description fits you. I hope that doesn't sound too presumptions. Please take the envelope and read what is on the front of it." He handed it to Claire. The writing on the envelope was very legible and stated, 'To the charming lady with a warm smile from the West Country. Please accept the enclosed as a small token for brightening up my afternoon.'

"As you can see there is no mistake. Please forgive me, but I have to return to the booking desk. Do enjoy the performance this evening," and with that he turned and left her on her own, clutching the envelope in her hand.

She looked down at the front of the envelope and once again read the note. It was not stuck down so she lifted back the flap and preceded to pull out a white ticket, which had a thin gold line around it. At the top was the name of the ballet, Swan Lake, followed by information relating to the time of the performance and the date. There was no mistake in the day. It was for that evening. She looked for the seat and row number but could not see it. She then let out a small gasp when she saw the word "Box". The ticket was for a box. She had only seen film stars and Royalty sitting in such places.

Once the initial surprise began to wear off, the practicalities of such an occasion began to hit her. What would she wear? She thought that she had brought clothes for all the occasions that London would present to her, cold, rain and a sort of a smart dress to wear at dinner in the evening in the hotel. She did not however possess what one would really call smart clothing classy enough to wear to the Royal Ballet. She would have to buy a new dress. It would certainly affect the financial planning of the rest of her stay in the city, but even if it meant going back to Plymouth a few days early it would be well worth it. This was a chance of a lifetime and her's was a very short one now. She would never again have such an opportunity so she decided to go for it.

Claire came out of the side entrance to the Opera House and slowly began to walk along the esplanade, which housed the expensive shops, trying to collect her thoughts. As she reached the far corner of the building she noticed out of the corner of her eye that she was passing a shop, which had ladies clothes in the windows. She looked up at the sign above the door. Nichole Farhi.The clothes in the windows appeared to be mostly winter ones. The 'in' colour this year seemed to be bright Autumnal rust. There was however, one exception to this beautifully arranged display. It was in the third window along. A solitary single long black dress with a thinly gold sequined neckline hung at the centre of the window space that was enclosed in cream silken drapes. Claire thought it was the style of dress that Princess Diana would have worn had she been going to the Opera. She looked for the price tag. It was cleverly facing up the wrong way thus not breaking the Trade Descriptions Act but enticing a would-be buyer into the shop. The price would probably have put most people off thought Claire. Nothing ventured nothing gained, so in she went.

As she entered the door of the shop a young female sales assistant detached herself from a group of three and came towards Claire.

"Good afternoon, Madame. May I be of any assistance?" she said with a warm smile.

"Yes," said Claire almost afraid to enquire of the dress in the window. "Could you tell me the price of the black dress in the window"

"Madame, may I suggest that you look at the price after you have tried it on? Even if you do not wish to purchase the garment at least you should have the satisfaction of seeing it on yourself."

A very clever sales ploy, thought Claire.

Claire did not have time to answer that question, as the girl led her to the window to make sure that it was the correct dress and then proceeded to ask her for her size. She then led her into an amazingly large changing-room, which was completely surrounded by mirrors and asked her to sit down. In a matter of seconds she reappeared with three dresses on her arm.

"I feel sure that one of these will fit, Madame. If not, I will bring another selection. When you have found the one nearest to your fit let me know and if need be I will get someone else along for their expert opinion."

The first dress was a little too tight, but the second one fitted a treat. She called for the sales girl and then walked out of the changing-room.

"That is perfect," said the girl. " If you wait one moment I will get the manager,"

She was back within a minute accompanied by a dapper little man in a very smart pinstripe suite.

"You were correct, Jayne, the dress appears to have been made for the lady. A perfect fit. I don't think there is any need for me to remain. Do have a nice day and a very pleasant evening," and with that he turned and went back to his office.

Claire looked at herself in the mirror once more before taking it off. Now came the awkward time of finding out how much the dress cost.

"I am rather afraid to ask how much the dress costs," she said to the girl.

The girl looked a little puzzled, as she was not used to being asked for the price of things in this shop. Almost all of her customers either gave a credit card without looking at the price tag.

"It's a bargain at £345" she said. She noticed the colour drain from the Claire's face. The lovely smile had disappeared. She could see not only disappointment but also sensed there was something else deep down. She felt for the first time in her career as a shop assistant a feeling of sadness for a client. Most of the clientele she dealt with usually had money to burn. This person probably had very little money.

"I wonder if Madame would sit down for a moment. I think there must be a mistake in the price. I am sure it was much less when I showed it to a lady yesterday. I will go and ask the manager"

Claire wished she had never entered the shop. Even if the dress had had the wrong price tag on she still would be unable to meet the price. She watched the girl make her way through the other shoppers towards the manager's office. Before she reached the door she stopped at one of the desks where the wrapping of garments seemed to take place and laid the dress on the flat surface. She then took hold of the sleeve of the garment and gave it a short sharp tug and then folded it in half and entered the office. She returned within a few minutes.

"We are extremely sorry but this dress has a slight flaw in the sleeve. It is hardly noticeable but the manager could not possibly allow you to purchase it in that state. I did ask him if there could be any form of discount on the purchase but he said it would have to be held back for the Spring sales. However, Madame could express great disappointment and say that there would be no time to look for another garment as you had to wear it this evening." Claire swore she saw the girl nod her head very slightly as if to encourage her to make that request.

"I can see that Madame would like me to do that. Please wait for a few more moments."

She eventually came back with the manager who profusely apologised for all of the inconvenience.

"If we allow Madame to take the dress you must appreciate that we would not be in the position to refund any money should you find that you do not like it on returning home." Again, Claire noticed a slight nod from the girl.

"As it will eventually find it's way into a sale and for the disappointment that we have caused you we can let you purchase it for £150."

Claire was dumbfounded. She noticed the girl was smiling profusely and was already preparing to wrap up the dress.

"That is extremely kind of you. Yes, I would like to take the dress."

As she walked out of the store she did not notice the manager who nodded at the shop assistant and give her an almost non-perceptible smile.

That night at the Ballet of Swan Lake a very elegant lady dressed in a black dress with a narrow gold sequinned neckline got out of a taxi and walked into the grand foyer. As she entered the grand auditorium many faces in the crowded area looked towards her. Claire blushed a little, as she was not used to being the centre of attraction. The performance was not due to start for another thirty minutes so she decided to visit the champagne bar. As she began to walk up the red carpeted stairs one of the Ushers stepped forward and spoke to her.

"Madame. Are you the young lady who paid a visit this morning to the champagne foyer? I was told to look out for an elegant lady who could easily be mistaken for a Royal Princes." Claire once more blushed profusely.

"Yes, I was here this morning," she said in a quiet voice.

"That's wonderful. Now that I've found you I can relax a little. Please follow me." The usher guided her to the top of the stairs and instead of leading her into the champagne auditorium he turned left and took her into a most beautiful glassed in area. "This is the Railway Carriage. It actually was a railway carriage at one time. We now use it for important guests. However, you are more important than that." He then proceeded to take her through another set of doors, which lead into a smaller room. Initially the scene took Claire's breath away. The room had three enormous chandeliers, which hung down from a vast ceiling. As the light shone upon the thousands of cut glass beads it was dispersed by the prismatic effect of the stones, which in turn threw tiny showers of sparkling droplets across the walls and floor areas. Claire felt as if she was in Wonderland.

"I am at your disposal for the entire evening, Madame. I will accompany you to your box and if you wish I will explain all about the Ballet as it takes place. Now would you like a glass of champagne?" Claire was speechless and only could manage a little nod of the head. "I know how you must be feeling at the present moment," continued the man. "I can remember the first time when I stepped into this room." He took Claire to the bar and ordered a whole bottle of champagne. By the time she had to enter the box for the beginning of the performance her head was beginning to feel very light.

The ballet was absolutely fantastic. During the interval whilst she was sipping yet another glass of champagne, she overheard someone enquiring if the lady in the black dress who sat in one of the boxes was Royalty!

At the end of the performance, just as Claire was about to get out of the seat, the curtains at the rear of her box were pulled aside to reveal the bar manager who had given her the glass of champagne that afternoon.

"I trust that Madame enjoyed the performance? May I be permitted to escort you to your limousine?" Claire was about to explain that she had come by taxi but the dapper little man beckoned her to follow him and was on his way out of the box and down the carpeted stairway. As Claire followed him she was aware of the other patrons looking at her. As they reached the door a man in a blue uniform stepped forward and pulled the door ajar. Claire stepped out into the cool evening air and noticed her friendly barman standing alongside one of the longest car she had ever seen. As she neared it the driver, who wore a light grey suit and a black cap, got out of his driving seat, stepped around the back of the car and opened the rear door.

"Good evening, Mr Jamerson. I presume this is the important young lady that I will be driving home this evening?" He said looking towards Claire.

"Correct, William." The manager then turned to Claire. "Young lady, just tell William where you are staying and he will ensure that you get home safely. It has been a real pleasure having you visit our House. Do come back another time. Au Revoir." Claire was lost for words. She noticed that she was becoming the centre of attraction and a small crowd was beginning to gather around the car. Embarrassed, she nodded to the manager, smiled and proceeded to get into the stretch limousine. By the time she got back to her hotel she was absolutely drained of energy but still on a high, which made it very difficult for her to drop off to sleep that night.

When Claire woke up the following morning she was in a lot of pain and very tired. The week was catching up on her. However this was soon forgotten when she saw the black dress hanging on the side of the wardrobe and the memories of the previous night came flooding back.

The telephone rang at the side of her bed. She knew that it was the switchboard of the hotel as she had requested an early morning call. This was her last full day in London as she had to return to Plymouth the following day on the 11.15 bus, so she meant to take full advantage of the whole of the day. After a light breakfast of toast and coffee she went out and hailed the first taxi that came into sight and with luck on her side it was empty.

She asked the driver for her to be taken to the Planetarium where she had made a booking for a ticket, which would also allow her into Madam Tussauds. She decided to go into the Wax Museum first as that would probably make her extremely tired walking from one room to another and so sitting later in the Planetarium would be a welcome rest period.

The waxed people were so life-like. She was amused to watch the faces of the children having their photos taken alongside their singing and film star idols. By the end of the tour Claire was beginning to feel tired and hungry so she went into the small cafeteria and ordered a toasted teacake and a cup of tea.

She spent about fifteen minutes again watching the antics of the other visitors and when she was quite satisfied that she had regained some of her lost energy she got up and went to the door of the Planetarium. She was in luck as the next show was to start in five minutes. The seats were very comfortable with a reclining back, which was designed to allow you to look at the constellation of the stars without getting a stiff neck.

The lights dimmed and the narrator began to explain the night skies around the British Isles and how they changed with the seasons. She wasn't paying a great deal of attention to the narrative. The seats were so comfortable that they were having a soporific effect on her. She was about to fall asleep. Her heavy

185

eyes slowly scanned the expanse of the ceiling not recognising anything in particular. At school she had never been taught of anything to do with the skies, other than cloud formations.

She didn't catch what the narrator was saying when he began to change the formation of the stars, but as the constellations gradually moved around and began to change their shapes her brain began to recognise something. She was now wide-awake. The sky above her was very familiar. She seemed to recognise all of the constellations even when they changed from one season to another. Claire was a little baffled by all of this as she had hardly ever watched the sky at night. The only time she could remember spending any time at all looking at the night sky was when her uncle had taken her out in the garden one late evening to look for Halley's Comet. She decided at the completion of the show she would go and see the narrator.

Once the auditorium had cleared Claire made her way to the centre of the room where the narrator was sitting at a large control box

"Excuse me. Would you be able to spare me a few minutes of your time. I would like to know a little more about one specific part of today's showing."

The lady looked up from the desk. "Why certainly. It's always nice to talk about the programme. What do you wish to know?"

"I do apologise," said Claire, "but near to the end of the programme I momentarily lost concentration and missed what you had to say about a certain constellation. It must have been about four minutes before the end."

"I'll tell you what", said the lady. "I have some time before the next performance. If you give me about five minutes I may have time to play back the last six minutes for you. You can have your own private performance." Seven minutes later Claire was once again watching the skies.

"This is it. If you watch the left hand corner a very bright star will appear and will travel across the screen at about thirty-five degrees where it will eventually meet another bright star. They will then part and the first one I mentioned will go on to meet the cluster of three that is at present in the top left-hand corner." Claire then went on to explain the movement of most of the stars before they actually made their way across the ceiling. At the end of the display the curator turned up the auditorium lights and peered around the hall.

"Is this some form of a wind up? I'm not on Candid Camera by any chance, or is this some kind of a joke? You have obviously been in here a number of times before." Claire had no idea what the lady was getting at and the two of them just looked at one another for what seemed an eternity. It was Claire who broke the silence first. "I am sorry if I have caused you any anxiety, but I have no idea why you are questioning me in this manner."

"Madame, only an expert in this field would have been able to explain the movement of the stars as you have just done. Even I would be unable to explain the order of events as you have. What you were looking at was a computerised programme on how the skies would have looked some four hundred years ago. Also the configuration of the stars was not for the United Kingdom. They were for South America. I would be most appreciative if you would allow me to share your little secret."

Claire was dumbfounded and no matter how much she tried to explain that she knew nothing of the stars the curator would still not believe her.

Just as Claire was about to leave she added, "Incidentally the star configuration that you have on the ceiling at this present moment is incorrect. That grouping there should be nearer to the centre and that very bright star there should be here," she said pointing with her finger.

Claire made her way out of the auditorium doors whilst the lady projectionist went to switch off the system. As her hand went to flick down the switch she momentarily stopped. What if the woman was right? It was obviously a ridiculous thing to think but if she did not check the coordinates she would wonder about it for the next couple of weeks. She reached for the internal phone.

"George, would you do me a favour please? I'd like you to play the programme of the skies four hundred years ago and just get the computer to do a double check on itself." What she was asking was the equivalent of a spell check for a page of prose.

Five minutes later George phoned back.

"You clever little girl. Have a look at your projection as it stands at the present moment. The computer has found something incorrect. I will get it to amend the programme."

The projectionist looked up into the night sky and watched as the star patterns slowly changed. She gave out a slight gasp, as the final alignments were identical to where the woman had predicted. Her prediction was an impossibility and yet she had been so accurate. It was a great pity that the woman had gone for she would have liked to have spent much more time with her.

The visit had taken over two hours and when Claire came out she began to feel tired and hungry. She looked around the street. Everywhere looked overcrowded so she decided to walk for a short distance until she came to a small café. Nothing appealed to her so she decided to return to Covent Garden as she knew there was at least three cafes, which she knew, would serve food to suit her tastes.

She caught a taxi and some twenty minutes later was making her way to the east side of the square. As she neared the corner she could distinguish in the distance the mellow sounds of some form of pipe music. It seemed to be coming from the corner of the square opposite to where she had originally seen the acrobats on the previous day. She did not intend going back over the same ground as she had much to see in the few hours she had left and so began walking in the other direction. It was very strange, for the further she moved away from the source of the music the louder it seemed to get. At first she thought it may have been due to the acoustics in the square and she thought that once she rounded the corner into the next street it would lessen in volume. She was totally wrong. It got even louder. It was as if it was calling to her.

She stopped half-way down the street. It was full of the deafening noises of tourists and traffic and yet this had little effect on the music from the pipes! It was most strange how the pipe music seemed to follow her no matter where she went. There was only one thing to do and that was to return to the square and seek out the source of the music.

Again it was very strange for as she backtracked her way through the dense crowds the sound of the music gradually decreased in volume She eventually reached the corner of the square from where the origin of the music came and saw quite a large contingent of tourists gathered around a very colourful group of Indian looking musicians.

The Indians had very dark tanned faces, quite weathered but very healthy looking. They were dressed in beautifully coloured what appeared to be blankets, more befitting to South America than London. She also noticed a group of school children standing nearby. They looked as if they were of the same ethnic group as the minstrels. One of them turned for a moment and looked behind her towards Claire. For a fleeting moment their eyes engaged one another and Claire had the feeling that she had seen this little girl before but knew that that was impossible, unless it had been somewhere else in London. Perhaps they had passed one another in a street. She dismissed that but still looked at the girl. She noticed that the girl had taken hold of the hand of the girl who stood next to her and at the same time whispered something in her ear. They both turned at once and looked at Claire. All three stood smiling at one another. What beautiful children, Claire thought, I wonder where their homeland can be?

The whole time that the school party was there, the two little girls did not once turn their eyes away from Claire. Even when their teacher took them off to visit another part of the square they still kept their eyes on Claire and kept doing so until they finally disappeared down one of the side streets.

Claire now paid more attention to the musical artists. Their music was so mellow that it almost brought tears to her eyes. She moved nearer so as to get a better view of their instruments. She had got within two rows of people from the front when the same uncanny thing happened again, but on this occasion, with far more effect. One of the pipe players standing at the back of the group was casually looking around the crowd that had formed in front of them when he caught sight of Claire. He smiled at her and when he glanced down at her old stone necklace he immediately stopped playing. It was as if he had been

189

turned into stone. A fellow flute player next to him noticed he had stopped playing and gave him a light nudge in the ribs with no effect. He then turned to him to see if he was OK, and at the same time continued to play. He could see by his friend's face that something had affected him and turned to follow the direction in which he was looking. He also met Claire's eyes and he in turn ceased to play.

Within a few more seconds the whole group of eight players had stopped playing and were all looking in her direction. Claire felt extremely uncomfortable and went to move away. Before she had taken more than a few steps someone touched her on the shoulder. It was one of the older members of the pipe players. He smiled in a gentle manner bowed his head and spoke to her in a foreign language. He then turned to one of the other members of the group who in turn went to a case and took out a disk of their music. He brought it to the older man and before he returned to his place he turned to Claire and gently touched her hand. He also said something to her that she failed to comprehend.

The old man once more spoke and pressed the CD into her hand. She put her hand into her bag and got out her purse to pay him. He immediately held her hand and waved his finger indicating that he did not want any payment. He then smiled again, said a few more words and returned to the group. In one last gesture the whole group turned to her and bowed their heads.

Claire was lost for words. Nothing like this had ever happened to her before. She was now the attention of the whole crowd. She needed to get out of the limelight so she turned and quickly made her way back across the square. On reaching the corner of the street, she turned one last time and saw the group of players who were still looking in her direction. They waved to her and she waved back and then she disappeared into the crowd.

The short break in London was beginning to take its toll on Claire. Each night she got back from her roving visits in the capital the more she felt tired and weak. The day before she was due to leave for home she did not even venture out of the hotel as her body seemed to be completely drained of its energy. She just sat around her room and in the lounge of the hotel reading and watching the people coming in and out. The latter she really enjoyed doing as the visitors were from all parts of the globe. It was fascinating to see how they differed so much in their body language and how they behaved when in a group as compared with being on their own. The noisiest were a group of Japanese who were extremely excited, as it was their first day in the city. Their poor old tour guide was having big problems getting them together and then keeping them in one place whilst he attempted to organise their transport arrangements.

The quietest were the American party. Claire had been brought up to think that all Americans were very brash and noisy but this group had dispelled that assumption for good. They had come back from an arduous tour around the centre of London taking in Horse Guards Parade, Trafalgar Square, Green Park, Buckingham Palace, No 10 Downing Street and Piccadilly Circus. No wonder they were so tired, Claire thought, as that route had taken her two days to accomplish.

The men in the group had decided to get drinks from the bar and returned into the lounge holding pint glasses of beer or Guinness, rather than their usual bourbon on the rocks. The ladies had retired to their rooms to get a rest before going out for an evening meal.

The men sat around in groups of three or four. One rather plump man, slightly older than the rest, decided to sit on his own in the corner, as he wanted to quietly read his magazine. He was casually dressed in a red sweater and denim trousers, which showed up his portly stomach as he lay back in his armchair. Claire paid little attention to him and spent her time looking at the others who were recapping on their experiences of the day. There was an occasional raucous laughter instigated probably by someone telling a joke, which seemed to annoy the man in the corner as it interrupted his concentration on the article that he was reading.

After a while Claire became aware that the portly man kept glancing towards her and she could see him squinting as if to get a better picture of her. He did not look her in the eyes. He seemed to be more interested in her dress not that she was look-ing particularly smart as she had not bothered to change into anything fashionable on that day knowing that she was not ven-turing out. She pretended to look at the other people in the room and at the same time keep a watchful eye on him.

Initially she thought he was looking at her jumper but then she began to realise that the centre of his gaze was her necklace, her favourite pebble. The man kept looking at his magazine and then back to her. This went on for a good five minutes until the party organiser arrived in the room to tell them that they only had fifteen minutes before they were due to depart for their evening meal. With that the men lifted their glasses to finish their beers and commenced to leave the room. The plump man in the corner forced himself to his feet, his stomach reaching well over his belt line, and made his way past Claire towards the door. As he reached Claire he made one last glance at her neck-lace, looked into her eyes and smiled and then did a strange thing. He bent forward and placed the magazine that he had so intently been reading on the small coffee table next to Claire's chair and pointed to her and the magazine. Without any words being spoken he then went out of the room.

How puzzling she thought. She glanced down at the maga-zine, which lay face down on the table. What had he read that interested him so much and which seemed to have some relevance to her presence in the room? Could there be some personality whom she resembled, perhaps one of those slim young women who graced the fashion catwalks? She chuckled to herself. She picked up the magazine and turned it over. It was the *Time* magazine. On the front cover there was a photograph of a man standing in front of some form of mural. It was the lower left corner, which suddenly caught Claire's eye. There was a large question mark and below it was her stone! The heading across the front page was:

LAST OF THE INCAS?

Has Professor Downing discovered the last retreat of the Inca Empire? What is the significance of the lone engraving?

For the next half-an-hour Claire sat and read the intriguing article about Professor Downing's efforts in looking for the last resting place of the Incas after their flight from the Conquistadors. The article told of the finding of the carved map inside the small statuette brought to the professor by an old man who had purchased it from an antique shop in Bournemouth, and how that lead to the jungles of the Amazon rain forests and then eventually up into the high mountains of Peru.

It then went on to explain the discovery of the lost city and of the carved mural on the rock face. Until then little was known of the history of the Incas, as they did not leave many recordings because they did not have the equivalent of our alphabet. They had made carvings similar to the Egyptians but no one had been able to decipher them until now. Professor Downing's discovery of the carved mural had enabled him to translate much of the past history of the Incas. His discovery was similar to the discovery of the Rosetta Stone, which had enabled scholars to decipher the Egyptian hieroglyphics. After having spent a year at the site he had now returned to London to spend time in the archives of the British Museum looking into further recordings of Inca carvings. The article then went on to describe the history of the Inca Empire and some background about Professor Downing.

It was now late evening by the time Claire had finished reading the article. The bell for dinner had rung so she decided to eat in the hotel that night and treat herself to a half bottle of Australian Chardonnay. The meal was just what she needed to rejuvenate her body. The first course was prawns served on a bed of lettuce with a small serving of crab, followed by roast lamb with all of the trimmings and finally a choice between crème caramel, ice cream or cheese and biscuits from which Claire chose the crème caramel.

The whole meal took well over an hour, which did not leave any time for a last wander around London before returning home the following morning, so Claire went into the lounge for a nightcap before retiring to bed. She ordered a brandy from the bar, which she thought might help her to sleep and then sat in the corner of the lounge from where she could study the rest of the clientele.

There were only a few businessmen in there initially but at about ten thirty the American group came in. This time the men were accompanied by their wives who were all smartly dressed in evening wear. Claire sat back amused by the antics of some of the men who were obviously competing for the attention of one particularly attractive middle-aged lady much to the displeasure of some of the wives. As she gazed around the room she noticed the little plump man who earlier that day dropped the *Time* magazine at her table. He was looking in her direction and as their eyes met he smiled, got up and proceeded to walk in her direction.

"May I be permitted to sit with you for a few moments? I am finding my friends a little noisy over there." His accent was very broad, much like the characters she had seen on television from the southern part of America. He had a very pleasant smile, which seemed to radiate over the entire area of his large moonlike face. His most distinctive feature was his beautiful white, even teeth which must have cost a small fortune.

"Please do." replied Claire, to which the man drew up a chair and sat on the right hand side of her. One or two of the American group looked across for a few moments at their friend's movement across the room and then continued with their conversations.

"I noticed you in the foyer a couple of days ago and then yesterday in here," the man continued. "I hope you don't mind me remarking, but I thought that you did not look too well this morning at breakfast and I thought I would come over to see if you were a little better now. You seem to have got a little more colour back into your cheeks since then. Do you feel well enough to accept a brandy from me, which is for medicinal purposes?" He gave another broad smile.

"That would be really nice," said Claire. He motioned to the barman and placed an order to include a pint of best bitter. "I love your English beer. Most of the beers in the States are bottled and do not possess the flavours of your beers. Whenever I

194

come across to England I try to taste as many beers as possible. I am not an alcoholic", he chuckled, " but I have acquired quite a taste for these beverages."

"Do you come across very often?" enquired Claire.

"About once every two years now that I have retired. I am keen on historical buildings and as England is steeped in history and has so many buildings with wonderful classical architectural features I tend to head for here rather than other parts of the globe. The only other rival to London would probably be Prague."

They chatted for well over an hour. Claire felt very relaxed in his presence, probably due to the number of brandies she had drunk in the small space of time she had been talking to him. Conversation drifted from interesting visits in London to what their favourite meals were.

By eleven o'clock most of the American party had retired to their individual rooms leaving only five people in the bar area. This did not include the barman who had shut up shop at the precise stroke of eleven having called last drinks two minutes too early.

The smiling man eventually brought the conversation around to the magazine.

"I see that you have been reading the *Time* magazine that I placed on the table near to where you were sitting yesterday," he said pointing to the magazine, which was lying on her lap. "I hoped that you would pick it up as I thought that you might find one of the articles particularly interesting. The one on the front page."

Claire glanced down at the front page and immediately focused on the inlay of the stone. The smiling man noticed her concentration on the corner of the page.

"Quite a resemblance wouldn't you say? I thought the necklace from a distance resembled the stone carving but under closer scrutiny I would say it is an identical replica. It is amazing how quickly entrepreneurs catch onto something. Did you buy it in London? It looks like stone. Clever what they can do with fibreglass and plastics nowadays."

Claire automatically reached up with her hand and held the stone in her thumb and first finger.

"It's not made of plastic. It is a real pebble." She then told the story of when she was very young and how she had gone to her favourite beach at Sandway and how the stone had appeared to come to her.

"What a lovely story. Amazing, in actual fact. Too much of a coincidence if you ask me. What did you think of the actual article by that professor? What was his name?"

"Professor Downing. I found it absolutely fascinating. They were an amazing civilisation. When I return home I intend going to the library and finding out more of the Inca people. It must have been one of the Professor's most memorable moments when he came across the ruined city."

"Did you read the whole article?"

"Yes," said Claire." I actually read it twice."

"Then you saw that he is giving a lecture tomorrow morning in the British Museum. I am thinking of going along to listen to him. You would be more than welcome to come along with me. It would make the taxi ride half the price." He chuckled to himself and gave her a wicked little smile.

"I would love to go along but I am returning to Plymouth tomorrow morning."

"That's the trouble with working. You can't please yourself when you wish to do things."

"No. I'm not working at the present moment. I am between jobs." Claire did not wish to go into the details of why she was not working and thus probably embarrass the man. A little white lie once in a while didn't hurt.

"There you are then. You do not have any excuse for not going with me tomorrow. All you have to do is to extend your visit for one more day. From what I can see the hotel is not too busy for this time of the year, so you should have no trouble in keeping your room for an extra day. What do you say to that?"

There was a long pause as Claire tried to grasp the implications if she did stay for another day. It would not affect anything really. She could easily change her booking on the train as she had an open ticket, and there was no one at home to worry about. She did not have a job and provided that she could remain in the hotel for another day there was nothing else that would prevent here from remaining where she was. She would love to hear more about the Inca people so she decided in just under a minute to stay. It amazed her how she had come to such a quick decision. A few months ago such a decision would have taken her hours in weighing up the pros and cons.

"Yes, I would like to accompany you to the talk tomorrow provided I can extend my stay here and provided you let me pay the taxi fare!"

The round faced man smiled. "Done, and as you seem so enthusiastic you can treat me to lunch for making you extend your holiday."

Before retiring to bed Claire went to the front desk and was relieved to find that her room was still vacant and so she booked it for one more night. That night, sleep did not come easily as she was so excited with the thought of the lecture.

She received her early morning call at seven thirty as she wanted to pack her bags before going to the lecture. She could then leave them with the hall porter and pick them up later and then go direct to the station. She was a little annoyed with herself for going to bed late the previous night. Usually she was in bed by ten-thirty and last night her head did not hit the pillow until well past one o'clock. Never mind, she thought, as she had allowed herself plenty of time to pack and have a leisurely breakfast.

The breakfast bell went at eight-thirty. It was possible to arrange for earlier calls but most of the guests came down at that time. By the time they had finished eating and gone for a final visit to the bathroom the city rush hour would have been over, which meant less crowding on the underground and easier access to taxis.

Claire had the full English breakfast plus toast and coffee as she would probably not have time for lunch. Her new friend came into the dining-room just after her, gave her a wave and gave the thumbs up sign before sitting with the rest of the American travellers. At nine-thirty they both met in the foyer and after a few greeting words went out into the street to hail a taxi. One came within a few minutes and ten minutes later they were standing on the pavement outside the Natural History Museum.

"What a magnificent building. It must have taken years to build," said the smiling man. "The only building to rival that in the States would be the Senate in Washington. We managed to transport London Bridge to the desert so I might make an offer for this establishment before I leave." This was followed by his little infectious chuckle.

Although this was Claire's second visit to this building she still felt overawed by its immensity and grandeur. They mounted the steps and entered the building between a set of enormous pillars. Inside were various plans of the outlay of the building and notices explaining where the morning meetings and lectures were to be held. Her newly found friend, who she had found out was called William, approached one of the uniformed curators and enquired where the lecture on Inca Culture was to be held. He took him over to a map that was displayed on the wall and pointed out the level and room in which it was taking place. William then thanked the guide and turned to Claire.

"We have three quarters of an hour to kill so why don't we have a cup of coffee and a cake in the cafeteria. I have been informed by friends who have visited London on a number of occasions in the past that if you ever want a good cup of tea and a light snack you can't go far wrong than visiting a museum or art gallery. Also the washrooms, or your so-called toilets, are always very well presented, not that I am suggesting that you go before the lecture. I must sound like a school teacher, sorry."

Claire laughed. She was enjoying being teased by him.

"Yes, I could do with a cup of coffee and although I have had an enormous breakfast I still feel a little peckish, so I might have a bun as well, provided that you let me pay the bill." He motioned her towards the stairs. The canteen was on the lower floor and not too busy as it was quite early in the day. The coffee was strong and they both settled for buttered toasted teacakes. It seemed that no sooner had they sat down than it was time to get up again to go to the lecture. They both made a visit to the bathroom and then proceeded to walk up to the second level to room seven.

Chapter Thirteen

Room seven housed the largest lecture theatre in the museum. Claire estimated that there must have been seating for over four hundred people. One would have to be a brave person to stand down in the depths of this theatre, she thought, and to be able to look up into an expanse of faces and then have the flair to hold their attention for possibly well over an hour.

Claire and William sat in the fifth tier of seating which was stepped at such an angle that no matter how tall the person was who happen to sit in front of you, one would always be able to see. The seats were made of a synthetic type of leather, which made terrible sounds if one slid around in them. Claire thought this was a major design fault as there was no possibility of fidgeting around during a long lecture. She wondered how many boring lecturers had received that form of treatment.

The room gradually filled until there were no seats left and the overflow was ushered to the rear of the banking. Claire hoped that none of them suffered with vertigo, as they seemed to be precariously perched way above from where she sat. The front three rows of seats had been reserved for the press such was the high profile of the lecture.

A sudden hush came over the gathering when a large teak door at the rear of the auditorium slowly opened to reveal two men neither of whom resembled the professor that Claire had seen on the front of the *Time* magazine. They moved across to the highly polished table whose only ornaments were a large cut glass jug which contained water and two tumblers placed there for the speakers in case of parched throats. The younger of the two held an armful of papers, which he placed on the desk. The other man, who looked very distinguished in his dark grey suit and longish silver hair, spoke in a cultured voice.

"Good morning, ladies and gentlemen. Welcome to this morning's lecture on the Machu Picchu Extension Site. Not a very inspiring name for such an amazing discovery but we have not been able to agree on what we should call it.

"I would like to start with an apology. I am afraid that Professor Jason Downing is unable to be with us today, as he had to return to Peru last night. If you have not already heard, there have been a number of landslides in the Machu Picchu area in the recent months and yesterday we received news that there had been a minor earthquake in that vicinity. No other reports have come out since then so we do not know if any of the Inca ruins have been affected. You can no doubt appreciate why the professor was so eager to get back. Judging by the number of press here today they have also got wind of the earth tremor. Rather than rush out there themselves and risk being injured in a landslide they appear to prefer to sit on a comfortable seat in complete safety and then try to convince their readers that the information that they have put into   print is from first-hand experience. No doubt they will claim exorbitant expenses for flying out there rather than a ten pence bus ride to this establishment."

Claire expected the press to react in a most vociferous manner to his statement but was surprised to hear most of them laugh out loud. They were used to this old professor and obviously enjoyed his sense of humour.

"If I may be permitted to continue," he said staring at the press in a most unnerving manner, treating them like a class of unruly pupils. "Fortunately for us we have been extremely lucky to find a replacement for Professor Downing at such short notice. This extremely young and fit athlete is none other than Doctor Jules Venning who, as some of you will know, was with Professor Downing's expedition when they discovered the Extension. Oh, how I detest calling such an historically significant site as this by such a name. I will endeavour to call a meeting immediately after this lecture to give the site a proper name. Perhaps the press could come up with something? I am sure the *Sun* newspaper would find that quite an easy task considering they named themselves after the Sun God. If you use such a connection as a leader on your front page I will expect some huge amount of remuneration from your editor." The three rows of journalists turned and faced the poor Sun reporter and once again let out a howl of laughter.

"Gentlemen, let us proceed. I present Doctor Jules Venning."

The Doctor took his place behind the large shining desk whilst the audience gave their customary round of applause. He did not seem at all perturbed by the vast wall of faces that was looking expectantly down upon him. He took his time arranging his various papers, poured a glass of water and took a small sip from it before beginning his talk.

"I feel quite guilty standing here before you. I should have gone back with Professor Downing but he insisted that we should not let you down by not making a presentation, especially seeing that there may have been a possible descendant from the Royal Inca family in the audience." He looked towards the poor old Sun reporter who shifted uncomfortably in his seat whilst his colleagues tried to stifle their amusement. He was certainly going to take some stick when he went for a recess.

"I won't spend much time with you on the history of the Inca Empire as no doubt you have read various articles in that field. I would however like to give you a little insight on their amazing building techniques. Their ability to move huge great stones and prepare them for building purposes still in this present day bewilders the most prominent architects. They were and still are great bridge builders. They had to be in order to travel across steep sided gorges with fast flowing rivers swollen with huge amounts of glacial waters. It was probably due to these bridges that the Incas survived for such a long time. When under attack they simply cut down the bridges. As this was the only way of crossing the rivers, the opposing warring parties gave up their pursuits, as it would have been an impossible to build their own bridge under the fire of the Inca soldiers.

"A few years ago I witnessed such a bridge being replaced by a whole village. The women and children collected grasses from

201

the hillsides and wove them into fine strands of string. The men then wove these strands into thicker strands until they were about ten centimetres in diameter and then stretched these across the river during the summer months when the river was at its lowest and thus replaced the older bridge. I mention this act of brilliance as we think this was the main reason why the marauding Conquistadors never discovered Machu Picchu.

"If you have ever been to Cuzco, the 'Pucara' or citadels that surround this city would no doubt have amazed you. The most majestic of these is the one called 'Sacsahuaman'. On close inspection of these buildings one is always mystified how a culture that did not posses the wheel was able to move such large stones and then, after so meticulously carving them to fit exactly, were able to lift them into place. It is almost impossible to slide a thin knife-edge between any of these huge building blocks. Even present-day technology would find it extremely difficult to replicate their works, in the inner reaches of the Fold Mountains."

The professor momentarily stopped talking and took a drink from his glass.

"If I may be permitted to digress at this stage and dwell for a few moments on the Inca Empire. The Incas descended from powerful families that were originally established around Cuzco in the heart of the Cordillera. It was the Inca Pachacuti who in the fifteenth century built the formidable Empire that was discovered by the dazzled Spaniards.

"The people of Cuzco referred to their Empire as 'Tahuantisuyu' the 'Land of the Four Quarters'. Cuzco was the 'navel' of the Empire and from its centre radiated four great sectors. They were orientated to the cardinal points. To the north stretched 'Chinchaysayn', to the south 'Collasuyu', where the Lapaqa Lords of Lake Titicaca lived. 'Cuntisuyu' extended to the west and finally 'Antisuyu'opened onto the Amazonian piedmont, which the Incas never really managed to subjugate despite several attempts.

"There was a succession of twelve Inca Dynasties at Cuzco, the thirteenth being Atahualpa. It was the ninth Sovereign

Pachacuti who rebuilt Cuzco, constructing roads and promoting the cult of 'Viracocha'.

"Why mention these facts? Well, we think it may give some light as to the origins of the newly found site near to Machu Picchu. This now brings me to why you gentlemen are here today," he nodded to the front three rows of journalists.

"Is it the Legend of Piatiti? For those who are not acquainted with this expression it stems from the story of a group of disaffected Incas who were supposed to have fled into the jungle taking thousands of llamas loaded with magnificent golden artefacts. Anyone who enters the forest east of Cuzco will come across countless tales of Paititi.

"One famous story is of a peasant who followed the trail of one of his lost animals for several days into the cloud forests. He eventually became completely disorientated stumbling through the dense undergrowth, finally collapsing in complete exhaustion. When he regained consciousness, he found that a band of hunting natives had found him and taken him to their village, Piatiti! Legend has it that the Indians presented him with a golden ear of corn and led him back onto his trail, which eventually took him home. He never was able to find the site again.

"'Titi' is the Agmara word for wild mountain cat. Legend has it that pumas or jaguars guard the lost city.

"An American journalist named Bob Nichols set off with two Frenchmen and travelled up the Shinkikibeni River into the Pantiacolla Mountains in search of the lost city. They eventually came across a massive rock face covered with ancient Petroglyphs. From there they followed a stone road until it was lost in a steep sided gorge, which proved to be impenetrable. Word got back via messenger of their exploits and they were never heard of again.

"A Japanese adventurer, Yoshiharo Sekino, met a group of Machiguenga Indians who claimed to have killed the American and his two French associates. These Indians are said to be the guardians of the Piatiti.

"So have we found the lost city of Piatiti? Let me pre-empt one of the questions that I feel you will undoubtedly ask, 'Why has it taken so long in this day and age of technology to find the lost city? Wouldn't a satellite have picked it out during one of its surveys?'

"The reason why it has taken so long is the situation of the site. From the air it would not have been noticed even flying in by helicopter, which incidentally is an almost impossible task. Due to its unique proximity to the jungles below it has for centuries been camouflaged by a carpet of thick lichen. The mist rising up from the jungle is rich in minerals which when mixed with the cooler air higher up in the mountain makes the perfect environment for the growth of the lichen. Only this form of vegetation will grow there so it has proved a relatively easy task to clear the site.

"What we found there has given us a far clearer insight into the history of the Inca people. Professor Downing's discovery of a huge mural carved in stone might be the key to being able to translate the writings of the Incas, which up until now has baffled historians the world over. He compares this discovery to the Rosetta Stone, which enabled historians to decipher the Egyptian hieroglyphics.

"Getting back to the site itself. There is no doubt at all that it is an Inca settlement. The buildings are constructed of large blocks of rock all of which meticulously fit into one another. How they managed to transport the blocks to this site remains a mystery. The most amazing discovery other than the mural was the layout of the town. It was identical to the layout of Cuzco, which suggests that the ninth Sovereign, Pachacuti, may have constructed it. It was constructed with a central square with four radiating segments just like that in Cuzco. In the centre of the square is a large flagstone which has on it the engraving which is featured on the front of the *Time* magazine. Whilst Professor Downing is having some success with the translating of the cliff mural he is completely baffled by the carving on the centre stone, which seems to resemble a pebble."

Claire's heart jumped a beat at the mention of a pebble.

The Doctor continued. "That's the only way we could explain it to someone. The emblem keeps popping up all over the place. It's the Doctor's personal enigma. He is determined to find out why it is included in so many writings even though it does not appear to have any form of translation. However this is a minor point so we won't dwell upon it.

"To the present time we have not discovered any great amounts of gold. In fact we have discovered no gold at all. We have, however, found numerous articles of historical value and importance, which is beginning to indicate that this settlement may have been the last stronghold of the Inca Empire. There is little that I can add on the discovery, which was described in the *Time* magazine. I am open to questions after which I will show you some slides that I took of the buildings in the settlement."

He was immediately bombarded by questions from all parts of the lecture theatre, which lasted a good fifteen minutes and would have continued had it not been for the intervention of the first old professor.

At the conclusion of the last question the doctor called for the lights to be dimmed and began showing a spectacular series of slides. The audience watched in awe.

"I have one last slide to show you. I call it 'The Annoyance' for each time I show it I know that it annoys Professor Downing." He put up onto the screen the flagstone at the centre of the square. It was Claire's pebble. As soon as she saw it she knew she had to go to Machu Picchu.

The professor sat down amid a loud show of appreciation from his captive audience.

The older professor then stood up. "I can see from your ovation that you enjoyed Professor Jules Venning's talk as much as I did. Thank you, Jules, for giving us your time this morning. We will keep you no longer as I know that you wish to return to Peru to be with the Doctor as soon as possible. Thank you all for being such an attentive audience. I look forward to purchasing tomorrow's edition of the *Sun* newspaper when I hope to be that much richer!"

Once again the reporter reddened up but managed a laugh along with his colleagues. Five minutes later Claire and William were back in the cafeteria having a nice cup of tea.

"Well, what do you think of that then?" said William.

"I thoroughly enjoyed the whole procedure. Absolutely fascinating."

"And the stone?" he questioned.

"What about the stone?" she replied.

"The stone in the centre of the square was a replica of your stone. That is too much of a coincidence, Claire. It's a pity we were unable to see the professor after the lecture. I'm sure he would have been fascinated to see your pebble. You surely can't let it go at that and simply go back to Plymouth tomorrow. You have to do something."

"I have decided to go to Machu Picchu within the week if that is at all possible."

She was amazed to hear herself pronounce those words. William was just as amazed, as he was not expecting any response from Claire and certainly not such a drastic one as that.

"Well, when you really make up your mind you really do! I will not be so presumptuous to ask if you know what that entails. I know that you are capable of anything from what I have seen of your character over the last few days. Good on you. Go for it." And that is precisely what she did. That night she sat down with a pencil and paper and planned out the next few days. For the moment the most important thing on her list was whether she would be able to stay for another at least five days. She picked up the phone next to her bed and rang the front desk.

"How may I help you?" came a very pleasant voice over the phone.

"This is room 45. Would it be at all possible for me to remain in this room for another five days, please?"

"Just let me have a look at our bookings. You seem to be making a habit of remaining for extra periods at our hotel. You obvious are enjoying your stay in the capital and we are just as pleased to have you staying with us. Yes, your room is not required until the weekend. I will book you in straight away. Is there anything else that we can be of assistance for you?"

"Yes. Can you tell me where the nearest phone box is as I will have to make a number of calls tomorrow morning?"

"Why don't you use the phone that you are using at the moment? We can give you an outside line and our rates are not much more than a normal call from a box. It would save you standing out in the cold and you could even have a cup of tea whilst making your calls."

Claire felt a little silly. Why did she not think of that herself? Never having possessed her own phone and always having to go down to the phone at the bottom of her road the thought of phoning from the hotel had just not occurred to her.

"What a great idea. That would be much simpler for me. Thank you very much for your help."

"We are here to make your stay as pleasant as possible, good night."

The next morning after another large cooked breakfast, Claire retired to her room and commenced to make her phone calls. The first was to her next-door neighbour.

"Hello, Mrs Pearson. This is Claire here. How are things at home?"

"Hello, Claire. Lovely to hear your voice. Everything is fine. I have been into your house a few times to check to see if everything is in order. All is fine. Weather hasn't been particularly good. We have had a lot of rain so all my washing is hanging all over the house. How are you? Are you having a lovely time? Is the weather better than down here? It always seems to rain here in Plymouth. Perhaps I should take a trip to London like you." Claire smiled at the last remark. No way would Mrs Pearson survive in this environment.

"Everything is fine with me, Mrs Pearson. So good that I have decided to stay on for another five days. I wonder if you could do me a few favours? I need to notify the milkman as I left a note asking him to start delivering tomorrow. Also if you could nip over to Robbie's the newsagent and stop my Evening Herald until further notice. Could you check my mail? I don't mind you opening them up as they will only be bills. If you come across anything else can you phone me on the following number. When you make the phone call ask the operator to reverse the call which means that I will pay for it so that it does not end up on your phone bill. Sorry to ask you to do so many things for me."

"My dear, that's nothing for me to do for you considering how much you have done for me in the past. I will start immediately you put the phone down. Now you just run along and enjoy yourself and forget this end of the line."

"Just one more thing, Mrs Pearson. If you are going past the doctor's surgery would you just nip in and say that I am just fine and enjoying my stay in London. Many thanks. Bye." And with that she rang off.

The next call was to her bank. She needed to sort out her finances. She got on to direct enquiries and after dialling a number and then pressing various buttons in response to numerous questions from a recorded message eventually got to someone who could deal with her account. She had no idea where the person was based but they knew her account number and after a few security checks asked how they could be of any assistance. It was so much better in the old days when you actually spoke to someone in your own branch. Far more personal, thought Claire.

"I would like to know how much is left in my personal account, please?"

"Just bear with me for a moment whilst I get it up on my screen. To the nearest pound you have two hundred and twenty five pounds in your current account and five hundred and eighty in your reserve account." Nowhere near enough thought Claire for what she had intended to do over the next month.

"How do I go about arranging a loan? You see I will need to borrow in the region of five thousand pounds over the next few days."

"I am afraid that I cannot advise on such information. You actually will need to speak to one of our financial advisors. There are numerous ways that you can borrow such monies but you will need to see someone who can explain the best method for you. What I suggest is for you to call into your local branch and arrange to meet such an adviser."

"That's impossible for me to do as I am at present staying in a hotel in London and my local branch of my bank is in Plymouth."

"Yes, that does present a small problem for you. Which hotel are you staying at?"

"The Royal Ascot."

"Just bear with me for a few moments and I will see if I can be of better assistance to you." He switched over to the 'Green Sleeves, musical recording and after a few minutes came back on the line. "I have been in contact with a branch of your bank only a few minutes drive by taxi from where you are at the present moment. They would be in the position to see you some time this morning if that is convenient with you. I will give you their telephone number. When you make the call ask for a Mr. Allen and mention our telephone conversation. Will that help you at all?"

"That's ideal. Thank you for all your help. I will get in contact with Mr. Allen immediately." She then rang off and proceeded to make herself a cup of tea from the kettle and various sugars and biscuits situated by the side of her bed that the hotel had supplied.

By ten-thirty she had arranged an appointment at the bank and within the hour she was sitting with Mr. Allen.

"Would you care for a cup of tea or coffee? I am due to restock on my caffeine reserves and around about this time my secretary usually makes me a cup."

"Thank you very much. I would appreciate a cup of coffee."

"Biscuits?"

"No, thank you. I had a large breakfast this morning before coming out which should last me for almost the rest of the day."

"Now, from my conversation with the young man that you initially made contact with I gather that you wished to borrow a sum in the region of five thousand pounds. With such a large amount involved I have to enquire as to how the money is to be used. I have already looked into your various accounts and made a number of enquiries about yourself. Would I be correct in saying that you do not have any other accounts such as Visa? "

"No, the only savings I have are with you. I have never had the need to use a Visa card or any other form of borrowing cards. I don't owe any money at all. I have always made it my policy never to borrow. I must tell you that at the present moment I am not employed and will not be working for the foreseeable future."

"I appreciate you being so honest with me. Your not having a position of work immediately narrows your field of borrowing. Do you have any form of collateral that you could use against the loan?"

"What do you mean by collateral? I haven't come across that terminology before."

"If I can give you an example. If you possess the deeds of your house and you do not have a full mortgage on the property we could hold your deeds and when the loan has been repaid with the acquired interest we would return the deeds to you. If, however, you were unable to repay the loan in the specified amount of time we may have to take possession of the house. We would then have to sell it, take out all outstanding monies plus any extra expenses. We would then return to you any monies left over. That would be the worst scenario for you."

"I do have my own house. My mother left it to me. The deeds are with my solicitor and there is no outstanding mortgage on the property. I would be quite willing to use this in order to borrow the money."

"To make things easy for you as you would like to borrow the money quite quickly, if you give me your written permission I will contact your solicitor today to make sure that the house is in your name and that there is no mortgage on. Also I will need to find out its present value so I will have to have it surveyed. If all is well we could solve your little problem within the week. Usually this procedure takes many weeks but I do have a few favours owing to me so I will call upon them. Now we have your hotel number so as to get in contact with you. If you sit down with my secretary and give her the details of your solicitor etc. we will get on with the enquiries immediately."

"That's very kind of you. Thank you for all that you are doing for me."

"Look forward to seeing you at the end of the week with your loan, Miss Axworthy."

They shook hands. Claire then sat down with his secretary for a further ten minutes and then went out into the busy streets of London once more.

During the next three days she started making various enquiries on whether or not a visa was required to enter into Peru, which was the more direct airline to fly with, what vaccinations were required, currency, medical insurance, etc. On one of her previous excursions into London Claire had noticed that one of the roads leading off from Piccadilly Circus seemed to have a lot of Travel Agencies and Airline Offices stretched along its length and it was there that she decided to make her first enquiries into the prices of flights to Peru. She had decided against going to a so-called "bucket shop" for the time being although they had a very good reputation for presenting cheap reliable travel with most of the leading airlines. She chose the travel agent which seemed to be the biggest and the busiest. She had to wait her turn in a queue and eventually sat down by a desk, which was manned by a smart young lady.

"Good morning, Madame. And how can I help you?"

"I would like to enquire which is the best and most economical way to get to Peru? I would very much like to visit the old ruins of Machu Picchu. I believe I have to fly to Cuzco first."

"Your information is correct up to a point. Initially you have to fly into Lima. From there you then have to fly to Cuzco, which is a most spectacular flight of about one hour over the Andes. Aero Continente, Lan Peru, and Trans Peru are reputable airlines for this part of the flight. You then have the choice of travelling to the ruins by a narrow-gauge railway from Cuzco to Aguas Calientes, which ranks one of the worlds' most scenic railways or by helicopter. The helicopter costs one hundred dollars each way whilst the train costs thirty dollars 'backpackers' express', fifty dollars 'autovagon' which includes drinks and snacks or the 'Inca Class' with breakfast and afternoon tea at eighty dollars. The rail fares are for return journeys.

"With regards to accommodation most people decide to stay in Cuzco, which is supposed, to be the oldest continuously occupied settlement in South America. From there you can visit

Machu Picchu on a day trip. The other option open to you is to stay in the Sanctuary Lodge, which was formerly the Machu Picchu Ruins. The cost to stay there would be on average two hundred and fifty dollars per night. It can justify its prices as it is situated just outside the entrance gate to the ruins. What I can do for you is to print out all of that information plus anything else which I think would be relevant to your trip. For example you could stay in the nearby Machu Picchu El Pueblo Hotel which is a series of bungalows along the Urubamba River, one hundred and seventy three dollars per room."

This young lady certainly knew her job, thought Claire.

"Yes, that would be ideal if you could gather all of that information for me. As I am staying in a hotel would it be possible for me to call back here later in the day and pick up the details?"

"No problem. I can have it ready for you in under the hour."

"That's fine then. What I will do is a little shopping and call back later."

Claire then went out into the crowds once more and began looking for a Boots.

She had heard from a friend a number of years ago that if you were thinking of going abroad and you did not have time to make an appointment with a doctor you could go along to a pharmacy to find out the necessary vaccinations that might be needed when visiting a foreign country. Apparently they had a booklet which was continually updated from the World Health Association indicating the possible types of infections one might catch in a particular country and what steps one should take before going there to combat this. The information that she received made it necessary for her to make an appointment with a doctor in order to be given the necessary injections which she did the following day.

Just over an hour later she returned to the travel agent to pick up all of the collated information.

"Welcome back," said the jovial young lady. "Trust you had a good shop. I've managed to get all of the information that you requested. There is one slight problem, which might arise during your trip, which I must advise you of. If you haven't already heard there have been some landslides over the last few months in the region. They have had a very bad one only yesterday. There is therefore the possibility that on arriving at your destination you might be prevented from travelling the final few miles to the actual ruins as the military may put the railway and all paths leading to Machu Picchu out of bounds. Our head office have asked us for the present moment to try to persuade travellers to postpone their trips for at least a few weeks until the situation in that area is made clear. My feeling is that if you can postpone your trip for at least a few weeks then do so, as you may end up paying a large amount of money and not reaching your final destination. If I were you I would take all this information with you and sit down tonight and work out the pros and cons of whether or not to go. I will give you my card which has a special number on it that will bypass the queuing sequence on the phone system and put you straight onto my phone here."

"That's very kind of you for putting in so much work on my behalf. I know that is your job but I think that you have been more than helpful. I will do as you have suggested and give you a call first thing tomorrow morning." With that, she again thanked the young lady, picked up the brochure containing all of the information and returned to her hotel.

During the afternoon she made a few more phone calls. One of them was to the Peruvian Embassy to enquire if they had any more information about the state of affairs with regards to landfalls around the ruined city and whether it was still possible to visit it. They were unable to give her any more news other than that that she already possessed. They suggested the same as the tour operator, put the trip off for the time being. That night Claire was a little disillusioned, as all of her well-made plans had seemed to have gone to waste. She spent the rest of the afternoon reading through the literature about the travel arrangements. By the time the dinner bell rang Claire was absolutely exhausted. She had contemplated not going down for the meal but decided that she would not bother to change her clothes and just go down for a quick bite and then retire to bed early.

She enjoyed the starter, which was a leaf of lettuce covered with prawns in a most delicious sauce. By the end of that she began to feel a little better.

"Good evening, young lady," said a voice from behind her left shoulder, which she immediately recognise as her smiling friend William." How have you got on with your enquiries today?" He could see by her tired look that things had not gone as well as she had hoped.

"Not too well. The Embassy and the travel agency are both trying to put me off from going on the trip for the time being. They have suggested to leave it for a few weeks until more is known of the landslides over there. The lady at the travel agency was quite right in pointing out that I could go all the way there and find the entry into the valley which leads to Machu Picchu was blocked off. I really do not know what to do."

"May I join you for dinner? Nothing worse than eating on your own unless it means eating with and old inquisitive natterbag of an American!" He smiled and she laughed.

"I would love you to join me."

"What are you having for your main course, Claire?"

"Roast beef and Yorkshire pudding."

"That sounds very appetising. I think I will have the same." He waved to one of the table waitresses. "I would like the same main course as this young lady. You needn't bother bringing a starter. Oh, I would also like a bottle of the house red, preferably an Australian Cabernet Sauvignon. If you haven't got that I will settle for a Chilean one, very good for the heart."

"Now, Claire, we have got to sort you out. This afternoon when you were out someone from Plymouth phoned asking to speak to you. It was a Doctor Bradden. He asked the receptionist, as you were not available, if there was anyone in the hotel who had befriended you during your stay in the hotel. She told him that she had seen us on a number of occasions talking in the bar and appeared to be getting on well together, so he asked to speak with me. He had heard from a Mrs Pearson who I gather is your next door neighbour that you had decided to stay on in London for a few extra days so he thought he would give you a ring to see how you were." He didn't mention that the doctor had asked him to keep a very special eye on her. The doctor did not disclose what was wrong with her but did say that she was a very brave young lady and that she should take every opportunity to do as many things as possible whilst away from Plymouth.

Whilst they ate their dinner they discussed in more depth what had happened during the day. William listened keenly and kept thinking of what the doctor had said about Claire. He had only known her for a very short period of time but agreed with the doctor that she was a very special young lady and he would keep a special eye on her.

They finished the Chilean red had a dessert and then retired to the lounge to have their coffee. As a special treat William ordered two large cognacs to have with their coffees. Both felt much more relaxed by the end of the coffee.

"Now, Claire I know it's none of my business but I would like to express my feelings as to what I think you should do. I am old enough to be your father and having never had any children I'm going to speak to you as perhaps a father would do to his daughter." He leant across the table and took her hand in his.

"When I look back over my life there have been a number of occasions when I should have done certain things that would have changed my life for the better and I did not. I was too calculating a person to make such dramatic changes at that time. I'm not saying that I am not happy at this present time but I could have been happier. Life is too short. I wish I were in your situation at the present moment. Claire, everything seems to be stacked against you but you must go against the tide. You have given yourself a mission in life now and you should follow it through no matter what. From what I have gleaned from listening to you and my conversation with Doctor Bradden you seem to have nothing to lose, so go for it. I rest my case."

Claire could feel the warmth and sincerity in his voice and thought that he would have made a really nice dad for someone.

"Thanks, William. I really appreciate what you have just

215

said. I had decided that I would travel to Peru even though everyone is trying to persuade me not to go. You have given me the final incentive to go ahead with my plans. Tomorrow I will get in touch with the travel agents and book my ticket." She felt the grip on her hand tighten.

"Good for you, Claire. You are going to be a very busy girl over the next few days. If I can be of any help at all just let me know. It's getting quite late and I have to travel down to Canterbury tomorrow morning with the group. We are having a look at your famous Cathedral. Should be back in time for the evening meal, so see you then."

They both got up and William gave Claire a little hug and kiss on the cheek. Yes, she thought, he would have made the perfect father.

William was correct when he said the next few days would be very busy for Claire. Her feet didn't seem to touch the ground She tried to get some further information on the landslides in Peru but with no success. The only information she was able to get was a few scanty reports from the newspapers. They gave the impression that there was chaos on the track leading to Machu Picchu. There had been a minor slip on the narrow approach road, which was proving extremely difficult to repair due to the problems with getting heavy machinery up the narrow road, which was jammed with tour buses. Things did not look too good. Claire however had decided to go no matter what reports were coming out of the district.

Much of the second day was spent getting together some form of wardrobe. She had come to London with mostly heavy clothing. She had nothing, which would prove suitable for a hot climate. It was going to take some good planning as to what to take. She only wanted to handle one medium-sized suit case plus a small form of hand luggage. She had heard so many people have problems with losing their cases in transit that she planned to have a reserve amount of clothes in her hand luggage just in case of the inevitable. Clothing had to cater for the hot humid time spent in Cuzco and the cooler temperature of the mountains. She had found out that the temperatures could

216

range from thirty degrees right down to freezing which meant having both summer and winter forms of clothing. She made sure that she had gloves, warm hat as most of ones' body heat goes out through the head, thick fleece with a form of silk lining, walking boots, the brown trainer type, plus two jumpers and warm trousers which were close-fitting like a track suit bottom. The rest of her packing was lighter clothing including a pair of shorts, which she had never before worn at home, plus the necessary insect repellents and ladies toiletries.

On the third morning she received a phone call from the front desk stating that her bank would like her to phone them in order to make an appointment. Two hours later she was sitting in the office of the bank facing the financial adviser.

"It's a pleasure to see you again, Miss Axworthy. All is well. I must admit I was pleasantly surprised to see how quickly we were able to get in touch with your solicitors and how quickly all the relevant paper work went through. The house was valued at forty three thousand pounds, which is more than is necessary for your loan. In actual fact you could have a far greater amount of loan if you so wished. All I have to do is to point out the various points in the contract and explain the additional amounts that will have to be added to the final loan. If this meets your approval all you have to do is to sign and the money is yours."

They sat for about fifteen minutes looking at the various binding clauses to the contract at the end of which Claire signed on the dotted line. There were then a few things to sign after which five thousand pounds was transferred to Claire's current account.

As she was leaving the office for the last time the financial adviser asked, "As a matter of interest, and you do not have to tell me if you wish to keep it confidential, what do you intend spending it on?"

"I'm going to Machu Picchu," and with those words Claire walked out of the office.

That night Claire was initially sad to find out that the American contingent was returning to the States the following morning. She had hoped to spend a little more time with William before he returned to his homeland.

At seven-thirty Claire went down to the dining room and was very pleased to see William sitting at her table.

"How is the intrepid traveller this evening? Have you made all the final arrangements?" he said with his normal broad smile.

"Yes. All is in hand. I have collected the airline tickets today and changed some of my sterling. I have even managed to book some accommodation when I arrive in Cuzco. I'm off in two days' time. I see that you are returning to America tomorrow morning."

"Wrong. My friends are going back tomorrow but I have extended my stay for three more days. You don't think I would let you leave this country without some form of a send-off? Can't have you departing from the airport on such an adventure without someone waving to you. We have two more days before you leave and seeing you have got everything in hand that will allow us to see a few more sights."

Claire was over the moon. The next two days she would never forget. They spent the whole time together visiting various museums, saw an amazing view of London from the Eye, went to a recital in the Royal Albert Hall, had lunch on the Embankment and then walked along to the Globe Theatre and then crossed the new Millennium Bridge and onto St. Paul's Cathedral.

Over dinner on the final night William made a little speech to Claire.

"Claire, it has been an honour to have met you. You have made my stay in London a most memorable one that I will never forget. I would like you to accept this little present from me. It's a small travel book of Peru. Not too heavy to carry and it will not take up too much room in you case. Don't open it until you get on the plane. Inside the front cover I have stuck a business card of mine with my address, e-mail address and telephone number. We will not look upon this evening as a farewell as I hope that you will come and visit me in America once you have finished your trek to Peru. Now tomorrow I will help you to the airport with your cases and make sure you get your plane."

Claire was very touched by his words and tried to hide it from him by making a joke, which didn't work as a tear still managed to find it's way into the corner of her eye. William noticed it but said nothing. He couldn't have spoken in any case as he had to fight back a lump in his throat.

Next morning at breakfast neither of them attempted the full English fry up. Instead they settled for some cereal and fruit. Ten-thirty the taxi arrived and by eleven thirty they were standing in the departure lounge. Neither wanted to say very much. They had agreed to keep farewells short. They gave one another a short hug. Claire could not resist giving William a little kiss on his cheek and then she quickly walked towards the departure doors not daring to look back again. She knew that he would keep an eye on her until the very last moment, which he did. That was the last he saw of Claire Axworthy, a young lady he would remember until his dying days.

Chapter Fourteen

Never judge a parcel by its packaging, a picture by its frame or a sheep by its clothing. First impressions can be extremely misleading. Not so with John McCormack. He looked tough and he was tough. He looked evil and he was evil. He looked extremely strong and he was extremely strong. He was about six feet three inches tall, weighed in at fourteen and a half stone, had a dark, rugged, weathered skin with only one feature interrupting his unlined face and that was a prominent jagged scar which ran down the left side of his face almost from his ear to his mouth.

Neuroscientists have published research that suggests that we are deeply affected by a face. At New York University, Dr. Elizabeth Phelps has established that when we see something alarming we react with a "startled response" or rapid eye blinks. Deciding how we feel about a face occurs in the amygdala, a part of the brain that behaves like a spotlight, calling attention to matters that are important to know more about. Depending on whether you are looking at the face of a friend or enemy, your boss or your lover, an emotional response is triggered. This response is critical because it prepares you for how to behave towards that person. If seeing a face sparks a rush of adrenalin it's a "fight or flight" response. Face processing is simply one of the most complex tasks our brain has to tackle in everyday life. Over the course of millions of years, the human brain has evolved to form a special area, the fusiform, part of the infero-temporal region of the brain, dedicated to facial recognition. The face is a human being's nametag.

Whenever anyone saw John McCormack for the very first time his face always sent huge amounts of adrenalin running through their body. Alarm bells started to sound in the amyg-

220

dala and immediately his face was transplanted to the forefront of the fusiform. No one ever forgot McCormack's face!

John McCormack was born in one of the poorer areas of New York City. His father was a painter and decorator in a local office block and had worked there for the past twenty-four years. It was here that had he met his present wife who worked as a cleaner and between them they produced John who was the idol of their lives until he joined the local teenage gang known throughout the neighbourhood and surrounding areas as the Barracudas.

Up until the age of nine John led a normal school-abiding life. His teachers looked him upon as almost the perfect child. He always handed in his homework on time and received top marks in all of his tests. He showed great promise in the academic world compared with his contemporaries, most of whom could not read or write. This was probably due to his parents who initially would not let him roam the streets until he had finished his school work, and even then he had to be in by nine o'clock, or before it got dark.

This was a very sensible decision by his parents as the neighbourhood in which they lived often had muggings during the night hours and sometimes during the day. Much of these crimes were committed by teenagers who were allowed to roam the streets at night with little or no parental control. It was one such group of delinquents that changed John's outlook on life. He had been sent down to the corner drug store to collect some groceries that his mother had purchased during the afternoon and which were too many to carry home in one go. He picked up two plastic bags, which were pulling his arms out of his sockets, as they were so heavy, and so made him rest every few hundred paces. On his third stop he noticed a group of youngsters on the opposite sidewalk who were walking in his direction. He also began to notice that whenever he stopped so they did.

It was during his fifth resting period that they crossed over the street and confronted him. They were seven in number and were dressed in similar clothing, light blue faded jeans, black tee shirts and black leather jackets which had a dragon's head

221

emblazoned on their backs. He would always remember the words of the leader of the group to his dying days.

"Hey short ass, proper little mummy's boy doing the shopping! Way out of your area. What do you think you are doing on our patch?" John was too frightened to reply. "Got no tongue?" said the big thug. " Anyone going through our patch has got to pay his way. What have you got in the bags?" And with that he snatched one of the bags out of John's hand and scattered its contents on to the sidewalk. "Well, not much here that's of any interest to us, so you will have to pay some other way," and with that he grabbed John by the scruff of his collar, pulled a sharp knife from his pocket and slid it's edge down the side of John's face. The skin parted and large amounts of blood ran down his neck and onto his shirt collar. In no time the blood seeped through the thin cotton almost as if it were made of blotting paper. "There", said the thug, "you wont forget this day for a while. Don't let us see you around these parts again. Now push off back to mummy, little faggot!" And with that the group of youths went off down the sidewalk laughing at what they had just achieved.

John was left in absolute shock. No one came to his aid and by the time he got home he was covered from head to foot in blood. When his Mum came to the door she almost fainted at the terrible sight of her son. However, Mum being a true mum rose above her initial fears and quickly set about cleaning up her son. She should have taken him to Casualty but that would have meant bringing in the police and her husband had always said not to get involved with them, as many were on the take and could not be trusted. Had she gone to the hospital John would not have had such a prominent scar down the side of his face.

The next day at school he became a bit of a cult hero as word soon got around that he had had a skirmish with the Barracudas and had got off with only a small cut on his face. The rumour eventually got to the upper school from where the bulk of their own neighbourhood's gang were selected. In due course, John was invited by being frogmarched to the boy's toilets to meet the General of the Fears Gang. John had seen him at times moving around the school collecting monies from the younger pupils. Some sort of protection money he assumed.

"Well, kid. Prize mark you got yourself there. What are you going to do about it?"

John didn't know how to reply to that, as he did not have the guts or physical presence to do anything against such over-powering odds.

"I'll tell you what you are going to do. You are going to join the Fears, that is if you have the right temperament. Once a member we can set about getting back at the scum bags that did that to you. However, to join us you have to be initiated." He then set about explaining what John would have to do, and as the plan was evolved so John became more afraid.

"Go home and think it over scar-face, and let us know if you want to join us. We will be in the school quadrangle after the last bell."

All that night John was in turmoil. He did not want to become one of them but he did want to get his own back. The next day he arrived at the prearranged meeting place and said he would like to join the Fears.

A week later John did not come home at the usual time of nine o'clock. At that time he was holed up in a dank, dark doorway twenty blocks away in the Barracudas territory along with twenty members of the Fears. The plan was for John to single out one of the Barracudas as he was making his way to their usual meeting point and stick him. Sticking someone meant just that. A sharpened screwdriver had to be plunged in to the leg in the region of the thigh thus preventing the quarry from running away. Once this had been accomplished the rest of the pack would emerge and put in the boot. If the person who was being initiated failed in their bid to injure their foe it was up to them to escape. In doing so they would still be able to join the gang for showing courage.

John began to shiver slightly. He didn't know if it was fear or cold but he wasn't enjoying the feeling. He had to wait for about twenty minutes and then someone appeared at the end of the alleyway. It was one of the gang, as he was wearing the uniform of black leathers and faded jeans. John drew back his breath as he recognised the big thug that had two weeks ago slashed his face. Poetic justice or a most horrible fate for him, he thought. There was no turning back now. He had to go through with the ordeal, even if it meant another pasting far worse than his initial one.

He waited until the unsuspecting thug was almost abreast of the place in which he was hiding. He had to be quick and decisive. He got into an almost sprint start position holding the screwdriver like a relay baton and took a deep breath. He came out of the dark like an international 100m runner and plunged the sharpened shaft into the rear part of the leg into the upper hamstring area. John expected the lad to fall to the ground, screaming in agony. Instead he just stood there holding his hand over the wound and looking straight into the eyes of his adversary.

"Why, you little bastard I told you not to come into my area. You should have stayed home with mummy. You sure as hell won't see her again!" Before he could utter another word John was on him. He must have stuck him a dozen times before he was pulled off by one of the Fears. He found out later that the thug was laid up in hospital for over two months. One of his lungs had been pierced and at the time of the incident he was diagnosed as being on the intensive care list with a fifty-fifty chance of survival.

The whole attack had been seen by all of the top brass of the Barracuda Gang. John's frenzy had left a marked impression on all of them. This was sure some kid not to mix it with. From that day John's whole attitude to life changed. He eventually became the leader of the gang. No leader had ever lived beyond the age of nineteen. He had three more years to live on that mathematical equation!

Life at home also changed dramatically. He became uncontrollable. Even his father who had had a tough upbringing could not deal with him. School became a chore and so he began to abscond from tutorials. It eventually got to the stage where he was going to be sent to a detention centre. He had to appear in court as a result of a grievous bodily attack on a fellow student. The expected sentence would have been eight months inside which would have proved the final nail in his coffin. He would have become a life-long criminal. Fortuitously for him, a new father had recently moved into the local diocese. Father Davidson was one of those people who saw some good in everyone. When it came to any mitigating circumstances the father stood up before the bench and explained that he would be willing to take John under his wing and make sure that he changed his ways. The judge gave John a suspended sentence of community service and also gave him a stern warning as to what would happen to him if he appeared before the bench again.

From that day forward John never looked back. Father Davidson instilled in him that the only way to succeed in the world today was to make sure that one was educated to the full, make a wide circle of friends and at all times be honest. John met all of these except the last one. He could not be honest at all times especially when it applied to business dealings!

By the age of eighteen he had made top grades in all of his subjects and then it was time for him to specialise. His views on life had certainly changed since being under the guidance of Father Davidson. A few years ago he would have jumped at the opportunity of leaving school and finding a job. Now all he wanted to do was to be better educated so that he could go out into the world of commerce, make big money and be in charge of people. In order to achieve all of this he knew he had to go to university, and so at the age of twenty, having saved some money by working in a local hardware store for a year he went off to Ohio University to follow a course in Business Studies and Law. This was a very astute decision on his behalf, as he knew he still had criminal tendencies and by studying law he would be able to keep himself just within the borders of law-abiding business dealings. In this area he knew that big money was made.

At about this time Justin Hackman was preparing to leave for the same university. Justin was the youngest in a family of five. He had two other brothers who were much older than him and both had left home and were leading successful lives in commerce. Justin's father owned a local, thriving business selling office furniture to all of the new corporations that were springing up in this once small town. In all, the Hackman family led a very comfortable life in one of the more affluent areas of the town where real estate was probably the most expensive in the county. It was here that Justin cut his teeth in the world of entrepreneurial pursuits. He first discovered his knack in making money when he was only six years old. His mother had bought him a battery-operated slide show, which projected single slides onto a screen. Justin did not posses a screen and so he used to use the white wall in the dining room. One day as he sat there in front of the screen he likened it to sitting in a cinema. It was then that he had his first inspiration into the world of making money. When his mum returned home that afternoon she was surprised to see a small line of youngsters queuing at the front door of the house. At the head of the queue she noticed Brian from next door who appeared to be in charge.

"What on earth is going on here, Brian?"

"We are having a film show in your dining-room," he replied.

Mrs. Hackman noticed that Brian was holding a piece of string in his left hand which had a needle attached to one end of it and in his other hand he was holding what appeared to be some tickets. She also noticed that the children that were in the queue were holding coins. She went into the dining-room and demanded to know what on earth was going on.

"We are having a film show, mum, and with the money that we make we are going to buy some new films and have a film show every Wednesday night. By the end of the year we will have made a lot of money."

Justin never forgot that day as he was made to give the film show free of charge and his mother gave all the children a free biscuit in the interval, which she charged up to Justin's next amount of pocket money.

Justin's next venture was going along to garage sales, buying a whole load of rubbish at the end of the sale which he used to get at a knock-down price and then proceed to have his own garage sale. At first his parents complained but when they saw how much profit he was making they allowed him to continue even though it was out of place in the area in which they lived. It eventually got to the stage of Justin's father actually going along to other garage sales on his son's behalf and buying up job lots for his son to sell. Hence the birth of a prolific entrepreneur.

Justin's father could see in his son the gift of spotting unique ways to make money and so he decided to back his son on any new ventures whenever he was requested to do so.

This gift was also spotted by one of Justin's schoolteachers who was in charge of the careers department. In collusion with Mr Hackman he planned Justin's path through the maze of educational corridors right up to the day when he went off to Ohio University to study a course in International Business.

Philip Jackson was a quiet, unassuming individual. He hated sport, didn't mix very well with his contemporaries and loved sticky buns, hence his leanings towards a spotty mesomorph. His one saving grace was his amazing ability in using mathematical formulas and calculations and so when any of his classmates found difficulty with their mathematics projects they automatically came to Phillip knowing that he would be able to fathom out the problem for them. He always came top in all of his exams and each year won the prestigious Isaac Browning prize for mathematics. He was one of a few pupils in the history of his college to actually be approached by the universities to attend one of their courses without taking an entrance examination. He eventually chose Ohio University as its name had fourteen letters. Phillip's favourite number was seven and he had decided that his chosen university should be divisible by seven!

That Fall the three of them descended upon the huge campus of Ohio State University and ended up in the same hall of residence, on the same floor and with adjacent rooms. During the first few days they only acknowledged one another with a nod or a smile as neither of them could see anything in their personalities that might prove compatible. It wasn't until the third day that they made any form of contact with one another. It was the evening of the Freshers Hop. None of them was looking forward to the occasion as they had not met anyone who had similar interests to theirs during the last few days at the various seminars and club gatherings that were organised by the Student Union in an effort to create some form of camaraderie between the new student intake.

It was almost time to return to their hostel and many of the students were a little worse for wear having illegally drunk copious amounts of liquor in the washrooms. The hop was not restricted to Freshers only and many of the students who were members of the various sporting teams of the university and who had had to report back early to get fit for the coming season had come along for a well-earned break. One of the groups attending was the football team who during the previous season had won all of the league trophies and who were idolised by most of the undergraduates.

One of them stood out above the rest as he was extremely large and had the reputation on the field as one person you never tried to get the better of. He was on form that night pushing his huge bulk to the bar and not caring who he shoved out of the way.

Unfortunately for him he bumped into little, fat Phillip and sent him sprawling across the floor and in the process knocking his drink out of his hand. The rest of the football group thought it was a huge laugh and started poking fun at him.

John and Justin who were standing at different ends of the bar noticed the whole incident. John felt sorry for the poor old fellow lying spread-eagled on the floor and with no thought for his own personal safety went across and held out a hand to Phillip.

"What's this? Another weak little Fresher comes to pay homage to the victorious football elitists. If I were you I would return to the bar from whence you came and order a fruit juice as it might have some effect on your scrawny physique." This was followed by rapturous laughter from the rest of the group.

"When you are at the bar see if they will serve you a bag of bubble gum for this over-inflated, anabolic steroid machine that's all mouth and no brain. No, change that order to a truck load of gum which might go towards filling his mouth!"

The big football ox turned around to see who had dared mutter such provoking words at him. He ended up facing a fairly tall guy who had a large scar down one side of his face.

"Who the hell do you think you are butting in to football business?" Those were the last words he muttered that evening. The next thing he knew was when he woke up in hospital the next morning with his jaw in plaster. He never again made any attempts to trouble the little fat Fresher from floor three in the Dwelly Fraternity.

That same morning three Freshers were sat in the downtown coffee shop toasting "One for All and All for One" Hence the motto of one of America's most aggressive engineering companies, "Global Engineering."

In the space of ten years the company expanded at an accelerating rate. In the initial stages it concentrated on advising large companies on how to improve their efficiency internally and how to market their products using new advertising techniques. Within five years they had become a household name in commercial circles and had amassed a large surplus of finances. The three directors had in the initial stages of forming the company decided not to reward themselves with huge salaries. Any excess money would be ploughed back into the company and be used for expansion in other areas. Those five years were the learning period for them and by the end of it they became experts in many fields' so much so that a decision was taken for them to actually expand into the commerce market.

They began in a small way by buying up companies that they came across which were experiencing problems in cash flow and were almost in the stages of calling in the receivers. They did not concentrate on any specific type of company. As long as they knew that they could make a quick profit they bought, often turning it around to a successful business and then selling it on. Some firms they bought and immediately closed down as a tax dodge. No thought was given to the employees who lost their jobs overnight. Hence they began to get the reputation of being quite ruthless. However larger companies still used their expertise as they were guaranteed to increase their own profits and that was all that the shareholders were interested in. It also meant fat bonuses for the directors of those companies.

During the next five years they concentrated on purchasing much larger companies, which dealt more with engineering projects. They also set up their own factories for producing the equipment and raw materials, which would be needed in these engineering projects. They eventually became a company known world wide for tackling extremely large contracts. They were not cheap but hugely successful in whatever they took on.

It was during their fourteenth year as "Global Engineering" that they made their biggest mistake in their diversification of their engineering products. John McCormack had been flying back across the Atlantic on one of his business trips. He had finished an extremely good meal and decided to take a brandy in the upper first class bar of the jumbo. He thought that it would help him sleep better during the final five hours before landing. Sitting at the bar with little else to do other than look at himself in the mirror which was placed behind a row of bottles for the effect of giving the bar the appearance of being twice as large, he picked up a magazine which had been left probably by another bored business man with no one to converse with. The magazine featured various celebrities who had hit the headlines during the past few years and what had happened to them since then. McCormack flicked through the pages finding none of them particularly interesting until he came to an article on the United Arab Emirates. The main feature was about the Sheik of Abu Dhabi and how he had brought his country into the twentieth century over a matter of only a few decades. How oil had been found and how it was changing the life styles of its peoples. What caught his eye in particular was how much revenue came into the country due to very rich oil deposits that were situated just off the coast. The article went on to describe how quickly the Emirates were expanding both in the commercial field and the tourist trade. This meant that there was a huge amount of building to be done, infrastructure to be developed and the means for the country to produce most of its foods. None of these things could take part without the supply of a huge amount of drinking water, which was proving to be a major headache. Many of the desalination plants were obsolete or coming to the end of their lives. The enormous demand for new plants had way outstripped world supply.

The article gave the impression that the Emirates would be unable to expand anywhere near the rate that the Sheik would have wished it, even though money was no object. On reading this McCormack's brain started to race. There was no chance of any sleep that night. As soon as he got off of the plane he made a number of calls in order to arrange a quick meeting with the other two partners who were at either ends of the country. The meeting was eventually scheduled for the day after next, which would give McCormack time to prepare an inviting brief.

The meeting took place in the penthouse of the central headquarters of the company in New York. First to arrive was Philip Jackson, the mathematical genius of the company. Next came Justin Hackman more flamboyant than usual dressed in a white silk suit. He was the man who had the gift of the gab in four languages. Extremely likeable personality hence very good on the commercial side of things when it came to the board meetings between possible merging companies where the tense atmosphere needed to be broken. These two exchanged pleasantries about families and the good old days at college with no reference at all to business, as they knew there would be much of that when McCormack arrived. John McCormack arrived some fifteen minutes later making the excuse that he was held up in the traffic. Coffee was brought in by one of the secretaries and then they sat down for business.

"This had better be good," started off Hackman. "I had to leave an important meeting with one of the Unions which is creating hell on the production lines of the Melling Factory. Only just acquired the company and this happens. They are refusing to do shift work even though we have offered them double time for the night shift."

"Call them all together including the drivers and give them one ultimatum, follow our policies or we close down the factory and sell it off piece by piece," chipped in McCormack.

No finesse at all, thought Philip Jackson, hatchet out and strike first. Typical McCormack. "Let's leave that problem until this meeting has dealt with the business that John is dealing with. Go ahead, John," said Philip in his quiet, reassuring voice.

McCormack placed his brief case on the shiny desk and proceeded to pull out three thick files, which he passed to the other two keeping one for himself.

"We are about to enter a field which will make us a huge fortune. We are going to supply the whole of the United Arab Emirates with fresh water. Read the file that I have prepared which will explain the situation at the moment and how the Sheik would like his country to develop in the very near future. You will see that expansion is impossible without the production of water. They have an abundance of oil but no water at all. And that is where we come back on the scene. We have the engineering facilities and the technical know-how to fulfil any requirements that the Emirates might put forward. We can collar the whole market."

The reading of the documentation presented to them took over an hour to digest after which it was decided to break for a light lunch and then continue an hour later. At the end of almost three hours of deliberations McCormack and Hackman were totally in favour of the move into the field of water production. Jackson, on the other hand, had his reservations. He was the cautious one of the three. He did not like putting all of their eggs into one basket. The thought of all of their assets being used to raise the funding for such an enormous project was mind-boggling. If things went wrong there would be no falling back onto other areas of their conglomerated business as there would be none left. Eventually Philip Jackson gave in and so began the selling off of many of their smaller companies with the accrued monies being channelled into the purchase of new equipment and new personnel who had experience in the water industry.

During the initial few years everything went as planned, even better. The prototype of the world's largest desalination plant was up and running well before the scheduled time and producing millions of gallons of the purest water each week. The financial ministers of the Emirates were more than pleased and placed an order for ten of the plants during the initial stages of the project with a promise of twenty more if the first batch successfully produced water with few teething problems.

Although all was on schedule Philip Jackson remained a worried man as the company was up to the hilt in debt. No payments were due from the Emirates until one year after the first opening of the plants. Money had had to be borrowed from some of the world's leading banks at interest rates above the base rate due to the complexity of the programme and the contractual position of not receiving any form of payment until one year after completion. On the plus side however was the large profit margin the company would gain. Other countries were also showing great interest in the project and were already making tentative plans to be the next in line for the plants.

The programme was successfully into its third year when the first major problem was encountered. It was McCormack who received the initial phone call. He was working late at the office when his secretary came on line.

"Really sorry to disturb you, Mr McCormack but there is a Horace Millington on the line. It's long-distance call from the United Arab Emirates and he said it was imperative that he talked to someone in head office who was in the top echelon of the company. He refused to say what it was about."

"OK, Phyllis put him through."

"Hi. This is John McCormack here and you can't get any higher on the echelon of the company than me. I own it! Now can this wait until tomorrow morning, as it is late at night here in the States and I am an extremely busy man?"

Horace Millington was temporarily thrown by the aggressiveness of the man's voice at the other end of the phone. This was the boss he had heard so much about and he hadn't wanted or even expected to actually be in contact with him. Perhaps this wasn't such a good idea after all. Too late now, he thought.

"Sorry, sir, but I think this is of prime importance to the company. You see we have discovered a fault in the desalination plant that could put the finalisation of the programme back at least two, three or even more years."

There was a slight lapse in the conversation as McCormack allowed the significance of the statement sink in. What he had just heard could possibly finish the company. He had to act quickly.

"You have done the right thing Mr Millington. Don't say anything more over this open line. I will take the first available plane out to the Emirates tomorrow. My secretary will make all relevant arrangements. Just make sure you are at the airport when I arrive. I'll hand you over to my secretary now," and with that he transferred the call to his secretary's desk with no further acknowledgement to his caller.

There were no available seats with any of the airlines in the first business class sections so McCormack had to travel tourist class, which did not put him in a very amiable mood. He had very long legs and so felt like a cramped up chicken in a battery shed. Alongside him was a young lady with a six-month-old baby, which spent the whole time crying. By the time he disembarked he was ready to take on the whole of the customs personnel single-handed. Although the terminal was air-conditioned it was still quite stuffy and McCormack could feel small beads of sweat forming at the base of his spine. July was not a good time to be visiting Abu Dhabi due to the high temperatures and the accompanying high humidity.

"Mr McCormack," came a voice from the other side of a large group of waiting relatives and men holding labelled cards. McCormack turned to see a rather insignificant little man in large horned rimmed spectacles walking timidly towards him. Timidly was an understatement as the fellow was absolutely petrified. Millington had been extremely apprehensive of meeting the man who had been so abrupt on the telephone and after making some discreet enquiries as to the reputation of the man had been even more worried. Now that he had seen him in person and noticed the scar on his face he was mortified. "Did you have a pleasant trip?" Poor fellow, he couldn't have started off on a more disastrous opening statement if he had tried.

"Let's cut the small talk and get on with the business," scowled McCormack. "Take me to wherever the problem is and you can fill in the details as we travel along."

Millington was unable to reply. He motioned towards the sliding exit doors of the arrivals hall and out to an awaiting limousine.

"OK. Lets hear it."

"Well, Mr McCormack, we first noticed the problem in our second desalination plant out near the port where we are now heading. The turbines had been running at three-quarter power for the past seven months with no teething problems at all. Then one morning one of the engineers noticed a high pitched note coming from possibly the drive shaft of number three turbine. He decided to shut it down which would have had little effect on water production for all he had to do was to increase the revs of the other four turbines.

"Having done that he called the technical supervisor in and explained what he had heard. The adviser started it up once more and immediately shut it down on hearing the noise. The machine was then stripped down and amazingly nothing could be found which might cause the noise. The drive shaft was checked for alignment and a special X-ray machine was brought over from headquarters to check for any stress fractures. Nothing. All bearings were replaced and then the turbine was reassembled and tested.

"The whole repair took five days. Once back in commission it worked perfectly well until about three weeks later when it happened again, but this time two turbines started playing up. Again both were stripped down, reassembled and restarted with no problems.

"Another four weeks went by and the same happened again this time only one acting up. Our first thoughts were that it could be some form of sabotage. We have had some of the local

235

fisherman complaining that their catches were down since we began pumping back in the saltier water from the desalination process. We mounted a twenty-four hour watch on the premises and no one came anywhere near the buildings. The next time it happened we decided not to do any work on the turbine out here. We shipped it straight back to the US to our research factory where the prototypes were made. They started it up and found nothing wrong with it. They ran it for two months with no problems. We were completely stumped.

"Then by sheer chance one of our technical staff was visiting a friend who was holding a dinner party and he happened to mention the problems he was having with one of his machines, not mentioning what it was and where it operated. Another of the visitors said he had experienced a similar happening with a turbo engine in a high-speed inter city train. The train had been in service in the UK and had no problems. The company won an overseas contract and shipped out a whole load of engines all of which immediately started getting problems.

"They eventually found that the environment of high temperatures and high humidity in which the machines were working caused the problem. All specifications and trials had been held in a cool climate. When things began to heat up all manner of problems began to appear. Allowances had been made for normal rises in temperature but not for the great extremes of temperature and humidity. The outcome was the withdrawal of all engines. They lost the contract and the company went into liquidation." The word liquidation sent a cold shiver down McCormack's back.

"So in layman's terms, what you are saying that under extreme conditions of temperature and humidity the turbine's workings expand which results in a high pitched noise. What would happen if we let the turbine continue to work?"

"We don't know as we have not taken the risk with such an expensive piece of equipment."

"How often do the Emirates experience such extreme conditions?"

"Not very often. We are talking about temperatures over forty degrees Celsius with eighty percent humidity. Perhaps once every twenty years give or take a few."

"Then it's more than likely that this phenomenon will not happen again for the next ten years at least?"

"Quite possible."

"OK, Mr Millington, you have done an excellent job here. You did the correct thing in notifying us immediately. Your swift actions will not be forgotten. I would like you not to tell anyone of these happenings for the time being until we have had time to think of all the consequences. What I would like you to do now is to make a comprehensive list of all personnel who have been made aware of the problems and fax it to me personally at head offices. I must get back to the States today as we have a very important meeting with the Saudi Arabian Minister of Finance. Thanks again." He shook Millington's hand firmly and left.

Horace Millington suddenly felt very relaxed. He had just been thanked by the big boss in person. Not such a bad chap as people made him out to be. Strange why he wanted a list of all personnel who had been involved with the problem turbines. He made a mental tally and decided there would be only about five people on the list.

That night McCormack sent an urgent fax to the other two directors. Whatever they were involved in they should put into someone else's hands and meet in head offices on Monday morning.

Chapter Fifteen

Andrea Concheta Gomez busied herself around the edge of her king size bed which was positioned in the middle of her very spacious hotel room. She had just been upgraded by the hotel management from tourist class to business class, which made her feel on top of the world. The new room was quite opulent and even had a white, leather suite of furniture adjacent to the bed. The other high-class touch was a Jacuzzi in the extremely large bathroom.

On the bed were neatly stacked piles of clothing. All had been ironed the night before. Andrea disliked packing clothes that she had already worn and had made it one of her priorities early on in her career to always do her washing no matter how inconvenient it may have proved at the time. It was not an uncommon sight for visiting cabin staff to come into her room and find every conceivable radiator or place of heating to be covered in clothing right down to her smalls. She was always careful whom she let in as on one occasion a group of her flight crew, including the captain and co-pilot, descended upon her for a coffee after a night out together. Most of the visitors were worse for wear and in no time were throwing the garments about the room. The captain ended up with a black pair of see through lacy pants over his head and the co pilot had run around the room wearing a red silk thong! The next day she dare not look any of the cabin staff in the face and the captain and co-pilot did not enter the plane until a few minutes before take off.

Although she had not ventured out of the four star hotel that day and had slept for a whole ten hours beforehand, she still felt extremely tired. Even after flying for eighteen months she still had difficulty in overcoming jet lag. She had tried many remedies handed down by leading doctors and psychiatrists on how to overcome the changes in the human body when eating and sleeping habits are drastically changed due to hormones being injected into the blood stream at the wrong times, sometimes competing against one another, with little effect. Months ago she had given up going out on the town with the other members of the flight crew. In her initial days with the airline it was not an uncommon occurrence for her to be in a nightclub until three a.m. and then grab a few hours sleep before boarding the next plane at eight a.m. The worrying thing for her was that the pilot sometimes accompanied them and if she was feeling like death she could at least rest in the service area of the plane. The pilot had to remain at his controls.

She was in the final process of packing before her flight to Quito. Over the past few months she had had numerous occasions to practice the age-old art of fitting too many garments into too small a space. On this occasion she was having to be far more precise in the way she folded her clothes as she had promised to take her uncle home a month's supply of duty free cigars and she did not wish him to have to smoke them in a flattened condition. She was not able to afford the luxury of a slightly bigger case, as it would not fit into the miniscule space provided for cabin staff. Andrea was an airhostess with one of the leading trans-atlantic airlines.

Andrea had not been home for over a year and she was getting very excited at the prospect of seeing her aunt and uncle whom she loved dearly. They had been her acting parents for almost as long as she could remember. Sadly her mother had died when she was only two years old. Her family had lived in a small village about twenty kilometres from the suburbs of Quito. It was a very impoverished establishment with no electricity supply and the only means of obtaining water was from a communal well which was situated on the outskirts of the village. The water had become contaminated and over a third of the village population had perished. No number of tests on the well water had produce any answers as to how the well had been poisoned. It was thought that over the years the walls of the well had gradually begun to disintegrate and rain water had filtered through impervious rock strata that had contained substances similar to arsenic which had then got into the clear drinking water and being of greater density had sunk to the bottom of the well. Its presence had had little effect on the villagers other than an occasional bout of stomach-ache and vomiting.

One summer it was extremely hot and the winter had brought little rain so the well had began to run dry. It was the lack of water in the well that had caused the final tragedy. The heavy bucket that was dropped into the well had begun to hit the bottom of the well and in doing so had disturbed the concentrations of arsenic to make the water a deadly cocktail.

Andrea was lucky to have survived with only a violent stomach-ache and vomiting. When she looked back she could remember that she had not felt very well for a few days before the tragedy and had been off her food and had had little to drink. That had saved her life.

Her father had had a nervous breakdown and was incapable of looking after his daughter so the village padre along with the village elders decided it would be better for Andrea to move to the city and stay with her aunt and uncle. From that day she had never returned to the village and had not seen her father again. He had apparently passed away not long after her departure. The cause of his death was never discussed.

Her aunt and uncle were absolutely delighted to have Andrea living with them. They were not particularly well off but they made sure that Andrea had a good education and mixed with the right peer group. She grew up into a model adult. Her mother would have been proud of her.

By one o'clock she had packed her suitcase and had taken the lift down to the ground floor where she waited for the rest of the flight crew

"Hello, young lady," a voice came drifting across the foyer from somewhere behind her. It was the captain who was wearing his very impressive uniform, which had three stripes on the cuffs. He was one of the oldest pilots with the airline and had a very good reputation.

"You must be Andrea, welcome aboard the team." She was

most impressed to see that he knew her name. Excellent leadership, she thought.

"Thank you, sir," she said not knowing how to continue with the conversation. Fortunately for her more of the cabin crew began to arrive and started to chat with the skipper. The remainder appeared a few minutes later and as soon as all of the billings had been paid at the front desk, they went out into the cold, damp air and waited for the shuttle bus.

The five-minute run into Heathrow took twenty minutes due to a lorry, which had run into a taxi, causing a huge tailback of traffic. By the time they reached the customs check in they were all slightly distressed. Andrea was the least disturbed probably because she knew it was her last flight for two weeks.

The man at the customs desk hardly raised his head when the flight team came through the search area. Although Andrea had never seen anyone stopped, she always felt a little intimidated by the presence of the custom officials even though she never went over the limit of duty free articles. In fact, she rarely took the advantage of taking goods home as she did not wear expensive perfumes, did not drink and did not smoke. It was having her uncle's cigars in her bag that made her feel even guiltier on this occasion.

The departure lounge was quite busy for this time of the year. The school holidays had not started and it was not a Bank Holiday weekend so she could not understand why so many people were milling around. The airline that she worked for was experiencing a period of flight cancellations due to a pilot dispute with their employers over wages. Perhaps that was it. That would mean a full plane with many irate passengers. This had the makings of a very tiring seven hours flight.

Once on board the plane Andrea packed her flight case into the small cupboard allocated for the flight crew and then went into the rear catering area for a briefing by the chef de mission.

It was an older lady who was in charge of this flight. One who Andrea had flown with before some three months ago and who she liked and admired for her good organisational qualities and her very friendly attitude towards the passengers. She could remember her dealing with a rather noisy executive in the first class section who had had too much to drink and had become quite obnoxious towards a younger member of the cabin crew. Instead of reprimanding the passenger, which would have delighted every one on board, she quietly whispered in his ear. This had an amazing effect on the gentleman for he immediately shut up and remained passive for the rest of the flight. What she had said to him remains a mystery to this day. This flight wasn't going to be as bad as she had previously anticipated.

The briefing took ten minutes after which the cabin staff went to their various allocated stations on the plane to get ready for their passengers. Andrea was in charge of checking that all of the meal containers were accounted for and that they were safely stowed away for take-off.

Once all the checks had been made the staff returned to the original meeting place to make their reports. No one had any problems so the chief stewardess told them to return to their positions in order to greet the passengers. Andrea was very pleased as she had been given the area at the bottom of the tunnel, which led from the embarkation area to the plane itself. She favoured this position as she could see clearly the passengers as they came down the quite steep slope.

Initially the first-class passengers came down the ramp. She was always surprised their dress code. One would have expected them to be very smartly dressed in the latest fashions and yet it was usually the complete opposite. The lower down the scale of passenger class the smarter they were dressed. The main exception to this rule was if the whole flight was tourist class only and then they were packed in like battery hens and as most had had a previous experience of this they tended to dress more casually in non-creasing garments.

First class was full by the time the business class began to come down the tunnel. Andrea tried to spot the people who might prove to be a little difficult during the flight. In the past she had been a bad judge of character and the least suspecting person had proved the most difficult to deal with. All passed with approval from Andrea.

Now it was time for the masses that always seemed to struggle on board the plane with huge amounts of excess baggage of all shapes and sizes none of which had ever defeated the cabin crew. They seemed to conjure up space out of nowhere in which to push the packages and at the end of a long flight pull them out in the same condition as they went in.

Andrea looked up into the tunnel once more. It was time for the tourist class to enter the plane. She watched with amused interest, as the family groups consisting of very small children were first to appear. It was paramount for the crew to get the youngsters settled first as they were usually very excitable in a totally new environment. They were then followed by the elderly who might need a helping hand with the stowing of their luggage and then last came the able-bodied although it never worked out completely to plan.

As she glanced to the top of the tunnel she became aware of what initially looked like an ordinary lady traveller dressed in an ordinary set of clothing. Her outfit was quite bland and worn by any other person would have blended into almost obscurity in the tightly pushing group. However, this was no ordinary person. There was something in the way she walked and in the way she held her head. As she grew closer Andrea thought that she must have seen her before but she did not recognise the lady's face. All of the characteristics portrayed by the lady's body language did not match up with the middle aged, slightly lined face. She moved, or a more accurate description would be to say that she glided, down the slope like a young girl in her twenties. She was almost regal. Had she come down a few minutes before with the first-class passengers Andrea would have said that she was somebody of extreme importance who did not wish to be recognised.

It was when she had almost reached the slight bend in the tunnel about five metres away from where Andrea stood that Andrea's brain began to race. People have said that when confronted with a dire emergency, such as drowning, one's whole life flashes in front of oneself in a matter of seconds. Andrea's brain had recognised something from the past. Something that had been of such great importance that it needed to be kept in a special compartment inside the complexities of the brain where it could be stored with no possibility of it ever being erased.

She was back in her childhood, sitting by a glowing fire in the house of her aunt and uncle. Her aunt was portraying a story, which had been handed down over the generations. It told of a heroic Incan Prince who had fought the invading Spanish many centuries ago and who had eventually disappeared into the forests never to be heard of again. It was told that he had met a beautiful young Indian girl whilst out hunting in the forest and had fallen madly in love with her. As far as she could remember the girl had given up her life in order for her Prince to remain alive. The story went on to say that one day she would return to the Inca lands to look for her Prince.

Andrea knew it was her. She was unable to move as the woman came closer. Their eyes met for a glancing moment and Andrea had the feeling that the woman had somehow recognised her.

In the back of her mind Andrea could recall that her aunt had said that when the Indian girl returned no one was to approach her. She had to find her Prince with no help from anyone. This was a story not only told by her aunt. She had heard it on a number of occasions at her friend's house and even at school when it was told by one of her teachers during "listening hour".

As soon as the mysterious lady passed by the open door to the plane Andrea came back to life. What seemed an eternity had lasted only a matter of seconds and yet she had recalled so many things. She did not have time to think any more of the incident as the maintenance crew appeared at the bottom of the tunnel and asked for permission to close the outer hatch of the plane. The head steward granted permission once he had been given the OK by the captain, and all of the cabin staff, who had reported to their various stations for take-off.

Andrea was positioned near the middle of the plane adjacent to the wing escape hatch from where she had a good view of all of the passengers in the tourist section. She immediately picked out the lady of mystery. During the whole of the video, which explained what one should do in the case of an accident, she kept her eyes on her. She knew that she was going against company policy but she could not help herself. Cabin crew were not allowed to fraternise or stare at any of the clientele in case it embarrassed them. This was a blatant breach of the rules on her behalf. Although she felt very guilty, she knew that the lady would probably not have noticed, so once the video was completed and the map of the flight course reappeared on the screen, she began to relax. She was soon back in the galley and, once all final checks had been made, gave a wave to the chief steward who having received the OK from the rest of the crew notified the captain who in turn announced that take-off was imminent.

Once in the air everyone seemed to relax and the staff set about preparing for the main meal of the flight. Roast beef, and fresh fruit salad was the order of the day. Any one who did not like the thought of eating beef or was a vegetarian had a further choice of a fish course or vegetable curry.

Andrea was due to serve the passengers on the right-hand side of the plane but managed to change to the left, as this was the side on which the lady sat. She was going to find it extremely difficult not to have a conversation with her. This, she knew, was not permitted. She would have liked to ask her where her final destination was.

The moment finally came when it was time to serve the last two rows of passengers. In the middle of a row of four sat the lady.

"What would you like for your main course, madam?" said Andrea trying her hardest not to stare into the face of the lady.

The lady looked straight back into the face of Andrea with a questioning smile. Andrea knew that her previous attempts not to appear too inquisitive had failed and yet the lady made no questioning remark. She merely said that she would like the beef and for a dessert the fresh fruit salad. Andrea slid one of the trays from out of the cabinet on wheels and passed it over to the lady. When she looked for a salad there did not appear to be any left.

"I am terribly sorry but we do not have any salads left."

The lady looked at Andréa and replied, "That is allright. I will just have a cup of coffee when you have time to serve it. Thank you." Andrea felt that she had let the lady down and she did not intend to leave it at that. So she went forward to the first class section and spoke to the senior attendant.

"Jayne, I have a special passenger in the rear section who would really appreciate a fresh fruit salad and we have run out of them. Any chance of one of your desserts? I did notice on your menu that you were serving strawberries and cream."

"What is so special about this passenger for you to come into this area?" said Jayne.

"I'll let you know when we land. Well, may I have a portion?"

"Yes you may, but it had better be a good excuse" She went to the kitchen area and returned with a small tray upon which was a delicious piece of strawberry flan and a large dollop of Cornish cream. Also at the edge of the tray was a most beautiful flower.

"As she is so special she may as well have one of these orchids. One of the first class clientele noticed me admiring it and asked if I would like it. She said that it came from a tropical area deep inside the forests, which border onto the upper slopes of the Andes. The horticultural societies had thought that it had become extinct but some explorer came across it a few months back. Beautiful, isn't it? It has a most distinctive fragrance. Hurry along now before I take it back and keep it for myself." Andrea held out her hands and carefully took hold of the tray.

On reaching the second but last isle Andrea turned and faced the lady

"Mam, I am pleased to have found you a dessert. Not quite a fruit salad, but it is fruit." and with that she passed it across to her. She watched the lady's face and could see that she was pleasantly surprised. She was even more surprised when she noticed the orchid.

The lady picked up the delicate flower in her fingers and held it beneath her nose in order to smell its bouquet. Her eyes closed for a few moments and when she opened them again Andrea thought they looked a little full, almost at the first stages of a tear. Perhaps she had done the wrong thing in bringing along the flower. The lady then looked up into Andrea's face, reached out and touched her hand and said,

"This is the most beautiful flower I have ever been given. It reminds me of something but I can't quite think what it is at the moment. It will come to me in a minute. Thank you very much, young lady." Andrea nodded and returned to her station in the canteen area.

For the remainder of the flight she kept a special eye on the lady passenger. The last she saw of her was when she made her way up the tunnel with the flower in her hand. Andrea knew that she would not see her again.

It took over an hour for Andrea to get to her aunt's flat. It seemed more than that as she not only was dying to see them both but was eager to tell of her experience on the plane.

Her uncle opened the door and gave her a huge hug. "Why, how you have grown in the last year. More beautiful than ever, if that is at all possible"

"You haven't changed, you old flatterer. Come on and let me in so that I can give aunty a cuddle." She pushed passed her beaming uncle and went into the living-room where her aunt sat at the window.

"I saw you come along the street. Your walk looked as if you were very excited about something," she said and gave her niece a little kiss on the cheek.

"Yes, Aunty. A strange thing happened on the flight over today." Before Andrea had time to continue her aunty interrupted the conversation.

"Yes, I know. She has at last returned. I knew as soon as I saw your face. You had the same expression as you used to have when I used to tell you the story of the Prince and the young Indian girl so many years ago." She held out her hand and took hold of Andrea. No more was said. There was no need. They both understood what they had witnessed that day.

Chapter Sixteen

"You blundering dipstick," shouted David Johnson as he threw his racket down in absolute pain. This was quite mild language for him, but there were three young ladies sitting in the viewer's gallery waiting to take over the court, which was most unusual as it was seven fifteen a.m. and no one ever appeared until gone eight o'clock. One of the ladies couldn't help letting out a small squeal of laughter when David threw down his racket. Funny how someone else's minor injury could cause one to laugh at the most inconvenient times. David was not at all amused and let the young lady know by giving her a stern glare.

"That's it. You've hit me three times this morning and this time right on my birth mark which was already hurting as soon as I got out of bed. I'm going off court now for a shower."

He turned to the ladies in the gallery.

"OK, girls you can come down now. It's very hot in here today so the ball is flying much faster than usual." He focused his comments on the one who had laughed.

"I'd keep my mouth closed if I were you as you could choke on a ball today!" He had such a nice way with women. Instead of being hurt by the comments she burst into laughter.

"At least I would not be able to squeal my head off with a ball lodged in my mouth like you have just done." Touché!

The changing rooms were even hotter and the showers didn't help much to cool him down. Everything was going wrong this morning for David. As soon as he had got up the birthmark on his arm had started to ache. Whenever he was a little stressed it always hurt. He had meant to have it removed by laser surgery but never got around to it. It had been the bane of his life. At school whenever he took his shirt off for Physical Education the other kids used to stare at it, as it was quite an unusual sight. It was dark red with a jagged line running diagonally across it. Whenever he got stressed out it changed colour to a crimson red. The kids had picked this up straight away and used to goad him just to see it change colour.

"Boy, I did hit the bulls eye this morning," said Pete Anning, his long time college pal. "Mind you, it was your own fault. Too slow getting to the T, not the usual lightning man around the court. What's up this morning, old boy?"

"I feel like an old boy. Didn't get much sleep all weekend. Worried like everyone else in the company. The top dogs are coming into head office this morning. They never do that. Rumours are flying around ranging from redundancies to head office closure and moving the whole set up across the border into Mexico where real estate is one fifth of the price and labour is almost free. Also the damn weather this morning prevented me from getting a cab. All that snow last night and the freezing temperature prevented any form of wheels from getting up my street, so I had to slither all the way to the subway, which I hate to travel on. Gets a little claustrophobic nowadays. That on top of your physical torture has put me in the ideal mood for work this morning!"

"I had noticed that by the polite way that you spoke to that delightful young bit of stuff that you tried to chat up on court just now. I'm going to have to give you a fatherly talk some time on the birds and the bees and how to win over one of the opposite sex. It's going to be a very difficult task but as you are a close friend I won't charge you the usual couch fees which are extortionate nowadays!" Pete Anning was a shrink and had his own practice. His preaching was brought to an abrupt stop when he was hit full in the face by a sweaty towel.

"Ah. Now we are perking up a little. Accuracy improving, so with a bit of luck I'll end up with your designer trainers." He ducked a lethal looking sock and went to the other end of the changing rooms to dry his hair under the blower. "Come on, you old fart, cheer up, breakfast is on me this morning."

David Johnson was the third child of the Johnson family, all boys who had graduated from university with honours degrees. His father had made sure that his sons were given the best that education could offer by sending them to a private boarding school and arranging for them to have home tuition during the school holidays. Life for these boys was all work and no play. During their schooling days they had been given little opportunity to mingle with the opposite sex and so lacked in social graces. Girls looked upon them as being aggressive, and did not appreciate that they were inept in being able to converse with women, as they had had no previous experience. And so the boys grew up to live only for their work and rarely went out on social evenings.

David did not enjoy his work at Global Engineering. He found the assignments given to him not at all challenging and extremely repetitive. David's expertise was in the field of computers and their uses in business. He had graduated with a First Class Honours from Harvard University and had been head hunted by his present firm. One of his professors had had a contact with Global Engineering and used to notify the company when someone with outstanding qualities was about to leave the University. Global Engineering had in the past picked up many a fine employee by this method before they had had any time to establish themselves in the world of commerce, thus saving the company initial high salary payments.

The rush of icy cold air hit him as he came out onto the street from the warmth of the squash club. He could feel his lungs trying desperately to extract oxygen into the millions of alveoli sacks that supplied his blood with energy in order to feed his tired muscles. He pulled the collar of his fleece jacket tightly around his neck, but still thin blades of icy air managed to pierce down between his shoulder blades making him haunch up like an old man. Still no cabs to be seen. All the ones that came his way were full of occupants all of whom looked warm and relaxed.

He edged along the sidewalk looking out for patches of ice. Eventually he came to a bus stop, which had a long queue of muffled passengers all of whom were puffing out streams of white condensed fog from their bright red noses. He had to wait for over thirty minutes for a bus, all of the time looking at his watch. No one would dare be late on this morning when the big three were attending head offices. He could see himself being the only one late and arriving just as they were getting out of their stretch limousine.

The bus eventually arrived, three in actual fact. All of them had had difficulty getting up one of the steep sided streets in the lower city area where the gritters had not been. By the time he got to the office he was cold and very frustrated. As soon as he walked into the front door of the building he could feel the anxiety of its occupants who were pretending to go about their work routine as normal. Even the doorman fumbled at the door when he approached.

"Good morning, Mr Johnson," he said with his usual jovial voice. "They haven't arrived yet," he continued with a smile. It never failed to amaze David how this man managed to remember his name in a building of thousands of workers. He had never given him a tip and rarely passed the time of day with him.

"Thanks, Brian. When they do arrive would you let off a rocket outside the building making sure that it's flight path goes past my office so that I can pretend to be working?"

"I can do better than that. I'll climb up the outside of the building and knock on your window."

The conversation cheered David up a little and he made a mental note to buy the fellow a small present at Christmas.

His cup of coffee was on his desk as usual. Well done, Mrs Rawlings, he thought. At least someone else managed to get into the office on time as well as him. For the rest of the day he worked solidly at his desk with the usual boring assignments. By lunch-time the atmosphere in the office was back to normal and all of the staff had forgotten about the big three.

The first of the directors to arrive was Justin Hackman. He came in quite early as he had flown over the previous day and stayed in the centre of town where he had an acquaintance. He kept her in a very pleasant flat in one of the high rise skyscrapers complete with a twenty-four hour doorman. The only thing he regretted about the arrangement was having to go in by the back entrance each time he paid a visit.

No one in the offices expected anyone to visit before about ten o'clock, and so were very shocked to see him walking down through their aisles of desks just as they were settling into their normal routines. He did this deliberately whenever he paid a visit to any of their establishments. It kept the employees on their toes.

They were already in a nervous state and his sudden appearance made matters even worse. How would they feel if the hatchet man arrived on their floor? He did his sudden appearance act on another three floors before going up to the penthouse offices where he arranged for a light breakfast of coffee and doughnuts.

Philip Jackson was next to appear. He arrived by cab. The thought of hiring a limousine to travel from the airport never occurred to him. He was always very frugal with regards to business expenses, always taking the cheapest form of transport and never staying in expensive accommodation when away from home. He was always shocked when he checked the expenses of his partners. What they spent on business entertaining and travelling expenses he could live on for the whole of the year. He would have to have a chat with them soon on their extravagant ways of life, even though the business was doing extremely well at the present moment. He went straight to the top floor with as little fuss as possible, and was soon tucking into the doughnuts even though they antagonised his digestive system.

John McCormack came in like a whirlwind. The whole of the building knew as soon as he entered the door so good was the grape vine in this establishment. Fortunately for the employees he was in no mood to meet anyone and so got straight into the express lift without even a cursory glance at either of the doorman and floor manager. On reaching the penthouse suite he went straight past the secretary and into the boardroom where he poured himself a stiff whisky.

Philip Jackson made a mental note to have a friendly word about McCormack's drinking habits at the same time as he mentioned expenses. Now was not the time, however. Whatever was troubling him was serious for him to be drinking so early in the morning. He eventually greeted the other two and then sat down at the long table.

"We have got big problems," was his opening statement. No niceties this morning.

"A few days ago I flew down to Abu Dhabi to take a look at one of the desalination plants, which was having some slight bother with one of its turbines. Slight would be an understatement." He then went on to explain all that had happened over the past year. By the end of his talk the other two were lost for words. Eventually the mathematician spoke up.

"What you are implying is that we are financially doomed. I said at the time that we should not have ventured into this scheme, but, oh no, you both wanted to make a fast buck. We were doing extremely well as we were, and would have continued to do so had it not been for the two of you!"

"Don't lose it, Philip. All is not lost yet. As I explained, the turbines only act up under extreme conditions and that only happens once in a matter of ten years. If the weather keeps to its usual track record it should not happen again for another ten years by which time we will be out of the guarantee period. We would then be able to bill them for wear and tear. In any case, by that time we would have found an answer for dealing with the mechanical problems. At the worst, we sell on the company at a huge profit and let someone else deal with the problem."

"What you have suggested is totally unethical," jumped in Philip.

"Are there any ethics in business? Its dog eat dog in the big time, pal," growled McCormack.

"OK. Let's not get our knickers in a twist. John, how can we get out of this situation? Surely too many people know of the problems and word is bound to get back to the Emirates Authorities. I can't see us keeping a lid on this for long."

"The answer to our problem is simpler than you would anticipate. There only four main players who have dealt with the turbos from start to finish and they have never met one another. All we have to do is to promote them into other fields away from each other. We then tell all the other staff that the problems have been solved and carry on as normal."

"That's all very well, but whoever takes over will immediately find out what has been happening and we won't get away with it a second time," said Hackman in a worried voice.

"Only if the person we put in has a technical brain. What if we employ someone who has had no training in technology at all? Why not put someone in who deals only with people and the business side of things. We could say that morale is running low at the moment over there and that we need a closer liaison with the Emirate Government. That would give us the excuse for putting such a person as the top dog over there. Also the beauty of that is that if things do go wrong, we have someone else to blame rather than ourselves. We need a scapegoat."

"Who?" said Philip now a little more amiable now that he could sense that there might be a possible way out even though it would be most unethical. He could not entertain the scenario of having to tell his wife that they would have to give up the private education for their children, move out of the district in which they lived and give up membership of the country club.

"Well, we don't want to advertise this new post as it may cause speculation. We need to keep it in the firm, so to speak. An internal posting with little fuss as possible. Someone who is fairly young and would jump at the chance of promotion away from company headquarters, and someone who has few skills in the field of engineering. A good cover-up would be someone who can speak the local lingo which would be a great helping in preparing the way for the official hand-over next year."

McCormack turned to Justin Hackman. "That is in your field. Can you get in touch with some of your drinking friends in the company and suss out if they know of anyone who fits that category? I suggest that we all meet the same time here tomorrow." They nodded in agreement, especially Hackman who could spend an added night in the sack with his mistress.

Word soon got around that the big three were staying for another extra day, which added flames to the embers re job cuts or something just as sinister. That night Hackman arranged a small dinner party for his friends and spent the evening in apparently light-hearted conversation, but in actual fact he was putting out feelers for the unsuspecting fall guy.

The following day matched the pattern of the previous day. Each member of the board arrived in the same manner and procedure as they had done the previous day. Jackson went immediately to the boardroom, Hackman visited three different floors and upset a number of routines and McCormack, looking worse for wear, had his stiff double whisky before coffee and doughnuts.

Eventually they sat down and the meeting commenced. It was Hackman who first spoke. He took a number of A4 sheets from his brief case and placed them neatly on the table in front of him. He had a look of confidence on his smiling face, which immediately raised hopes in the other two who had come to the meeting with the worst of fears.

"Gentleman, we have found our man. He meets the criteria to a 'T'. Last night I held an informal meeting with some of the section heads. I treated them to an all expenses meal in one of the best restaurants in the area, making sure that good wine flowed the whole evening."

Jackson inwardly groaned at the thought of the huge bill that had been run up that night.

"I said that the company had done extremely well during the year and so they were all due for a healthy bonus at Christmas. By the time the coffee had arrived all were in the best of spirits, excuse the pun, and conversation was freely flowing. I then began making discreet enquiries on management within their departments and the various people they dealt with during the course of a normal day. Nothing serious which might flag up a question in the back of their alcoholic brains and which they might remember the following day. Eventually one name came up. David Johnson. He has been working for the company since leaving college. Works in the field of computers in the Overseas Business Department on the eighth floor. He is a graduate from Harvard University where he attained a First Class Honours Degree. At the present moment he is not happy in his work. Finds it very repetitive with little challenge. We have got him just at the right time. I have been given the impression that he would jump at the chance to work abroad on a new project. I suggest that we get him up here right away and offer him the position of overall director of the project. What do you two reckon?"

"Are you sure that he has no technical know-how on turbines and that you can close all other avenues which might lead him to the original problems?"

"Stop worrying, Philip. I said that I would deal with the people who were closely involved with the project's difficulties," said McCormack with a nasty smile on his foreboding face. "Have you got a personal file on this guy Johnson that we can browse through to see if there are any areas which would effect our little plan?"

Hackman pushed some sheets across the table to each of them. "You'll find all of his details there right down to his preferences in clothing, food and drink." They all sat silently for the next fifteen minutes whilst they inwardly digested the file in front of them. McCormack eventually broke the silence.

"I will not ask you how you got all of this information but it certainly allows us to get a good insight into the fellow. I would say he fits the picture perfectly. How about you, Philip?"

"I would agree, but I still feel we are skating on thin ice."

"Philip, there is no other way out for us. We have to give this a try. Let's get him up now," added McCormack. After another ten minutes of deliberation they called in the secretary from the outer office.

"Jayne, be a good girl and phone up the Overseas Business Department and ask them to send up a Mr David Johnson please," said Hackman with a glint in his eye. Never stops fishing for sex thought Philip.

On the eighth floor business was as usual until the phone call came to the office manager.

"Is that Mr Browning of the Overseas Business Department? This is Jayne Ackerman. I'm the personal secretary to the Governing Board of Directors."

Browning swallowed hard, fearing the next few sentences.

"I believe that you have a Mr David Johnson working in your department. Would you be so kind as to ask him to come up to the board room, please?"

"Certainly, Miss Ackerman. He'll be there within the next few minutes," he said in a relieved tone to his voice. Usually he would send along his secretary when he needed to speak to one of his subordinates but on this occasion he decided to do it himself. As he walked down through the aisles of desks he was aware of many pairs of eyes watching every move that he made. He felt quite self-conscious.

"Ah, Mr Johnson. Would you stop work for a few moments and report to the boardroom? The directors would like to speak to you." A hush descended over the whole of the office. Was he the first for the chop?

David looked up from his work in disbelief. Why on earth did they want to see him? He had a good track record with the company, always kept a low profile and never complained about his job in public. He put down his pen, pulled on his jacket, straightened his tie and walked towards the elevator feeling even more conspicuous than Mr Browning had felt a few moments earlier. He got into the lift and looked at the panel of buttons in front of him. He took a deep breath and pressed the top button which was labelled 'Board Room.'

When the doors of the lift opened, he was greeted by a smartly dressed secretary who led him to two large mahogany doors which upon which was fixed a large brass plaque with the letters, "Board Room" She knocked, and proceeded to push them open. David was surprised at the size of the room. It seemed almost as big as the office in which he worked and that housed twenty desks plus operators. This room had an enormous table running down its whole length and at the far end stood the three board members. Seeing the door open one of them made his way to David, holding out his right hand in the process. He shook David's hand firmly.

"Welcome to the boardroom, David. I'm Justin Hackman, that is Philip Jackson and this is John McCormack," he said pointing to the other two who came forward and shook David's hand. David felt a little unnerved when he looked into the eyes of the hatchet man. He looked as evil as people had described him to be. Not the sort of person to get on the wrong side of, thought David. He was now puzzled as to why he had been summoned. If they had intended to give him the sack they would not have gone through the ritual of shaking his hand and trying to make him feel at home.

Hackman continued. "We have been looking at your progress in our company. All reports indicate that you are an extremely reliable employee and a diligent worker. We have also looked at your qualifications and feel that you have not been well placed in the firm. It's about time that you were rewarded for your work. We're proposing to make you work even harder by offering you an overseas posting. You have probably heard of the project with the United Arab Emirates." Anyone who hadn't, thought David, must have had their head buried in the sand for the past few years, such was the enormity of the contract.

"Well, we would like you to take over the management of it. We need someone who can speak Arabic and who is good at mixing with people. As you probably know we are nearing the final stages of completion and need someone out there who can tie up all the loose ends and organise the signing over processes."

David could not believe what he was hearing. One minute he was expecting to be thrown out and now he was being offered an amazing posting.

"I don't know what to say. I'm in deep shock." The three of them laughed with one accord.

"You don't have to make any decisions for the moment. What we suggest you do is to take a few days leave and go away somewhere quiet and have a long think. We will give you all the actual details of the post, including salary, which will not compare at all with what you are earning at the present moment! Also details of a very substantial allowance for looking after extremely rich business men, chauffer-driven car, hotel penthouse suite or if you prefer it a house with house staff, etc, etc. I expect by now your head must be spinning, so say nothing and go back to your desk collect up all of your personal belongings and take a few days off." He held out his hand and shook David's firmly and then led him back to the elevator not giving him enough time to even think about accepting or declining the offer. "We will touch base in a few days time."

The mention of David's head spinning was an understatement as it was almost about to twist off from his neck. By the time he got back to his desk he was beginning to think a little more clearly. His boss on the floor must have been informed that David would be taking a few days off and was already standing by David's desk with an offer to help him to get things together. The rest of the office staff pretended to work but were all trying to fathom out what was happening. David collected up all of his belongings, said thank you to his boss and his secretary and went off for a few days break already knowing full well that he was going to accept the offer!

Chapter Seventeen

He returned to the office three days after meeting the board of directors and accepted their invitation to become the manager of the project in Abu Dhabi. He had been placed temporarily in a small office with his own secretary until he was ready to fly out, and was now in the process of planning his trip. There were numerous things to do. He needed details of the personnel that he would be working most closely with. He needed to buy a whole new wardrobe of clothes and most important of all he needed to know a lot more about Abu Dhabi. His secretary had been given the assignment of collating all she could find on the area in which he would be operating, including its history. These details arrived on his desk a day later. That morning he requested that he should only to be disturbed for extremely important matters and as he had known his secretary for a long time he knew he could totally rely upon her judgement. He then sat down at his desk with a cup of strong coffee and commenced to read the file that his secretary had produced.

The United Arab Emirates consists of seven Emirates; Abu Dhabi the capital, Ajman, Dubai, Fulairah, Ras al-Khaimah, Sharjah and Umn al-Qaiwain of which Abu Dhabi is the largest by far. These Emirates were almost unheard of even as late as the nineteen-seventies. Up until then it was a very impoverished country, which relied upon pearl diving as its main industry. The Gulf was in actual fact the leading area in the world for producing pearls until the market was hit by the production of cultured pearls in Japan.

The life of the pearler was a harsh one and fatalaties were frequent. Only the odd few people made a fortune out of the industry. The divers used to spend months on board old wooden ships in very cramped conditions with poor dietary foods.

Often after a season of severe hardships a diver could come off of a boat owing more than when he went on, if the catch was a bad one. He was expected to pay for his own keep whilst on board ship, and the owners of the ship made sure that he rarely received a good wage so that he would have to come back during the next pearling season.

The British were the main influence in the area and they made sure that the Trucial States, as they were called in those times, were not allowed to develop.

With the finding of oil things changed very slowly at first. Millions of dollars came into the country but little found its way down to the common people. The majority of people were undernourished as the supply of milk was poor, and few fruits and vegetables were available. For the inhabitants away from the coast, who lived at oases, conditions were even worse as most perishable foods, which had to be imported, could not survive the long camel trips in the heat of the deserts. Even the local fish had to be eaten within hours of being caught.

The men usually wore a single garment called a kandoura or dishdash, the children next to nothing and the women owned at the most two kandouras, which they usually made themselves. There were no schools in the nineteen-fifties so children grew up with no education at all. The majority of people lived in tents with woven mats made of palm fronds used on the floors and as a windbreak from the biting, cold winter winds.

These Spartan conditions changed however, with the new leadership of Sheik Zayed. He was an intelligent man who could visualise how his country could progress with the discovery of oil, or black gold, as it was known by the locals. With the proceeds of the oil revenue he established an education system for the children and a health scheme for all to benefit from. He improved the infrastructure of the country with new roads and buildings and made sure that the local businessmen were given the opportunity of making profits rather than it all going overseas. It was an incredible feat to change a country almost overnight from a small encampment of impoverished people into one of the most affluent countries in the world today. Abu

Dhabi is now a thriving modern city with beautiful buildings and luxurious hotels.

David was looking forward to the climate most of all. He was fed up with the dark cold winters and the hours spent cooped up in some stuffy car waiting for the change in the colour of the traffic lights in order to take him to the next set only a few meters down the road. He longed to feel the sun on his bare arms and not having to wear a collar and tie day in and day out. There would be times when he would have to dress formally but he had heard that everyone dressed casual in the office and he had no intention of changing that rule.

At the end of a month he was ready to go. He had had the final briefing from McCormack on what was expected of him. He was to leave all technical problems to the design department. Should any problem arise he was to inform McCormack immediately who would then deal with it. And so he eventually boarded a plane to Abu Dhabi. The flight was uneventful until they were within fifteen minutes from their destination when the pilot came on the air to announce that there was to be a slight change in the flight pattern.

There was a heavy ground mist at the airport in Abu Dhabi and so they had been diverted to Dubai. The pilot then handed over to the chief steward who then went on to explain the travel arrangements for getting the passengers to Abu Dhabi. Air-conditioned coaches were already organised and express facilities had been laid on in the terminal to get them through customs quickly. There would also be facilities for passengers to make any necessary phone calls to waiting friends. The coach journey would take less than two hours. He went on to say that refreshments would be provided before joining the coach and the journey through the desert would give new visitors to the Emirates an insight into the desert terrain. David was not at all perturbed as he had not made any prearranged times for going into the office. All he wanted to do was to get to his apartment, unpack and catch up with some sleep. He did not want to meet his new colleagues until he was feeling in tiptop shape.

The terminal at Dubai is an amazing place with probably the

best selection of duty free merchandise in the world. As you walk through the terminal you are surrounded by the latest Porches, Mercedes and four-wheel drives all being raffled with no profits being made. The internal façade of the main building is all marble with expensive-looking shops. You have the feeling of being in an exclusive hotel. The travellers are quite cosmopolitan in their dress. Many of the local people wear their national dress and many of the women are covered from head to toe in black with their faces completely covered and only their eyes showing.

The coach journey did allow one to get a feeling for the country as the steward had explained. David actually saw camels wandering in the wild with no owners in attendance. There were road signs indicating to beware of such stray animals. To knock one over could result in a gaol sentence. All along the entire drive there were shrubs and trees, which had their own individual water supply. Wherever one sees a tree in the Emirates it will be accompanied by a hose, which at pre-arranged times, will sprinkle its roots with a fresh supply of water. Presumably, thought David, if you ever got lost in the desert, look for a tree and then start digging. Occasionally he saw flocks of goats, which he assumed belonged to the nomadic tribes who still wandered the desert.

About half way along the journey the driver of the coach pulled into a small filling station but did not stop at the pumps. Instead, he parked adjacent to a mini mosque. David watched as the man took off his shoes, washed his feet and then proceeded to kneel on a small mat which he had brought with him and began to pray. David had read that the men had to pray at least five times a day and these times were usually published daily in the newspapers. He was also made aware of the important dates in the Islamic calendar, Al-Israa wal-Miraaj, which marks the Prophet's ascension into heaven and Mawlid al-Nabi, which was the Prophet's birthday. In Ramadan, which was the Muslim month of fasting, work hours were reduced and there was no consumption of food or water between sunrise and sunset. At the end of the month Ramadan was followed by the Eid al Fitr holiday, which can last as long as an entire week. Also at the end of Hajj, which is the period in the final month of the Islamic year, all government offices stayed closed so it was no use trying to arrange an important business meeting during that time.

During the flight David had noticed that some Islamic passengers had even placed their prayer mats down in the isles of the plane and began to pray. The interesting thing David noticed was that when they prayed they had to be facing Mecca and on the small TV screens on the plane there was always a sign indicating the direction to Mecca.

The coach driver's prayers took about five minutes and then they were off once more. Including the stop the journey took just over two hours. They had the choice of being dropped in the centre of the town or at the airport as some were due to be met by relatives and business colleagues. David was being met at the airport so he had no option, which meant probably going straight past his apartment only to be brought back to it an hour later. He was correct.

He was met by a company secretary who had arranged to get him through customs and immigration quickly rather than line up with the numerous immigrant workers whose papers took twice as long to scrutinise as compared with a holiday visitor. This amiable young man collected his baggage from the carousel and led him out into the humid heat where he began to sweat profusely and continued to do so until he got into an air conditioned car whereupon he began to feel cold. He was going to have to get used to the dramatic changes in temperature quickly he thought, as perspiration began to show on his shirt, in the pit of his back and under his arms.

After driving for about twenty minutes they came into the city limits which were an amazing sight. There were no high-rise buildings, as the Sheik would only allow buildings to reach a height of twenty stories thus keeping the city uniformly tidy from an aerial aspect. The actual buildings were, however, breathtaking. Many had reflecting glass in various colours and all appeared to be relatively new.

263

The limousine in which David was travelling eventually pulled up adjacent to the prestigious Lexus building on As Salam Street. David noticed that the street names were in Arabic and English. He was met by a doorman who showed him into a large lobby, which had mirrors reaching up to the ceiling giving the effect that he was standing in a huge glistening auditorium. He introduced himself to the doorman who led him to the lift and pressed the button to the penthouse suite.

The views from the top were absolutely stunning. He could see out over the entire city as far as the sea in both directions. The suite was very tastefully decorated and had two bathrooms and two bedrooms in case of guests staying. That night he did not do any unpacking. David just had a quick shower and went straight to bed. He intended to sleep until midday but was awoken at seven o'clock by the sound of a recording from the local mosque calling the men to prayer. He got out onto the balcony to watch the sun rise and was amazed to see how many people were coming from all directions to the mosque in order to pray. In the UK on a Sunday morning one would have had to use a powerful pair of binoculars in order to see anyone going to the local church.

By nine o'clock David had showered and had had a light breakfast. He was very pleased to have found the fridge well stocked up with a variety of foods, which would last him for the next few days until he found the local shops. He took the lift down and then commenced to walk in a circle around his building. On the corner was a small shop, which appeared to sell almost everything. The owner was of Indian origin and an extremely pleasant man, who introduced him to the local papers, which were both in English and Arabic. He was mildly surprised and pleased to find how much detail was printed about news from overseas. The journalism was as good if not better than a lot of the newspapers at home, so he knew that his Sunday mornings would be pleasantly spent lying in bed with toast and coffee.

The first few days he spent acclimatising himself with the locality in which he lived and the people and their customs. He

264

had decided not to make any contact with the main office until he had got over the time differences and climatic conditions. After all he was the boss and he could do almost as he pleased. That in itself would take a lot of getting used to.

On the third day he had his first stroke of luck. He was coming down in the lift when it stopped on the fifth floor to allow a very attractive young lady in. She smiled and they struck up a conversation. She was called Nicola and was teaching in one of the local private schools. Before setting off for school she asked if David would like to be shown around the city one evening as she explained that someone had done that for her when she arrived and it had made it so much easier for her to settle down to a normal routine. He accepted the invitation and two nights later they met.

She took him first to the nearest supermarket, which was the Coop. All of the locals shopped there as the prices were extremely competitive. He remembered what he had been told by one of his uncles many years ago when he was setting out on his various travels around the world, and that was to watch where the local people eat and drank because they were the best judges of value for money.

Nicola also introduced him to the British Club where many of the expatriates hung out. The land on which it was built had been given to the club free of charge by the Sheik who owned all of the land in Abu Dhabi. Over the years it had been developed to having a large swimming pool adjacent to its own private beach, a library, large functions room, sailing club, tennis courts, and squash courts. Once a week it held some form of a social evening, which was always well attended and proved very lively on occasions when the expatriate school teachers let their hair down after a stressful week. David soon became one of the teachers' socialising group and for the first time in his life actually enjoyed going out with members of the opposite sex. He owed a lot to Nicola who became one of his best friends.

By the second month he had paid visits to most of the buildings and offices within the company and had established his authority in such a way that most people were not afraid to approach him if they were experiencing any problems with their work. Arrangements were well in hand for the handing over of the desalination plants to the Government in a year's time, which allowed David to enjoy his work almost stress free.

David had made one coup, which the management were extremely pleased with, and that was finding a date by which the Sheik could actually attend the opening ceremony. On those occasions when the Sheik attended, the whole Government was expected to be in attendance, so it was going to be a very memorable day for the company and the directors.

When David originally accepted the post he had thought it rather strange that the actual desalination plants were not part of his jurisdiction. He had been specifically told to leave the entire running of the plants to the senior engineer and as David had no experience in the field of engineering he had decided to do just that. That was until a fax was sent by mistake to his office instead of head office in New York. It was addressed to one of the directors and simply said, "possible problems with third generator in number six plant". David kept a copy of this which he knew he shouldn't have done and then sent the original on to head office. Strange that the fax had not been sent to him, he thought, as he was in charge of the project overall and that it had been sent to one of the directors instead of the Head of Overseas Projects. He decided that if he had a few spare hours in his daily schedule he might pay a visit to the plant.

Another two busy weeks went by during which he was working most nights up until eight o'clock, and this prevented him from doing any form of socialising even at the weekends. By the end of that period he was exhausted and decided it was time for him to take a short break from the office. He was due to at least a week off work but informed his secretary that he would be away for only a few days. He wasn't going out of the country, and would probably spend most of his time down at the club catching up with his suntan and getting back into the gym.

By the second day at the club he was getting restless. He was not really a person to sit around all day doing nothing. His life since leaving school had been non-stop work and he always found it extremely difficult to wind down. He was one of those people who seemed to thrive on stress. It was during the afternoon when he suddenly decided to break the monotony of his day.

He was sitting in the air-conditioned bar sipping a pint of Fosters and reading an article in the local *Gulf News* about drilling off the coast for a new oil well, when his eye caught the words fresh water. His brain immediately switched into the area used for storing non-essential data and drew out the thoughts on the desalination plant, which had had problems a few weeks ago. The complex was about a few hour's drive down the coast so he made up his mind to call in later that afternoon. As it was not going to be an official visit he decided not to let them know beforehand as it might upset their usual routine and it would be interesting to see how they usually ran their operation.

The drive was an uneventful one. He did not run over any camels and no freak dust storms blocked his vision on the fast three-laned motorway. He was glad he was driving one of the company's four-wheel drives as the last five kilometres was over a bumpy undulating sand track which had been sprayed with a thick bitumastic type of oil which helped bind the loose sand together. Other than the blackened road there was no other indication of any form of life in the area.

Occasionally he came across a few prickly looking bushes and that was all. He kept thinking what it might be like to be lost in the desert. It wouldn't take much to wander off this narrow track. One gust of wind just as he was about to go over the top of one of the steep sand dunes could send him rolling down its steep side where he would be trapped until someone came across him, and that might be too late.

He shivered and concentrated on the black line ahead of him. Eventually he came to a fenced off area with a sign indicating that only personnel from the plant were allowed to enter. There was no one on the gate so he drove in and parked by the only building which had windows. As he got out of the car someone shouted from the corner of one of the larger buildings, which he assumed housed the generators used in the desalination process.

"Do you have any authority to be here?" echoed a rather officious voice across the large open space. It was the site manager, Jim Drisco, who had just come out from inspecting one of the turbines and was a little hot and bothered.

"The name is David Johnson. I'm the area manager. I should have given you some form of notice to say that I would be calling in but I didn't decide until the last moment. Sorry if I took you by surprise."

Jim Drisco looked a little sheepish on finding out that he was facing the big boss from head office in Abu Dhabi.

"I'm the one who should be sorry Mr Johnson. Never expected you to be this far out from civilisation. We don't get many visitors out here, a few young college lads visiting their parents sometimes borrow their dad's four wheeler and go sand dune hopping and stray into our sector. What brings you out here then?"

David decided not to mention anything about the problems they were experiencing, as he was not supposed to know.

"Had a few days to fill up and thought I would pay a visit to one of the plants. I am organising the handing over of them in about six months time and thought that I should know a little about them. I've got no experience at all in the technology area and wouldn't know a wrench from a turbine."

Thank goodness for that, thought Drisco. Don't want anyone sticking his nose into this plant at the present moment even if it was the boss himself. He would have to mention this to the top man, McCormack, who wanted to know of anyone out of the ordinary who visited the site.

"You are welcome to stay as long as you like and have a look at the process inside the turbo house. I'll get one of the lads to take you around. I can't let you go on your own due to health and safety regulations and there are some areas which could be dangerous. Come on into the office and have a cold drink. No beer, I'm afraid, as all installations are strictly dry if you forgive the pun." He smiled at that and led David into the cool of the air-conditioned office.

"If you will bear with me for a moment, I will go down to the workshop and find someone to show you around. It may take a few minutes so feel at home and turn on the T.V. if you like. It's satellite and I think there is a baseball game on one of the sports channels. The channel changer is on top of the set." David took his drink to the set, turned it on and began to flick through the channels.

Once out of the office, instead of going to the workshop, Drisco made his way to his sleeping quarters, took out his mobile phone and dialled the number that had been given him by McCormack. It was the middle of the night in New York and a not too happy a man answered the call.

"McCormack here. It's two thirty in the morning so this had better be good."

"Really sorry to disturb you, Mr McCormack. This is Jim Drisco from the United Arab Emirates. I'm in charge of the desalination project and you asked me to get in contact with you if anyone unauthorised came down to the project and started asking questions." McCormack immediately came to his senses on hearing this bit of information, the sleepy haze suddenly disappearing.

"At this present moment I have a Mr David Johnson who is the overall manager of the whole operation out here. He turned up with no previous warning and said that he was just dropping in to see how things were going. He said that he had no former training in the area of engineering and as he was due to hand over the scheme to the authorities he felt he should know at least something of the mechanics involved in the desalination processes."

McCormack jumped into the conversation. "You did the right thing to get in contact with me. I want you to play everything low key. Have you got anyone there who has difficulty in speaking the language and who could show him around? Make sure that you do not get involved with him. I suggest that once the visit commences you get a message to him saying that you had been called out to one of the fields on an emergency, and that you would get in contact with him when he returns to head office in Abu Dhabi. He's right when he says he knows little about the mechanics of the turbines, so you probably won't get any more visits from him. Keep in contact with me and let me know the outcome of his visit."

McCormack rang off and then sat back in his chair. Bloody Johnson, he thought. He was told there would be no need for him to visit any of the sites as they were being supervised by experts. Why was he sticking his nose in at this late stage of affairs? All was going well since the last set of problems. Probably nothing in it. He knew he could leave it in the hands of Drisco, as he had had dealings with him before and he had always come out on top. He soon convinced himself that there was nothing to worry about and went back to bed.

Jim Drisco went straight to the canteen after his call where he knew one of the local natives would be working. The chap he was looking for had a reasonable knowledge of English but not enough to hold a conversation on the technical terms relating to turbines and how they worked. He would be ideal for the job in question.

Albert, as the staff affectionately knew him, as his name in his native tongue was far too difficult to pronounce, had been working on the site from the initial stages of laying down the foundations. He could lend his hand to anything and had proved invaluable to the company. Although he was officially employed as unskilled labour he was paid above the going rate and held the trust of all the firm's employees. At that moment in time he was helping the kitchen staff to put up a new set of shelves in one of the rear cupboards at the back of the kitchen.

"Albert, I'd like you to leave what you are doing. Got a very important job for you to do for me. We have a special visitor who would like to be shown around the site, and the best person for doing that is you, seeing that you have been here from it's birth. I think they dug you up here when the first spade went into the sand." Albert laughed as he had over the years learnt to appreciate the humour of the foreigners and enjoyed being at the receiving end of their friendly jokes. No one ever took advantage of Albert as he had such a warming personality.

"Certainly, Mr Drisco. Would you like me to take him below

the sand to where I live and show him around?" He could give as good as he got. Jim Drisco ruffled the mass of wiry black hair on top of Albert's head.

"Enough of that. We don't want our visitor Mr Johnson going back to Abu Dhabi with sand in his eyes, do we?"

By the time they got back to the office David was dozing in the low old settee having got fed up with flicking the channels. The heat of the day was beginning to take its toll even with the air-conditioning working at full blast.

"Sorry to keep you waiting. Had a job to find Albert here, who is going to show you around the site. Caught him in the hairdressers attempting to get his hair straightened and then dyed blond." They all laughed in unison. "Right, Albert, take Mr Johnson anywhere he wishes to go but keep him out of harm's way. Those turbines are turning at thousands of revolutions per minute and would make mincemeat of your shirtsleeve plus your arm in the space of no time. Don't forget to put on the yellow helmets. We stringently follow Health and Safety rules in this establishment. When he's had enough of all the noise and heat bring him back here and ask the office to page for me."

"OK, boss," said Albert with a smile radiating all over his sun tanned face. "You come with me, sir. We get helmets, then go to turbine room."

As soon as they went out of the office Jim Drisco phoned his secretary and told her that he had been called out on a semi-emergency and that he would probably not be back until the following day. He explained about their unscheduled visitor and what she had to relay to him once he returned to the office. He then surveyed the outside parking area making sure that his visitor was nowhere in sight and then made a dash for his car and drove off for the rest of the day.

The turbine shed was certainly a noisy affair even with the earmuffs on. David was impressed at the immensity of the machine and how much water finally came out into the huge holding tanks where it then was pumped out to its various destinations. There was no chance at all of asking Albert any questions about the mechanics of the process whilst in the building, so he decided to leave all questions until they were back in the quiet, cooler office block. In the space of an hour they visited two other machine sheds and other areas each having their own specialised jobs to do in the purifying of the salt water. David found the whole visit very interesting and wished he had gone there during the early days of his move to Abu Dhabi. As they were nearing the end of their tour they passed an even bigger building, which seemed to be shut up.

"What's in this building," said David.

"Big turbo, but him no work."

"What do you mean by, 'him no work'?" enquired David.

"Big machine break down a year ago so we shut it down and leave it. Men are at present taking it apart and shipping it away by lorry. Mr. Dunkley say all machines be like that in a few years."

"Who is Mr. Dunkley? Where can I find him?"

"He soon leave after machine break down. Don't know where he goes."

David decided not to continue with this line of conversation for the time being, as the fellow obviously did not know any more than what he had previously said. He decided to take it up with Jim Drisco when they got back in the office. However, when they eventually got back he was very disappointed to find that Drisco had been called out on other important business.

He thanked all concerned, had a last refreshing drink and left in his four-wheel drive to bounce back up the narrow oil covered track before it came in dark. He did not wish to spend the night in an upturned vehicle shivering in the almost freezing temperatures and waiting for some unwelcome scorpion to pay a visit. All the way back he could not take his mind off of the disused turbine and the words of Albert that the others would fail. The thought of that happening would be devastating for the company and for himself, as he was overall in charge. He was annoyed with himself for not having gone around the sites during the first few weeks of his posting. In the morning he would make a call to head office and speak to whoever was in charge of the turbine production.

First thing the following morning he went into the office early so as to be able to contact head office before their lines got too busy. He sat down at his desk and glanced at the mail that was neatly laid out in front of him by his meticulous secretary. On top was a phone message that was marked urgent, so he decided to read it before making his call to New York. He was surprised to see that it was from one of the directors, McCormack. It simply read 'phone as soon as you arrive back in the office, urgent.' Strange, thought David as he picked up the phone, as he was about to phone head office. Probably just a coincidence. It only took a few seconds and he was through to the main office. He must have been given some sort of priority number.

"Good afternoon, this is Mr. McCormack's office, how may I help you?"

"David Johnson here. I was asked by Mr. McCormack to get in touch with him."

"Ah, yes. I have a directive here for me to put you through to Mr. McCormack even if he is in a meeting. Just bear with me for a moment."

David sat back in his seat and wondered what was so important that necessitated the interruption of possibly an important meeting in head office.

"Johnson, this is John McCormack. I tried to reach you yesterday but was told that you were out on some jaunt in the desert. It was extremely important that we got in touch with you as a major problem raised its head about the hand over of the project to the Emirates Government. We had to deal with it without your guidance. Thankfully we had someone here at the time that had been working in Abu Dhabi before your posting there, so that got us out of a tight spot. We have decided that in future as we are so near to the hand-over date that you should remain in the city at all times just in case of any future emergency.

Incidentally we are sending over an expert on the desalination plants so that you would not have to deal with any technical problems should they arise. We need your full attention working on D-Day when we hand over the running of the turbines to the Government. I hope I don't come across as

273

being too dictatorial, but we are getting a little on edge back here in head office. Do I make myself clear? A lot of our resources have been placed into this project and we can't afford for anything to go wrong, no matter how small at this stage in the proceedings."

David took a deep breath before replying. He got the distinct feeling that McCormack had somehow found out that he had been out to the site and was warning him off. He decided to play this very carefully. McCormack had to be put at ease otherwise he would have the place swarming with spies.

"Sorry about yesterday. As you know I have no technical knowledge of the workings of desalination plants and decided to take a look at one. I did not wish to be in the position of being unable to converse with one of the diplomats over here about the simple fundamentals involved in the production of fresh water. As it turned out my visit gave me a good understanding of the principals involved. I went out to Plant Seven where a Jim Drisco arranged for me to make a most comprehensive tour of the area. I was most impressed how smoothly things were running.

"I know now that when I attend any future meetings with Government officials I will feel much more confident if any conversations arise on the more technical side of the operation. I always take with me someone who has had direct dealings with the running of the turbines, but even then I have always felt quite vulnerable. So I hope that you can see why I made the trip. There is no need for me to stray away from my offices in the future and I can understand why you may have been perturbed yesterday when you could not get in touch with me. Please accept my apologies Mr McCormack."

"Accepted. You probably did the right thing in getting yourself genned up on the technical side of things. Just did it at the wrong time. Well, keep in touch if you do have any problems. Now that you have my number you can get directly in touch with me in an emergency. Must get back to my meeting now. Look forward to seeing you on the big handover day."

Bt the end of the conversation David was damp with sweat. He didn't want to have to go through that procedure again, not with the notorious McCormack acting as a KGB interrogator. He would have to tread very carefully in future as his movements would probably be monitored by some one in the office who would have been assigned to their position by the likes of McCormack. Why should one little visit have caused so much hassle, enough to get the hatchet man going for him? He decided to let things quieten down and then perhaps make a few discreet enquiries about some of the points that had arisen out of his visit.

The following morning he called his secretary into his office as soon as she arrived for work.

"Mavis, when I was out during yesterday afternoon did anyone phone in for me from head office?"

"No Mr. Johnson. In fact it was a very quiet afternoon. I only took three calls and they were for Mr. Harrison."

"OK. Thanks for holding the fort for me."

David retired into his office and sat at his desk mulling over in his mind all that happened the previous day. Now, what was the name of the guy that Albert had said who had been in charge of the turbine sheds until his recent replacement? He had to name associate in order to remember. Animal, donkey, Dunkley. In order to find out a little more about the man he turned to his computer and typed in his password. He then typed in personnel and scrolled down the alphabet until he hit Dunkley. Robert Dunkley, Marine Engineering, and that was all. David pressed his line to his secretary who responded immediately.

"Mavis, I want you to get me some details about a Mr. Robert Dunkley. I need to know where he is working at the present moment and how to get in contact with him. Try and be as discreet as possible please."

"It so happens, Mr. Johnson, that I have got a close friend working in the personnel department at head office. They owe me a few favours. I'll give them a phone in a few hours time."

"Thanks, Mavis. You're worth your weight in gold. Remind me to put something extra in your Christmas stocking."

Mavis was glad he could not see her blush at the thought of something extra! She found her boss extremely attractive, but there was an age gap of some twenty years so she appreciated that there would be no inroads for her in that area. She was puzzled why no other young lady ever appeared on the scene. Probably because he was always working, silly man.

The details of Robert Dunkley appeared on David's desk the following afternoon when he returned from his lunch break. He was always surprised at the efficiency of his secretary. He buzzed her and congratulated her on her expediency.

Robert Dunkley was now living in Sweden and was the chief engineer in charge of running a large pipeline from a tanker terminal on the coast across a mountainous hill where it then supplied a vast hinterland with fuel for the production of electricity and heating for a population which was spread out over a very large area. Sweden, until most recently, relied upon huge hydro-electric schemes from its vast water supplies plus nuclear reactors. Now due to the movement of Green Peace and a few other smaller groups that were pushing for more care to be taken to protect the planet from pollution, there was a move in parliament to start closing down nuclear reactors and replace them with other forms of energy. Global Engineering had seen this as an opportunity to use their technologies for moving vast quantities of oil into the hinterlands via a pipeline. All oil had to be imported and the only means of transport was via lorry. The company had put forward a viable alternative to the use of lorries, which were unable to operate for at least half of the year due to the adverse climatic conditions. This proposal was accepted which landed the company with a most lucrative contract.

David noticed whilst reading through the notes on Robert Dunkley that there was a phone number for the central office of operations and next to it Mavis had put in brackets the time differential. Good old Mavis. David decided to try to contact the man as soon as the time was suitable, as he did not want to wake him in the middle of the night and put him in a bad mood. He made the call the following day. At first he was completely thrown for the voice at the other end of the line spoke in Swedish.

"I'm sorry but I can't understand what you are saying"

"That's perfectly normal, sir. You must be American as you

have a more of a drawn-out accent as compared with the English accent. Now how can I help you?"

"That was a quick change around in your language brain and may I say that you have a far better command of the English language than myself." David had certainly learnt a lot from his good friend Nicola in how to deal with the opposite sex. "Would it be possible to speak to Robert Dunkley who I believe is based in your head office in the engineering section which is overseeing the pipeline project?"

"Yes, he does work out of here. If you give me a few moments I'll see if I can locate his whereabouts." With that she put him on hold and the annoying music of Greensleeves came over the air. No matter where one went in the world the same music seemed to haunt you, or so David thought. He made a mental note to check to see which type of music was played in Abu Dhabi.

"I'm very sorry but Mr Dunkley is away for about three weeks. He has had to go out to the pipeline and I'm afraid there is no way of contacting him."

"Isn't he on a mobile phone?"

"Yes but we have found that they do not work in that area. Something to do with the static produced by the metallic contents of the mountain that they are working on. Would you like me to leave a message with his secretary for when he returns?"

"No thank you. It's not very important. I will get in contact at a later date."

"Whom should I say called?" said the secretary who felt annoyed with herself for not having asked the question as soon as she took the call. David decided on the spur of the moment not to leave his name on the off-chance that McCormack may have had a spy even in this neck of the woods.

"Just a friend from the past" and with that he put down the phone.

What now? thought David. The completion date and the signing over of the project was only a few months away and now this had to happen. They must know about the problems with the turbines at head office so why was he not informed? He began to feel most uncomfortable. The consequences of the turbines beginning to play up before or even after the project had been handed over to the government were horrendous. The first person people would come running to would be the overall leader of the contract in Abu Dhabi and that was himself. Would head office back him up? Not the likes of McCormack. Was he being set up? He had to know more about the problems with the turbines.

There was no hope of getting any information from the technical department in New York as this was too near to McCormack's patch. The only one who could give him the information that he needed was Robert Dunkley and he was in the outback. There was only one thing to do, and that was to go and pay Mr Dunkley a visit, even if it meant trekking into the interior in search of the fellow. He picked up the phone and once more and dialled for his secretary.

"Mavis, would you come into my office for a moment please?"

Mavis picked up her pad and pencil and went into the adjacent office. Instead of being asked to sit next to her boss at his desk where she usually sat for the dictation of notes, he guided her to the area of the large office, which was used when dealing with clients. There were four large leather armchairs, which were chosen in order to make any visitor feel completely relaxed.

"Mavis, come and sit down here," David said, with a warm smile which immediately put her at ease as she thought that she might be in a spot of trouble as she was never invited to sit where the visiting board members sit.

"What I am about to say must never be repeated outside this room. There is no need to reply to that, as I know that you are extremely trustworthy. I am in a serious dilemma, which could have grave repercussions for the project here and in turn for the whole of the company. I am not at this stage able to tell you any details of the problems we face but will confide in you after the next few days have elapsed. I am having to go to Sweden for at least four days and I do not want anyone to know where I am. That is where you come in. I want you to give the impression that I am meeting up with some relations in Singapore, who are on their way to Australia. As I am due to a week's holiday I had decided to fly over to there. If anyone does enquire as to my whereabouts you could add that I looked extremely tired and needed a short break to recharge my batteries. Do you think you can handle the little white lie, Mavis?"

"You should know by now that you can rely on my help at anytime, Mr Johnson." She could not help blushing and hoped that her boss did not notice.

"I really appreciate that, Mavis. Now there are a number of things that I need you to do in relationship to my trip there. Any finances must come out of my own private account and have nothing to do with the firm's monies. I would like to fly out the day after tomorrow and land in the capital, Stockholm. From there I have to get to the camp, which is near the head of the River Ljusnan. Time is of the essence so I will use the quickest means of transport, which is by seaplane. Not looking forward to that part of the journey, but I cannot spare the time to travel by road, if there are any roads in that area. Probably have to take to the water for the last part of the journey. If there is any chance of a helicopter then I'll take that. Sorry it's a lot to do in such a short space of time but I know you like a good challenge."

Within the next hour Mavis had made a booking for the flight to Stockholm, chartered a small seaplane and even managed to hire a small speedboat with a skipper to take him on the final stage of the trip. She then arranged for some travellers cheques to be delivered to the office and a cab to pick him up from his apartment. Two days later he was on his way.

The first part of the journey was quite relaxing sitting in the business section of the aircraft. Meals were better than the usual in club class, probably due to the airline being a small one. Good quality in meals and service often is more appealing than saving a few dollars on the airfare. David went through customs and immigration without any hold-ups and then out into the empty foyer of the terminal. There were a few waiting people holding up placards and he noticed his name almost immediately.

"Hi. I'm Mr Johnson." David said to the rather over-weight driver who was smartly attired in a dark grey suit.

"Welcome to Sweden, sir. My car is at the first parking lot only one-minute walk away. Allow me to take your baggage. Our drive to the heliport is about half an hour so you can either sit back and take a short nap or be absolutely bored with a running commentary on the wonderful countryside through which we will be travelling." He gave a friendly wink and commenced to pick up David's suitcases.

For the next thirty minutes David was given a very interesting talk about the topography through which they were passing through and how it affected the infrastructure of the area. The heliport was adjacent to a stretch of water along which were moored small colourful seaplanes. David wished he had been able to charter one of the helicopters but none were available so he was forced to put his trust in one of the flimsy looking planes, which were bobbing about on the water at the end of the quay.

Dracona Airflights had a fleet of five aircraft and spent most of its time flying out trappers in the winter and homeowners in the summer who had built in the outback and which were inaccessible by road. Their aim it seemed was to cut themselves completely off from the outside world for a period of time and live off of the land, although most of them apparently took along huge amounts of food just in case of an emergency!

David thanked the taxi-driver and made arrangements to be picked up two days later at the same time. He could have been back the same day if all went as planned, but he had to be prepared for all eventualities and gave himself plenty of extra time. He went into the office, which looked in the need of his secretary, as there were papers and various books and maps spread over all available space. He saw a bell on the desk and gave it a ring. He heard some movement at the back of the building followed by the appearance of a man in dirty grey overalls, which was covered in oil.

"Excuse my Sunday best. You must be Mr Johnson. We are due to fly you out within the hour, I believe. I'll get this gear off and get ready for the flight. Make yourself a cup of coffee. There is a full pot on the stove in the rear of the building and the milk is in the fridge behind the door. Won't be long."

David did as he was told and made himself a strong mug with two sugars as he felt he would need the extra caffeine and sugar intake. He was beginning to feel anxious about the next flight.

"There, that didn't take long. Now the flight will only take about fifteen minutes, but we will still have to dress up in all of the gear as it gets quite cold up there and the heater in the plane does not work very well." He handed David a large fleece lined all in one suit much like a baby wears to bed, a fur hat, gloves and earmuffs.

"The earmuffs are not to keep your ears warm. It's to prevent your ears from getting damaged by the noise of the engines. We don't have the insulation of the Jumbos on which you no doubt usually travel. Now to put you at ease, none of my planes have ever failed to fly and as you see all have successfully landed in one piece. The difference between a Jumbo and one of my craft is that should the engines of a Jumbo fail you just plunge to the ground much like a stone, whereas in one of my machines we glide down and there is always water on which to land. So sit back and relax. Any questions before we set off?" David was so petrified that all he could do was shake his head.

The trip was amazing. It was a little bumpy taxiing out to the centre of the lake but once racing the engine into full power the plane slid gracefully across the water leaving a large V like wave behind it. The climb was exhilarating which ended in a sharp banking to the left so as to miss the forested hill at the end of the lake. Below the view was spectacular with hundreds of small ribbon lakes separated by impenetrable dark green conifers. Higher up the pass he could see white glaciers with vivid blue melt water streaming out of their heads and smooth bare rock angling high on either side of them. David hoped that they did not have to fly above that level.

The morning mists were just beginning to evaporate to show the snow-capped tops of the mountainous ridge, which he knew they did not have to fly over. David felt that he could have stayed up in the plane for the whole day such was the beauty of the panoramic picture below him. In what seemed no time at all they began to descend towards an extremely narrow gorge where the river suddenly narrowed. He could see one small dwelling place right next to the river which had a small landing pier at the end of which was tethered some sort of a boat. On hearing the plane someone came out of the building, got into the boat and slowly began to motor out into the centre of the river. The plane banked sharply to the right and then seemed to dive straight at the water. The pilot had to do two more sharp manoeuvres before they landed and taxied towards the small aluminium boat, which was to take David to his final destination

"Welcome to Morgan Springs," said the man in the boat in a strong Australian accent. "That was quite some flying into the narrows of this part of the river. Thought at one time you were going to land half way up the cliff over there." David nodded in agreement.

"Can you come back and pick me up the same time tomorrow?" David said to the pilot.

"No problem provided that the skies are clear. Do you need any supplies?" he said turning to the boatman.

"No thanks. I've got all that I need at the present moment and should I run out I can pick up some things up at the pipeline head where we are going now. See you tomorrow, same time, same place and try not to run me down," the boatman said with a smile.

David took off his flying togs and got down into the boat, which had a powerful Evinrude 70hp outboard on the transom. They quickly moved off to allow the plane to taxi to the centre of the river. The pilot revved up its engine to almost full throttle and sped off down the river. It seemed to take ages before it began to lift off the river and in no time it disappeared over the brow of the hill. Tranquillity once more descended into the valley and the only sound was the lapping of the water against the bows of the boat.

"Did I hear an Australian accent a few moments ago?" said David who was sitting in the centre of the boat and looking aft to the boatman.

"Very astute of you," he said with a broad smile. "Came to this country five years ago on a walk about and have been here ever since. Love the freedom of the place and did not want to return to the dry hot summers back at home. Found this piece of land, which was dirt cheap and set up home. Just my luck that they began building the pipeline up the river which adds supplement to my hunting revenue. The company uses me quite a bit for ferrying their men and small deliveries of equipment from here up to the site. Anything large is brought in by helicopter, which is very expensive so they use me as much as possible. You work for the company then?"

"Yes. I've come up for a day to see how things are going. I can appreciate why you have chosen to live here. Its idyllic but I don't think that I could handle the winters."

"They're not so bad as it's very sheltered here and there is nothing like a large roaring log fire when it's freezing outside. We will be at your destination in a few minutes. Its just around the next bend of the river."

David turned to look upstream and as they rounded the bend he could see a group of aluminium buildings huddled up against the steep sided cliff. He could see a few people moving around so he wouldn't have to go into the forest looking for someone, thank goodness. The boatman landed him right up on the beach. They shook hands and agreed to meet the following day.

"Didn't know we were expecting any visitors today, Phil, did you?" said Robert Dunkley to his assistant projects engineer. They were about to enter one of the pump rooms and stopped when they heard the drone of the outboard motor.

"No. We're not due for anything today or even for the next two days and then we are expecting a shipment of pressure valves."

"Well, it gives us an excuse for not going into the dungeons", as the pumping stations were known to most of the work force, "so lets go down and meet the guy and see what brings him this far out of civilisation."

The two of them casually walked down towards the landing stage and by the time they had got there the boat had cast off and was speeding back from whence it had come. A lone figure holding a small bag stood at the end of the quay and waited for them to approach.

"Hello," said Phil Saunders. "Nice to have a new face about the site. Presume that you have come for a summer holiday. Accommodation is excellent and the cuisine is next to none. Night life however is a bit dull, no TV and no dancing girls." The two men laughed at the "in joke" and David smiled not really knowing whether to reply with a joke which might be misconstrued as him being a little cocky.

"I wish I had the time to take a holiday. I'm not here actually on business but I am a member of the same firm as you. I've just flown out from Abu Dhabi and would like to speak to a Robert Dunkley, if that is at all possible."

Philip Saunders looked at his boss. "Well you're in luck as this is the very man himself. Allow me to introduce the one and only Robert Dunkley."

Robert Dunkley held out his hand and firmly shook David's hand. "I hope you haven't come all this way to tell me that the pipe line is to be closed and that you are once more rewarding me with a promotion!"

"Sorry?" enquired David not fully appreciating what he was on about.

"Apologies. Just making a joke about something that happened in my past life. You must be pretty hungry after your trip in the boat and your flight in the old kamikaze flying boat. Grub should be up in the canteen in about five minutes. We'll take you along to the bunkhouse first so that you can have a little clean up and then we'll eat, during which you can tell us why you have made this visit if it can wait that long."

"No rush as I can't get back until tomorrow and was hoping to scrounge a bed for the night if you have one to spare. If not I have brought my Boy Scout Survival Manual with me and can

284

easily rig up a hut for the night." They all laughed at that and made their way to the sleeping quarters.

David was mildly surprised at the interior of the aluminium huts in which the work force lived, could have passed as a three star hotel, with it's subdued wall lightings, plush carpet and settees. The walls were covered in some form of a light blue fabric so as to prevent any form of condensation and which gave the room a feeling of being twice as large to what it was. That along with large mirrors, which hung at either end of the eating room, made the place even bigger.

The meal was as good as any that David had had in many of the hotels that he had stayed in whilst travelling around the world. There was a choice of three different starters, two main courses and an array of deserts followed by a cheese board. By the end of it he felt quite bloated.

"Now that you have replenished your energy levels perhaps you would tell us why you have come all this way just to see me," said Robert Dunkley. David looked at Phillip Saunders and was about to request that he would prefer to have a private conversation when Robert spoke again. "Don't worry about Phil. We have no secrets from one another. We have worked together on many a project before this one and have always confided in one another, so shoot away."

David looked at Phillip and expressed an apologetic smile.

"It's to do with the project in Abu Dhabi. Recently I was visiting one of the sites when someone informed me that the turbines were not possibly designed well enough to do justice to the project. The informant was not the brightest of people but seemed to know what he was talking about."

"I bet that was Albert. So they missed one. Probably thought as you did initially that he had a screw loose and so could not be of any threat to the company. They couldn't have got rid of him in any case, as he was a local."

"So there was a problem with the turbines?"

"Yes, one hell of a big one. We sent four back to the workshops in New York during the initial stages to be taken apart piece by piece. Nothing wrong was found. They were then put

285

back together despatched back to the Emirates and started up again. Within a few months they suffered the same symptoms. Strange thing was the problems disappeared as quickly as they had started. I was praised for my work and sent out here on a much higher salary. I was however very sceptical of the whole scenario and so kept in touch with one of my friends who was working for the company but not actually in the turbine group. He kept his ear to the ground and fed me back little snippets of information, which kept indicating that the troubles with the turbines had not been sorted out. You now will appreciate my little joke when you initially arrived at this complex. I can well appreciate why you had to come out here to see me. When is the handover ceremony? I know it will go ahead as to delay it would mean the loss of a huge amount of finances to the company and once word got out that we were putting defective equipment in the workplace it would damage our prospects worldwide. I wouldn't like to be in your shoes when the first turbine seizes up or even disintegrates. No chance of getting promotion like me before judgement day?" he said with a look of sympathy towards David.

"Thanks for being so frank. I don't know what I will do at this present moment."

"From what I have heard you only have two options if you don't mind me intruding into this conversation," said Phillip who had remained silent during the whole of the conversation. "Rob has often spoken of the project and of the head men in our company. That guy McCormack sounds the sort of person who is capable of adding personnel who get on the wrong side of him to the missing persons bureau. You could take a chance and hope that the machines do not meet up with high temperatures and humidity until you have gone on to other things and then some other poor chap will take the can. Your other option is to blow the lid off the whole thing, which would mean you losing your job with little chance of getting another one and you would have to keep looking over your shoulder in case McCormack was lurking in the shadows. I would take the first of the two options, as I am not a very brave person."

"That's really cheered me up, Phil. Thanks for a really good choice. Do you have any more views, Robert?"

"I initially thought along the same lines as Phil and so took the easy way out as I did not relish the thought of having no job prospects if I had gone to the Emirates Government and told them what was happening. There was also the added possibility of being put in prison as I was the person in charge of the project at that time and could have been held for supplying shoddy workmanship and equipment. I would dearly have loved to see McCormack land in the mire but there was little chance of that as he would have put the blame on myself or someone else who was involved in the design of the turbines. I would advise you to get out of the company at the first possible moment even if it does mean going along with the company until the project has been handed over to the Government. Not much help, I'm afraid, but you have no other choice as far as I can see."

There were a few moments of silence and then David spoke.

"I appreciate your help and I am going to have to return to the Emirates and take a long look at my prospects if there are any at all if I should let the cat out of the bag. Let's try to forget about it for a while. We have a few more hours left before the sun goes down and I would like to soak up some of the beauty of the lake and woods before I return on the boat tomorrow. No doubt you have a lot of work to catch up on so would it be all-right for me to take a walk along the lake shore?"

Phil was about to say that he did not do any work after dinner but decided to allow David to go on his own in order to give him a little time on his own to try to work out his problems and he was in no better a place if he wanted a little solitude for as soon as he returned to the Emirates he would be going flat out preparing for the grand handing over ceremony.

"Yes, I do have some important changes to make to some of my drawings so if it is OK with you I will decline the opportunity to walk the lake."

Five minutes later David was on his own beside of the lake and out of sight of the camp. There was not a ripple on the water, which gave the lake the appearance of being a huge mirror, which reflected the surrounding trees and the sky above. He sat there watching the clouds drift across the lake's surface and finally disappear into the tree line on the opposite side of the lake. Occasionally a flock of wild geese appeared overhead flying in their customary V formation. David marvelled how whenever the lead bird changed direction so did all of the other birds in unison as if they were receiving direct telephonic messages. He tried to shut out his problems about the company for a few minutes but was unable to do so. The more he thought about it the more his mind became fuddled until he could think no more, so he had to leave the tranquillity of the lake and make his way back to he bunkhouse in the hope that sleep would blank out his problems for a few hours.

The following day he had a full fried breakfast, promised the two overseers that he would phone them as soon as he had made a decision as to what he would do to solve his problems and then got onto the speedboat and disappeared across the lake.

"Anyone phone whilst I was away, Mavis?"

"Yes a few local calls but nothing from head office, Mr. Johnson. No one actually asked where you had gone so I did not offer that information. Did you like Sweden?"

"Beautiful country. I will go back and spend much more time there when I next get some spare holiday time. Lots to do, I expect. I'll go through my mail first. I would appreciate a cup of coffee in about an hour's time by which time I will need you to take some notes to send out to the various dignitaries that will be coming to the ceremony in a month's time. I will need the list of names that head office has suggested should be invited. The invites should go out in the next few days so that we will be in a position to book accommodation and flights for them if that is necessary. David and out." His final jocular statement was to try to give the impression to his secretary that all was well and that he was in total control of things. She knew better and had already decided to keep a very watchful eye over her boss and give him as much protection as possible over the next hectic month.

Chapter Eighteen

During the next three weeks David had little time to think of anything else other than the handing over of the project to the Government of the United Arab Emirates. The ceremony was to take place at the prestigious Continental Hotel, which was the largest hotel in the Emirates and had the facilities to cater for very large conferences. David's main function in the proceedings was to ensure that all guests arrived at the hotel at least an hour before the arrival of the Sheikh and were seated in the main function room half an hour before the Sheikh made his appearance. The reason for this was the elaborate safety precautions that were always taken whenever the Sheikh made any visits within the Emirates. Although his subjects loved him dearly there was always the possibility of one fanatical loner attempting to make a name for himself as had happened in many other parts of the world.

An hour before the arrival of the Sheikh all roads to the hotel would be shut off. Then at intervals of fifty metres there would be an armed member of his forces stationed in positions where they could see anyone within two hundred metres. A half an hour before he was due to enter the hotel all corridors would have been shut off and manned by members of the Special Forces, which were an elite group of soldiers who were trained by past members of the British SAS. At least David did not have to worry about the safety of his royal guest.

There would be a strict protocol in the seating arrangements of the guests. David had had to get one of the government officials to advise him in this area. All members of the Royal Family were to sit in the front row and behind them in order of priority sat the Sheikhs of all the other principalities. Behind them sat their own advisers and behind them would sit the guests of the company. The three directors would sit at the top table with the Sheikh plus his top Government Advisers. To the side of the top table would be a group of six company members who were involved with the project and who along with the three directors would have to sign the final agreement. One of these people would be David. In all there would be over two hundred people including the press and local television crew. This project was such an important moment for the Emirates that the Sheik had requested that the signing of the contract should be seen throughout the Emirates, as it would be beneficial to all of his subjects in one way or another.

As the day to the signing gradually became closer so David became more agitated. The office staff began to notice a slight change in his personality and put it down to the fact that he was suffering from stress due to the huge commitment that he had made over the past few weeks organising the mammoth tasks of accommodation, transport, seating arrangements etc. What they did not appreciate was what was continually circulating inside David's brain. He was not at all worried about the arrangements for the day, he actually revelled in the organisational side of things. What worried him was the fact that he had decided to go against his conscience. He knew that what he was about to do was unethical. People were going to suffer, not only the rich but also the poor. If and when the turbines did malfunction, crops would suffer from lack of irrigation, which in turn would affect the livelihood of the farmers and all who worked for them. Although the country's revenue was from the production of oil the Government was attempting to diversify into other forms of revenue in preparation for the time when the oil supplies began to run dry or the price of oil dropped drastically on the open market. When this did happen it would be the fault of his company and himself and he would have to live with that for the rest of his life. He had put himself into that predicament and it was too late to do anything about it.

The night before the official signing, David had arranged for all members of the team plus their other halves to meet with the Board of Directors for a celebratory dinner. This was to be held at the Forte Grand Hotel in the centre of Abu Dhabi where the directors were staying. David was not looking forward to meeting the full board once again.

During the initial stages of the dinner all seemed to go very well. The set meal of sea food starters, roast sirloin of beef, followed by one of the most delicious choice of deserts that David had ever tasted, which was always David's favourite part of any meal. That along with a different expensive wine with each course had the desired effect of making everyone totally relaxed. Various speeches were made by the directors praising all of the hard work that everyone had put into the project, and how the publicity from such a huge undertaking had circulated around the world of high finance and raised the already high prestige of the company to even greater heights.

Once the speeches were finished the disco took over and everyone let their hair down and had a great evening. By the time most of the people were ready to go David's anxieties had all disappeared. All he had to do now was to have a last word with the directors to make sure that they had received the final arrangements for the following day and then retire to bed. All went initially well. The three directors in turn shook David's hand and congratulated him on the impeccable arrangements that he had prepared for the hand-over and how he had run the show over the past year. David felt really pleased with himself as he left the group of directors and returned to the rest of the gathering for a last glass of wine. Ten minutes later as he was about to depart when McCormack pushed his way through the noisy mass of half-cut employees and held out his hand to David.

"Let me once again congratulate on your work for the company," he said with an expressionless face, his blue eyes focusing menacingly into David's eyes.

"By the way, did you enjoy your little trip to Norway?"

His grip increased in power. David felt the hairs at the nape of his neck begin to stand on end and felt that he had caught his hand in a vice such was the strength of the man. Without waiting for a reply from David, McCormack released his grip, turned and went back to the other directors. He must have said something to them with reference about David as they all turned at the same time and stared in his direction. David could not bear the tension any more and made a hasty retreat towards the door to the elevator. He made a decision there and then that once the handing over ceremony had finished he would give in his notice.

The day had finally arrived. David was up at seven a.m., had a light breakfast and was in the office just after seven thirty. He wanted to check to see if any messages were there for him, which might have any bearings on the day's procedures. Nothing was in the in tray and the computer and fax machine were blank so he went to the outer office and made himself a strong cup of coffee and began to relax. By nine o'clock the office was once again working at full throttle. At precisely eleven o'clock a limousine pulled up outside the main entrance to the building and David called to his secretary to see if she was ready as she was required to make notes on the day's procedures. They had some time to spare so David asked the driver to take the scenic route along the Corniche, which ran alongside the water.

The Corniche is one of the longest paved walkways in the world and is irrigated to provide lush green lawns bordered by exotic bushes. Often whole families would meet up with all of their other relations to picnic and generally socialise. Although the building of the promenade had been extremely expensive it had proved a very successful venture by the Sheikh as it gave his citizens a place to relax and for the itinerant work force it gave them a free recreation area in which to relax.

At eleven-twenty the limousine arrived at the front of the Continental Hotel and the smartly attired doorman opened the car doors for David and his secretary. The lobby of the hotel was quite full with visiting tourists and already some of the invited guests were beginning to assemble at the far end of the hallway where beautiful oriental ladies were serving coffee. David made his way to the far side of the coffee area so that he could see the entire visiting dignitaries as they arrived. He was very impressed by the tasteful displays of freshly cut flowers and how they blended in with the décor of the foyer. David was relieved that the greeting of the guests was not part of his agenda. The directors had arranged for professionals who were trained in the art of politely ushering the guests on such occasions to the places they should be at the designated times, and on this occasion one could not afford to be in the wrong place at the wrong time when the Sheikh was due to arrive.

David excused himself from his secretary for a few moments so that he could go and inspect the hall where the actual signing was to take place. Already there were armed guards on the door who looked menacing with their mini-machine guns held at the ready in front of their camouflaged uniforms. As he approached, one of them unslung his carbine and pointed it towards David. These guys were not to be tangled with, thought David, who made a sign towards his lapel badge. It was coloured gold which meant that he was one of the chief organisers and could go into the banqueting hall at any time before the beginning of the proceedings. The guard nodded when he saw the badge and stepped aside to allow David to enter the room. David had been in there a number of times during the two weeks leading up to today and each time he was always amazed at the sheer size and beauty of the room.

The carpet was of thick turquoise twill, which left imprints as one walked over it initially, but within minutes returned to its original smooth texture. The decor gave the appearance that one was in the desert with real palm trees and bushes surrounding the borders of the hall. The walls were decorated with the finest of gold leafing, almost transparent, which shimmered in the soft lighting. Row upon row of plush dark green velvet covered seats filled the whole of the floor space and at the front of the hall on a slightly raised dais was an ornate golden chair upon which the Sheikh would sit. In front of that was a large highly polished dark oak table a good six metres in length and at its centre was a solitary golden pen resting on a parchment of paper which was the official contract. In less than an hour's time David would be holding that very pen in his hand and then he would be asked to sign the contract.

The reality of the occasion suddenly hit him. Up until that

moment David had been so busy during the past two weeks that he had been able to block out the guilt that he had felt when he finally knew that the project had very bad flaws in it. Now it all came flooding back to him and now it was too late to do anything about it. He felt that he was about to sign his soul away. A movement behind him momentarily blocked out his present thoughts. It was one of the guards who beckoned to him that he should return to the main assembly point as the time was nearing when the Sheikh would be arriving at the hotel entrance. It would soon be time for all of the guests to take their seats.

On returning to the coffee area David was surprised to see so many people in such a relatively small space. He pushed his way over towards his secretary who seemed to be relieved to see him.

"I'm glad you have returned. The directors were asking of you a few minutes ago. I assured them that you had only just taken leave of this room in order to check out the main banqueting hall. I got the impression that it was in the back of their minds that you might not have turned up for the occasion. Is everything all right, Mr Jackson?" said Martha in a very inquisitive voice.

"No problems at all. The main hall is looking absolutely splendid, fit for a king or should I say a Sheikh," David said with a little grin to try to cover up his anxieties.

"I think it must be about time we began to enter the hall, as the Sheikh is due to arrive in the next fifteen minutes. There seems to be some movement to the left of the door so let's begin to make our way over now. I would prefer it if you did not go anywhere near to the board of directors, Martha."

The hall filled up quite quickly. All but the two front rows were filled to capacity. David was sat to the side of the big table and had an excellent view of the main entrance from where the Sheikh would make his first appearance. His three directors were already in place sitting on the left hand side of the glistening oak table. David kept feeling that all three from time to time were specifically looking at him even though he did not make any eye contact with them. McCormack looked even more menacing than he had done the previous night. David began to sweat at the base of his spine. He could feel his shirt sticking to his skin and knew it was not due to the heat within the room as the building was adequately air-conditioned. He was beginning to feel scared. A sudden hush fell over the gathering. David looked towards the door and noticed that a tall Arab dressed in a dark, long flowing dishdash and wearing some sort of ceremonial dagger about his waist was standing in the centre of the doorframe. He must be one of the Sheikh's ceremonial bodyguards, thought David.

After a few moments when he was assured that all had seen him and that silence had descended upon the large gathering he moved to one side and allowed the entourage to enter. First came the members of the government all dressed in white robes. Next came the relatives of all the Sheikhs and then the individual Sheikhs of the seven kingdoms who were all dressed in black with a gold headdress. There was then a moment's pause and then a command sounded from somewhere at the front of the hall which brought everyone to their feet. Through the door came six tall bodyguards followed by one of the Sheikhs closest advisers and then finally the Ruler of Abu Dhabi. He looked splendid in his golden robes, holding his head on high as he walked to the front of the hall and took his place on the raised dais. David could understand why his royal subjects held him in such high esteem. Here was a man who had done so much for his country and his people in bringing them into the twentieth century in the space of a few decades and making sure that they were all cared for. He was regarded world wide as being a shrewd but fair businessman and one who could be trusted in honouring any form of business transaction.

For the first time for many a month David's arm began to ache around his birthmark. This usually only happened in the past when he was suffering with stress and that was what was beginning to happen to him at that very moment. It was seeing the Sheikh in person and knowing what type of man he was that the full guilt of what he was about to do sank in. David began to feel a little nauseated and his skin felt very clammy. He looked around the gathering and his eyes made contact with

McCormack who was looking directly at him. David looked away hoping that the man had not noticed his possible change in face colouring. Only a matter of fifteen minutes and it would be all over, thought David, and he was sure that he could hold out for such a short period of time. Those fifteen minutes seemed like an eternity to David.

Speeches were made by various members of the company and government, none of which registered with David, as he was so preoccupied with his feeling of guilt.

The time finally came for the official signings. First went the three directors of the company followed by members of the government. David sat rigidly in his seat and watched the golden pen flow across the parchment at the centre of the table. Then it was his turn and the other four people who were sitting next to him to sign. Once they had completed the task the final signing would be the Sheikh himself.

David was actually the penultimate person to sign as he was in charge of the whole of the project in the Emirates. As he got out of his chair with the other members on his table he felt as if a projectile had hit him in his upper arm. His birthmark was reacting more painfully than when it was hit during the occasion when he was playing squash back in New York. Damn, how he wished that he had had it removed by plastic surgery years ago.

He stood at the back of the short line and witnessed each person in front of him signing his or her name on the parchment and all the time dreading the moment when he would be holding the pen in his own hand. That moment then arrived. He picked up the pen from the table and poised it above the parchment and there it remained for he was unable to put ink to paper no matter how hard he tried. Guilt had frozen him as if he were some form of a marble statue. One could sense the change in atmosphere within the room. What on earth was this fellow playing at? He was holding the whole procedure up and keeping the Sheikh waiting. Suddenly McCormack got out of his chair, went over to David and firmly took hold of his arm. He then looked towards the Sheikh, bowed his head and spoke in a quiet voice.

"Your Royal Highness, I do apologise on behalf of Mr Johnson. He should not have attended this meeting as he was taken ill last night but insisted on coming along today. I will steady him whilst he adds his signature." He then guided David's hand to the spot where he was due to sign. If the audience was perturbed by the state of play so far it was about to get the shock of its life.

"I will not sign!" said David in a loud clear voice, which could be heard throughout the hall. McCormack released his grip in disbelief. A unified gasp came from the rest of the guests who started to talk amongst themselves. The only two people who showed no emotion at all were the Sheikh and his aide. As the initial noise from the exclamations and chatter began to subside the aide slowly rose from his chair and moved towards the microphone that was resting on the table in front of the Sheikh.

"Ladies and gentlemen, I propose that you allow the Royal Cortège to leave the hall and then if you would all proceed to the banqueting hall and take some refreshments we will see if we can continue the proceedings in perhaps half an hour."

This proposal was in fact a command so everyone arose to allow the Sheikh to leave, and then the guests made their way along to the refreshment area. The only people who were not allowed to leave the hall were the three directors and the five men who had occupied the table adjacent to the top table and who had signed the parchment. They were escorted individually to different rooms within the hotel.

David sat on his own in one of those rooms for over two hours. During that time he had a lot of time to think about what he had just done and the consequences of it for himself and the rest of the firm. Although he was extremely worried he still felt immensely relieved as if a huge burden had been taken off of his shoulders. There was no point in planning what he would do next as that was up to the government officials. All of them were in a serious position and he knew that soon he would be in for a thorough grilling by the special branch of the police force. He had offended the Sheikh and David could not think of anything worse that he could have done. He buried his head in his hands and tried to think of something, which would take his mind off the predicament that he had landed himself in.

There was a knock at the door but no one made any attempt to enter.

"Come in," shouted David not really wishing for anyone to enter. It was the Sheikh's aide who presented himself. He walked slowly over to David showing no emotion in his face at all.

"You are free to go. We have arranged for the collection of your passport so you may not leave the Emirates until we have had time to sum up the situation. Your other colleagues will be remaining also. They will be staying in the Post House Hotel if you wish to get in contact with them, but I do not think you would want to do that at this moment in time." There was the slightest of movement at the corners of his mouth as he said that, almost as if he was trying to stifle a smile.

"When you have made the necessary arrangements for your accommodation we would like you to ring the following number and let us know where that is." He handed David a piece of paper that had a telephone number printed on it. " I will now leave you in peace," Again the resemblance of a smile attempted to change the austerity of his face.

David sat back in the chair and tried to make some form of a plan for the next few days. He did not want to go back to his flat as there was the good possibility that his directors would attempt to contact him and he certainly did not want to see McCormack who had by now probably put out a contract on him! The only person he could think of getting in contact with at the moment was his very good friend Nicola.

He suddenly felt hungry. He hadn't eaten for over eight hours and as it was too early to phone Nicola as she was probably still at school so he decided to ring for room service and order a sandwich. Two sandwiches later plus a glass of cool lager he began to feel a little better. He waited until seven o'clock and then gave his friend a phone. He was in luck as her voice came onto the phone instead of the usual answering machine.

"Hello Nic. David here."

"Stranger. I thought that you had gone and done a runner."

"Could do with doing that at this very moment but wouldn't get very far without my passport."

Nicola could tell from his voice that something was amiss.

"Are you all right, David?"

"Not really. Would it be convenient for me to call around this evening for a little chat? I know that it is half way through your school week and won't be disappointed if you said no." Liar, he thought, as he needed desperately to talk to someone.

"No problem. If you come over in the next hour you can share a meal with me if you don't mind eating a mild curry."

"That would be just fine, Nic. Really appreciate you seeing me. I'll have a quick shower and be over in the hour." He rang off and suddenly began to feel much more relaxed.

The meal was absolutely delicious and after a bottle of Cabernet Sauvignon David began to pour out his problems to Nicola. It took over an hour for him to tell the whole tale by the end of which they were both exhausted.

"That was some story, David. Took a lot of guts to do what you have done today. Most people would have taken the easy way out and said nothing. What on earth are you going to do now? First thing is to find you somewhere to live for the time being. I would allow you to crash out on the floor here were it not for the strict laws over here. I may be able to help out, though. Do you remember that boisterous blonde who made you dance on the table at the rugby club ball? Well, I think she has gone home for a couple of weeks and her flat is empty. I can get a key from her friend Maxine and if you promise not to invite your friend McCormack around for a few drinks you can hide away there until the government sorts out the whole business."

David smiled at her remark of inviting McCormack around for a few drinks. Keen sense of humour, Nic.

The next evening David had moved his belongings into the flat. He left no forwarding address with his next-door neighbour and did not notify his office. He had no intention of phoning in his whereabouts until he was out of Abu Dhabi, even if it meant his salary being curtailed. By the third day he was beginning to get restless. He had notified the authorities where he was living immediately he had moved in and since then heard nothing. He was afraid to go out into town in case someone from the company saw him. It was Nicola who again came up with a good idea. No one at the British Club, where the two of them were members, had any connections with his company and during the day time few people went down there so why not enjoy the sun and beach and lie around the pool area. The food was always very reasonable and of good quality so one could spend the whole day down there and not get bored. There was also sky TV and a library.

So for the next two days David took a cab to the club early in the morning and Nicola gave him a lift home in the evening. It was on the third day that something strange happened. Nicola had arrived at the usual time of three-thirty and had gone straight into the gym for an aerobic workout. By the time she came out it was getting a little late to go back to the flat and cook so David suggested they stay down at the club and have a light meal. After the meal, as it was such a lovely evening they bought two drinks and went and sat down at the beach to watch the sun go down over the distant sand dunes. They had been sitting there for about half an hour when Nicola cut across David 's conversation.

"Excuse me interrupting, David but that seems strange. Look, across the water there at the top of the sand dunes. Aren't those soldiers? They don't usually practice manoeuvres so near the city."

They both sat there and looked over at the men who were some four hundred metres away. They seemed to have taken up a perimeter formation as if they were guarding the approaches to the narrow straits of water, which separated the man-made sand bar from the club area.

"They don't seem to be doing much. Very clever how they got to that position without us noticing them, as they would have to have come across some very open ground. Hey, look. There's some form of landing craft coming across from the spit. It's heading this way. All very exciting isn't it, David."

David nodded and watched the craft come across the narrow stretch of water and actually run up onto the beach of the club. As soon as the boat made contact with the sandy bottom the front came down and out ran a group of soldiers in full combat kit. They immediately fanned out and took up strategic positions around the outskirts of the club. At the sight of this both David and Nicola began to feel a little apprehensive. Next from the rear of the club a whole host of police appeared and began to mingle with the people who were left on the beach. They seemed to have a short conversation with each individual person who then packed up their belongings and made their way back to the clubhouse. Eventually one of the police, who appeared to be in charge of the group, approached the two of them.

"No need to be alarmed. We have been asked to move all persons off the beach for the next hour. If you would be so kind as to return to the clubhouse where refreshments have been laid on at no charge. Mr Johnson I would like you to remain please."

David looked at Nicola and neither of them spoke but both had the same thoughts. How on earth did the policeman know that he was Mr Johnson? The golden rule in the Emirates was that no one ever argued with a policeman. Nicola packed her belongings, squeezed David's hand, and went off in the direction of the clubhouse. Just before she disappeared from view she took one last look over her shoulder and noticed another strange thing. Coming down through the narrow water inlet was the most beautiful boat she had ever seen. It was a native Dhow painted in gold with large billowing white sails. Flanked on either side of the boat were two small powerboats, which appeared to have large machine guns mounted on their foredecks. Only one boat would have had such an escort as this, thought Nicola, and that was the Sheikh's Royal Yacht!

At the same moment that Nicola noticed the Dhow so did David. He sat there with his policeman and watched it gracefully sail to a position opposite to the club beach, where it dropped its sail and laid anchor. For the next few minutes there was a hive of activity on the decks. Sails were neatly furled; a line of seamen took its position on the prow of the boat and a smaller shaped Dhow was lowered from the stern. Into this was placed a walkway and all movement then ceased on board. After a few more moments two people walked down the walkway into the smaller Dhow, which then drifted away from the mother ship and gradually made its way across the water to land on the part of the beach nearest to where David was sitting. David could now see who was sitting in the middle of the Dhow. It was the Sheikh and his aide who had been the master of ceremonies at the recent signing of the parchment.

David was lost for words, not that he could think of anything to say at that precise moment in time. He just sat there and watched the Sheikh alight from the boat with the help of various servants. Once on dry land the Sheikh was led to where David had been sitting. The Sheikh looked at David for a few moments and then held out his hand.

"I would like to shake the hand of someone who has been of great service to the United Arab Emirates. What you did last week took a great deal of courage. I can't begin to imagine what must have been running through your mind over the past few months. I know that you realise that your days with your company are coming to a close. Whether or not there will be a company in a year's time is another matter. No doubt you will be forced to move into another field of work. I have come here for two reasons, David. The first as I have already said is to thank you for what you have done for our country. If you had not stood up and stated that the project was faulty we would have suffered great financial losses and my subjects would have experienced much suffering. So we are indebted to you. We know that life in the near future for you will be quite difficult. If we can be of any help at all now, or in the future, you must give us a call. My chief adviser here will give you a telephone number, which is only given out to a few trusted friends, so guard it well and remember no matter what the request is feel free to call and if it is within reason we will honour it. Thank you once more." The Sheikh held out his hand, shook David's firmly and then turned and went back to the boat.

"Take this card. On it is a number, which will give you a direct line to the palace. It has a direct link to a satellite, which allows complete privacy. Goodbye, David Johnson. May Allah be with you." He put his two hands together made a small bow and returned to the boat.

The last David saw of them was when the golden Dhow disappeared around the end of the sand dune. David sat on the beach for a long time trying to take in the last fifteen minutes. He then became aware of someone approaching him over the soft sand. It was Nicola.

"Well what was that all about, Mr Importance?" she said with a broad smile.

"I'll tell you later when I have had time to think. Come on. Let's get out of here and go out to Ikea where we can get a McDonalds, or if you prefer we can go to Hero's at the crown Plaza" He was hoping she would choose the latter as England were playing the All Blacks on television.

Six days later David took off on flight BA62 at 12.20 to return to the States. He did not like saying farewell to Nicola as she was a very special friend and he would miss her pleasant company. He hoped that she would one day meet the right guy.

For the next eighteen months David flitted from one job to another. He had to choose mundane jobs as he had lost all confidence in applying for posts, which would require him to send off his CV on the international network. People were still talking about the downfall of Global Engineering and he was sure that his name would be included as the main culprit for its failure. No one would wish to take a chance on employing him, he thought, as all companies had their little dark secrets.

Life was getting him down. He could not find a post that gave him any form of job satisfaction and coming home to a one roomed flat, which was very dark and had extremely uncomfortable furniture, was making him very depressed.

It was during one of his depressive moods that he came across the *Time* magazine. He had mistakenly got off the subway at the wrong stop and so had decided to walk a few blocks rather than waste his money on a cab. As he rounded one of the corners he almost knocked over a news-stand and made the owner jump.

"Hey, boy. Don't be so eager to buy a paper as I have plenty today," said the rather plump newsvendor. David felt a little embarrassed and decided that he should at least buy a paper.

"Sorry. I'd like the *Evening Star* please." He handed over a note and waited for his change. He pushed the loose change into his trouser pocket, tucked the paper under his arm and was about to depart when out of the corner of his eye he caught sight of the front page of a magazine. It was almost the case of his subliminal memory selecting that specific magazine as there were dozens more of a much more colourful nature on the same rack. He stopped and went over to the magazine. It was this week's edition of *Time* magazine and on the front page was a photograph of his birthmark!

"Hey," said the plump paper man. "I don't allow people to flick through the magazines." It wouldn't make any difference if you did, thought David, as with that business attitude you would be lucky to sell one.

"Don't worry, I'll take it," and it would be the last ever form of reading material he would buy from this stall he decided.

As soon as he got home he put on the kettle for a cup of coffee, put a boil-in-the-bag meal into a saucepan of water and turned the ring up high, and then proceeded to flop down into a hard chair. A small amount of light was struggling to find its way between the half drawn curtain and the adjacent skyscraper. There was enough however to enable David to read his magazine. He sat there staring at the front cover. He read the subtitle, which explained that the photograph had been taken of an Incan rock carving in a city that had been lost for over four centuries.

David read the accompanying article which told the story of how Professor Downing had discovered the lost city in the Amazon jungle which had eluded expeditions over hundreds of years. The article went on to tell how the professor was the only person to be able to translate the inscriptions on the cliff face. When asked how he felt after this amazing discovery he simply said, "Extremely pleased with the whole expedition and the discoveries that we have made. There is one little thing that's annoying me though, and that is this carving here which does not fit in with any of the transcripts and which keeps appearing from time to time in other Inca writings which we have found in the surrounding area." The journalist obviously decided that at a later date the Professor's puzzle would be solved and by featuring it in his present writings he would be in a very good position to be chosen to write the sequel to it. So he had featured the carving on the front page of the magazine.

David reread the article again before going to bed so fascinated was he by the resemblance of the carving to his own birthmark. If you had superimposed the stone marking over his birthmark it would have matched it identically.

That night he found it extremely difficult to get any sleep at all as his mind kept wandering back to his birthmark and the Inca carving. By the end of the week he was really up tight as he had had very little sleep and during the day even his job would not take his mind off of the magazine article. By Sunday night he was at his wits' end. There was only one way to solve his problem and that was to go to the Andes! No matter how absurd this seemed to him in his present predicament he knew there was no other way. For the rest of the night he spent his time working out his financial position and how he could improve upon it.

The next day he phoned in to his work place, reported that he was sick, and then made an appointment to see his bank manager. After telling him that he needed a small loan in order to purchase a car, which in turn would enable him to travel further afield to a better job, he was given a loan. Three weeks later he was standing in the arrivals hall in Cusco.

Chapter Nineteen

Claire sat in the departure lounge and tried to gather her composure after the farewell with her newly found friend, William. She would certainly make contact with him when she returned from her visit to Peru. That was provided her health held out. She had been so busy over the last two weeks that any thought of how she felt had not entered into her thought pattern. Now she suddenly felt absolutely drained and was looking forward to collapsing in the seat of the plane. Half an hour elapsed during which time she just sat there looking at the other people rushing off to the duty free shops looking for last-minute bargains and returning with heavy looking plastic bags which attempted to pull their shoulders out of their sockets.

The television monitor eventually showed Claire's flight and that it was time to board, so she collected up her small travel bag and magazine and went towards the departure zone. Once her ticket had been checked she went through the sliding doors and began to walk down quite a steep enclosed ramp at the bottom of which stood some of the cabin staff. Everything smelt new and the thick carpet combined with the slope made normal walking twice as difficult. As she neared the entrance to the plane she noticed that one of the smartly dressed airhostesses seemed to be staring at her. She looked at the attractive young face, which smiled back and the very slight nod of the head seemed to indicate to her that the young girl had recognised her from a previous meeting. Claire could not place the girl at all but smiled back and then stepped into the plane.

The journey was very relaxing for Claire. She slept for the first part of the flight and missed the early dinner that airlines usually serve almost as soon as the undercarriage was up. She noticed that the young airhostess kept looking her throughout the flight and who appeared to give her preferential treatment over the rest of the tourist class. She was even presented with a most exotic flower, which was placed on her tray when she had requested a dessert. As she left the plane, instead of the customary smile and "thank you for travelling with us" the young airhostess stepped forward, took Claire's hand in both of hers and gently squeezing it said,

"You will find him."

The statement caught Claire by surprise. She had no idea what the girl was talking about. Before she was able to reply she was herded up the slope by the remainder of the passengers who were eager to get off after being cooped up over such a long period of time.

The air terminal at Cuzco was extremely busy and very hot and humid. It took over half an hour to collect her bags, clear customs and find a taxi. The driver did not seem to understand English but as soon as Claire showed him the name of her hotel he seemed to know in which direction to drive.

Ten minutes later she was standing in the hotel lobby. It was off the main street, which was fine by Claire, as the traffic in the main thoroughfare would probably have prevented her from getting a good night's sleep. The hotel itself had only a two star rating but looked quite clean and respectable. The lobby was bare of any furniture other than an inviting Coke machine. The floor was made of white shiny marble and in the far corner stood a plant with large green leaves. On the wooden desk, which ran down the entire side of the foyer, was a brightly polished bell with a sign next to it, which Claire assumed meant ring. She pushed her hand firmly down on the bell and a highly pitched resonance echoed throughout the entire hotel. Minutes seem to pass and then eventually the small door in the corner of the foyer opened to reveal an old lady. Claire was surprise to hear her speak good English.

"Welcome to our hotel. I hope that you have made a reservation, as we are completely full up. We seem to have twice as many tourists in the city this year," the lady said without looking up.

"I phoned the hotel a few weeks ago and made a tentative booking. The name is Axworthy."

The old lady picked up a book from the desk, opened it and glanced down the list of names.

"No. No one by the name of Axworthy. I do all of the bookings for the hotel myself. The rest of my staff is forbidden to take bookings. I am afraid we cannot accommodate you. If you like I will call a taxi and then I suggest you ask the driver to take you to some nearby hotels that may have an odd few vacancies."

Claire by now was extremely tired and not being of the argumentative type picked up her bag, said thank you to the old lady and went towards the door. The old lady finally looked up and caught her breath as she watched the woman walking away from her. It was the walk that caught her eye initially.

"No, wait a moment. I've just had another look at the list and I see that one of the rooms is not booked out until Friday. If your intentions are to stay for only a few days then we can accommodate you."

As Claire turned around she noticed that the old lady had raised her head and was looking at her necklace. It was the same look that had been on the faces of the airhostess and the young man who had been playing the pipes in Covent Gardens.

"Yes, that would be ideal as I only intend to stay for a few days."

"I suppose you will be venturing up into the mountains to Machu Picchu? That's where all the tourists go."

She didn't wait for a reply from Claire. She came around the desk, picked up Claire's bag and nodded for her to follow her. She went up two flights of stairs, which lead onto a well-polished wooden floor, and pushed open the first door they came to.

"You will find this room very pleasant. Not too noisy and at night you will get a cool breeze coming down from the mountains. I suggest that you do not go out at night on your own. I will get you some food if you wish."

"I'm not too hungry but I would appreciate something to drink and perhaps a light snack for later."

The old lady placed the case by the bed, gave Claire her key to the door and went out without saying another word. Half an hour later she returned with a pot of herbal tea, a small salad and some form of sweetened bread.

"What time would you like a call for your breakfast?" said the old lady in a very gentle voice. "I can make it at any time suitable to you as I rarely go out nowadays."

"About nine o'clock will be just fine. Thank you for the drink and meal."

That night Claire sat down at the small table in the corner of the room adjacent to the window through which drifted a pleasant cool breeze and began to study her small dossier about Machu Picchu.

Her first readings were from a recent newspaper article that was discussing the pros and cons of introducing a cable car to transport the sixty-five thousand pilgrims who make their way up the rigorous Inca trail each year. The eight million dollar scheme would help solve the problems of the huge wear and tear of the trail and also the large amount of plastic bottles and paper that was strewn along the five hundred-year-old path. It would also whisk the travellers to the peak in six minutes thus replacing an arduous twenty-five minute bus ride on a land-slide-prone access road.

She had two choices of reaching the summit. The first was by helicopter, which cost about one hundred dollars each way, and the second was by a narrow-gauge railway from Cuzco to Aguas Calientes that ranks as one of the world's most scenic routes. Claire decided on the latter, which cost thirty dollars for the backpacker. On reaching the top the only accommodation available was in the nondescript Sanctuary Lodge, a thirty-two roomed hotel costing on average two hundred-and-fifty dollars a night. Her financial situation would allow only three nights maximum so whatever she was looking for would have to be accomplished within that time span. The only other expense was fifty dollars for a permit. The fee was used to cover the costs of maintenance of the trail and collecting up litter!

Other than money, Claire's major problem would be her health. On reaching the end of the rail track she would have to trek just over thirty-five kilometres which was two full days' walking, with a one night camping stop. It was also extremely important not to try this arduous journey until one had acclimatised oneself to the rarefied atmosphere. The guidebooks suggested at least a two-day acclimatisation period otherwise one would certainly suffer with headaches, nausea and insomnia. It was suggested to keep away from alcohol, which causes dehydration, and heavy foods, and drink plenty of mate de coca, which was a tea made from the coca leaf.

The trail itself needed no guide as it was well sign posted and there was no obligation to join an organised tour. The actual walking was generally reckoned to be a strenuous hike with no rock-climbing or glacier walking involved, but there were numerous steep ascents and descents. It could be dangerous in certain places where there were sheer drops next to the path, but if one was careful there was little chance of a fall. An odd bear sometimes makes an appearance plus an occasional pig or dog. A good insect repellent is a must as the flies can be extremely fierce. Toilets are non-existent so one has to be sure to bury all excrement well away from the actual trail itself. Most important of all take plenty of drinking water.

Once Claire had read all of her notes she began to make a list of what she would need to buy the following day. The list included good walking trainers, waterproof clothing, backpack, clothes for warmth, first aid kit, insect repellent, etc. The list seemed never ending and soon began to eat into her reserve money. By the end of the evening she was quite depressed as she was almost insolvent. It was just after that that her guardian angel came to her rescue.

Claire had had a shower, then cleaned her teeth and was about to turn the light out when she noticed a small envelope that was lying on the floor next to her case. She crossed the room, picked it up and then sat on the edge of her bed. It was addressed to her and signed by her good friend William. It must have been inside the book that he had given to her when she departed from the hotel in London. She tore open the top and inside was a very short note and a slip of paper.

Dear Claire.

If I attempted to give you the enclosed cheque I know that you would have refused to take it. Your trip will be a very expensive one and my contribution towards it will allow me to be part of your grand adventure. Take care, young lady, and thank you for giving me the opportunity to spend some most memorable moments with a very courageous lady. May the Gods of the Andes be with you!

William.

Claire unfolded the cheque. It was for a thousand dollars! A large lump formed in her throat and she sat at the edge of the bed and cried.

"Thank you, William," she whispered, hoping that her thoughts would eventually reach him wherever he was at that moment in time.

The next two days Claire spent going around the various sports and camping shops buying all the things on her list. Thanks to the very generous contribution from William she was able to buy the best and have some money left over. She then made her booking on the bus and train and that night made her final preparations. The evening meal in the hotel was beautifully cooked and presented. The old manageress brought it to her table herself.

"We have cooked you one of the region's local dishes, seeing that it is your last night with us. The journey that you are taking is a very special one so I would like to give you a little present." She proceeded to take off a necklace and gave it to Claire.

"It has been in my family for a very long time. I would like you to wear it, as I know that it will bring you luck. By wearing it will mean that a part of me will be sharing your venture, as I have never been up the mountain."

Claire knew that the lady did really want her to take the necklace so without making any fuss she put it around her neck and did up the clasp. The old lady noted that it rested alongside the stone that Claire already had around her neck and was inwardly pleased.

At nine o'clock a taxi came for Claire and the old lady helped her take her bags down the steps and then gave her a final little hug. Again Claire could not get over how kind people had been to her during her travels.

The bus ride and the train trip up the mountain were absolutely spectacular. The panoramic views were far superior to anything that she had seen at the cinema featuring the Andes in Vistavision. The travellers were of all nationalities. The ones that fascinated Claire the most were the local people who were wearing their traditional colourful dress. This was a normal working day for them and so they were accompanied by their children and wares for the market, which included livestock.

When the train arrived at its destination everyone got out through any opening that they could find, including the windows, and began to make their way out of the station towards the small cluster of buildings which were situated at the start of the path up to Machu Picchu.

The area seemed to be extremely busy. There were far more people than Claire had anticipated, at least double the amount which had got out of the train. Near to the area where the path started up the mountain she noticed that there was some form of a commotion. People were waving their arms in the air. Someone was stood on a chair and was attempting to address the irate crowd. She made her way over to the area and stood next to a group of students who were well kitted out with equipment, obviously hoping to tackle the trail and stay for a period of time.

"Excuse me," Claire said to the nearest one in the group who was a girl with dreadlock hair and was wearing a colourful hairy jumper. "What's going on over there? What is the man on the chair saying?"

"Bad news, I'm afraid. That is if you are intending to go on to the top. Apparently there have been a number of landslides between here and Machu Picchu and the local guards are allowing no one to go onto the trail until they have done a complete survey of the damage. They say that there is still a lot of rain forecasted and that there is still a strong possibility of more mudslides. All the accommodation here has been taken and the authorities are refusing to let anyone camp in this vicinity. They are going to put extra trains on to take the people back to the town."

Claire was devastated by the news. She only had enough money and food to last her another three days at the end of which she had planned to return to the UK.

"Is there nothing that can be done? Is there another way up to the top?" enquired Claire.

"Yes, if you are a bolshy student," added one of the other students. "There is another way up but it can be quite dangerous in places. It is the original track to the top, which has been closed off for quite a few years. One of our group here did it two years ago and said that he would never do it again especially in these conditions. We are going to try it in two days' time if things don't change. Might see you back in the town as we are intending to go back on the next train and get some extra supplies."

Claire nodded as if indicating that she would be returning at the same time. However she had already made up her mind that she was going to the top even if it meant the hard way on the old track.

"Just out of interest where does the old track start from?" Claire said to the girl.

"About five hundred metres out of the village from the way you came from the train. If you retrace your steps and keep an eye out on your left you will see an old sign that is obliterated with a large red painted cross over it. That is the start. Don't even think about it lady," she said with a look of concern on her face.

"Don't worry. I'm not that silly. Bye for now. If I don't see you back in the town I'll see you on the summit."

Within the next hour Claire was a good mile up the old track. No one had seen her walk up past the old sign so she felt that she could take her time. She walked on for another hour and was quite surprised how fit she felt. It was as if she was in someone else's body. She hadn't felt so well for years. During the initial stages of the track it was relatively easy going. The ground underfoot was a compact mixture of earth and fine gravel, which gave the bottoms of her walking boots good grip. However as the path increased in steepness the gravel gradually disappeared it left quite a smooth surface. This was fine when dry but where Claire was encountering areas that had become wet from nearby streams and waterfalls she was beginning to find it hard to keep her footing.

Just after her second stop for a rest and a drink of water Claire was rounding a very sharp turn in the path when her feet went away from under her. She fell to her left and started slipping across the path towards the steep sided valley. She grasped anything that she could get hold of which would slow down her fall and eventually came to rest right on the edge of the cliff. Another metre and she would have plunged to the valley floor some thousand metres below. She sat there for over a minute just looking down over the sheer drop. Was this the moment to turn back she thought? No, she had come this far over the past four weeks and she was not going to give up that easily. After all, she only had months to live so it would be far better to go out swiftly in such beautiful surroundings rather than slowly in some hospital bed.

These thoughts immediately raised her spirits and so she began to see what damage she had done to herself and her kit. Her head felt a little sore and as she ran her fingers over her forehead she discovered quite a large bump, which she bathed in some icy water from a nearby stream. Her hands were cut in a number of places and her left ankle felt painful when she put weight on it. On removing her boot she found that the ankle was swollen on the outside. Again she used the cold stream water to bring out any bruising and then took a crepe bandage from out of her kit bag and put a tight strapping on it. Her clothing was ripped in a number of places so she began to resemble a hobo. When she tried to put her boot back on she could not get it over the bandage and so decided to change into her trainers. The boots were quite heavy so she decided to leave them at the side of the path as they might come in useful to another traveller.

The next part of the climb became easier as the path began

to level out and eventually led into a long, flat narrow valley whose sides were etched in cultivated, stepped fields which were being worked by the local Indians.

Much higher up the valley Nanchu sat in her favourite seat on top of one of the stone walls which divided one field from the other. From there she could look right down the valley and see when the horse drawn carts were arriving to load the corn for the villages lower down in the valley. Her mother was a few fields away planting next year's crop and in the adjacent field to Nanchu was her grandmother who could still do a fair day's work even though she was ninety-one!

Nanchu had been sitting there for about half an hour when she noticed in the distance someone walking down the centre of the dirt track towards her. As the person got nearer Nanchu could see that it was a woman. She had never seen her before but she felt that she should know her. It was when she got close to her and she was able to study the way that she walked and the manner in which she held her head on high that Nanchu knew who she was. She immediately jumped down from her position on the stone wall, ran across the next field, jumped over the gate and made for her grandmother.

"Nanchu, I've told you before not to jump off the wall like that as you will injure yourself. Now, why are you so excited?"

Nanchu grabbed hold of her grandmother's hand and held it tightly.

"It's her, the lady who you told me about in your stories. She's come back to find her Prince."

The old lady smiled at her grand-daughter and wished that she had such a vivid imagination. She looked in the direction to where Nanchu was pointing and saw a rather dishevelled woman bending down in the middle of the road and drinking from a plastic bottle. She must be one of the tourists going up to Machu Picchu, she thought. Very occasionally one of them would come along this track having wandered from the main route. It was when the woman stood up that the grandmother began to take more notice of her. She looked almost regal even though her clothes did her no justice at all. As soon as she began to walk she knew that her stories of the past were about to come to life. Without speaking to her grandchild she knelt on the ground as a sign of respect. The lady working next to her had not heard any of the previous conversation and was surprised to find her friend kneeling on the bare earth. She looked in the direction to where she was looking and immediately knelt down beside her. Nanchu was now extremely excited and left her grandmother's side and ran over to where her mother was working.

"Mummy, she's here and look at grandma." Her mother looked at her daughter and then towards her mother who was kneeling on the ground. For a moment she was afraid that something had happened to her mother and was about to rush over when she noticed the woman who was walking up the middle of the track. She froze for a moment and then she began to appreciate why her mother was kneeling down. A small tear formed in the corner of her eye and then started to run down her face. Like her mother she knelt down. Within the space of a few minutes almost all of the womenfolk in the valley were kneeling. The few men who were also helping in the fields stopped their work and took off their caps. The whole valley had come to a standstill.

Claire screwed the top of the bottle back on, pushed it into the top of her kit bag and stood up and faced up the valley, which looked even steeper than the first part of the walk. As she set off she became aware that something was not quite right. She looked to her left and noticed that the peasants who had been diligently working their fields a few minutes ago were all now facing in her direction. The majority of the womenfolk were kneeling and the men had their heads bowed. She thought it must be some form of a ritual, which they perhaps did before the sunset.

Claire turned towards where they were facing expecting the other workers to be facing in the same direction away from her. She was surprised to find them facing towards her, which made her feel a little uncomfortable. Had she intruded upon their valley and was this their way of showing their discontent? With that a little girl ran across the fields and proceeded to climb over the wall adjacent to where Claire had stopped. The girl then walked slowly up to Claire and held out a small flower.

"My mummy thought you might like this flower. It is from all of us," she said in her own language, which Claire did not understand. Claire held out her hand and took the pretty flower from the little girl.

"Thank you," she said with a gentle smile on her face. Claire found the moment very touching. She reached into the side pocket of her kit bag and took out a sweet, which she handed to the little girl who took it excitedly and then ran off across the fields and held the hand of one of the women who was kneeling. They were all still looking in Claire's direction and continued to do so until she eventually reached the top of her climb and walked out of the valley.

That night Claire slept under the stars. She had read in her guidebook that due to the altitude and the coldness of the nights there were no insects or animals, which would prove a nuisance to campers. She could not be bothered with putting up a tent and so put on extra clothes and then climbed inside her feathered sleeping bag. She would never forget the beauty of that night spent gazing up at the stars. There was not a breath of wind and no sound at all came up through the valley. She kept thinking of the strange happenings that had taken place in the valley below during that afternoon and of the pretty little girl who had given her the flower, which now lay on the ground next to her head.

Claire kept getting the feeling that she had been here before, especially when she looked up at the stars. She had missed a lot of beautiful things when growing up but would not have swapped them for her childhood walks through Mount Edgcumbe Park.

The early morning sun shone into Claire's face and the warmth woke her up. She had slept soundly and was ready for the next and, she hoped, final part of her walk. She was surprised not to feel at all tired or stiff from the previous day's trek. A light breakfast was followed by a cold wash in a nearby stream, which made Claire feel absolutely exhilarated, and soon

317

she was off walking at a brisk pace towards the summit. She reached her destination nine hours later, which took her completely by surprise, as there were no indicating signs that one was about to enter into the Inca ruins.

Machu Picchu was breathtaking. The whole setting was idyllic with the structures of the buildings still very discernible amid a carpet of thick lush mosses and grass. There was hardly anyone in sight. Obviously the main track to the site had still not been opened to the general public and the people who were moving around all seemed to be wearing some form of uniform indicating that they worked here.

"And where did you come from young lady?" came a voice from behind her. Claire turned to face a mature-looking man who was dressed in a khaki safari suite.

"I came up the old path. I'm looking for Professor Downing. Is he around anywhere?"

The man looked at Claire and wondered what this dishevelled woman who looked as if she had been through World War Two had in common with the Professor.

"Sorry, but the Professor is up at the new site and is not expected back for at least a week. I'm afraid there is no way of getting in contact with him as the fellow refuses to keep his mobile phone switched on. He finds it extremely distracting when it rings and he says it throws him out of his working mode. The only time he uses it is when he needs extra supplies or to talk to one of the research professors, and he has never been able to grasp the technology of checking to see if there were any messages left on the answering machine. Unfortunately, you will have to make an appointment to see him when he does return, as no one is allowed to stay here for more than a day. If you leave me a message I will make sure that he receives it."

Claire knew that time was not on her side and if she did leave a message there was no guarantee that the Professor would get in contact with her. She knew that the authorities would not allow her to venture up the trail to the new site. She would have to go on her own.

"That's very kind of you. I will write out a note now and then if it is OK I would like to take a wander around this site before returning to the lower valley?"

"No problem. You see that hut over there," he was pointing to a wooden building with an aluminium roof, which shone brightly in the sun's rays. "That's my office. I will be there for the next two hours. Drop in the note before you leave."

Claire nodded. In two hours she would be well on the way to the upper site and if they decided to go after her she would make damn sure that she would arrive at her destination long before they caught up with her.

The walk was much harder than during the previous two days as she had to negotiate very narrow cliff paths with dangerous overhangs where water came cascading from above making the surface underfoot very treacherous. By the time she came out of the narrow valley and into a more open plain she was looking even more dishevelled than when she arrived in Machu Picchu. Her clothes were in a far worse state, being covered with mud and a green slime from the mosses, which grew all along the cliff face. Fatigue had now set in and it was only sheer will-power that kept her going. Fortunately for Claire she had covered the most demanding part of the trek and in front of her was another flat valley floor similar to the one lower down. The only difference was that at the far end of this valley she could see some dwelling places.

Claire sat down for a few moments in order to regain her energy levels, which were helped along by a mouth-watering Mars bar followed by some form of drink, which was advertised as having energising ingredients. When Claire set off again she walked at a much slower rate in order to conserve the little amount of energy reserves that her body had stored.

As she walked up the valley towards the houses she became aware of one sole figure that had come out of one of the dwellings and appeared to be going about their work. After a few moments the woman stopped working and turned to face Claire. It was as if she had recognised her as she held up her hand and then started shuffling across the road towards her. Claire could see that she was very old as she had a very bent back, her hands were swollen up with arthritis and her face was lined with numerous deep wrinkles.

As she approached Claire, she held out her hand. As Claire took hold of it the old lady knelt down onto the ground and spoke to her in the local language. As the woman looked up into her eyes she pointed to Claire's necklace and began to quietly cry. Claire had no idea how to deal with the situation at first but then took hold of both hands of the old lady and gradually helped her to her feet. The woman again spoke to Claire and then started leading her across to her house. Claire was expecting for her to be taken inside but instead she was led around the side of the building and on towards the edge of the jungle.

Claire tried to convey to the old lady that she did not want to travel in that direction, but the woman kept tugging at her with an unusual amount of strength for someone so old. The woman continued to pull Claire along and into the dark jungle for about five minutes and then suddenly stopped. In front of them was what appeared to be an impenetrable wall of green vegetation. The old lady then reached forward and preceded to pull back a curtain of lianas to reveal what seemed to be a stone stairway, which had been carved into the sheer rock face. The old woman then pulled Claire to one side and started pulling at the thick mosses, which covered the ground of the clearing in which they stood. Claire was dumbfounded at what came into view.

On the stone floor was a carving of a stone, which was the same as her necklace. The old woman became very excited and kept pointing at the stone carving, the necklace and the steps. Claire's heart began to beat wildly. She understood what the old lady was trying to convey to her but did not relish the prospect of attempting to climb the steep steps in front of her. Again it was if someone was taking over her body as she suddenly found herself being willed towards the steps. She turned to thank the old lady but she had vanished back into the jungle. There was no going back now as she might get lost in the depths of the jungle and if she went up at least she would eventually come out into the open. And that is how Claire Axworthy eventually reached her goal.

Chapter Twenty

The old woman lived in the almost extinct village of Quitta. Many years before it had been a thriving town at the confluence of two large rivers where the Indian tribes of the jungles brought their wares for bartering. People from the so-called civilised world provided them with the essentials for surviving in their inhospitable environment. Tools for making clearings in the forests, guns for hunting as many had lost the art in the use of a bow or blowpipe, and European forms of dress. When the loggers came to destroy the hardwoods of the jungle they drove the Indians further into the jungle and so the town lost its viability. Soon there was little if any employment and so the younger element of the society moved away to seek their luck in the larger cities that bordered the coastal lands. Now there were only a handful of older people remaining. Their only means of livelihood was providing fresh fruits and meat from the jungles for the tourists who travelled through their village.

The old lady was born in this village over eighty years before and expected to die there. She lived in a small house built of mud mixed with the fibres of grasses to give it strength in order to withstand the continual weathering from the strong winds during the hot summers, which whipped up the sands and used them as a grinding material, and from the torrential rains during the winter months. The roof was made of matted grasses, which had been made by her own bare hands over the years. The floor was one of hard baked mud, which was covered in straw matting to give it some form of insulation against the cold of winter. There were only two rooms, one used for cooking and the other for sleeping.

She lived alone as her husband had died many years ago.

Although she lived a very lonely existence she hope that one day she would see him again.

It was early morning and the mists had just begun to lift out of the valley below. It was a beautifully clear day and in the distance one could see the white snow-capped tops of the mountains glistening against the blue azure backdrop of the cloudless sky. Although the temperature in the village was in the upper eighties the temperature up in the mountain peaks never reached above freezing. A solitary bird of prey glided gracefully on the currents of the warm air rising from the steep valley below, looking for some unsuspecting prey.

The old lady was going steadily about her morning rituals, which she had done for the past sixty or so years. First she baked some bread for the next day and then had a simple meal of beans and a slice of bread from the previous day. Years ago she would have had to put the goats out to pasture before getting the breakfast for her husband and herself. Now she did not have to go through that tortuous ritual as they had been sold many years ago to provide her with the essentials to survive. Her husband had passed away ten years ago at the age of seventy-three. She missed him terribly as he had been by her side throughout their marital years keeping her happy and amused. He had been the perfect husband and had been a pillar of strength when she had been told that they would be unable to have children.

Over the years to compensate for her problem of barrenness, she started looking after the children of the villagers who had to spend their times in the fields. Before she offered her services the villagers used to take the children along with them, even during the coldest of winters. She became the equivalent of the village schoolmistress as she not only cared for their well-being but she also attempted to give them some form of a simple education as there was no formal educational system available to the children so high up in the mountains. She would cook for the children and show them how to weave the grasses from the hillside to make matting for the floors in their houses. For this service the villagers used to bring her and her husband some of their harvestings and when her husband did pass away they made sure that she never went without food.

The bread she made from her crude oven was the best in the village and would have graced the shelves of Harrods. It had a crispy brown coating, which came from years of carbon coatings on the surface of the inside of the oven. Once out of the oven, the bread was placed on a low wall outside the house for it to cool off. The smell of the freshly baked bread used to waft down the hillside and into the centre of the village where it used to make the mouths of the villagers salivate. Everyone knew when the old lady was baking.

Once the household chores were completed she would then walk to the edges of the jungle and begin to collect berries to be used in one her own cake recipes. Once this ritual was completed, which usually took about an hour, she would place the straw woven bowls of berries at the edge of the clearing and then disappear into the forest for about another hour and then eventually reappear with a bunch of the most exotic flowers. Where she got them from nobody knew, as they were afraid of venturing too far into the forest in case they lost their way. There were also numerous rumours that tribes who practiced cannibalism still roamed in those forests. Also there were superstitious stories handed down through the generations of a lost civilisation deep in the forest, which was protected by a ring of huge stone statues of jaguars and birds of prey. Some children did try to track her on one occasion and got lost. It was the old lady who eventually found them. From that day no one had ever tried to follow her again. Had they done so they would have found themselves in paradise.

The old lady had years ago stumbled across a small clearing in one of the densest parts of the forest. The clearing had a small stream running through it, which nurtured an abundance of tropical flowers of all sizes and colours. It was from here that she used to pick her flowers to decorate her humble house. It was during one of these visits that she wandered slightly off her usual track and almost bumped into a stone carving of a ferocious animal.

Each day after that, she would collect her flowers and on the return journey she would visit the stone animal which she gradually cleaned away all of the vegetation that had grown on and around it over the years. In time it regained its prowess and once again became a guardian of the lost civilisation. The finding had made the old lady more adventurous and in time she found another two stone animals all of which she cleared of vegetation. Although they were of different shapes she noticed that they all had one similar characteristic. They all looked in the same direction and that was into the denser part of the forest where no one in the past had dared to venture. During her visits she became more and more confident in the jungle and looked upon the statues as her guardians. Each time she paid them a visit she got the impression that they wanted her to follow the direction in which they were facing, so one day she plucked up courage and began cutting into the thick undergrowth clearing a maximum of two metres each day.

Eventually, after having hacked a good two hundred metres into the dense jungle her machete struck something very hard which sent shock waves down the entire length of her arm. She momentarily dropped the steel tool that she was holding onto the soft decaying ground of the jungle. When she stooped down to retrieve it she noticed that where it had struck the ground it had taken a large piece of rotting undergrowth away to reveal what appeared to be a dark brown rock. As she proceeded to scrape away the ground around it she found that the rock was in fact a stone, which had been carved into a square shape, and this in turn was adjacent to another stone of the same shape.

As she cleared away more of the vegetation she began to uncover a whole area of these stones, which obviously had at one time been some form of paved walkway. It was about a metre in width and led in the direction of the statues. At the position where her machete had made its first impact, she began to gently cut into the thick twisting lianas that seemed to spiral up the entire height of the forest. With each stroke she kept hitting a hard surface and eventually she came across a solid mass of rock which rose up above her. The climbing lianas had attached themselves to it in order to reach the sunlight high up in the jungle canopy.

It took her almost a month to make a large clearing around the base of the cliff face. She also discovered that the steep sided rock had a precarious set of narrow steps carved into it and which she had no intention of venturing up. Her other major find was at the very base of the rock face where there was a much larger stone which had a raised centre upon which was carved an almost circular disc which had a jagged line running across its centre. The old lady assumed it must have been some sort of sacred stone and she decided that each day she would place on it a floral offering to the gods who had inhabited this region many years ago. Perhaps they would help her one day to achieve her longing ambition to be reunited with her husband.

Since these findings the old lady became more content with her life. The only change that was noticed by her neighbours in her daily rituals was that when she returned from her visits into the jungle she would brush over the hard baked earth outside of her little house and then proceed to make some form of a drawing by using the reverse end of her broom. Occasionally a friend would venture over to pass the time of the day with the old lady and inquisitively look at the drawing, which was circular in shape and had a jagged line running across it. What it represented they never ventured to ask and just put it down to the whims of a very old lady.

Chapter Twenty-One

The Andes have two large ethnic groups, one speaks Quechua, which was the language of the Inca Empire and the other speaks Aymara, whose peoples settled mainly around Lake Titicaca and neighbouring Bolivia. There are numerous ethnic groups in Peru. In the Amazon Jungle there are an amazing fifty-three ethno linguistic groups. One of these ethnic groups is white and called the Morochucos of Pampa Cangallo. These people have light coloured eyes and hair and speak Quechua. Legend has it that they are the descendants of a renegade band of conquistadors who inhabited an isolated stretch of the Sierra. Gonzales Yandeze was a descendant of this tribe and now lived high up in the mountains.

The route to most of the villages in the Andes usually comprises of a narrow, graded earth road, in the summer baked concrete hard from the fierce dry-season sun, and in the winter awash with torrents of rain, slick with mud and often closed by rock slides. These roads wind tortuously through the mountains, making complicated switchbacks up and down their flanks or follow deep river valleys. The vehicles that ply them, the means of transportation readily available and affordable to most of the inhabitants of those villages, are sometimes small, rattle-trap buses, retired from service on proper roads somewhere else and consigned to end their days travelling perilous mountain routes. The other form of transport is heavy, multi-ton trucks with wooden sides and a gate and ladder on the back, which carry everything from grains and potatoes destined for the markets in the cities, to livestock and people.

The villages at the end of these roads in the Peruvian Andes are inhabited for most part by the Quechua, descendants of the population once ruled by the Incas. Although these people have adopted some of the twentieth-century amenities such as European dress, and aluminium pots and pans, radios and flashlights, they nevertheless still follow a life similar to their ancestors in the sixteenth century.

Life in these villages is very harsh. It is based on the need for growing one's own food in order to survive the winters. Villagers have to be prepared for some years when too much rain or drought damages crops. Only the larger towns have electricity or even generators. Most have some form of fresh water and those that don't have to make strenuous treks to the rivers below. The houses are made from baked mud bricks with hard packed earthen floors and thatched roofs. The rafters are usually blackened from years of open fires over which the meals were cooked. There is little furniture although an affluent family may have a bed or table. Women sit or squat on the floor and the men sit on benches carved out of the mud walls. Their most prized possession is a radio, which is their only connection with the outside world. Very occasionally one might see a mobile phone!

A typical day begins in the darkness when the woman of the family rises and stirs the embers of the previous night's fire, fetches water and puts a kettle on to make mate which is a form of heavily sugared herbal tea. Breakfast consists of mote, which is made of dried boiled corn and maté. As the rest of the family eats, the woman would then start to prepare the next meal of the day, usually a rich soup made from potatoes and hot peppers and a hearty glass of chichi, which is a homemade corn beer.

Gonzales Yandeze lived in such a house high up in the mountains. His family were farmers and from the tender age of five he was put to work in the fields. He learnt to hate the summer season most of all, as this was the growing season which meant much hard work preparing the fields followed by back-breaking work planting the seeds. It was also the rainy season, which brought hail and mud that made working conditions at times almost impossible.

The village's communal-held potato lands lay in the Puna, often up to three hours' walk from the village, which for a boy of only five years of age seemed like a marathon. On top of this he was expected to do a full day's work at the end of the walk. The walk home was even more difficult as his body had used up all of its reserves during the long working day. What he did not realise at the time was that his body was gradually adapting to all these hardships and would eventually turn him into a very strong and formidable young man.

When it became time to harvest the crops almost the entire village moved over to the crop fields and lived in tiny, temporary huts, almost like camping. They took most of their cooking utensils with them so that they did not have to return to the village each night after work. So short was the time they had between collecting in all of the produce and the beginning of the winter that time spent travelling between the fields and the village was not cost-effective and could mean not having time to gather in all of the produce before the winter winds began to damage them. When the harvest was over the grain was stored in large huts, which were raised off the floor to protect it from rats and water, which sometimes came rushing down over the hardened mud from higher up in the mountains.

During harvest time the only people to remain in the village were the very old, the very young and usually children who were just into their teens who could look after themselves and who were put in charge of looking after the livestock. During these times Gonzales came into his own as he was a good organiser and gained the respect of all of the other young minders and so established himself as the village leader until the elders came back from the harvesting.

At the end of each season Gonzales used to pray for a bumper crop as this would mean that the village had enough grain not only to last out for the whole of the winter but also would have enough to sell in the nearest town. With the proceeds from this, the villagers were able to purchase new equipment and a few odd luxuries in order to make their humble way of life a little more bearable. During these times the young ones were given the opportunity to travel down to the town with the elders and take a look at the so-called civilised part of the world.

Gonzales found life extremely exciting there. At night for

instance people did not go back into their houses, as there was street lighting, which enabled them to stay out of doors for much longer periods of time. They all seemed to be so much better off as they all wore expensive looking clothing and their houses had much more furniture in them. The shops were all full of things he had never come across before. Then there were the huge lorries and buses, which used to take the produces and people further down into the valley to the much larger towns, which were known as cities. One day, thought Gonzales, he would go down into the city and never again return to his village or to his life of such arduous work.

Other than the trips to the town there was little else to look forward to up in the mountains. The only form of entertainment once he had grown out of playing games with his friends was on the seventh day of the week when the whole of the village would congregate in the square. There a large wooden fire would be lit and the elders would tell stories of the past. Gonzales favourite stories were about the times of the warlike Incas and how they had conquered all of the tribes of the mountains and the valleys below to become the strongest fighting nation in the history of the Andes. He didn't like the story of the eventual downfall of the Inca Empire at the hands of the marauding Spaniards.

Probably his favourite story was the one of the Prince who carried on fighting long after the conquest of the Spanish and how he had led some of his followers into the dense Amazon forests and settled in what was now known as the Lost City of the Incas. The story went on to predict that someday the Prince would return to the lands from where he had been driven away. Gonzales used to question his grandfather as to when he would return and if he did how would one recognise him. His grandfather's reply was that when the Prince did return he would be recognised only by the ones who were believers. As Gonzales grew older he knew that he would never see the Prince, as he did not believe in the stories from the past. All that he wanted to believe in was the day that he would eventually leave the village and his family.

The day Gonzales eventually left the village was a day he would never forget even though he tried on many occasions to remove it from his memory banks. The whole of the village turned out to see him off. Although he had little to take with him he had arranged for one of his friends from the town who owned a beat up old pick-up truck to collect him. He intended to leave in style. Just before getting into the truck having said all of his farewells to his family his old grandfather came to him and held him by the shoulders.

"You will come back one day, my son, and you will see the Prince."

No chance, granddad he thought, and got into the truck and disappeared behind a cloud of dust.

Since that day Gonzales had a number of jobs, which took him from town to town until he eventually settled in the city of Cusco where he became the most feared baggage handler in the entire airport. His rise to top dog was due to his leadership qualities, audacity and physical strength, all of which he owed to his upbringing in the mountains.

Chapter Twenty-Two

There was only one flight on that particular morning and Gonzales was determined to get the biggest tip. The previous night he'd been out with the lads and had spent a fair bit of money. One of his friends was celebrating his twentieth birthday and they wanted to give him a good send off to unconsciousness! Gonzales' head was worse for wear and when he was in one of those moods it did not pay anyone to cross him when he was working in the baggage collection area.

He had been sitting in his usual place on top of a metal postage box, which gave him an excellent vantage point for spotting possible clients. He would watch for smartly dressed men in suits and then follow them to the baggage collection point and as they reached forward to take their cases from the conveyer belt he would step in and take it before they were able to grasp the handles. It always worked. Even the hardiest of travellers knew by looking into his eyes not to argue with Gonzales and they would make damn sure that they tipped him well.

He eventually spotted two potential targets and was about to jump down from his vantage point when he saw David out of the corner of his eye. The guy was casually dressed in not particularly expensive clothing. He was obviously one of those back packers who were travelling the world on a shoestring. Those sort of people never tipped very well as they had little funds and needed every penny just to survive. Normally, Gonzales would have dismissed such a person immediately but on this occasion he noticed there was something different about him, which much to his annoyance distracted him from his original two targets.

He began to give the fellow his full attention. It was the man's mannerisms that made Gonzales think that he must have met him somewhere before. Perhaps he had carried his bags on a previous occasion although he usually never forgot a face. It was when the man picked up his shoulder bag from the floor and began to walk towards the baggage collection point holding his head on high and somehow made him look regal that things hit home base with Gonzales. His mind raced back to the compartment in the brain, which stored memories, and he could see his old grandfather speaking to him, as he was about to leave the village to go to the big city.

"You will come back one day my son, and you will see the Prince."

A strange feeling swept over Gonzales, which made his hair feel if it was standing on end. Someone had just "walked over his grave" as the old saying went. The man he was looking at was the Prince. He just knew it. His grandfather was right after all. Without further thought he jumped down from the postal box and rushed through the crowds to the baggage area just as one of his fellow porters had taken the man's suitcase in his hand. Gonzales pushed his way through the busy throng of people and grabbed the bag out of the porter's hand who knew not to put up any form of argument.

"Hey. What do you think that you are doing? I have already got a porter so give the bag back to him immediately."

As David spoke he made a motion towards the offending porter to get his bag back but the man had already turned and was off across the arrivals hall. David had no choice but to follow the offender towards the sliding doors that led out to the taxi ranks. As soon as the doors slid apart David was hit by a blanket of heat and high humidity, which momentarily slowed him in his efforts to catch up with his bag. Fortunately the baggage handler stopped at the same time and turned to face David who had had premonitions of his bag disappearing into the crowds never to be seen again.

"Where are you staying?" said the formidable baggage handler to David, who was now trying to get his breath back.

"I do not have a booking for a hotel. I had intended to make inquiries in the airport before you so rudely grabbed my bag and made off with it."

Such a response would have invited an immediate terse reply from Gonzales but he saw the funny side of the occasion and smiled.

"I can't see any reason for smiling, young man. Your actions have caused me a great deal of inconvenience, and if you are expecting some form of a tip you can think again!"

At this point Gonzales smile turned to a laugh. This man has got nerve, he thought, to speak to him like that. Good job no other of the baggage handlers were around otherwise he would have had to have done something about the situation in order to protect his tough image.

"Had you enquired at the information desk you would have found that all of the better hotels would have been fully booked months beforehand. More than likely you would have also discovered that even the grottier hotels were fully booked. This weekend is a celebration of one of our Saints and people come in from all of the neighbouring villages. It is a good job that you came across me. You can stay at my place."

David could not believe his ears and Gonzales could not believe that he had just said that! What a bloody cheek to think that he was going to stay at this baggage handler's house whom he had never met before and who had walked off with his bag without his permission.

"No way, sunshine. I don't know who you are and where you live. For all I know you could be some form of crook that lures people into their home and then robs them."

Steady, mister. Don't push your luck, thought Gonzales.

"Yes, I can appreciate your concern and I do apologise for my actions."

That was the first time that Gonzales had ever made any form of an apology to anyone since leaving his home village.

"I suggest that you go back into the arrivals area and make some enquiries about possible accommodation. In the meantime I will look after your bags and if you are unable to find anywhere I will take you back to my flat. That would prove far safer than sleeping on the sidewalk. If you ended up doing that you would certainly lose your bags and probably your clothing as well."

The thought of sleeping rough in this country did not appeal to David in the least, but he had no intention of going back to this chap's flat.

"OK, we'll go back to the terminal and you can guard my bags but make sure you do not stray from my side." Gonzales nodded and thought, "Stray from your side? I'll be glued to your side".

After twenty minutes of phoning the various hotels that he had been given by the Tourist Information Offices he had achieved nothing, so he was stuck. He still did not want to go off with a complete stranger so he thought that he would try to make some discreet enquiries about his baggage handler. He decided to ask one of the other porters.

"Can you stay here for a few moments whilst I go to the nearest cash point? It will only take me a few moments."

Within the space of a minute he had stopped one of the baggage boys who was loitering near the departure door

"Excuse me. Do you see that person over there who is looking after my bags? Do you know him?"

"Oh, yes. Everyone knows Gonzales. Don't cross him as he can be one mean man."

"Is he a trustworthy person?" said David feeling a little guilty at asking such questions about a complete stranger and to a complete stranger.

"I would trust him with my wife if I was so lucky as to possess a wife. I would trust him with my life if the occasion ever arose but I would hate to ever make an enemy of him. Why, is he giving you any trouble?"

"No. Thanks for your help and please accept this." He pushed a dollar bill into the man's hand and went back to his own baggage helper.

"OK, I would like to accept your offer of accommodation for tonight for which I am willing to pay the going rates for a hotel." If he was going to stay with the fellow he might as well be generous and thus keep on the better side of him, thought David.

"Right. Follow me. If you're willing to pay for a cab, which won't cost more than five dollars we could be home within six minutes otherwise we walk which would take us about half an hour."

"Cab will be fine."

In seven minutes David was standing in a small flat, which had very little in the way of furniture but was surprisingly tidy and clean. During the ride in the cab he had noticed that the area was quite shoddy, not the sort of place to go out exploring the streets, not that there was any likelihood of that, seeing he would only be there for one night.

He was there for four nights and enjoyed the experience immensely. His baggage handler, who he found out was called Gonzales, was the prefect host. He had purposely taken time off from his work to show David around the city and had helped him with his preparations for his visit to Machu Picchu. By the end of the last night they were very pally.

"Well, Gonzales, I will be off tomorrow morning so I would like to square up with you tonight. How much do I owe?"

"Nothing at all for the accommodation. What I would appreciate though, is the fare for the mountain train, which would enable me to travel with you for part of your journey. I have always wanted to go up the mountain and never had the opportunity."

David looked at Gonzales and thought it rather strange that he had picked this particular moment to take such a journey. He had been off work for five days now and could have easily have asked for four times the amount of a rail fare. He remembered what the young baggage handler had said at the airport, "Don't cross him."

"OK. That's a deal, provided that you allow me to pay for all of our food?"

They both found the rail trip spectacular along the steep sided mountain ridges and as the journey progressed so their friendship became stronger. They both told each other about their lives and divulged where they thought they had gone wrong. It was quite a soul searching experience for both of them.

During the four days of running around the city David had kitted himself out to walk the route to the old ruins but was not prepared for the endurance test that was about to present itself to him.

When the two of them reached their destination and got out of the train they were both surprised at the number of people who were milling around the station. Chaos seemed to reign. Gonzales went over to someone in a uniform and enquired as to what was making the people so excited. He also asked in which direction to go in order to reach the upper mountain plateau.

"In answer to your first question," the officious-looking man replied. "There are not enough trains to get everyone back tonight, and in answer to your second question, the path has been put out of bounds as there have been landslips further up the pass which is making the track extremely dangerous."

Gonzales looked at David who was obviously disappointed with the news. Both knew that David had to get to the ruins but neither had discussed the reason why.

"No matter what happens we will get you to your destination. If the path is out of bounds then we will find another way up. There is a café over there. You go and get us a drink and something to eat and I will go and make some discreet enquiries."

David made his way to the small café and by the time his food order had been placed on the table Gonzales was back and looking quite pleased with himself.

"Good news. There is another way into the ruins and that is by travelling along the narrow gorge over there and then coming over the top of the ridge and into the rear of the plateau. It will not be easy but it is possible. I will accompany you for the first part of the journey and make sure that you are on the right track. We will go as soon as we have finished this food, as you will need as much daylight as possible. No need to worry about me as I was brought up in surroundings similar to these."

The first few miles were easy going as they were following a well-worn path, which ran alongside of a fast flowing river that had cut a steep sided gorge through the hard rock over the centuries. David thought it was strange that he felt so much at home up here in the mountains even though he had never spent any time in such an environment before. He was expecting to be extremely tired and short of breath but felt perfectly all right which he put down to the many hours that he had spent dashing around the squash court.

It was when they were rounding a sharp spur in the valley that they met their first hazard. A fall of rock had taken the footpath away which meant them having to fix a rope around each other in case one of them fell into the river below. Gonzales' strength helped save David on two occasions when his footing gave way and he began to slither towards the river below. Had Gonzales gone first there would have been no way that David would have been able to pull him back up the smooth rock face. They both sat down after their narrow escape and took a well-earned drink from a water flask and gorged themselves on two digestive biscuits.

It was now beginning to get a little dark and both knew that Gonzales would have to start retracing his steps soon. Neither wanted to say goodbye to each another. It was David who made the decision.

"It's time to leave me, old buddy. I should be back in about five days when I will look you up once more."

Gonzales could not bring himself to speak, as he knew that this was the last time that they would see one another. He did not expect David to return from the mountaintop. He had no idea what was going to happen but he knew that David somehow was connected to the Inca Prince of whom his grandfather had spoken on many occasions when they were sitting around the fire during the winter months. The other reason why David would never see him again was that on his return to Cusco he intended to empty his flat and return home to his village where he would once again attempt to settle back into a peasant's way of life. He would also look forward to meeting his grandfather again and telling him of how he had met and travelled with the Prince.

Gonzales held out his hand and took hold of David's hand and shook it firmly. They looked one another not needing to speak as their eyes portrayed their feelings. David pulled Gonzales towards him and gave him a manly hug. Without a word being uttered they both turned away at the same moment

337

and started to walk in opposite directions. As David reached the next bend in the river he turned to take one last look at his reliable baggage handler but he had already disappeared around the landslip.

David now felt very alone and as it was getting dark decided to bed down for the night. He erected his little tent higher up the side of the valley as he had been warned of the possibility of seasonal flash floods which gave no warning to the unsuspecting walker and which could suddenly came rushing down the valleys taking everything in their path.

That night David got very little sleep. He was cold even though he had purchased a feather-down filled sleeping-bag. He kept thinking of all that had happened to him over the past two years and how his life had changed so drastically. "Shut up," he said to himself. "Get some sleep as tomorrow is going to be a tough day." With that thought in his mind he eventually manage to drop off for a few hours.

The following morning David awoke in a thick freezing fog, which made him shiver even before he got out of his sleeping-bag. After a quick breakfast of cold water and two oat biscuits he set off feeling quite sorry for himself.

He walked for almost ten hours and eventually in a very poor state appeared over the brow of the valley top. His spirits were immediately raised from what he saw. The ruined city of Machu Picchu was more magnificent than any guidebook had attempted to portray to the traveller. It nestled on a lush green mossy carpet surrounded by high mountain peaks. The ruined city was empty except for a few people who were milling around doing various jobs. There did not appear to be any touristy types so David assumed that the pass was still out of bounds. He made for what appeared to be an office and knocked on the door.

"Come in," shouted a male voice from the other side of the dark wooden door. David pushed open the door and was mildly surprised at the mod cons within it. Cooker, microwave, television were only a few of the electrical appliances that he saw on first glance, much like his old office in Abu Dhabi. Quite civilised, he thought.

"Can I be of any assistance to you?" came a voice from behind one of the office chairs, which suddenly swivelled around to exhibit an oldish man dressed in a safari suite.

"I'm looking for Professor Downing. Is he anywhere around on the site?"

"Not another one. You're the second person today to make such an enquiry. No, I'm afraid that he is up at the other site, which is not open to visitors. I am afraid that there is no way of getting in touch with him. All that you can do is to leave a message and I will make sure that he makes contact with you. Now please, don't think me rude, but I have a lot of work to do and the day has been one of numerous distractions. If you jot down some notes in the pad on my desk over there I will show it to him when he returns sometime next week."

David made a few notes with reference to the discovery of the new Inca city and then let himself out. What next, he thought. If the professor was up at the new site then he would have to go up there. He didn't have a clue as to where that might be so he looked around for someone who he might ask as to the whereabouts of the new ruins. David happened to notice a young girl working inside one of the ruins and made his way over to her.

"Excuse me. Can you give me some idea in which direction the new ruined city is? I am writing an article for the *National Geographical* magazine and I have to cover all aspects of Machu Picchu and its surroundings." Quite good, thought David, for a cover story made up on the spur of the moment.

The girl looked up from her work and smiled.

"You see that dilapidated gate over there; well that's the way down and up to the site. However we have been issued with strict instructions that no one is allowed up there for the time being. Something about landslides."

She then turned away and once more got engrossed in her work. David slowly made his way across to the gate and noticed that the path sloped quickly downwards. If he was able to get down the first ten metres of the path without being seen he would then be able to continue his journey in his own time. He looked around and the only person in sight was the girl that he had just spoken to and she was bending down facing the opposite direction to where he stood. As quick as a flash he was through the gate and down the path before anyone had noticed.

David had been walking for about three hours when the ending to his great adventure happened in the space of a few seconds. One minute he was walking along a level part of the track and the next he slipped on a patch of wet earth and was rolling down a steep incline, eventually coming to rest against a large boulder adjacent to the river. An excruciating pain came shooting up his right leg. He looked down and noticed that his foot was positioned at a most grotesque angle to the rest of his leg which made him feel quite sick. It didn't need someone with medical training to diagnose a break in the ankle. He was mortified. Whether he would get out of that situation alive did not occur to him. What he was annoyed about was the fact that he would now never reach his destination. The pain gradually began to subside a little, just enough for his brain to function in another direction.

There was no way out of this situation unless someone happened to come along, and that was most improbable as the path was out of bounds. He could be there for days, even a week by which time he would have starved to death. David had never felt as low as he did at that present moment in time. He put his head into his hands and began to cry, something which he had not done since he was five years old. The effect of this helped to rid his body of the enormous amount of stress that he had stored up over the past few months, and by the end of five minutes he began to feel a little better. The pain from the ankle was still there but now his brain was thinking about survival.

He once read that the first step in survival technique was to assess one's possessions and see if there was anything that could be used to attract someone's attention. What an idiot! He had a mobile phone in his rucksack. He fumbled around inside his bag and eventually his fingers felt the smooth edges of the phone. He prayed that it still had some power in its batteries. He was in luck. It was showing fully charged. The narrow gorge might prevent any signal from getting out but it was certainly worth a try. Now what should he dial? If he dialled for the local authorities they would immediately whisk him off the mountain and back to the city for treatment and so he would never reach his destination. There was no one he knew in Cusco other than Gonzales and he was not on the phone. He got out his diary and began to flick through the pages hoping for something to give him inspiration. It hit him straight between the eyes. The Abu Dhabi number.

"If you ever need any help, no matter what it might be, then phone this number and if it is at all possible we will help" he remembered the Sheik's minister saying to him. It was worth a try. He quickly dialled the number and waited. Suddenly the phone came alive and he could hear a woman's voice talking in a foreign language, which he assumed to be Arabic.

"Hello, can you hear me?"

"Yes, sir. How can we help you?"

"This will sound extremely ridiculous but I have fallen down a cliff face in the Andes and have broken my ankle. I need help."

"Please hold the line for a moment."

"Hello. This is the assistant Secretary for Internal Affairs. To whom am I speaking and how did you get this number?" a man's voice came down the line instead of the woman's.

David quickly explained who he was and how he had initially got hold of the number. The line went dead for a few moments and then another voice came onto the line. David recognised it as the Sheik's principal secretary, the one who had given him the telephone number on the beach at the British Club.

"David. I wondered when you would give us a call. You certainly seem to have been in the wars. Your present situation offers us quite a challenge. What we would like you to do is to leave your mobile phone on line and then sit back and wait. Have faith in us, my good friend."

During the next four hours David kept looking at the screen on his mobile phone to see how it's batteries were lasting out. He was worried that if they did run out he would then have no means of getting in contact with the rescue party that he hoped was on its way. He had no idea how they would find him and was surprised when the Sheik's aide had not asked for any indication as to where he actually thought he might have been.

David's greatest anxiety began when the sun started to disappear over the tops of the mountain range. Once darkness had set in, there would be no hope of finding him until the sun came up the following morning by which time his phone would be dead. He pulled his sleeping-bag from out of his kit-bag plus any extra pieces of clothing that he could get on and then sat back and waited. Darkness descended and with that David gradually gave up any hope of being found at all.

He must have dozed off for a time and was brought back to his senses by a distant, far-off noise. At first he could not quite distinguish it, but as he listened he could gradually pick out the sound of rotor blades. A helicopter was on the search for him. David looked through his kit bag for something, which he could use to attract the pilot's attention should he fly over the narrow sided valley in which he lay. He could find nothing and wished that he had purchased the small torch that the shop assistant had tried to persuade him to buy when he was equipping himself with his camping gear. The chance of the helicopter flying over his position and for him to be spotted in the pitch-black valley were worse odds than winning the National Lottery, thought David.

For a further five minutes David could hear the helicopter gradually getting nearer as if it was coming up through the valley towards him. Suddenly there was an horrendous noise above his head and some form of a powerful searchlight lit up the whole of the valley about him. Dust and twigs started to fly around and made it impossible for David to see what was going on above him as the huge rotor blades beat down upon the area in which he lay. The machine seemed to hover for ages and then suddenly he was aware of someone standing next to him. In fact there were two people.

"OK, we've located him. Can you push off for a few minutes whilst we take a look at him?" David heard one of them say and assumed the person was in contact with the pilot. Almost immediately the noise from above disappeared and the valley once again returned to its normal peaceful state. David looked at his rescuers who were dressed in harnesses under which was some form of a camouflage flying suite. The one who originally spoke came over to him and bent down.

"Hello, David. You haven't chosen a very good spot to set up camp. I would suggest that when we get you out of here that you book in at the first possible Boy Scout Jamboree and get some lessons on the Art of Good Camping," he said with a friendly smile.

"You must be someone really important for us to be called out at this hour and from such a long distance away. However, we will not go into that. Now what have you done to yourself? If you explain it to my colleague here, who is a trained paramedic, he will endeavour to make you a little more comfortable before we hoist you up into our bird."

During the next five minutes the paramedic had diagnosed that David had indeed broken his ankle. The medic gave David some form of a pain-killing injection and then proceeded to cut his boot from off of his foot. The procedure was extremely painful for David even though he had had the injection. However once a tight strapping was placed around his ankle the pain began to subside.

"Right. Are you ready to be hoisted up into the helicopter? All that you have to do is to hold on tight to John here, and he will do the rest. You can't fall anywhere as both of you will be harnessed onto the wire."

David nodded but did not relish the thought of swinging around in the confined spaces of this valley whose sides were littered with sharp, jagged rock formations.

"Phil here. Time to come in and pick up the baby. Let's go."

The helicopter was back in the space of one minute, and thirty seconds later David and the medic were being hoisted up into the belly of the hovering beast. As soon as his feet made contact with the floor of the machine someone grabbed hold of David and proceeded to drag him into the inner sanctuary of the bird. Once the other members of the rescue party had been hoisted up, the helicopter swung around and made off for its base.

"We won't delve into why you were in that nasty situation down there. Our job is to make you as comfortable as possible and get you to a hospital. Is there anything we can do for you? Anyone that you would like to contact?"

"Yes, I'd like you to deliver me to the newly discovered Inca ruins near to where you found me."

The personnel looked at one another in a questioning manner.

"I don't think we can do that. The orders that we were given were to pick you up and deliver you to a hospital. You have a nasty break in your ankle and if we don't get you to hospital as soon as possible complications could set in."

"I'm not bothered with the state of my ankle. It is imperative that I get to the ruins today."

"As I said before, you must be someone very important. All stops were pulled out in order to find you. One of the NASA satellites was used to locate your precise position using your mobile phone as a guiding beacon. I'll have to make a call before we can consider taking you to the ruin."

The officer who had made initial contact with David went forward to the pilot compartment. He returned a few minutes later just as the helicopter began to bank sharply to the right.

"I have been told that we have to comply with whatever you wish, provided it is within the realms of safety, so we are now making in the direction of the ruins. The pilot has already been notified of our new destination and he has already changed his flight plan. We have been asked for you to sign an indemnity letter stating that you are going of your own accord and that we are not liable for anything that might happen to you. Flight time is only ten minutes by which time there should be enough light to ensure a safe landing. My medic here will give you an extra strong shot to enable you to walk with as little discomfort as possible. To make sure that you do as little damage as possible to the ankle we are going to put you in a tight splint, which will make walking quite difficult. When you have completed your assignment give us a call on this number and we will arrange to pick you up. Right, let's get sorted out for landing procedures."

Chapter Twenty-Three

The afternoon was just perfect, thought Professor Downing, as he sat outside his office and looked out over the ruined overgrown city, which was just beginning to take shape. For the past few months he had been given a squad of over thirty people to work under his directions. All of them were experts in the field of archaeology and all were enthralled at being selected to work on this incredible new find in the jungle. They had done an amazing amount of work in such a short amount of time and so the Professor was not too disappointed at the present hold-up in the excavations. In actual fact he was very pleased with the recent landslides lower down in the valley as it had meant that he had the site to himself and no one would be coming back to the camp for at least four days. There were not many occasions when he could enjoy absolute solitude in such idyllic surroundings.

It was mid-afternoon when his solitude was broken. At the time the Professor was sitting reading one of his papers which he had prepared for a lecture that he was due to give to a group of business men in Cusco. He had just finished reading the third page and was in the process of making a few alterations when out of the corner of his eye he thought he saw a movement at the far side of the site. As he focused his attention on the area he was surprised and then annoyed to see a person walking slowly in his direction. As the person got nearer he could see it was a woman, and an untidy one at that. The Professor had had no notification of a possible visit of anyone to the site and so assumed that the woman had made her own way there without any given authority. Well, she wouldn't be here for very long, he thought to himself! No one would spoil his few days of absolute peace. He put his papers back into his brief case, pushed it under his chair and then proceeded to walk down the grassy slope towards the woman who had now seen him and was walking towards him. Before he was able to speak and show his annoyance at her being there she spoke.

"Professor Downing?" she said and refrained from adding "I presume" which she thought would be a little too corny.

"Yes," he replied, the wind having been slightly taken out of his sails.

"I have come all the way from Cornwall, in England to see you and I don't really understand why," said the rather unkempt-looking woman.

"It's because of this," and she proceeded to pull at her necklace so that the stone appeared from beneath her sweater. When the Professor saw it he immediately recognised it as a replica of his mystery stone carving.

"It didn't take the commercial men long to jump on to this band wagon. They know they're on to a winner. Where did you purchase it?" The professor was mildly interested now but his body language still conveyed an air of annoyance.

"I've had it since I was a young girl. I found it washed up on a beach near my home in Plymouth, little fishing village called Cawsands."

The Professor's faculties were now in full working mode. How could a replica of his stone have been made years before he had even discovered it? He was now deeply intrigued.

"You must be completely exhausted with your travels today. Come along with me, young lady. I have a fridge, which has a stock of cold drinks, or I can make you a nice cup of tea." The Professor's attitude towards Claire had swung full circle in the space of a few minutes.

"I'd love a cup of tea. The last decent one I had was back in London." Claire followed the Professor back up the mossy slope to the wooden veranda, which was situated adjacent to a metal cabin.

"Sit yourself down here and I'll go inside and make a pot of tea. Would you like a digestive biscuit with it?"

"Yes please," said Claire gradually warming to the Professor. He came back five minutes later carrying a metal tray upon which were two cups of steaming tea and a variety of delicious looking biscuits. Claire had not eaten for over four hours and without thinking tucked into the delicacies in front of her.

"Start from the beginning and tell me all about your finding of the stone," said the Professor who had also tucked into the food. Claire talked for over an hour and told him about her uncle who had had the stone made up into a necklace, about her mother, her trip to London and many other trivial things. It was when she mentioned about her visit to the Planetarium and how she had gone to the projectionist and pointed out that their star constellation four hundred years ago had some stars in the wrong place that he really sat up and began to listen. He was even more surprised when she said that when the projectionist checked the computer programme it had slight imperfections, which had moved some of the stars away from their correct positioning. Once amendments had been made to the programme and the constellation was projected back onto the ceiling the rogue stars positioned themselves to where Claire had initially stated they should be.

By the end of the woman's story the Professor was totally intrigued. If anyone had come along to him in England and told him of this story he would have just laughed at that person and sent them on their way. But now he was actually witnessing the tale in person and did not have the slightest idea of how to deal with it. The woman had come all this way for his help and he was at a total loss.

"That's a most intriguing story, young lady. It could be a meaningless coincidence of you finding a stone, which is identical in design to the Inca carving which keeps appearing in different locations in this area, or it could have some form of spiritual meaning. I would be in favour of the first, but you never can tell. Why don't you stay up here for a few days and take a look around the ruins? Something might inspire you, which might throw some light on your stone. Feel free to wander wherever you wish but stay away from the upper extremity of the city, as there is a sheer drop of over three thousand feet to the jungle below. In the mean time I will make sure there is a clean bed for you in one of the other cabins. You will not be disturbed as no one is due to return here for another five days at least. If you want to have a shower there is one in that cabin on the end of the block."

Claire went off to the block to get cleaned up whilst the professor looked for fresh bed linen. Although he had just lost his solitude he was not annoyed, as he quite liked the woman. She appeared to be a shy person who possessed a great deal of determination. Not many people would have attempted the journey that she had taken over the past few weeks, especially on their own.

That night the Professor cooked one of his favourite meals, spaghetti bolognaise and put a bottle of red wine on the table. The meal proved very tasty and they managed to finish the whole bottle of wine. By the end of the dessert they were completely relaxed with one another's company and were soon telling each other stories about their past lives. They talked into the early hours of the following morning until they both began to get very tired.

"Tomorrow you can lie on if you wish. I will show you where the breakfast things are and then you can help yourself. I will probably have a lie on so you can forget about me until about lunchtime. Is there anything you might need before tomorrow?"

"No. I've brought everything with me. Thanks for a lovely evening. I've enjoyed every moment. See you tomorrow then," and with that she went out of the canteen and over to her cabin. Within fifteen minutes they were both fast asleep.

Claire was up at the crack of dawn. She went over to the shower block and was pleasantly surprised to find the water hot. However she found it extremely cold when she stepped out into the unheated room, which was just getting over its nightly exposure of sub-zero temperatures. By the time she had dried off and got into a clean set of clothing the sun was just beginning to send its warm fingers across the frosty grasses. The night before, Claire had decided to have a very early breakfast and then start exploring the site.

The frost was still on the ground when she came out of the canteen and so as she walked across the grass she left a very neat set of prints behind her. The air was invigoratingly fresh on the lungs and as she breathed out, the warm air mixed with the cool mountain air causing a billowing white cloud about her head. The warm air from the valley below was just begging to rise and as it met the colder air above it began to form a blanket of fine mist that spilled down the centre of the valleys like the searching tentacles of a ghostly octopus.

It was so magical up here in the mountains, thought Claire. She had a strange feeling as if she had come home to her place of birth. Just at that moment the tranquillity of the scene changed dramatically when a huge ugly looking machine came up out of the valley below, hovered for a few moments just above ground level and then raced low over Claire's head and landed at the far end of the ruins about eight hundred metres from where Claire stood. As Claire watched only one person came awkwardly down from the machine and no sooner had his feet touched the ground than the ladder was withdrawn and the noisy thing took off once more and was gone within twenty seconds.

A few minutes before that the Professor was turning over in his bunk to adjust himself for another hour in his cosy warm bed when a deafening roar shook the tin sides of his cabin.

"What the bloody hell is that?" he shouted to himself as he leapt out of his bed and threw on his clothes. As he came out of the door he was just in time to see a camouflaged army Sikorsky helicopter disappear down over the lip of the plateau. "Bloody army," he thought, "why don't they do their manoeuvres somewhere else instead of trying to give me a heart attack so early in the morning. If it comes back again it'll get a brick through its rotor blades!" It was then that he saw someone hobbling down the middle of one of the mossy roads. 'Who the bloody hell is that' he mumbled to himself. He was really annoyed by his second unwanted visitor of the day. 'Hobble as you may old chap but you'll be out of here as soon as I have had chance to shout into your precious little ear. You had better have a good excuse for being here otherwise you may end up with another damaged leg.' The Professor was furious.

The one step jump from the ladder of the helicopter sent a

shudder through David's entire body. He swiftly moved away from the rotating blades above his head and watched as they picked up speed and lifted the huge machine back into the cloudless sky and whisked it out of sight down into the valley. He was amazed how quickly the deafening noise disappeared. Silence descended on the scene within seconds. By now the sun had risen much higher in the sky and because the air was so pure its rays were emitting an unusual amount of heat, which caused David's body to begin to overheat. He still had on the flying suit, which he proceeded to remove. The splint on his ankle made the manoeuvre much more complicated than it would have been had he been fit, but he managed it eventually. The effort made him even hotter so he also removed his jacket and stood around in just a T-shirt and shorts.

At first glance around the site he could see no one else and then he noticed someone near the centre of the ruined city making his way towards him. The person seemed in a hurry as he was taking quite large steps, and as he got nearer David could see that the effort was beginning to make him tired. Large amounts of white condensation were emitting from his mouth and nostrils giving him the appearance of someone who was extremely distraught.

"What the hell are you doing on my site at this God earthly hour?" he shouted at the top of his voice, his whole body shaking with anger. David was quite taken aback by the attitude of the old man who looked as if he had just tumbled out of bed judging by the back of his shirt which was flapping around his bottom and one end of his shirt collar stuck inside his jumper.

"I've come up to take a look around this site and would really like to talk to Professor Downing, if he is around."

Just as the Professor was about to reply and point out that he was in actual fact the Professor that David was looking for, he happened to glance at David's upper arm where a marking caught his eye and which sent his brain racing. As David turned slightly away from the Professor to take a better look out over the ruins the Professor was able to study the marking more closely. It was obviously some form of a birthmark but a most unusual one at that. On closer scrutiny the Professor was shocked to see it had the same markings running across the centre of it, as did his mysterious stone carving. For a few moments he was lost for words. In the space of a few hours he had had two complete strangers descend upon him from nowhere, both of whom possessed markings identical to his stone. What on earth did all of this mean? He thought to himself. How come they had both arrived at this precise moment in time? They both had had to endure extremely difficult hardships in their travels to get here and yet they had made it against all the odds. The professor was now even more baffled than when the woman had arrived yesterday. His whole attitude to the present situation now suddenly changed.

"Look. I'm really sorry about my initial outburst a few minutes ago. I've had a bad week worrying about the recent landslides and how it is affecting the progress at this site. You look as if you need some form of respite. Come on down to my cabin and I'll fix you up with some grub. Here let me carry your bag, as you do not want to put too much weight on that leg of yours. Incidentally, I am Professor Downing. Pleased to meet you," he said offering his hand which David took and shook.

David was amazed at the Professor's change in attitude towards him. One minute he was a raving madman and the next he was greeting him as if he was a long-lost friend.

The Professor led the way back to his cabin taking the easiest route, so that David did not have to put too much strain on his leg. Even so, by the time they got to the hut David was feeling very tired and the pain-killers were beginning to wear off resulting in a mild throbbing feeling, much like toothache, which was travelling up the entire length of his leg.

"Take a seat there, and rest your leg on this box," said the Professor. "I will get some food for you plus a hot drink. Coffee OK?"

"Yes, that will do just fine. Thank you."

David sat back and relaxed in the chair. It was a magnificent view from the Professor's veranda for one could see out over almost the entire city with the exception of the area directly behind them, which was at a slightly higher level to where they were. There was no one else in sight and the only sound was from the birds circling high above. Their wingspans looked enormous compared with the birds David had seen in the States, so he assumed they must be Condors. At the outer edges of the city he could see small wisps of mist curling across the grasses from the valleys below adding a slight eeriness to the scene.

"Milk and sugar?" enquired the Professor from the doorway to the cabin.

"Both, please," said David, his mouth slightly salivating at the thought of something to eat and drink.

Once the tea things had been set down onto the low table adjacent to David and the Professor had poured out the first cup of coffee the two of them fell into a deep conversation. The Professor was extremely interested in why David had decided to come to his city and in the back of his mind he was wondering if it had anything to do with the girl.

They had been chatting away for over half an hour when the Professor asked, "Had you planned to meet anyone here? I was wondering if the lady who arrived yesterday might have been anything to do with you. Like you she came out of nowhere. She is out at the present moment walking about the site. At lunchtime you will get chance to meet her. You may have noticed her whilst you were sitting here when I was preparing the food?"

"No. The only things that were moving were those large birds up there." David pointed to an area above their heads where three birds were circling.

"Magnificent hunters, the condor. Their feathers were prized by the Inca Kings who had them woven into the headgear of their personal guard so that they majestically stood out from the rest of their warriors. My, look at the time! Soon be time for lunch. I'll have a quick look to see if I can locate the young lady and let her know that lunch is imminent."

The Professor stood up and turned towards David and then stopped abruptly. "I told her not to go near the far end of the excavations as there is a sheer drop of over a thousand feet and there are no safety fences in place at the moment."

David rose to his feet and looked in the direction in which the Professor was facing. He could just make out someone standing motionless at what appeared to be the edge of the precipice. She seemed to be looking down into the mists, which were slowly ascending from the valley below and just beginning to lap at the edge of the cliff.

"Professor, would you like me to go over and ask her to move away from the edge?" said David having seen how anxious the Professor was. If the old man made any attempt to approach the girl in that frame of mind, he thought, he might startle her, which could result in a nasty accident. David had read an article many years ago about self-hypnosis and the sort of things, which might bring it on. He remembered the part about fog and mist, which tended to disorientate a person and give them a false sense of direction.

"Don't worry, Professor. I'll hobble across there and have a chat with her. You sit down there in your chair and keep a watch on us." David made sure that the Professor was not going to follow and then proceeded to walk up the grassy slope towards the woman.

The closer David got to the woman the more apprehensive he became for her safety as the mist from the valley below was beginning to drift higher and occasionally block her from view. He knew that he would have to be very careful once he got within earshot of her as he did not want to startle her because she was now standing at the very edge of the cliff. From what David could see she was definitely in some form of a trance. She was just standing there looking out into the mist.

The appearance of the huge, noisy helicopter had broken the majestic spell of the site for Claire. She had watched it land at the far side of the site and seen a man descend awkwardly down a ladder and crouch low to the ground. She was greatly relieved when eventually the ugly thing disappeared in the direction from whence it had come. As the new visitor started slowly walking towards the main cabin block, Claire noticed the Professor marching up the slope towards him, probably to welcome him to the newly found city.

Claire turned away and focused her attention on examining the uncovered remains of the buildings. Although the sun had risen higher into the morning sky, Claire began to feel cold. She was not really dressed for this altitude. When she had put her head outside of her cabin that morning there was no wind and she was given a false impression of the prevailing temperature and she did not bother to put on any warm clothing. Now that the wind had risen a little she was beginning to feel cold and her skeletal muscle network was beginning to quiver in an attempt to generate some form of heat. In order to stave off the cold she decided to take a brisk walk up the hill to the very end of the site hoping that the effort would make her feel warm once again.

For the first time in two weeks Claire suddenly began to feel weak. By the time she reached the top of the ruined city it was as if all her ailments had returned to her body. She found breathing difficult, her limbs felt weak and her head began to feel a little fuzzy. The closer she got to the edge of the cliff the worse she began to feel. They say that one's past rushes in front of one's eyes in matter of minutes when the time has come to pass into another world and this is what was happening to Claire at that very moment.

As she neared the very edge of the precipitous drop the mist began to caress her body, which had a calming effect on her and which in turn took her mind away from her physical pains. She began thinking about her mother and uncle and her house in Devonport and all the friends in her street and the games that they played together. Memories came flooding back, the family trips through Mount Edgcumbe Park, the finding of her stone, Dr Braddon, her trip to London and her visit to the Planetarium, her new friend William, and so it went on, memories of all the happy things that had happened to her during her life.

She stared out over the mist and knew that she did not wish to return to Plymouth in order to die. It was time for her to go now. She inwardly felt that this was the chosen place. Somehow she knew that she had been here before. It was a place, which had been sacred to her, and yet she could not remember why.

The mists were now beginning to swirl around her as if

beckoning her towards the edge where she knew she would at last be at peace with the world.

David had now reached the brow of the hill, which was shrouded in a light, bright mist. Occasionally when the wind created small clearings in the fine water droplets, he was able to catch glimpses of the woman who was now standing extremely close to the edge of the cliff. He knew that she would eventually topple over unless he did something very quickly. He would have to approach her slowly for if he suddenly appeared out of the mist she would probably take fright and instinctively step backwards.

The mist was now beginning to affect him and play tricks on his eyes. As it swirled it revealed small glimpses of the woman who now appeared to have changed in appearance. David's first impressions of her were that of a pale, middle-aged woman with short greying hair and dressed in a blouse and slacks. What he was now seeing was someone much younger who had very dark skin and had long, black hair, which flowed down the length of her back. She seemed to somehow have changed her clothing, which he knew was totally impossible in such a small spate of time. She was now dressed in a long white dress, which was made of a very light silky material and seemed to be caressed by the light winds that were dancing around her.

Quietly, as the mist enveloped her once again he took a few more steps towards her hoping that he was going in the correct direction and that she had remained in the same position. He paused momentarily and became aware of a most beautiful exotic fragrance, which he recognised but could not quite identify.

Suddenly the mist cleared and there she was directly in front of him, almost within touching distance. She was standing with her back towards him and although he could see little of her he knew that he was looking at the most beautiful woman he had ever come across.

At that moment she must have sensed that he was there for she slowly turned to face him and it was then that he saw the full beauty of her face. She must be an Indian girl from down in the valley as she had some form of a tribal marking on her cheek which made her even more beautiful. It was when she raised her head and he was able to looked into her eyes that he knew that he had come across her somewhere in his distant past She was the woman that he had given his heart to so many years ago. As he gazed at her he noticed a tear had formed in the corner of her eye, which then commenced to trickle down the smooth skin of her cheek. He held his hand out towards her.

It was time. Claire made as if to step out into the mist but stopped momentarily when she became aware that someone else was nearby. She could hear no sounds at all other than the whisper of the light winds and yet she sensed that there was somebody very close at hand. She glanced over her shoulder and in the mist she thought that she could see a figure, which was slowly making its way towards her. As she watched, the mist began to clear and only a distance of about five metres from her stood a most magnificent person. It was as if she had stepped back in time for in front of her was a soldier in full battle armour. From her childhood history books she knew that she was looking not only at an Inca warrior but a most impor-tant one at that, as his chest plate was made of shimmering gold. As he stepped nearer to her he held out his hand in order to take hold of her hand. Claire in turn reached forward to place her hand into his. When she glanced down at her hand it was as if it did not belong to her. Her hand was not one of a middle-aged woman but that of someone very young.

Claire momentarily froze when she looked and caught sight of her reflection in the warrior's gleaming golden chest plate. Instead of seeing a tired fraught woman she saw an elegant Indian woman who was attired in a long flowing white dress. Claire looked down once more at herself and noticed that her skin had changed to a smooth dark sheen. She ran her hand down over the material of the garment that she was now dressed in. It appeared to be made of a very fine silk, which seemed to caress her fingers.

It seemed as if she had been standing there for an eternity. She now knew that she had somehow been to this place before but could not place when. Claire looked up once more and when her eyes looked into the eyes of the Inca warrior, who was now standing immediately in front of her, she suddenly realised what was happening.

"I knew that one day you would return for me," Claire whispered softly.

The Inca Prince smiled and took her hands in his and gently pulled her towards himself. As their faces touched he noticed the fragrance in her hair. It was the scent that he had come across so many years ago in the jungle clearing where he first set eyes upon her. He was at last united with his first and only love. The Prince took her head in his hands and lifted it up so that he could look once more into her beautiful eyes.

"I kept my promise that one day I would return for you. I will never leave you again." He pulled her once more towards himself. As their lips touched, they both remembered the first time that they had held each other on the rock in their little clearing in the forest. At that moment they both knew that they would never leave each other again.

The Professor watched David make his way slowly up the hill until he was almost within talking range of the girl. It was at that moment that the mists began to swirl in and obstruct his vision. Over the next few minutes he witnessed the strangest of things. For a very brief moment the mists parted and standing dangerously near the edge of the cliff were two completely different people. One appeared to be an Indian girl dressed in a long flowing dress, like the robes that the maidens wore for an Inca sacrificial ceremony, and the other was a warrior who was dressed in one of the most spectacular uniforms of the Inca Army. A few moments later the mist closed over the scene.

The mist was obviously playing tricks on his eyes, thought the Professor. As he continued to watch the mist suddenly dispersed to reveal nothing other that the grassy edge of the cliff. The native girl and the Inca warrior had disappeared. The Professor looked around the surrounding area but there was no one in sight. It was then that it suddenly dawned on him that they had both fallen over the edge of the cliff.

Not bothering to put on protective clothing the Professor raced to the path, which would take him to the bottom of the cliff. The climb took him thirty minutes by which time he had taken the skin off four of his fingers and both knees in his mad scramble to see if either of them had perhaps miraculously survived the fall, although he knew that that was an impossible hope.

The trek through the jungle took another ten minutes and finally he found himself nearing the edge of the clearing. He slowed down anticipating the worse and gingerly began pushing aside the lianas, which had for so long protected the area from unwanted visitors. As his eyes became fully accustomed to the gloom, which was caused by the thick undergrowth and the tall trees, the Professor focused his gaze on the stone slab that he had discovered so many months ago and was relieved to see that there were no bodies. He managed to pick out the jagged line, which ran across its centre and noticed that something was lying on it.

As he proceeded to move to the centre of the stone slab he saw a single flower that must have been placed there very recently as it still looked fresh. It was a rare orchid. The Professor crouched down and as he picked it up he became aware of its beautiful fragrance.

Immediately his brain started to race back over the last few days and he began to put together all of the things that had puzzled him; the lady's necklace with the pebble, the jagged marking on the man's upper arm and how they both resembled his stone and now the disappearance of the two of them. He suddenly remembered the old lady who lived in the village not far from here and the story she had told him of how one day an Inca Prince would return for his loved one. At last he had finally solved the mystery of the stone, which had the jagged line running through its centre.

Whenever the Professor walks through the perfume section of a large city store, the fragrance always takes him back to the little clearing in the jungle. On one such an occasion his wife enquired why he had a small tear in the corner of his eye, to which he just smiled and gave her a loving hug.